Guy Walters was a journalist for eight years on *The Times*, where he travelled around the world and reported on a wide variety of subjects. He is married, lives in London, and is now a full-time novelist.

The Traitor

Guy Walters

headline

Excerpt from *Autumn Journal* by Louis MacNeice,
published by Faber & Faber, is reproduced
by kind permission of David Higham Associates.

Excerpt from *Erotocritos*, translated by
Theodore Ph. Stefanides, is reproduced by kind permission
of Papazissis Publishers S.A.

First published in 2002
by HEADLINE BOOK PUBLISHING

10 9 8 7 6 5 4 3 2 1

ISBN 0 7553 0056 4

Typeset in Goudy by Avon Dataset Ltd, Bidford-on-Avon, Warks

Printed and bound in Great Britain by
Mackays of Chatham plc, Chatham, Kent

HEADLINE BOOK PUBLISHING
A division of Hodder Headline
338 Euston Road
London NW1 3BH

www.headline.co.uk
www.hodderheadline.com

This book is for
ANNABEL

Acknowledgements

FOR HISTORICAL ADVICE and guidance, I must thank Adrian Weale. He has taken my appropriation – and subsequent subversion – of the subject in very good spirit, and I am very grateful.

For medical matters, I turned to Dr Peter Kyle, and his daughter, Vanessa Andreae. They were both exceedingly helpful and allowed their brains to be picked without the slightest complaint.

His son-in-law, Tobyn Andreae, was immeasurably helpful in matters of plot. He knows how thankful I hope to be.

I could not have had a finer and more rigorous editor than Marion Donaldson. She must take enormous credit for any enjoyment the reader may gain over these few hundred pages. I would recommend her to any author.

My agent, Tif Loehnis at Janklow & Nesbit, is a wonder. She has exhibited enormous faith and kindness, and has set me on a path that I hope to be very long. She is worth every percentage point.

My parents, Martin and Angela Walters, my brother Dominic, and my parents-in-law, Richard and Venetia Venning, have given me so much of the confidence and support needed to carry out such a venture. I can never full repay them.

Finally, and most importantly, there is the person to whom this book is dedicated.

Prologue

June 1986

HUGH WAS AWAY, and there was nobody to help get the children up. That sounded like Simon shouting upstairs, no doubt being picked upon by Giles, his twin. Louise would still be in bed. Only twelve, she had already reached that adolescent stage of permanent indolence. This morning was going to be a shocker, she could just feel it – they had to leave in an hour. Roll on the spring term, when they'd all be back at school.

'What?' she shouted up the stairs.

'Giles is throwing all my soldiers out the window,' came a sobbed reply.

'Giles! GILES! Stop that! Now get dressed and one of you go and wake up your sister.'

She went into the kitchen and filled up the kettle. All her actions at this time were automatic. Put teabags in pot.

Open fridge, get out milk and orange juice. Put on table. Go to cupboard next to sink. Get out five bowls and five plates. Stop – no Hugh. Only get four. Lay table. Get cornflakes out of cupboard under clock. Look at time. Half past seven. Put cornflakes on table. Look out of window. Watch soldiers raining down from boys' bedroom. Ignore it and look at paper. Hear post arrive. Go to hall, shout at children, pick up post.

She rifled through them. Nothing interesting – a newsletter from her Oxford college, British Gas, a couple of letters for Hugh, and then, curiously, a final envelope addressed to 'Miss Amy Lockhart'. That was her maiden name. There was a badly printed insignia on the top left corner and the words 'On Her Majesty's Service' running along the bottom in maroon. It was probably from the taxman. She took them into the kitchen.

The kettle had boiled, and she poured the water into the teapot. As it brewed, she studied the envelope. The insignia seemed to be of an eagle on top of an anchor, crossed out by what might have been a couple of swords. Not very Inland-Revenue-ish, she thought. It was quite bulky, and the envelope could barely contain whatever was stuffed into it. She poured herself a cup of tea and sat down at the table.

A huge crash came from above, from the boys' bedroom. A moment's silence and then some really loud screaming. Resigned, she went upstairs to find Simon sitting on the floor in tears, next to a knocked-over chest of drawers. Giles was reading an Asterix book on his bed, still wearing his pyjamas, looking the innocent.

'Giles pushed me into the chest because I tried to stop him throwing my soldiers out the window.'

'Giles? Did you?'

'No, Mummy – I've been reading, I promise.'

'I don't believe you for a second. If you don't both get dressed and downstairs in five minutes, I'll make sure your father slippers the pair of you when he gets back.'

She stared at them. Giles stared impudently back, but reluctantly got up as slowly as possible. She left the room and went across the corridor and pushed open Louise's door. The curtains were drawn and Louise was still in bed.

'Come on, young madam, time to get up,' she said as she opened the curtains.

'But Mummy,' came a voice from under the blankets, 'we don't have to get up for ages. I can miss breakfast if I want.'

'No you won't.'

'But Daddy lets me when you're away.'

'No he doesn't.'

'He does.'

'Well, he shouldn't. Now get up.'

A surly grunt. With that, Amy pulled off the sheets and blankets with one vigorous tug.

'Mummy! What are you doing? How dare you? Stop being such a fascist!'

Amy paused.

'What did you call me?'

'A fascist.'

'And what is a "fascist" exactly?'

'Why, don't you know?'

'No, I don't. I'd like you to tell me.'

Louise stayed silent.

'Go on,' Amy urged. 'What's a fascist, Louise?'

'Give it up, it's just a word.'

'No, I won't. Come on.'

'Well, it just means that you're really bossy and stuff.'

'Does it now?'

'Yeah.'

'Don't ever call me a fascist again, do you hear? You've obviously no idea what it means. I'd rather you called me a bossy cow than called me that.'

Louise went silent, shocked by her mother's intensity.

'OK, OK - sorry.'

'Good - now get up.'

Amy went back downstairs. Fascist indeed. Where had she got that from? Presumably they all called their teachers that.

She sat down and picked up the envelope. She slit it open with a spoon handle. It was from the Ministry of Defence - so that was the insignia. There were at least a dozen sheets of neatly typed paper. Even before she read it, she knew what it would be about.

Dear Miss Lockhart,

I am writing to you concerning your father, Captain John Lockhart . . .

Her eyes started to fill. She had waited nearly a quarter of a century for this, and it was hard to believe it had

4

arrived. She looked out the window. Another soldier fell
down.

August 1934

*The graffiti makes it clear they are not wanted. 'Smash
Fascists!' 'Get Rid of Blackshirt Thugs!' If he were alone, he
would be feeling scared, but with his band of brothers he feels
strong, ready to give these Jew bastards what-for. They have it
coming, that scum, they really do, taking away their jobs and
charging all those high prices. They're out for revenge, and
some Hebrew blood will be spilt tonight.*

*And what a lovely warm night for it. They certainly cut a
dash walking down Commercial Street, the twenty of them,
fine upstanding fellows ready to defend the sacredness of
Albion's soil. They aren't wearing their black shirts – this is
'unofficial' business, a little bit of extracurricular if you like.
Party line is against violence, but then most members of the
British Union of Fascists prefer a punch-up to a knees-up.*

*All they need now is a Jew, a nice fat Jew who can be taught
a lesson. This is the place for it – lots of rag-trade Shylocks
ready for a good kicking. But where the hell are they all, these
sons of Israel? They must have had a tip-off, because the streets
are empty. Could there be an anti-fascist in their ranks, a
bleeding Communist, in league with the Jews? As far as he is
concerned, this proves it, proves that the Bolshies and the Yids
are all in it together.*

*One of the mob throws a rock through a shop window. The
breaking glass sounds good, and a cheer goes up. The shop*

5

name is Solomon – a sure sign that it deserves the rock. A Star of David gets painted on the door with the words 'Jews Out'. Another cheer. They'll soon get the message, these leeches, and bugger off somewhere else.

They continue walking, curtains twitching as they pass. It smells foul round here – can't these people keep themselves clean? Another window gets broken and . . . Jesus! What the hell was that? Did someone just hurl a rock at them? Where in God's name did that bloody come from? He thinks he knows, he thinks he saw one of them running down that side street.

'Come on, lads!' he shouts. 'Get the little shit!'

More cheering and he leads them into a run, turning right down the side street, entering a row of slum housing, a few shocked pedestrians standing still.

'Get 'em all!' and the blows come down, indiscriminately.

'Fucking Jewish scum!'

The mob are nicely worked up now; nothing can stop them, not even the police. He spots the rock-thrower again, turning down another street. This is a like a maze, are they being led into a trap? He doubts it. Blood is all he wants – how dare a Yid throw a rock at an Englishman!

'Keep running! We're gaining on him!'

He's glad he keeps himself fit. No Jew is going to outrun him, and this one will be the first to know it. He can see him clearly now, thirty yards away, his little legs doing their best. He looks a real shorty, this one. Good, he'll be even shorter in a few minutes, if he ever walks again.

There are four of them in the lead now. Some of the others are finishing off the ones back there, and some are a little slower. Shameful. He must make sure they get some proper PT.

Twenty yards now, then ten, and then the lad turns round, panting, looking back at them with fear and boldness in his eyes. He must be only fifteen.

'Just leave us alone!' the lad calls out.

'Fuck you!' one of the men shouts, and the four of them pounce.

Oh yes, this is good, this is what they came here for. This little Jew-boy will regret throwing that rock. These new boots are proving worthy additions too, judging by the screams the boy gives at each kick. His face is coming up nice and red and purple under the gaslight. There's blood in his mouth too – internal bleeding that is, which means they are really giving it to him.

The boy tries covering his head but it's no help. Two of them pick him up and hold him between them, while the others take turns to hit him. The boy cannot even say 'Stop' any more, just a strange groaning. He looks a real mess and he's slipping in and out of consciousness. They cannot see his eyes any more, just a mass of bruises and cuts. Should they kill him? he thinks. Why not? Nobody will throw rocks at them again.

A whistle! The four men look back. They see the silhouettes of at least six policemen.

'Coppers!' he shouts.

They're running once more, but this time faster than before. He is running like a superman. He feels supreme now, he feels great. They will never catch him. For he is too quick, he is too clever. One day, when the country is theirs, they will run from no one. But until then, he will live underground, plotting and waiting.

Chapter One

November 1943

LOCKHART WAS ANXIOUS. They had been navigating the same three miles of coast for two hours, and still there had been no signal. The night air was clear and the sea was calm. The captain had insisted they were in the right place, although Lockhart didn't believe him.

'Who are you going to trust?' asked the sailor. 'Me, or a bunch of drunken shepherds?'

Lockhart held his tongue. Pompous naval halfwit. He didn't want to start lecturing the man on Cretan bravery. He turned, and continued to scan the inlets for the three flashes of torchlight.

The air was scented with thyme. The aroma brought back good memories, but now wasn't the moment to reminisce. The last thing he wanted was to miss the signal and find himself kicking his heels back in dusty Cairo.

Perhaps Manoli and his gang of *andartes* had been captured, tortured, shot, their families raped and deported. Those too frail to move would have been burned alive inside their homes. Lockhart slowly exhaled.

The little crewman next to him started tugging at his sleeve and pointing. Lockhart looked through his binoculars to see the dim light of a flashing torch.

'Get the captain to take us in,' Lockhart ordered under his breath.

As the crewman made his way aft, Lockhart tried to discern anything around the light, but it was too dark. He should have been helping to ready the dinghy, but something wasn't right. And then he realised the obvious: the torch was flashing four times. He looked again. There was no doubt – it was the wrong signal. Bugger. It could be a German trap, or, just as easily, a simple mistake. He went aft to find the captain.

'Bad news,' Lockhart announced. 'It's the wrong bloody signal.'

'Christ,' the captain sighed, shutting his eyes and pinching the bridge of his nose. It had been a long night and he still had to get back to Cairo.

'It's flashing four times instead of three. I'm sure my man knows the drill – he's done this before.'

'Your Cretan friend probably can't count.'

'And you can barely sail, so why don't you just shut up and do as you're told?'

Lockhart glowered at him, detecting a small, cynical smile through the captain's dark ginger beard. Lockhart held his stare.

'All right then, *sir*,' the captain said. 'What would *you* like to do then?'

Lockhart paused. The captain was making him bloody-minded. He didn't want to stay on board, but a decision made in anger could see him trussed up in the back of a German lorry, en route to a bloodstained cell in Heraklion. Sod it, thought Lockhart, Manoli had probably just made a mistake.

He looked the captain straight in the eye.

'I'm going ashore.'

The captain snorted. 'Whatever you say.'

Lockhart regretted his decision as soon he went back on deck. He had let some damn-fool sailor wind him up. He bet Theseus never had this problem when he sailed to Crete. Lockhart tried remembering his Plutarch – what was the name of Theseus's pilot? He had read it only the other day, thinking that he too should have sacrificed a goat to Aphrodite before he left.

He looked through his binoculars again. There, still, were those same four confident flashes. He felt perversely reassured. If the Germans had discovered the location of the landing point, then they would have known the correct signal too. Was he trying to justify his rash decision? Perhaps. But he had come too far now. It would be too much of a climbdown to go back.

The crewmen were readying the dinghy. On to it was lowered food, weapons and ammunition, a radio, clothing, and – most crucially for those spending the winter stuck in small mountain caves – spirits and cigarettes. As Christmas was coming up, the supply officer had even slipped in a Christmas pudding at Lockhart's request.

Lockhart checked himself over. He was dressed as a native – baggy breeches known as 'crap-catchers', a black bandanna, a thick shirt and an embroidered waistcoat. He had even grown a moustache, although it was not up to the hirsute magnificence of the typical Cretan example. Slung over his shoulder was his Sten gun and round his chest a belt of ammunition. He slowly cocked the weapon and engaged the safety catch with his right thumb.

There was one more thing, one thing that he had promised himself to get rid of. He felt the point of his left collar. It was still there, that small bump, his ultimate escape route – his suicide pill. They called them 'cough drops' at Arisaig, their training centre in Scotland, although this was a medication that killed in five seconds. In theory, it meant that you never talked, you never suffered and your friends stayed safe. It was supposed to be the honourable thing to do, because everybody cracked, running out of things to tell, until all that was left was the truth. But many of them threw the cough drops away, determined that they would never talk, and would suffer anything rather than take their own lives. If there was life, far better to hang on – let someone else kill you. Lockhart unpicked the stitching on his collar and removed the little grey capsule. He looked at it briefly, and then threw it into the water. As it landed with a tiny high-pitched splash, Lockhart hoped some poor fish didn't regard it as a tasty morsel.

'We're ready to go now, sir.'

Lockhart looked at the little crewman. There was a tremor in his voice, and his eyes were unnaturally wide. He must have been only twenty, yet here he was risking his young life in the middle of the Mediterranean for a man he had never met.

'Fancy some bravery juice?' asked Lockhart, pulling his hip flask from his breeches.

'Sorry, sir?'

'Well, if we're going to get blown to bits by whoever it is on the beach, then I'd prefer to have some Talisker inside me, wouldn't you?'

The crewman smiled gauchely – he plainly had no idea what Lockhart was talking about.

'Do you want a *drink*, man?'

'Oh, yes please, sir,' the crewman replied, taking the hip flask.

He swigged it, and Lockhart was surprised to see that the whisky didn't make him cough and choke. Richard had always said that Talisker was a lot smoother than Lockhart's 'filthy' Glenfiddich. It looked as though his brother had been proved right. The crewman handed the flask back.

'Thank you, sir, that was very nice, sir.'

'My pleasure,' said Lockhart, taking a neckful. 'Right – let's get on with it then.'

They made their way to the side of the boat. Lockhart looked around the deck. The captain waved a perfunctory goodbye. Cretin. Lockhart nodded back, turned and swung himself on to the scrambling rope. The dinghy was almost too packed for him and the crewman to board. Lockhart sat on an ammunition box in the stern, while his companion pushed them away with an oar. Unslinging the Sten, Lockhart steeled himself for an imminent volley of shots.

They were two hundred yards from the shore, and the crewman was rowing the heavy dinghy with great difficulty. Over his shoulder, Lockhart could see the torch, still flashing that exasperating four times. He gripped his gun tighter, trying to make out perhaps the shape of a German helmet, but there was nothing visible. Whoever was there was well hidden.

Lockhart looked back at the boat. They were now too far away to go back. If it was a trap, and the Germans had seen them leaving, then they would open fire. Lockhart didn't fancy his chances sitting on a box full of hand grenades. At least he wouldn't feel anything, he thought. No, they had to keep going in.

A cough. Not a loud one, but loud enough to carry across the smooth waters. The crewman looked startled. Just as he was about to speak, Lockhart put his finger to his lips. Lockhart squinted again – they were a hundred yards away and the cough had seemed to come from the right of the torch. He tried playing the sound back in his head. Had it been a German cough or a Cretan cough? Was there a difference? Lockhart knew he was clutching at straws.

With fifty yards to go, he ordered the crewman to stop rowing. As they bobbed, Lockhart noticed the flashing becoming more rapid, more insistent. The crewman looked up at him, bewildered. Lockhart scanned the beach – he began to make out three figures near the light. They didn't appear to be wearing uniforms; their shapes looked more baggy, informal, as if wearing peasant clothes.

Lockhart gesticulated to the crewman to continue rowing. It could yet be Germans in disguise, but Lockhart was now more confident. Nevertheless, he levelled his Sten gun at the three figures, waiting for a suspicious move. If that happened, he would open fire. There would be no indecision. The SOE training school at Arisaig had taught him to use weapons as part of his body, and to react without a pause.

'Hurry up, John!'

The crewman stopped rowing. It had come from one of the shapes, now only thirty or so yards away. Lockhart broke out into a big smile. It was that hairy brute Manoli! He looked at the crewman, who had shut his eyes in relief.

'Come on, keep rowing,' whispered Lockhart. 'There's a glass of raki for you when we get this lot off.'

'What the hell is raki?'

'It's a sort of local fuel. Don't worry – it's bloody dreadful.'

The men on the shore started wading towards them. They were dressed like Lockhart, and carrying either Marlin sub-machine guns or rifles over their shoulders. At their head was Manoli, Lockhart's old friend from the digs, his six-and-a-half-foot frame wading firmly through the surf. Lockhart jumped out of the dinghy.

'You took your time getting here,' said Manoli, gripping Lockhart by the shoulders.

'It was nice of me to come at all considering you gave the wrong bloody signal.'

'But we did as instructed – we flashed four times.'

'It should have been three,' said Lockhart, and then added with a smirk, 'You great big idiotic peasant.'

'And you're a pathetic excuse for a man,' replied Manoli, pulling Lockhart's moustache. 'The runner from Mr Yanni said it was four times.'

'Never mind,' said Lockhart. 'Come on, let's get the dinghy ashore.'

The two men added their weight to pulling the dinghy in. Eight more *andartes* had come down from the rocks, along with five mules. It was quite a party, and their tired faces looked excited at the cargo.

'What have you got for us here then?' asked Manoli, as they dragged the craft up the sand.

'Christmas pudding,' Lockhart replied.

'What?'

'You'll find out next month.'

By two o'clock the mules had been loaded. The creatures looked as though they were about to collapse.

'Are they going to make it?' Lockhart asked.

'Of course!' Manoli replied. 'My mules are the best in Crete. I've never known one to give up – if they do, they will make an excellent stew.'

'In that case they'd better bloody make it.'

The party left the beach, the tide starting to erase their presence. Lockhart wasn't relishing the long hike. Even though they were only walking five miles, they had to make their way up muddy goat tracks to a height of two thousand feet. The Cretans measured distance in time, and they had a habit of underestimation that irritated Lockhart. Manoli had said two hours, but Lockhart knew five would be more likely.

The paths would take them to their hideout, a cave in the side of Mount Kefala, near Alones, Manoli's village. Lockhart remembered it from peacetime, visiting Manoli's parents in their one-roomed whitewashed cottage. It was Easter, and they had served up lamb and endless bottles of raki. Lockhart had never been so drunk – not even at May Balls in Oxford. He dimly recalled falling into a coma underneath a tree, and being woken up by Manoli telling him it was time for more raki. Lockhart had unappreciatively vomited at the mention of the word.

Lockhart smiled to himself as he walked in the middle of the file. Manoli was leading briskly, and the beasts were struggling. Despite Manoli's boasting, they needed a lot of encouragement, and the men were constantly thrashing them into action. They were walking through scrubland peppered with the ubiquitous thyme bushes. Lockhart was concerned by the lack of cover, but Manoli had assured them that the nearest Germans would be in Plakia, a good seven miles away. Lockhart kept his gun at the ready, although the Cretans had slung theirs nonchalantly over their shoulders.

After half an hour they reached a road. As Manoli ordered the file to halt, Lockhart ran up to join him. They made their way to a ditch at the roadside.

'I didn't think we were going on any roads,' Lockhart whispered.

'We're not,' said Manoli. 'But we have to cross this one. It's the main coast road to Plakia – there's no way we can avoid it. It's all paths again after this.'

They sat still and listened. All was silent, except for the wind. As Lockhart's ears strained, he thought he could hear a car.

'Can you hear that?'

'Hear what?'

'The car.'

Manoli shut his eyes.

'I can't hear a thing. Are you sure you heard something?'

Lockhart listened again. Nothing. Perhaps his ears were playing tricks.

'It seems to have gone – how about giving it a few minutes?'

Manoli nodded, and went back to tell his men. There was little cover for the mules, but, grateful for the rest, they were keeping still. The men lay on the ground, their rifles aimed towards the road. After a few long minutes, there was still no sound. The car had been all in Lockhart's mind.

There was a wood on the other side, for which he was grateful – finally they could get into some decent cover. Manoli rejoined Lockhart in the ditch.

'Right, let's do this quickly,' said Lockhart.

'Agreed.'

Manoli waved his men forward. They got up swiftly, and quietly goaded the mules forward. Seeming to sense the danger, the beasts moved quickly towards the road. They crossed without too much cajoling, although the final one was proving reluctant.

Lockhart remained on the road, looking down the slope in the direction of Plakia. The road went round a blind corner after fifty yards, but various sections could be seen as it snaked down the valley. It looked clear. He turned to inspect the progress.

The final mule was still being obstinate. Despite its handler's best efforts, the beast wouldn't budge.

'Can't you move that bloody thing?' Lockhart stage-whispered to the man.

'It won't move,' groaned the *andarte* as he strained on the mule's rope. Lockhart looked back down the road. What he saw made his blood freeze.

Two bends away, he could quite clearly see headlights, moving at great speed.

'Car!' he shouted. The mule's handler stopped.

'Car! Keep pulling!'

Lockhart ran up to shove the mule by its haunches. Manoli ran out of the wood to help them. Lockhart looked back – no car. That meant it had only one more bend to travel until it came to the bend before their stretch. They had a minute at the most, and still the sodding mule wouldn't move.

The three men pulled and pushed, and eventually the beast decided to lift its hooves. Lockhart turned round – this time he could see the lights. The car had one more bend to go.

The mule was nearly walking, but with Manoli's exertions, the animal and its load was actually being dragged into the woods. Lockhart looked again – the car was invisible. It would only be seconds until it rounded their bend.

As Lockhart jumped into the trees, he became aware of the muted yellow of the headlights. The light rudely entered the wood, and the powerful Daimler Benz motor invaded the silence. All the men had their rifles trained on the car. Manoli had ordered them not to shoot, but Lockhart half expected one might get nervous and let off a round.

What Lockhart hadn't expected was for the car to slow down and then come to a stop alongside their hiding place. Lockhart's finger crept inside his trigger guard as he heard voices coming from the black staff car. He turned his head towards the anxious Cretans, and gestured towards them to hold fire.

The front passenger door opened, and out stepped a German officer, smoking a cigarette. Lockhart recognised him immediately to be an oberstleutnant – a major. The officer walked casually towards them, his boots slowly crunching along the stony road. He stopped at the ditch before the wood and looked down at his trousers.

'Ich habe schon zu viel Bier getrunken!' he shouted back to his driver. Lockhart, with his fluent knowledge of German, knew what that meant: the man had had too much beer.

Laughter came from the car. With that, the drunken officer clumsily unbuttoned his trousers and proceeded to urinate, swaying slightly as he did so.

If the German hadn't looked up, he might well have lived. The sequence of events was so rapid that Lockhart later couldn't recall what started them. Manoli maintained it was the sound of a mule, but Lockhart thought that it was nervous laughter from one of the *andartes* that had caused the officer to look into the wood.

The German's drunken eyes met Lockhart's, and just as they were registering a glassy surprise, Lockhart opened fire. The impact sent the oberstleutnant's body hurtling back towards the car. And then there was a pause, as Lockhart and the partisans looked down at the twitching body, the man's penis still leaking urine.

Lockhart ran towards the car, aiming at the driver through the passenger window. The young man had frozen. It had only been twenty seconds since his officer had stepped from the car, and now he was looking into the barrel of a British machine gun.

'Hands up!' shouted Lockhart.

The driver continued to look back at him, rigid with fear.

'I said put your hands up!'

The man didn't move.

Just as Lockhart was about to shout again, the car windscreen shattered. The driver's face instantly turned into an unrecognisable mess. Lockhart looked to his right, towards the front of the car. There was Manoli, the barrel of his Marlin smoking.

'Fuck all of them.'

Lockhart nodded slowly, looking back at the fresh corpse.

The rest of the men began to extract what they could from the car and the bodies. Within a minute, money, cigarettes and the men's pistols had been removed. Even their boots were taken. In a rushed attempt to conceal it, the car was then pushed into the ditch, with the body of the oberstleutnant restored to the passenger seat.

'They'll kill many for this,' said Manoli. 'Ten of us for every one of them, and I expect they'll burn down a village. And then there'll be the rapes and the tortures.'

'We didn't have a bloody choice,' Lockhart replied.

'I know, I know,' Manoli muttered darkly. He walked back to the wood, and Lockhart thought he heard him stifling a sob. The band followed. They were silent, shocked at the violence. For some, it had been their first engagement with a hated enemy. All were eager *andartes*, but the rawness of the killings had turned even the strongest of their stomachs.

Lockhart spent the rest of the hike in a daze. Despite the intensity and seriousness of his training, he had partly convinced himself it was all a big adventure. And now he had killed a man, added another to his list. He felt a long, long way from Anna, wherever she was.

They had first seen each other across a pile of rubble. Lockhart had been helping to remove the thick layer of earth covering a Minoan floor near the palace at Knossos. It had already taken the team of four Cretans and two Englishmen a week to uncover a mere twenty square feet, and it was dawning on Lockhart that archaeology was harder work than he normally cared for. He was spending his summer down from Oxford at the site, and he feared that all he would see of Crete would be this bloody floor. He only saw the sun at lunchtime, when the team would sit on the piles of rubble to enjoy a simple lunch of retsina, olives, bread and cheese. And it was one lunchtime, at the start of his second week, when he first saw her.

She was being led on to the site by the head of the digs, the tedious Dr Buchan. She wore a pair of long shorts, walking boots and a thick white cotton shirt. A large sunhat hid her face, and over her shoulder she carried a small knapsack. She looked slightly ungainly, her long legs tripping over the piles of ancient masonry. Lockhart and his companions started to laugh at her stumbling efforts to keep up with Buchan's long strides.

The laughter stopped when the curious couple drew near. The team stood up to receive them, all eager to see what lay underneath that large hat.

'Gentlemen,' Buchan began, 'this is Miss Anna Green, who will be joining us for the rest of the summer.'

She looked up defiantly. From then, Lockhart knew he would be more than happy to spend his time cooped up in a filthy ruin. She had a strong face – handsome even – and yet she was still pretty. Her large brown eyes looked straight into Lockhart's. Unfortunately for him, his companions felt equally mesmerised – they too stood silent, all speculating on what the summer might now bring.

'Miss Green has just spent a year at the British School of Archaeology in Athens, where she has already earned quite a name for herself. I'd ask you all to remember that she is not here as an entertainment, but as a hardworking professional.'

Lockhart noticed that their new colleague had lifted her chin a little, giving the slight impression she was looking down at them. Know-it-all, thought Lockhart. Buchan then addressed Lockhart directly.

'John, could you show Miss Green around the rest of the site?'

'I certainly will, sir,' Lockhart replied, doing his best not to smile too obviously.

'Miss Green, this is John Lockhart, who is here from Merton College for the summer. I'll leave you in his hands.'

A titter from the ranks.

They shook hands, Lockhart feeling self-conscious at the five pairs of jealous eyes behind him.

'How do you do?' he asked.

'Very well, thank you,' she replied.

The formality felt absurd amongst the rubble.

'Let me introduce you to everybody. Ah, this is Manoli Pentaris, who has been working here for . . . how long is it now, Manoli?'

'Three years.' The big Cretan grinned under his moustache, which was already vast for a twenty-three-year-old. He kissed Anna's hand with a flourish, which caused her to raise her eyebrows in amusement. Lockhart was aware that Manoli had a reputation as a ladies' man. He spent most of his spare time chasing girls in the bars in nearby Heraklion. Lockhart knew that he would be the first to regard their new arrival as 'an entertainment'.

Lockhart introduced Anna to the other Englishman, Andrew Worstead. Like Lockhart, Worstead was also still at university, at King's College in London. Lockhart liked Worstead, although many didn't. He could be chippy and aggressive, as he imagined most people were out to get him. Lockhart suspected that he had been teased about his weight at school and was thus cursed with an inferiority complex. But when he was relaxed, Worstead was good company – witty and, like Lockhart, a good drinker. The Cretan climate didn't suit him though. He found the heat hard to deal with, and his shirt was permanently drenched with sweat.

Thus it was a sweaty palm that shook Anna's.

'How nice to have you here, Miss Green,' he beamed, laying on the charm a little thick, Lockhart thought. He doubted that Worstead would be much of an adversary.

After Anna had met the rest of the group, she and Lockhart made their way around the site. As he told her about the various rooms, he noticed that she wasn't really listening. Lockhart did his best to sound authoritative, but as he was talking about the origins of the antechamber, he realised that he was wasting his time.

'You can't have been studying for very long,' she said. 'In fact it may even date from much earlier than that. Look here at the shape of these bricks.' She squatted down and pointed them out. 'Do you see how different they are from the ones back there?'

She looked up at Lockhart and smiled, a little too smugly for his liking. She really was bloody know-it-all.

'I bet you were head girl at school,' said Lockhart.

'How did you guess that?'

'I wonder.'

25

'Are you making fun of me, Mr Lockhart?'

'Maybe, Miss Green.'

Lockhart was smirking at her, and she was clearly doing her best to look serious.

'Because if you are, then I shall—'

'What? What will you do?'

'Then I shall put you across my knee. I was allowed to beat people as head girl, you know.'

As she said it, she tapped his chest. He wanted to grab her hand and kiss her there and then, but he thought better of it. His time would come.

Three weeks later, it did. Lockhart had borrowed a motorcycle, and one Sunday morning, they rode out to see the spectacular monastery at Arkadi. After a couple of hours walking around the cloisters, with Anna having now assumed the mantle of lecturer, they decided to climb a few hundred feet to the top of Mount Petrotes.

Rewarded with a clear view of the Ida range, they ate a picnic which Lockhart had deliberately made more liquid than solid. Halfway through the second bottle of retsina, Anna lay back and looked at the clear sky, a breeze blowing her brown hair across her face.

'Well!' she began. 'Aren't you going to take advantage of me now that you've lured me to the top of this mountain?'

'Oh – if I must,' Lockhart replied, trying to sound calmer than he felt. He looked straight at her.

'Well, get on with it then.'

He needed no further encouragement.

He swore he would never forget the motorcycle ride home, with Anna's arms clutched tightly under his shirt, the setting sun casting their long shadows in front of them.

Manoli had neglected to tell Lockhart about the bats. The entire roof of the large cave was a twitching mass of leathery wings and fur. Canopies had been erected to shelter the men from the droppings. Despite feeling exhausted, Lockhart eyed the creatures warily.

'Couldn't you have found a cave without this ugly lot?' he asked Manoli.

'I rather like them. They keep the same hours as us, and they behave very well.'

'I just hope they're not vampires.'

'No,' laughed Manoli. 'But we could make an offering to Carna if it would make you happy.'

'You and your bloody nymphs.'

It was seven in the morning, and the band had just arrived at the hideout. The remainder of the journey had passed uneventfully, although they had briefly rested at a small church at the foot of Mount Tsilivdikas, where Lockhart had taken the opportunity to pray for the first time in ages.

Lockhart looked around. Some of the men were eating bread and cheese, and others were turning in for the day. He couldn't work out if he felt more hungry than tired. He lay down underneath a splattered canopy and found that he couldn't sleep. He stared at the damp rock a few feet away, watching water droplets snake their way down to a small puddle. It reminded him of a passage by Louis MacNeice.

> Sleep to the noise of running water
>   To-morrow to be crossed, however deep;
> This is no river of the dead, or Lethe,
>   To-night we sleep
> On the banks of Rubicon – the die is cast;
>   There will be time to audit
> The accounts later, there will be sunlight later
>   And the equation will come out at last.

MacNeice too had read Greats at Merton, although he had left before Lockhart had arrived. For a time, Lockhart had wanted to emulate the poet, especially after he had read MacNeice's excellent translation of *Agamemnon*. But he knew that he would never get near, especially after Anna had been characteristically frank about his scribblings.

The air was cool in the cave, and he started to shiver slightly. He tucked the thin blanket around his shoulders, which did little to help. He thought of Anna, his best critic, and little Amy. That was too painful. Sleep would be a release, a temporary relief from the images of the dying oberstleutnant and his driver.

He was woken by Manoli, who was shaking him hard.

'Wake up, John.'

'What time is it?' Lockhart yawned.

'It's nearly midday.'

Lockhart looked to the mouth of the cave. It was a bright winter's day, the type of day for a bracing cross-country run, about the only keen thing he ever did at Winchester. Other sports had held little appeal – he left those for his older brother Richard. Richard. He had been killed in Tunisia last December, incinerated in his tank. Lockhart still hated the baldness of the telegram that left him as the only living member of the family. Mother had died in the flu epidemic of 1918 when was five, and father was taken away by a heart attack in '36. It was Richard's death that had spurred him out of military intelligence in Whitehall over to SOE in its eccentric Baker Street flat. The transfer had been hard to obtain, as the department valued his languages, but Lockhart was adamant that he should fight.

He started to cough. The men had lit a fire, and the cave was filling up with smoke. They had no choice: a fire outside would mean instant detection. Even if the Germans did not spot it, they would have heard soon enough. There were plenty of villagers who were willing to collaborate.

'I don't suppose you've got some breakfast going?'

'Indeed we do,' Manoli replied proudly. 'Some of that delicious pudding you brought us.'

'But that's for Christmas, you ignorant peasant!'

'We might not be around by then – I thought it best to enjoy it while we can. Besides, I was too intrigued.'

Manoli brought Lockhart a hunk of the pudding in a grey mess tin, and a cup of black coffee.

'Happy bloody Christmas,' Lockhart toasted, and tucked in with his fingers. It was the worst Christmas pudding he had ever tasted. Cairo must have made it out of camel dung. Still, the *andartes* seemed to be enjoying it.

After breakfast, Lockhart and Manoli sat at the back of the cave, out of earshot of the rest of the band.

'So what plans do you have for us?' Manoli asked.

'There's not one big plan, I'm afraid. My orders are to have as much fun as possible. You've seen all those explosives I've brought. I'm sure we'll be able to do some damage with that lot.'

Manoli chuckled. Lockhart thought his laugh rang hollow. It was not the same laugh as that of the lecherous young archaeologist from ten years ago. Manoli still remained a source of joy, but it was underpinned by grimness. His brother had been a victim of the German reprisals carried out a month after the invasion of May 1941. General Student's paratroopers had expected to be welcomed with open arms by the Cretans: instead, many of them were shot as they were drifting down. Even the priests had joined in with the fighting, one of whom was Manoli's brother. He had used his church in Rethimno to shelter resistance fighters, but he had been betrayed.

The penalty was swift. The men found in the church were led into the town square to be hanged. Manoli's brother had pleaded with the German officer to spare the men's lives, offering his life in exchange. The officer, an Oberstleutnant Walther Dietrich, agreed, and Manoli's brother was indeed hanged. His body was left there for two weeks. The men were shot shortly afterwards.

Manoli heard about his brother's death while he was hiding in the hills outside Rethimno. He did not speak and barely moved for two days. On the third day he went back to Alones, where he told his parents. The villagers said they could hear the wailing from the top of Mount Kefala. His parents warned Manoli not to let his heart grow cold, but the advice was fruitless. The loss had changed him, eradicating much of his laughter, making him hard. His father died a year later at the age of fifty-seven. Manoli blamed his death on the Germans. His mother pleaded with him not to continue as an *andarte*, but his mind was made up. He would kill as many of them as he could.

Lockhart looked at his old friend.

'How are you, Manoli?'

'Not so bad.' The big man slumped.

'And your mother?'

'She's not too bad. I haven't told her you were coming. You know what she's like – the whole of Crete would know by lunchtime.'

'At least she's still gossiping.'

'Oh yes, that hasn't changed. But the gossip is no longer about who's run off with who, or whose son has been caught stealing sheep. It's all about death. Just death.'

'I'm sorry, Manoli.'

'Don't be. You're here, and that brings me a lot of happiness. How is Anna?'

Lockhart looked at his boots. He'd known Manoli would ask him sooner or later. He took a deep breath.

'The truth is, I don't know, Manoli. I don't even know if she's still alive.'

Manoli frowned.

'How do you mean? Has she disappeared?'

'Worse. She's been taken prisoner by the Germans.'

'How?'

'She was in Holland when it was invaded. She was there with her mother, trying to persuade her to come and join us in England. But just as she was about to leave, the paratroopers landed and she was stuck. I didn't hear a word from her for two months, and then the Foreign Office told me that they had heard via the underground that she was alive. I remember asking a chum there if they could do anything, and all he said was, "What do you want us to do? Declare war again?" I nearly decked him, but he had a point.'

'But why is she in prison?'

'About two years ago, I found out via the Resistance that Anna had been locked up in Vught concentration camp in Belgium. She had been caught working on an underground newspaper, writing articles about the evil of Nazism.'

'Is there anything you can do?'

'Nothing. I can do precisely nothing. My fear is that Anna with her defiant nature will not have endeared herself to her captors. What makes it even worse is that Amy keeps asking when Mummy's coming back home . . .'

'How old is she now?'

'She's just turned six. She can hardly remember her mother. In fact, when she was a little younger, she thought the photograph of Anna actually *was* Anna, and she would talk to it.'

'So who looks after her?'

'I did for a while, but it was hopeless. She's now with Anna's sister, who's a gem.'

They sat in silence. Manoli placed his hand on Lockhart's shoulder.

'I try not to think about it,' said Lockhart. 'And I try to keep myself as busy as possible. But as soon as I stop, even for a second, my brain starts bringing up terrible images. I think that maybe she's been shot. Not knowing if she's alive or dead is a very cruel trick indeed. Sometimes I think it's better to think she's dead, but I feel so guilty when I do. But when I think she's alive, I'm tortured by thoughts of what they might be doing to her . . .'

Manoli looked at his old friend. Although he was only thirty, Lockhart's hair was starting to go grey. His face looked leaner than he remembered – the puppy fat had disappeared. Manoli thought he looked more handsome for it, but as with too many, the war had given his eyes a faraway look. But the swagger remained, complemented by a new firmness and a quiet authority. The war had changed them into men they had never thought they would be. They had both foreseen peaceful lives of digging up past civilisations, and now they were killing to protect their own. That was what Manoli hated most of all: that the Nazis had taken not just lives, but the futures of those who were still living. It was like being made to grow up all over again.

* * *

Berlin had been especially cold all November, but this morning seemed colder than ever, thought Hauptsturmführer Carl Strasser. The forecast said it would stay at ten degrees below all day and he didn't doubt it – he could even see his breath as he lay in bed. Still, at least he had a bed, a luxury he didn't have in Russia, where it would hit forty below. Strasser had been with the SS Das Reich Division, fighting with them from November 1941, until last March, when he was posted back to Berlin.

It was still dark outside. He looked at his watch. It was six o'clock, as he knew it would be. He had woken up at that time for months now, but he always liked to check. He was due at work at the SS Hauptamt – headquarters – on Berka Strasse at half past seven. As it was only a ten-minute walk from his barracks, he had time to have a leisurely breakfast down in the mess room. He wouldn't have a shower – the water was bound to be cold and he couldn't face it. A cold shave was bad enough, but a cold shower, no way. This time last year he would have killed to have got clean, to have washed off even a few lice. But barrack and office life was making him soft once more, and to be honest, he didn't regret it one little bit. He had paid his dues.

He got up and walked across the small room to the washbasin. As he ran the water, he looked at himself in the foxed mirror. A face much older than his twenty-seven years looked back. The blue eyes looked baggy and tired and the complexion was an off-grey. He had looked healthier at the front, where he had sustained the small scar on his right cheek. A Russian shell had hit a nearby field gun, the shrapnel killing two of his NCOs. Strasser had been lucky – those men had taken the brunt of the blast, sheltering him from the worst of it. He had also taken a few pieces in his right leg, but they had been dug out successfully, leaving him with a slight numbness. After the explosion, he had lain in shock, looking down at his uniform, trying to work out whether the pieces of flesh and bone splattered on his tunic were his.

He felt to see if the water was getting hot. It wasn't. Ever since the air raids had started, hot water was scarce. Strasser knew that it was the small things that would drain the morale from his fellow Berliners, no matter what the Führer or their gauleiter, Dr Goebbels, might say. Last week, he had tried to get a new bulb for his bedside light, but old Karl in the stores had said there weren't any. In the end he took a bulb from an unused lamp at headquarters. It was ridiculous. Every day, Strasser was organising the shipment of vast quantities of ordnance from the factories and labour camps to the front line and he couldn't even get a new bulb. And he was an officer in the SS – how much harder was it for ordinary people? He began to doubt whether all those armaments on all those sheets of paper even existed, and whether he wasn't part of some vast game involving imaginary armies.

It had been a bad year for the Reich, thought Strasser. In January, von Paulus had capitulated at Stalingrad, and in the spring the war in North Africa had been lost. The treacherous Italians had signed an armistice with the Allies in August, and then there had been another defeat at the hands of the Russians at Kursk. And now there was the bombing, although last night they had been spared. The weather must have been too bad, even for the Lancasters.

After he had shaved, Strasser splashed some freezing water over his chest and under his arms. That made him feel a little fresher. He opened his door, and hanging up in the corridor was a clean undershirt, left there by his mann – his private – who had also polished his boots overnight. The mann was a lad of eighteen called Heinrich whom Strasser shared with another hauptsturmführer. Heinrich had been injured when he was training – shot in the foot – and to his great shame he would never be able to fight. He was a true believer in National Socialism, and he looked Aryan through and through. His Heil Hitlers were so earnest that they had at first caused Strasser to laugh. Heinrich had looked worried – was he doing it wrong, Hauptsturmführer? Not at all, not at all, Strasser had replied, telling the young mann that maybe he was a bit too loud for that early in the morning.

He got dressed. His move back to headquarters meant that he no longer wore a field-grey tunic but a sky-blue one instead. The trousers remained grey, as did his cap, complete with the death's-head insignia. He had been promoted too, so now his left collar bore the three pips of his new rank, rather than the two of obersturmführer. His right collar bore the SS runes – two lightning flashes of silver braid that made men like him stand above ordinary Wehrmacht soldiers.

His belt and holster hung on the back of the door. In it was a Walther P38, which he preferred to his old Luger, which had a habit of jamming. The P38 was a lot heavier, but then it was a lot more powerful too – it must have claimed the lives of at least twelve Russians. He put the belt on, and felt the reassuring kilogram of pistol rest on his left hip. His field-grey overcoat, which also bore the SS runes and his rank, was hanging in his cupboard. It still felt a little damp from the snowstorm he was caught in yesterday evening – he should have left it out to dry. He folded it together, and draping it over his left arm went down to his breakfast of eggs, ersatz coffee and bread.

As he stepped out on to the street, it started to snow. Strasser cursed his luck – his overcoat would probably end up rotting at this rate. There was a strong wind too, which stung his face. It was still dark and it was certainly still cold – this was no morning to go to work. Perhaps he would treat himself to an evening at Kitty's place on Giesebrechtstrasse – Leni there would cheer him up. It would cost him a fortune, but she certainly knew how to make him forget everything else.

Berlin was still waking up. As he walked, he could see lights switching on through the gaps in blackout curtains. There were only a few cars around, mostly staff cars, their dim headlights lazily mirrored in the slushy streets. Shops were beginning to open – he passed a baker's he remembered being owned by the Taubers. As a boy, Strasser had loved eating their bagels, toasted and covered with thick brown honey. He hadn't realised the Taubers were Jews until their shop was smashed up, and Stars of David painted all over the shop front. The Taubers had long since left – a shame, because he missed their bagels. Still, it was for the good of the Reich that they had gone, he was told, although he had found that hard to accept at first.

He reached headquarters at precisely twenty-five past seven. He recognised the two guards standing at the front doors, who spent this time in the morning permanently saluting. He saluted them back, and walked into the atrium. White columns draped with swastika banners reached eighty feet up to the ceiling. A vast marble staircase rose up at the end, with a portrait of the Reichsführer SS, Heinrich Himmler, looking down it.

There was a short queue at the security gate, and Strasser joined it, getting his pass ready. Standing in front of him was his closest colleague in the Beschaffungsamt – procurement – section, Hauptsturmführer Max Esser. He was unmistakable from behind as he only had one ear – the other one had burnt off somewhere near Kursk. Strasser tapped him on the shoulder.

'Good morning, Max,' he said breezily. 'How are you this morning?'

Esser turned round – his eyes lit up when he saw it was Strasser.

'Terrible. Absolutely terrible. Where were you? I thought you were going to join us at the pictures. We ended up making a night of it and now I feel like shit.'

'You don't look great, I must admit.'

'Thanks, Carl.' Esser smiled. 'I can always count on you to give me the honest truth.'

'But I was lying!'

'So, I don't look too bad then?'

'No, Max, in fact you look shit – really, really shit.'

Esser playfully punched Strasser in the stomach.

'Just you wait, Carl, one day we'll get you out and pour a bottle of schnapps down your throat, and then we'll see how you look.'

'You're on. So long as you pay.'

The two men showed their passes to the guard at the gate. He nodded them through, and they made their way up the stairs, continuing their banter.

Strasser shared an office with Esser and a ferocious-looking secretary, the gargantuan Frau Buch. She held the rank of a junior NCO – a gefreiter – and even Strasser would admit she looked terrifying in her uniform. She worshipped the Führer, so much so that she had hung twenty pictures of him on the office walls, making the place into a shrine. Unlike her hero, however, she chain-smoked, with the result that she had a cough like a panzer starting up. Frau Buch was in her early fifties, and she treated the two young officers as errant children. In return, they endlessly teased her and indulged in horseplay such as throwing paper aeroplanes at her desk.

Frau Buch's ashtray was already half full when Strasser and Esser entered.

'Good morning, Head Matron,' grinned Esser.

'And what happened to you last night?' she enquired, a cigarette dangling from her lower lip.

Esser looked pleadingly at Strasser for support, but Strasser was sitting down and smiling to himself.

'I went to dinner with my mother,' Esser replied.

'Balls you did,' Frau Buch spluttered.

'Now, now, Gefreiter, that's no way to talk to an officer,' said Strasser, not looking up.

The other two went silent. Was he joking? He looked serious enough. Carl could be like this, Esser thought, suddenly blowing cold, getting all 'Party'.

Strasser looked up and smiled.

'I do think we should be careful though,' he said. 'I wouldn't like our colleagues in the next-door offices to think that discipline in our little world had completely broken down.'

'Quite right,' replied Esser with mock severity. 'Gefreiter – get on with your work or you'll end up herding Jews in Ravensbruck.'

'Yes, sir, my esteemed Hauptsturmführer.'

'That's much more like it,' said Strasser, and the three of them settled down to work, Frau Buch's typewriter clattering away. For the next two hours, Strasser and Esser worked mostly in silence, occasionally checking a fact with each other.

Just before ten, Strasser's telephone rang. He let it ring a few times as he was in the middle of a calculation, and then picked it up.

'Yes?'

'Hauptsturmführer Strasser?' asked the female voice at the end of the line.

'Yes.'

'This is Obergruppenführer Berger's office. Could you come up and see the Obergruppenführer right away?'

Strasser's heart missed a beat. Berger was the head of SS recruiting and the SS Hauptamt.

'Yes, of course – I shall be up immediately.'

Strasser put the phone down. Esser and Frau Buch were looking expectantly at him.

'That was Berger's office. I've got to see him right away.'

'Did they tell you why?' asked Esser.

'No they didn't. And before you ask, I have absolutely no idea.'

'Armenoi,' said Manoli. 'There's a big fuel and ammo dump at Armenoi.'

Lockhart and Manoli were talking business again – the temptation to wallow in their private miseries had nearly bettered them. They were studying a map that Manoli had sketched.

'How heavily is it guarded?' Lockhart asked.

'Quite lightly, as the Germans do not think we have the means to raid it. I suppose there must be around thirty or forty troops there. It's a busy place, with lorries always going in and out.'

'What about locals? Do many locals work there?'

'A few – they are mainly used for building huts inside the compound.'

'Couldn't we disguise ourselves as a work gang?'

'We could, but there are always rigorous checks of the gangs for just this reason. I think it's too risky.'

Lockhart chewed his lip.

'Presumably it's surrounded by barbed wire. Electri-fied?'

'No, I don't think so,' Manoli replied. 'But there are regular patrols around the perimeter.'

'How big are these patrols?'

'Normally a couple of men. Usually with a dog.'

'So, if we took care of a patrol, we might have enough time to cut through the fence, cause havoc, and run back into the night.'

'We might, yes.'

Manoli looked up.

'Have you done this before, John?'

'Oh, Richard and I used to do this sort of thing every day when we were small.'

But Manoli wasn't laughing.

'All right, Manoli, yes I have,' said Lockhart guardedly.

'Where?'

'In France, in the summer.'

'What did you do?'

Lockhart eyed Manoli warily, not because he didn't trust him, but because he was conditioned to not talking about his work.

'It was my first mission, although it wasn't an arms dump, it was a power station.'

'A power station?'

'That's right – it supplied the power to a massive steelworks. Our bombers had been unsuccessfully trying to destroy it for weeks. My orders were to link up with the Resistance and do what the RAF couldn't do.'

'And did you?'

'Yes – yes, we did, but . . .' Lockhart's voice trailed off.

'But what?'

'But we lost a lot of men.'

'How many?'

'Seven out of a party of twelve, but before you say anything else, that's small compared to the amount of civilians who were being accidentally killed in the bombing raids.'

Manoli looked grim.

'How did you lose them?' he eventually asked.

'When we were escaping we ran into a German patrol – it was just bad luck, that was all.'

Manoli breathed out.

'And you led this mission?'

'Yes. But I have to tell you, Manoli, that it was considered a great success.'

'Despite your losses?'

'Despite our losses. I hear the power station is still out of action. That means no more steel out of that plant, which means fewer tanks for the Germans, which means fewer lives lost in the long run. In the end it's just maths, just numbers.'

'And now you think you can lead me and my men into a German arms dump, blow it up and be back in time for tea?'

'That's up to you. I never said they were my men. If you'd prefer, we could just sit in this cave, and radio Cairo for some nicer Christmas pudding.'

Manoli stayed silent.

'Look, Manoli, I know what you're thinking. The last time you saw me, I was a cocky student, and here I am, a few years later, telling you and your men to risk their lives blowing up German ammunition dumps. I still can't believe it either. Even though I am one, I don't feel like an agent, but that's what I've had to become. It's my duty, Manoli. I'd wasted far too much time farting around in so-called intelligence in Whitehall, but now I'm actually *fighting* this war. If I didn't speak Greek or know this place, I'd probably be just a regular soldier, like Richard was. And it just so happens that my duty now involves coming over here to help you in giving the Germans a hard time. That's all I want to do, to help.'

Manoli cradled the back of his head in his hands.

'That may be fair, but let's not be too ambitious. My men aren't real soldiers.'

'I know, but they're committed, which is worth a lot of training. What do you say, arms dump or not? Come on.'

Manoli sighed. 'The arms dump. Let's blow up an arms dump.'

The band spent the next few days learning how to use the explosives. Lockhart had brought enough plastic explosives to eradicate half the island, let alone a fuel dump. The *andartes* were sceptical about the sticky, dough-like substance, so Lockhart took the risk of using a small amount to blow up a rock. The demonstration was a success, as the rock was obliterated. The only mishap was a falling fragment hitting one of the men on the head, knocking him out. He revived to be met by a throbbing headache and his companions' laughter.

Lockhart also taught the men how to cut a throat, although some of them appeared not to need the lesson.

Manoli had warned him that at least two of their group were murderers, but with a common enemy, an unholy alliance had been formed between farmer and criminal.

Although not refined, the men were clearly capable fighters. Centuries of bloody feuds on the island meant that many Cretans were born warriors. Children as young as six knew how to use a rifle, and during the invasion, teenagers fought alongside their fathers and uncles. It was said that the only good thing to come out of the occupation was that the islanders were no longer killing each other. However, the ancient Cretan art of thieving continued unabated, as the shortages got worse.

With their preparation over, the band left the cave. Lockhart knew that the men were as ready as they would ever be. They might not be up to the standard required at Arisaig, but Lockhart had neither the facilities nor the time. The men handled the weapons and the explosives well, but he was worried that they lacked the discipline to take orders during an engagement.

The route to Armenoi was tortuous. Once again, Manoli had underestimated the length of the journey. It took three nights, stumbling along broken paths used only by sheep and goats. Many of the men's boots were in bad shape, and Lockhart feared that two of them would not make it. When they removed their boots at the end of a night's walk, their feet were raw and bleeding. The antiseptic cream from his medical kit was soon exhausted, and Lockhart cursed that he had not taken the boots from the young crewman who had rowed him ashore.

The nights were cold too, and the wind, funnelled through the mountain passes, was vicious. No matter how many layers Lockhart put on, it was never enough. But he was lucky – some of the men's clothes were flimsy, and they made a brave show of not complaining.

By day, they sheltered in caves, which were as cold as the nights. Those that they used were too small to light fires in, so they slept tightly packed together. The smell of the mass of male bodies reminded him of the digs at Knossos – there was something uniquely foul about Cretan sweat, Lockhart thought. And no fires meant no hot food, which sapped morale still further. But they had cigarettes, which helped.

These conditions caused Lockhart to marvel at the stamina of the runners, who undertook journeys such as this week on week, month on month. They had done so for the past two years, taking messages from one group of *andartes* to another. Usually wiry and small, they made twice as much speed as Lockhart's group. They travelled alone, and seemed to exist on very little food. Their feet were horrific to behold.

As they tried to sleep, Manoli would quietly recite the *Erotocritos*, a seventeenth-century Cretan epic poem, the ten thousand lines of which he knew by heart. One passage stuck in Lockhart's mind.

> Observe how Eros works his magic spells,
> And how all love-sick mortals he compels.
> He quickens their desire and gives it might,
> And teaches them to wrestle in the night.

He cheapens gold, to blemish he gives charm.
And to the weakling lends a warrior's arm;
He makes the coward dare, the sluggard race,
The awkward he endows with every grace.
Love made Rotokritos to hold his ground
And to defy the ten who gathered round.

Lockhart was constantly impressed by Manoli's knowledge of the classics. Sometimes he felt a fraud. There was he, with a doctorate under his belt and a classics don for a father, and there was Manoli, the son of a shepherd, for whom the classics were not just texts, but living, spoken works.

They reached Armenoi early on a Sunday morning. Manoli's plan to hide in a small chapel on the hills outside the town relied on their arriving twenty-four hours earlier. Instead, they had to make do with a large ditch in an olive grove. Lockhart didn't care for it, but there was a good view of the dump, which lay about three hundred yards away down a slight slope.

As the men slept, Lockhart and Manoli took the first watch in order to observe the goings-on beneath them. As he looked through his binoculars, Lockhart felt his heart quicken. The dump was about the size of two football pitches, surrounded by barbed wire. The main gate was a constant source of activity, with trucks kicking up lingering dust clouds. The compound contained huge stacks of fuel drums, and a large, heavily guarded storehouse in the middle.

'That has to be the ammunition store,' said Lockhart, passing the binoculars to Manoli. 'That big hut in the middle.'

Manoli adjusted the focus. 'It looks pretty hard to get to – it's a long way from the fence. Perhaps we could just throw some hand grenades at it and run.'

'They'd just explode harmlessly on the outside. No, we've got to get inside and actually lay the plastic explosive.'

'How in God's name are we going to do that?'

'We'll have two things on our side – surprise and darkness. We'll need to split into two parties. The first takes care of the oil drums nearest the main gate. That will create a diversion for the second lot to try and get in the storehouse. It won't be easy, but I can't think of a better way.'

The Cretan breathed out. 'We were right to eat your Christmas pudding early. I don't think any of us are going to be here this time next month.'

'Stop being so pessimistic, Manoli. We're not dead yet, and I certainly don't intend to be. We'll be in and out in five minutes – they really won't know what's hit them. Come on – how good can these Jerries be if they're the ones chosen to look after a fuel dump in Crete? If they were real fighters they'd be in Italy or Africa, not here.'

Lockhart hoped he sounded convincing. As they discussed the details of their plan, he felt an unusual nervousness creep up on him. It wasn't the same fear he had when he landed, but a deeper dread that made him think this was his last day. By tonight, he'd be strung up in a town centre and left to rot. His hand shook slightly as he drew a plan in the grit at their feet. He knew Manoli had noticed it.

It was half past two in the morning – half an hour before they were due to attack. The eight men crouched in the ditch, repeatedly checking their weapons. Lockhart instructed them to put some mud on their faces, and in the moonlight the whiteness of their eyes and teeth made them look almost demonic.

Lockhart crawled up to the lip of the ditch and surveyed the perimeter fence. He watched the patrol make its way along the fence's near side, the breath of the men and their Alsatian swirling around them. The interior of the compound was well lit but quiet, although Lockhart could just hear the crackling sound of a badly tuned radio coming from the guardhouse near the gate.

The first part of the plan was to eliminate the patrol, which made a circuit every fifteen minutes. Lockhart and two others would lie behind some scratchy bushes near the corner of the compound, and as the guards passed, leap out and slit their throats. Lockhart and the murderous-looking Christos were assigned to the two guards, and the other *andarte*, Niko, would kill the dog. As the corner was a good five to six minutes' walk away from the main gate, the guards there would not notice the absence of their colleagues for that period of time.

According to Lockhart, that should give them enough time to cut through the wire, toss some grenades in amongst the fuel drums near the gate, set the plastic explosive in the storehouse and then get the hell out for a five-hour route march back to the previous night's cave. If there was any problem with the storehouse, then Lockhart had ordered the men to leave it alone and hope the fire from the burning fuel drums would take care of the ammunition. He doubted that Arisaig would have approved of the crude tactics, but he was certainly going to set his part of Europe ablaze.

Lockhart made his way back to the group.

'Everything looks as it should be,' he whispered.

'So no guards and a Red Cross parcel each,' Manoli whispered back.

'That's right, and Betty Grable says she is getting a little bored of waiting.'

They smiled in the darkness, both men knowing their banter was a scanty covering for fear.

Lockhart beckoned Niko and Christos. Their breath stank of raki. Lockhart thought of reprimanding them, but there seemed little point. Besides, he could have done with some himself.

'It's now quarter to three,' he said to them. 'Check your weapons one last time. Leave behind everything except for your guns, knives and explosives. Is that clear?'

The men nodded. They looked nervous. Lockhart tried not to show that he felt similarly.

'Are you sure you know what to do, Manoli?'

'Quite sure. As soon as you have got rid of the patrol, we'll come down to the wire to join you.'

Manoli gripped Lockhart by the shoulders.

'Good luck. I'll either see you in a few minutes or never again,' the Cretan said.

At first, Lockhart wanted to make the obvious joke, but he stopped himself.

'Thanks, Manoli. Good luck too.'

Niko and Christos signalled that they were ready. Lockhart checked himself over one last time, and the three men went up to the edge of the ditch.

The guards had come back round to the near side of the fence again. They seemed relaxed – one of them was smoking a cigarette, and their laughter drifted up the hill. Lockhart handed the binoculars to Christos.

'Do you see your man, Christos? Yours is the one nearest us, the one with the cigarette.'

Christos nodded and passed the binoculars to Niko.

'The dog is going to be hard, Niko,' Lockhart said. 'Are you all right to deal with it?'

'It shouldn't be too difficult,' Niko replied. 'I just need to bash its head with my gun.'

'And can you both see where we're going to hide, the small bushes near the corner of the fence?'

The men exchanged the binoculars, and muttered silently to themselves. They nodded to Lockhart. Their eyes were wide open.

The guards were nearing the far corner, about to turn away and out of sight.

'Move when I move,' Lockhart ordered.

He watched as the men rounded the corner. As soon as he saw the last glint from their helmets, he stood up and started running down the slope. His heart was beating maniacally, and his legs felt peculiarly shaky as he did his best not to trip over. He heard Christos and Niko behind him, their breath coming in sharp bursts. They seemed to be making a racket, but nothing stirred within the compound.

The bushes were getting closer now, and Lockhart thought they looked inadequate. Surely they would be spotted immediately? He consoled himself that the guards were probably feeling too relaxed to be observant, and it was movement that was noticed at night, not shapes. So long as they kept still, they should be safe.

They made it to the bushes in just over a minute. They slid down on to the stony surface, sharp pebbles digging into their stomachs and chests. Lockhart estimated they would now have a five-minute wait until the guards came round again. He looked down the length of the fence in the direction from which they would be walking.

They lay panting for a few seconds, accustoming themselves to their new location. Lockhart soon noticed their breath was lit up by the arc lights from inside the compound. The bushes would look as though someone was boiling a kettle in them, he thought. At Arisaig, they had taught him to put snow in his mouth, but there was no snow here. He turned to point it out to Niko and Christos, and then tucked his mouth under his shirt. They did the same.

He aimed his Sten gun down the length of the fence. If the dog spotted them, they would open fire and then run for it. There was no point waiting for the guards to react. Arisaig rules were to get the violence in first. Christos and

Niko pointed their rifles in the same direction, their fingers slowly moving in and out of the trigger guards. Lockhart looked at his watch – two minutes to go. He laid his knife by his side. As soon as the guards passed, he would exchange the gun for it, get up, run up behind his man, clamp his left hand over his mouth, jerk back his head, and then draw the knife deeply across and into the man's neck. It should take less then ten seconds. In theory the victim would not make a sound. In theory.

As if running to a timetable, the patrol rounded the corner two minutes later. Lockhart heard Niko draw in his breath sharply. Christos made no sound and seemed calm. Had he killed before? Lockhart hoped so.

Lockhart began to make out the faces of the two Germans. They looked older than he had imagined. Perhaps these really were, as he had told Manoli, the dregs of the Wehrmacht. One was talking, and the other was laughing occasionally. It sounded like a long-winded joke or anecdote. Lockhart prayed that whatever it was would last long enough to take them past the bushes. If the story ended before then, they might look around.

The one member of the patrol that wasn't listening was the dog. Lockhart feared the Alsatian more than anything else. He couldn't take his eyes off it, its tongue hanging out as it padded dutifully along. It was keeping its head to the ground, no doubt as bored of the circuit as its masters were.

Lockhart had never owned a dog, but he knew what one looked like when it had smelled something. The

Alsatian's head jerked forward in their direction, its whole body pulled by its nose. Its lead tightened, it started barking. The guards stopped their conversation and looked towards them. Arisaig rules, thought Lockhart. Goodbye, Germans; sorry, dog. He opened fire.

Manoli saw the flash of the guns' muzzles in the bushes. Watching breathlessly through the binoculars, he saw the two Germans and the dog knocked back by the gunfire. Lockhart and his men must have emptied their magazines into them.

He looked over to the compound. Lights were going on all over it, and he could hear orders being shouted and dogs barking. After a few seconds, some partially clothed Germans appeared from the guardhouse near the gate. They were carrying machine guns and hand grenades. This lot weren't as dozy as Lockhart had suspected, thought Manoli.

He looked back at the bushes. Lockhart and the two others had already got up, and were running back up to the ditch. It would take them at least a couple of minutes to get there. Would it be enough time? The guards were already out of the compund, and were running around the fence towards them. They numbered at least twenty, and they were bound to see the three *andartes* fleeing up the hill. Manoli felt helpless. He would only order the rest of the gang to open fire if the Germans spotted Lockhart. To fire now would give away their position, and there was still a chance that those running wouldn't be spotted.

* * *

Lockhart ran as he had never done before. Although he was quick, he was not as swift as the two Cretans, who were slightly ahead of him. The loose ground made progress difficult, and the men stumbled frequently. The ditch still looked very far away, and he began to detect the sound of frantic activity behind him. Would it be best to lie and hide in some low scrub? But instinct took over. He kept running.

For a split second before he heard the shots, he could see their effect – fragments of stone and dust kicked up from the ground around him. The rattling crackle of the sub-machine guns drove a panicky terror into him, reminding him of the escape from the power station in France. So this was how his life was going to end. Any second now, he would feel an immense thump in the back and then blackness. No pain, just blackness.

There was now no choice. Manoli ordered his men to fire. It had the immediate effect of stopping the Germans. They hit the ground and waited, as another volley whipped over their heads.

Manoli noticed that Lockhart and the two others had also gone to ground. They were still a good hundred yards away, in amongst some scrub. They would be able to crawl up to the ditch, but that would take several minutes. In the mean time, the best Manoli could do was to offer covering fire.

Lockhart lay in the scrub, panting. He couldn't see where Niko and Christos had got to, and he didn't want to shout to find out. He heard bullets whizz over him from both directions. That Manoli had opened fire gave him great comfort, but he was now in the worst possible situation. He was on his own, and caught in crossfire. If he got up, he would be dead within seconds, perhaps killed by a Cretan bullet. If he stayed, the Germans would eventually overrun Manoli's position and he would be found as they did so. The only thing he could do was to drag himself up the hill, tearing his front on the sharp rocks and the gorse.

Although the ground cut into him savagely, Lockhart could not feel a thing. It was only when he had reached some stone slabs that he realised how rough the going had been. As he paused on their cold surface, with the sound of gunfire all around him, his mind drifted back to another life. He looked at the slabs closely, slowly realising they were slab stelae, erected over Minoan tombs as markers. The irony. He appeared to have made an archaeological discovery in the middle of a gun battle. What he hadn't noticed, during this reverie, was a grenade about to land fifteen yards ahead of him.

The *andartes* in the ditch were fighting well, but Manoli knew that there would come a point when they would have to flee. The Germans were fighting back ferociously, and were making steady progress up the hill. When they got within grenade-throwing range, that would be the time to go. To wait for Lockhart and the others would result in death or capture. That was what logic told him, but he couldn't bring himself to leave his comrades.

The Germans were within fifty yards of where he had seen Lockhart go to ground. Through the binoculars he thought he could see a dim shape moving through the undergrowth, but he wasn't sure. He could only look for a few seconds at a time – the German fire was constantly raking the top of the ditch. As he ducked down, Manoli heard the explosion.

He thought his eardrums had burst. Even though it had not landed that close, the force of the grenade smashing into Lockhart's body momentarily deafened him. For a few moments he lay there, not daring to open his eyes, his brain trying to evaluate what had happened and whether there was any damage to his body. He couldn't tell if he had lost a leg or merely suffered a scratch. Shock was shutting parts of him down, and his rational side fought against it. He had to keep moving, he told himself, but his brain wouldn't let him.

He lay in suspended animation for several more seconds, his hearing gradually returning. Gunfire and shouts crept back into his brain, reminding him where he was. He knew there would be more grenades, and he wouldn't be so lucky next time. Slowly, he brought himself up into a low crouch – his body still seemed to be working. He ran as best as he could, trying to keep at the same level as the scrub. To have continued crawling would have been too dangerous – he now had to get away from the grenades.

Manoli kept his head down for a few more seconds after the explosion. Then he tentatively got up and scanned the battleground. A small cloud of dust and smoke hung in the air, and it was hard to make out if anybody had been hit. He trained the binoculars on the slope and noticed someone running. It looked like Lockhart. He searched for Niko and Christos, but of them there was no sign. Perhaps they had been hit, or were lying low. He looked back to Lockhart. There was nothing. Manoli scoured the scrub frantically, but there was no movement. Where had he gone? The firing started again. Perhaps it was time to run.

He had only fifty yards to go. If he could just make the ditch, he would be safe for the time being. They could hold the Germans off for a while and maybe make good their escape. A grenade exploded over to his right, far enough away to cause no harm, but near enough to make him dive down.

As he got up, Lockhart saw a black shadow a few yards to his left. He ran towards it, praying that it was what he thought it was. The archaeologist in him recognised it to be the opening to another tomb. The soldier in him saw it as shelter. He peered down into the blackness. How big a drop down was it? He had no choice. The sound of the machine guns was getting closer – he wouldn't make the ditch.

He lowered himself through the narrow opening and let himself fall. The drop must have only been six feet, but he landed badly and his left ankle began to ache. Reaching out in front of him, he began to edge his way forward into the blackness.

He was going down a slight incline into the side of the

hill. If this was like other Minoan tombs, then he would soon come to a small burial chamber. The air smelt stale, reminding Lockhart of so many tombs before. It made him feel at home. Had this been under ordinary circumstances, he would have been highly excited. Now he merely felt relieved. He made his way forward, the sound of the gunfire retreating. He was stepping into another world, a sanctuary from fear and death.

Lockhart stopped. There was little point in going any further. There could be more drops and he was safe where he was. He sat down and leaned his head back against the cool wall. His legs began to shake uncontrollably, and he tried stifling his sobs. He wanted to scream out, a mixture of shock, rage, sadness and emptiness overwhelming him. Images of Anna and Amy plagued his head. A voice was telling him he would never see them again. He was too exhausted to argue with it.

The second grenade had exploded too near for Manoli's comfort. He knew they had to leave the ditch – there was nothing they could do for the others. The Germans outnumbered them and were better armed. To stay would be suicide. If they ran now, they would have a good start on their pursuers. To ease his conscience, Manoli decided that he himself would stay. He could hold the Germans back with the Marlin for several more minutes while the others fled.

Manoli ran along the ditch, issuing the order. The men looked surprised and reluctant.

'But what about the others?'

'What can we do?' Manoli asked. 'They are closing in all the time. We'll all die. Mr Lockhart would want us to go.'

The men could see the sense in that, but they felt guilty at leaving their comrades.

'Go!' Manoli shouted. 'Just go!'

As the men got up to run, Manoli slung the Marlin over the edge and let rip with three long bursts in three different directions. Somewhere nearby he heard a scream and a German voice crying out in agony. That should stop them for a while.

Lockhart heard the screaming. It was only a few yards from the opening to the tomb. The sound chilled him – they were the cries of a man who was feeling the horror of knowing these were his last moments.

'Help me, help me! Please, please help me! I'm dying!'

And then the screams continued, the whole essence of the man channelled into that desperate call for help. But Lockhart knew that no help would come. Nobody would run into a line of fire. It had gone eerily quiet – no firing, no explosions, just the sound of a dying man filling the smoking air.

The screaming stopped after a couple more minutes. Lockhart felt his shoulders drop, and then tense up again as the firing started. But this time it was only coming from the German side. The *andartes* must have run for it. He knew he would have done the same, but that did not stop him feeling vulnerable.

He sat rigid, not daring to move. The firing was nearing the tomb. He pointed his Sten gun towards the entrance, his hands shaking violently. He told himself to keep calm, but Arisaig had never prepared him for a situation like this. Perhaps he should have stayed in Whitehall, prancing around St James's in his captain's uniform.

After quarter of an hour, he gently lowered the barrel. The Germans had passed him. He listened to the volume of shouting and firing diminish – they would be beyond the ditch. Now Manoli's troubles would really be starting. Lockhart slumped forward, his chin falling on to his chest.

As he drifted off, the name came to him. Nausithos. That was it – the name of Theseus's pilot. That he had remembered here and now seemed to Lockhart almost funny.

June 1937

He has never seen such a big house. It must be the size of the whole street in Tooting, and just one family lives here. He too will have a house like this, when they take over. He'll come down from London, where he will be a minister in the new fascist government, and ride a horse, a great big black horse, and Eileen will have the finest clothes. It will make up for the years of poverty and struggle. This is what he deserves, he reckons, nothing less will do for him, a true leader of men.

The taxi draws up to the steps and a footman comes down to open the door. He grabs his small suitcase, steps out tentatively and offers to shake the footman's hand. The footman stares back at him, leaving his hand by his side.

'Do you have any more luggage, sir?'

'Just this,' he says, holding up his suitcase.

'May I take it, sir?'

'Don't worry, I can manage.'

The footman raises an eyebrow. 'Would you follow me, please.'

Together they walk up the steps to the front door. It is a beautiful day, and he looks across to the parkland surrounding the house. This is the real England, a land of oaks and deer, not a place for skulking Jews and Bolshies in their slums. This is the place where greatness breeds and where dynasties are founded. What a glorious new England it will be!

The butler greets him in the hall.

'Sir George and Lady Pendle are in the conservatory at present, and they have asked me to show you to your room first. Sir Oswald is already here, as are several of your other colleagues.'

The staircase is lined with portraits, showing that the features of the Pendles have barely changed in three hundred years. Light shines in from a glass cupola above. It reminds him of the very grandest buildings in London. Blimey. This place is a palace, not a house. Is this really how a lot of them live, in places like this? No wonder they feel born to rule.

His room is surprisingly small, but it is comfortable. He washes his face and looks at himself in the mirror. He's wearing his best suit, the one he wore at church before he gave it up. It's a bit hot for August, but he wants to look his best, to fit in with the rest of them. His hair is short and tidy, but he gives it a good brush anyway. He opens his suitcase – along with his washbag and underwear, it contains another shirt and a pair of flannel trousers. At the bottom there are *several sheets of neatly typed paper – his speech. He is really going to impress them tonight. He wants the Union to go further than ever, to adopt more extreme policies. He is sure that Sir Oswald is going to like it, although it may be a bit strong for some.*

They don't notice him at first. There are at least twenty of them, all laughing in that loud way that always makes him feel so uneasy. Eventually, Sir Oswald spots him, and strides over, a broad smile forming under his dark moustache.

'Aaaaaah! There you are! Did you have a good trip down?'

He goes over and shakes Sir Oswald's hand. The Leader looks the picture of health and is very much at ease.

'Very nice, thank you, Sir Oswald.'

'I'm so glad. I say, have you come from a funeral?'

He looks around – everybody else is wearing light summer suits or tweeds.

'My other suit is at the cleaner's.'

It is a lie, and he knows they must know it is a lie, but what else can he say? That he has only got one suit?

'Never mind – so long as you are comfortable. Now then, we're all having a drink before lunch – what would you like?'

He doesn't know what to say. Normally he only drinks beer, but everybody else seems to be having cocktails.

'I think I'll have a cocktail.'

'Any particular one? Jessop here can make you anything from a Stinger to a punchy Mint Julep.'

Is Sir Oswald doing this on purpose? Surely he knows that people like him don't drink cocktails? He looks at Sir Oswald's glass – it looks nice enough.

'I'll have what you're having, Sir Oswald.'

'Gin and French? Whatever you say. Jessop – could you get the man a gin and French? Now come along and I'll introduce you to a few of our benefactors, especially Sir George, who has heard so much about you.'

He is glad that he hasn't brought Eileen along. She would be an embarrassment, and besides, he wants to concentrate on making a good impression and not worry about her behaviour. She'll learn one day, when he has reached the top. Hopefully, she could become like one of the ladies here.

Later, his speech is met with polite applause. Sir Oswald tells him it was 'capital', but he doesn't feel so sure and goes to bed early. He hears laughter as he walks slowly up the stairs.

November 1943

'Where's Daddy?'

'Daddy's not here, darling.'

'But he was here last birthday.'

'I know, but he's had to go away, Amy, he's gone to help fight the Germans.'

'Why?'

'Because he's a brave man, fighting for his country.'

'And where's Mummy?'

'She's gone too, gone to help *her* mummy.'

'Where?'

'Why don't you just blow out your candles? Come on, deep breath, and then blow!'

*   *   *

Amy blew out the candles, watched by her Aunt Ellie, Uncle Peter and their two children, her cousins Harry and Sam. What she did know was that Auntie Ellie was her mummy's sister, and that she didn't like Harry and Sam, who would tease her because she was a *girl*, tease her because *she* didn't live with her own mummy and daddy.

Daddy used to come and see her, sometimes every few days, bringing her a toy or occasionally some chocolate. She loved it when Daddy came – he was always so funny, and he looked so smart, wearing his Army uniform. Why did Uncle Peter not wear an Army uniform? Amy asked. Because Uncle Peter, said Daddy, was doing something far more important, which meant that he had to wear a suit and tie. What did he do then? Aha, that was a secret – a secret that little girls weren't allowed to know. And that would annoy Amy, who would stamp her feet, and say that that wasn't fair, that it wasn't fair that little girls shouldn't know things. Once she remembered Aunt Ellie saying, 'Oh, she's Anna's daughter all right,' and Daddy laughing. But Daddy didn't come here any more, and Aunt Ellie and Uncle Peter would never tell her where he had gone, and just said that he was 'very brave'.

There was a picture of Mummy on the wall in her bedroom, the bedroom she shared with Sam, her younger cousin. She couldn't really remember her mummy, and once she said something that made Aunt Ellie cry.

'Mummy's dead, isn't she?'

'No!' Aunt Ellie replied. 'You mustn't say that, Amy.

Mummy has just gone away for a little bit, and she'll be back soon.'

'Back with Daddy?'

'That's right, darling – back with Daddy – and then you can go back to your own house, with both of them.'

'When will that be?'

'Very soon.'

'But when? When?'

'Soon, Amy, soon. Come on, it's time for bed.'

And she would lie in bed until Sam had gone to sleep, and when he had done so, she would get up and take down the picture of Mummy from the wall. She would open the blackout curtain next to her bed, and if the moon was out, she would look at the picture for a long time, tracing her little fingers over her mummy's smiling face. And when she got tired, she would fall asleep clutching the picture, feeling the hardness of the frame on the pillow next to her.

Sometimes, Aunt Ellie would get up in the middle of the night, and check up on them. Each time, she would find Amy clasping the picture, and she would attempt to remove it, release it from her niece's grasp as gently as possible. But Amy's grip was too strong, and Aunt Ellie, try as hard as she might, found that there was no way she could take the picture of her sister away.

Chapter Two

November 1943

OBERSTLEUTNANT WALTHER DIETRICH lit a cigarette, put his feet up on the desk, and closed his eyes. It had been a long night, chasing partisans all over the hills. They had shot two of the bastards as they were running from the arms dump, but God knows how many had escaped. Three of his men had been killed, and he wanted blood. It didn't matter whether it was the blood of the partisans or the civilians – they were all in it together. He had already issued the order to take thirty hostages, but before he shot them, he would have breakfast. Never go to work on an empty stomach, his mother had always told him. Perhaps he would have a snooze as well. What was the time? Nine o'clock. Yes, that would be good: a quarter of an hour for breakfast, a couple of hours' sleep, and then up in time to kill the rabble. He was too tired to hear all that pleading and wailing. It would only make him irritable.

His batman brought in coffee and boiled eggs. Their shells were too hot and he dropped one of the eggs back on the plate with a small *ouch*. He blew on his index finger, waggling it in the cooling jet of air. That was better. He then bashed the eggs with the spoon and gingerly unshelled them with a few more *ouch*es. Their yolks were slightly runny – just how he liked them. He took a swig of coffee and belched gently. He noticed how foul his breath smelt with its mixture of caffeine, egg and tobacco. If Rosa was here she would have complained and refused to kiss him. Oh well, that was one of the benefits of being away from her, not having to worry about domestic niceties. Whores never complained.

He finished his coffee and stood up, bringing another chair near to his. He then sat again, pulled his boots off – they smelt almost as bad as his breath – and put his feet up on the other chair. The bright morning light disturbed him. He reached for his cap, leant his head back and placed the cap over his face. Much better. Apart from the fact he had to endure his breath again, he was now comfortable. He was asleep in five minutes, snoring volubly.

Ten minutes later he was being shaken awake by his batman.

'Oberstleutnant,' the young man urged, 'they've captured one of the partisans.'

'What?' Dietrich asked blearily.

'One of the partisans has been captured – he's in the cells.'

Dietrich swung his feet off the table, knocking the empty coffee cup on to the floor, where it smashed.

'Clear that up, Schmidt,' he barked. 'And pass me my boots – I don't want to walk on this floor now.'

Schmidt did as he was told, and bent down to clear up the fragments as Dietrich heaved his boots on.

'In fact, this office is a mess. Have it cleared before I get back.'

'Yes, sir. It will be done right away.'

'Good.'

Dietrich turned on his heel and walked towards the door, grinding small shards of cup into the tiles.

The parade ground of the Rethimno barracks was quiet. Much of the garrison, which was nearly a thousand strong, was either on manoeuvres or chasing the *andartes* responsible for last night's attack. Others would be trawling the town for suitable hostages.

Dietrich passed a row of lorries. Some mechanics had jumped back to work upon spotting the oberstleutnant's approach.

'I want them all fixed by this evening,' Dietrich shouted. 'I shall even test one myself at random.'

The mechanics saluted, their eyes bulging in worry and disbelief.

Dietrich reached the prison. Before the invasion, it had been a storage cellar for wine and olive oil. It was cool and dark, and could accommodate nearly two hundred prisoners in the cages the army had installed. The two guards at the door clicked to attention as Dietrich entered.

As he made his way down the steep stone steps, his eyes took a while to get accustomed to the dimness. The air was still and stank of sweat and urine. The soldiers who worked down here were usually on punishment duty – being a mere guard was a disgrace.

At the bottom of the steps was a small room, containing a desk and some chairs. A heavy door at the back opened into the main prison. Dietrich found four men standing to attention, one of whom was an officer, Oberleutnant Gunther Fasshauer. All of twenty-three, Fasshauer was a rising young star, and Dietrich liked the fact that he was capable and respectful without being oleaginous, unlike some of his other junior officers.

'So then, Fasshauer, who have you got for me this morning?'

'One of the terrorists from last night's attack, Herr Oberst.'

'Where did you find him?'

'He was hiding in an old tomb about two hundred metres from the arms dump. One of the dogs sniffed him out. He came out when we threatened to throw in a grenade.'

'A tomb?'

'Indeed, Herr Oberst, I was surprised too. That whole area seems to be littered with them. No one had known they were there.'

'You are becoming a bit of an archaeologist, young Gunther!'

'I hardly think so, sir, but we did notice some broken pots down a couple of them as we searched.'

'Interesting, Gunther, very interesting. There could be some valuable stuff down some of these tombs. Go back there this afternoon with as many men as you can get your hands on and give them a thorough inspection. I'm sure Berlin would be grateful to receive some more treasures from this island.'

'Yes, sir – I could do with some culture.'

'Couldn't we all! Now then – let's meet this partisan of yours.'

A guard unlocked the door and led them into the dimly lit prison. A long corridor ran between the two rows of cages, all of which were crammed with dispirited and tattered Cretans. The stench was foul – the buckets in each cell were overflowing. Dietrich took out his handkerchief and covered his nose and mouth. The groaning and pleading which filled the room ceased as he walked past. Hollow eyes looked at the man who controlled their fate.

'Are some of these fresh from this morning?' Dietrich asked Fasshauer.

'Yes, sir – so far twenty have been hauled in. The rest should be here in the next hour.'

'Good. Where is the partisan? I hope he's been kept apart.'

'Certainly, sir, he's in solitary at the end here.'

At the back of the prison lay two small rooms, both about the size of large cupboards, which was what they had been. Now they were punishment cells, with no light, no buckets, and a small hatch at the bottom of each door through which food would be passed twice a day if anybody remembered.

The guard drew back the iron bolt and pulled the heavy wooden door towards them. Dietrich stood for a few seconds in the doorway, letting his shadow cast itself on the form in the corner of the cell. He walked in to examine his catch. Like all Cretans, the prisoner had a moustache, although this one did not seem as large as most. His hair looked finer too – not the normal thick and wiry mop found on the local heads. His clothes were in slightly better shape, although his waistcoat was ripped so that it hung off one shoulder. Dietrich looked into the man's eyes. They looked back at him sharply, intelligently. This was no ordinary *andarte*, thought Dietrich.

'What's your name?' he asked. Dietrich's command of Greek was fair – he had been on a course prior to his posting, but he sometimes found the Cretan dialect impossible to understand.

'I don't have one.'

That earned the prisoner a sharp smack to the nose with the back of Dietrich's hand. The prisoner let out a suppressed grunt and blood started to pour from both nostrils.

'What's your name?'

The prisoner looked impudently back, wiping his nose with his sleeve.

'I told you, I don't have one.'

Dietrich was used to this. In fact, he found these pathetic displays of bravado somewhat tedious. Most of them did talk eventually, so why did they bother to hold out? Almost wearily, he punched the prisoner hard in the face. There was a crunch of gristle as the man's nose broke and a dull thud as the back of his head hit the wall. The prisoner yelled out, his eyes squeezed tight in agony. He clenched his teeth, doing his best to control his show of pain.

Dietrich turned to Fasshauer.

'This one thinks he's a bit of a hero, doesn't he?'

'He does indeed, sir. May I ask him a question?'

'By all means.'

'Where are you from, you little piece of shit?'

The prisoner didn't reply.

'I asked you where you were from,' shouted Fasshauer. He then bent down and whispered, 'If you don't tell me, I'm really going to hurt you.'

The partisan looked up at Fasshauer. Although his eyes were streaming, a resolve shone through.

'Go and fuck your mother, you cuckold,' the man mumbled, his voice obscured by a mouthful of mucus and blood.

Dietrich and Fasshauer looked at each other in amazement. This was the strongest insult a Cretan could utter.

'You seem to be losing your touch, Gunther!' Dietrich laughed.

Fasshauer was enraged. Even though he knew his commanding officer wasn't blaming him, he felt livid at the nerve of this pathetic bleeding huddle.

'Go and fuck yourself!' he shouted, and with it, he stepped back, and kicked the prisoner in the groin.

The prisoner screamed high and loud. Dietrich knew that the sound would reach the parade ground. He heard screams like this every few hours, but the '*Kugelstoss*', as he called it – the 'bollock kick' – was always the loudest, the most pain-filled.

Dietrich looked at his watch. It was a quarter to ten. He still felt tired, and he desperately wanted to have that little sleep before he executed the hostages. He yawned.

'I'm getting a little bored of this man, and I could do with some rest. I'm going to lie down for a couple of hours.'

'Shall I lock him up with the hostages, Herr Oberst?'

'No – leave him to lick his wounds for a while. I think this one is a bit more interesting than your run-of-the-mill peasant – maybe he's a big shot. We can carry on with him later. But make sure he gets nothing to eat or drink.'

'Yes, sir.'

Dietrich left the cell. He walked slowly between the cages, looking down at the floor. Something bothered him about this prisoner; a sixth sense told him that he was different. What was it? Was it the clothes, the hair or the voice – or all of those things? He walked out into the sunlight, chewing his lip. He neither noticed the frantic activity around the lorries, nor was he aware that his office was now spotless. Once more, he took off his boots, put his feet on the chair and placed his cap over his face. Another scream came from the prison. Fasshauer must have given the prisoner another kick in the groin. Dietrich nodded off.

Lockhart awoke from what passed as sleep to find nearly every part of his body aching. His testicles hurt the most – he didn't dare look to see what state they were in. He reached for his nose, gingerly touching it. Even that gentle exploration caused a bolt of pain to shoot up it, spreading over his entire face. The back of his head felt sore and puffy – he had sustained a huge bruise from when his head had snapped back from the oberstleutnant's punch.

The cell was dark, the only light seeping in under the door. If his nose wasn't blocked, then Lockhart would have smelt the fetid mixture of stale urine, vomit and faeces. The floor felt slimy and damp, caked with the effluence from previous inhabitants. He could hear vague noises from the prisoners in the cages outside. That he wasn't alone gave him slight hope, but he knew that he was housed in little more than a transit camp between life and an unmarked grave. Any hope in a place like this was false.

He half wished he still had the cough drop, feeling the torn stitching around the point of his collar. But he was still alive, and he had to stay that way, for the sake of Anna and Amy. He had to see them again, had to reunite his family, make it whole again. For them, he would endure anything, suffer the most vile excesses that could be imagined. Manoli's *Erotocritos* came to mind:

> Love made Rotokritos to hold his ground
> And to defy the ten who gathered round.

He turned his mind back to his body. His groin was hurting more and more. His nose still ached, but he knew it wouldn't get worse. But he had do something about his testicles – big Jock, the doctor at Arisaig, had told them all about it, drawing a cross-section of a scrotum on the blackboard. It had caused a titter around the class of young men.

'Now, gentlemen, the *balls*,' Jock had boomed out in his thick Glaswegian accent. 'How to deal with a kick to the balls – although as most of you appear not to have any, this won't be a problem.'

Another laugh. Jock knew how to grab an audience's attention.

'The most likely outcome of a kick to the balls,' Jock had continued, 'is what us medical men call testicular torsion. In layman's terms, that means a twisted bollock. Now a twisted bollock is a very bad thing, because it also twists the spermatic cord that supplies the bollock with blood. A twisted cord is a blocked cord, and with no blood, your balls wither on the vine. It only takes six hours for a bollock to die. It then gets gangrene, and then you're in heap big trouble.'

By now, Jock's audience had gone quiet.

'So, if anybody gives you a kick to the balls, you've got to act quickly. Normally, you'd be anaesthetised and operated on immediately, but it's unlikely your captors will offer you such care. So, you'll have to untwist it yourself. Make no mistake, gentlemen, this is the single most painful thing that can happen to a man. It will hurt like the biggest buggery and a buggery is what you'd rather be having. And even if you manage to untwist it, it still might twist again sometime in the future, which means you'll have to untwist it all over again. In an operation, the bollock is sewn on to the inside of the scrotum to stop it ever happening again – but I don't see any of you trying to do that.

'Now, I can see all of you are dying to know the procedure. It's very simple. The offending globe will be swollen and sore, and will probably have risen up inside your scrotum. Take it between your fingers and your thumb and grip it very gently. By now, you will be screaming your head off. Don't worry, it gets worse. Now, simply roll the ball ever so slightly left and right, until you can feel which way it should untwist. As you untwist it, you should notice the ball beginning to drop back down. Keep twisting until it wants to go no further, although it might be hard to tell, as any movement will cause you a lot of pain.

'If you're lucky, any swelling and redness will begin to disappear over the next few days. In a couple of weeks, your balls could even be back on active service, but none of you ugly lot would be so lucky. Now, has anybody got any questions?'

Lockhart recalled that there had simply been a silence. They had all joked about it that evening at the mess, but Lockhart guessed that every man had lain in bed, as he had done, praying that he would never be in such a situation, but gently practising Jock's technique all the same.

And here he was, knowing that he would have to do as Jock had taught them. He tried to convince himself that the pain was subsiding – that it was only a little bruising which would soon go away. But he was feeling nauseous, another symptom that Jock had described. He had to act quickly, before any permanent damage was done.

Lying flat on the floor, he slowly pulled his trousers and underwear down to his knees. Even the movement of the fabric over his genitals caused acute bursts of pain, and for a few moments he lay there panting, steeling himself for the agony to come. He reached down to his groin, and as gently as he could, felt his genitals. One of his testicles had swollen and was much higher than the other. The lightest touch was enough to make his eyes water profusely. He wanted to scream out, but he had to stop himself. If a guard came in and saw him, he would probably get another kick.

If it was going to be done, it had better be done quickly. He stuffed his right collar in his mouth and bit hard. Once more, he moved his hand down, and grasped the testicle between his thumb and fingers. He paused, letting his body become accustomed to this level of pain, trying to make it accept it as normal before proceeding to new agonies. He started to turn the testicle.

Lockhart guessed that he should turn it away from his body, and he guessed right. He gritted his teeth, and allowed himself to let out a stifled scream. The pain was ridiculous, and he had to use all his will-power to keep going. Every muscle in his body had tensed up, lifting much of him off the floor. He continued turning, and as he did so, he could feel the pain easing off slightly. Was he there? When was he supposed to stop?

After a slight pause, he continued. The testicle was beginning to feel looser, which had to be a good sign. With a couple more slight manipulations, it refused to turn any more, so he stopped. This must be it – he didn't want to twist it the other way. He took his hand away, and let his body relax. His groin was on fire, but the pain was starting to relent. Only time would tell if he had done the right thing. One day he would tell Jock all about it. It was worth staying alive just to see his reaction.

As he sat up against the wall, Lockhart heard three volleys of distant rifle fire.

Strasser left the office, feeling the quizzical looks of Esser and Buch burning into his back. He was as mystified as they were. Had he done anything wrong? Since coming back from the front, he had behaved himself. There were the whores and the occasional rowdy evenings, but nothing that wasn't usually given the blind eye. SS men weren't supposed to drink, but with the war going the way it was, permanent obliteration was a fact of life for many. Strasser could hold his drink better than most, so much so that Esser thought he watered his drink down on the sly.

It must be the whores, but Strasser had been careful about that too, restricting his visits to once a week. Any more often and he would appear depraved, not to mention penniless. He had been careful too, even with Leni, not to tell them anything. Many were the rumours that Kitty's place was run by the SD, the internal security body. How else would Kitty get such good wines and brandies? people asked. Strasser felt confident that he had never told a whore anything, apart from complaining about Frau Buch's incessant smoking.

As he closed the grilles on the outside of the lift,

Strasser reasoned that he wasn't being summoned because he was in trouble. He pressed the button marked '6'. No, this must be an opportunity for him, but in what capacity? The only thing he could think of was his ability to speak English, but there were plenty of others who could do so.

His thoughts were interrupted by the lift reaching the sixth floor. He stepped out into a silent corridor and headed towards a pair of giant doors, the sound of his boots echoing off the whitewashed walls. A dull grey light was washing in through the small windows – Strasser could see that it was still snowing. It had been snowing the last time he had come up here, to collect his promotion from Berger. It was the first time he had met the Obergruppenführer, and he had immediately seen why the head of the SS Hauptamt was so feared. A short, fat man in his late forties with a husky voice, Berger cut a sinister figure. His hair was cropped all the way round, leaving a mop perched on top of a squat and ugly face. He had more or less managed a smile when he presented Strasser with his certificate of promotion.

Strasser reached the doors, paused to smooth down his uniform, and opened them. He was presented with a well-lit wood-panelled room containing four uniformed secretaries, and by an equal number of junior officers. Portraits of Hitler and Himmler were placed on the far wall – Strasser noticed that they had been arranged so that the two men were facing away from each other.

One of the secretaries looked up from her typewriter. 'Hauptsturmführer Strasser?'

Strasser looked at her. She must have been only twenty

and had cold grey eyes that chilled him. This was a girl who would do anything for her Führer, he thought. If she wasn't working at the SS Hauptamt, she might well be ensconced in a *Lebensborn* home, where single women could procreate and bring up children sired by permanent SS 'procreation helpers' – *Zeugungshelfer*. Naturally, it was a task that every SS man wanted to do, but only the most racially pure could apply. Strasser had met such a man in Russia, who had boasted that he had fathered thirty-two children for the Reich. 'Who knows, perhaps they will be able to form their own SS corps in a few years' time,' he had joked, but Strasser hadn't laughed – he thought the *Lebensborn* campaign absurd, an opinion he didn't voice, not even with Max.

'Yes, Fraulein, reporting as requested.'

'Wait one moment, please.'

The girl got up from her desk and went over to another set of giant doors. She opened one, and holding the door handle and the frame, she leant into the room, her left foot leaving the ground. The movement tightened her skirt over her hips, causing Strasser a moment of lust. He really must see Leni as soon as possible – he didn't normally find himself going for SS ice maidens.

He heard a mumbled exchange of words and then the girl leant back and looked over to Strasser.

'You may go in now,' she uttered, without any trace of warmth.

'Thank you, Fraulein.'

Strasser swallowed, hoping that the girl had not noticed this slight display of trepidation. As he walked over to the doors, he noticed one of the junior officers smile at him. Strasser nodded and weakly smiled back. Why was the man smiling? Was it gallows humour?

He knocked on the door.

'Come in!'

Strasser did as the husky voice ordered him. He stepped in to see Berger sitting behind a large desk, with the ubiquitous portrait of the Führer behind him. A large wood fire blazed to the left of the door, making the room stifling. The windows were covered in condensation. Strasser clacked his heels together and performed his best Heil Hitler.

Berger looked up from a large file on his desk, breathing heavily through his broken nose while he scrutinised Strasser's face.

'Heil Hitler, Hauptsturmführer. Shut the door and sit down.' Berger gestured to the chair in front of the desk.

The Obergruppenführer's face was impassive – Strasser still couldn't tell what the nature of his fate might be. As he walked over, he saw Berger extract a document from the file.

'Before I say any more, I must remind you, Hauptsturmführer, that the conversation we are about to have is top secret. Nobody else, not even those in your department, is to know what we have spoken about. Is this clear?'

'Certainly, sir.'

Strasser let himself breathe out a little. This couldn't mean that he was in trouble, but he was now unbearably curious.

'Perhaps it is best if I let you read this. It will be quicker.'

Berger passed over a heavy sheet of paper. As Strasser started to read, he could feel Berger's eyes once more scrutinising him. It was rumoured that Berger had been a boxer, and Strasser didn't doubt it – he must have won many a bout because of the harshness of his stare. Strasser tried to ignore it and looked at the top of the document – it bore the insignia of the Foreign Ministry, and it was stamped 'Top Secret'.

To: SS-Obergruppenführer Gottlob Berger,
           Head, SS Hauptamt
From: Herr Arnold Hillen-Ziegfeld,
           Special Representative,
           England Committee
Copied to: Dr Fritz Hesse, Chairman,
           England Committee
Subject: The Legion of St George
Date: 23 October 1943

Herr Obergruppenführer,

I write to you on the highest authority concerning a matter of the greatest sensitivity and importance to the war effort.

As I am sure you are aware, we have been recruiting English prisoners of war to help in the fight against the Bolsheviks since the beginning of this year. It is a plan personally approved by the Führer himself, and we have had some success in implementing it.

We have established two camps near Berlin, as satellites of Stalag IIId, in which those men who are considering fighting against Stalin are housed. Special Detachment 999 is a villa for officers on the Kaunstrasse in Zehlendorf and Special Detachment 517 is a larger camp for NCOs in the suburb of Genshagen. Conditions at these camps are far more pleasant than in normal stalags and oflags, and we find that the provision of a few basic comforts helps to make the prisoners more amenable to our ends.

In addition, we have established, under the auspices of the Army High Command, a facility at Stalag IIIa at Luckenwalde. It is here that we have had most success, and so far, through coercion and intimidation, we have twenty-two men – all NCOs – who are willing to fight the Bolsheviks.

At present, these men are assembled into a unit called the Legion of St George. The idea for the unit was that of the broadcaster John Amery, although he now has no input.

We are at the stage when the unit can be formally adopted by the Waffen-SS. Although the unit has been provisionally under the control of the Wehrmacht, it is felt by the committee that it should be built up along the lines of your foreign legions in the SS. The Führer has insisted that the Legion should only see active service when it has reached a strength of thirty men, but we are confident that figure will soon be reached.

Our only disappointment is that we have yet to find a suitable officer to lead the unit. Until then, it is hoped that you will be able to appoint a German SS officer on a temporary basis. The man who you select will need to be of the highest calibre and discretion. He will of course need to be fluent in English.

There is little doubt that the propaganda value of the Legion of St George will be enormous. However, we do not wish to see the unit remaining as just that, and we expect the men to be trained up to your high standards in the same way as any other SS soldier. The unit will be sent to the Eastern Front as soon as it reaches the required strength, and will form a dedicated band of Aryan brothers in the European struggle against the Jewish Bolshevik conspiracy.

I look forward to receiving confirmation of your readiness to enter the Legion into the glorious ranks of the SS.

Heil Hitler!

Hillen-Ziegfeld

Strasser put the document back on the desk and looked up at Berger, who was still staring at him.

'So what do you think?' Berger asked.

Strasser was flummoxed. Did Berger really think this was worth the effort? Maybe he did. Berger hated the Russians. Strasser remembered he had written a pamphlet called *The Subhuman*, in which he had described them as 'the afterbirth of humanity existing spiritually on a lower level than animals'. That may well be so, but Strasser knew that whatever species they were, they certainly made good soldiers. Any new force to help defeat them was welcome – the SS already had Danish, French, Spanish, Dutch and Belgian divisions, so why not an English one? But Strasser doubted that many Englishmen would join forces with the Reich.

He sat on the fence: 'I am surprised that they have managed to find so many Englishmen willing to join us.'

Berger snorted. 'I agree with you, Hauptsturmführer. But this Hillen-Ziegfeld is an arrogant little shit, prone to embellishment and even lying. For all we know, these twenty-two men could be complete halfwits not worthy of joining the SS. But orders are orders, and I'm making you the man to lead them. You shall act as liaison officer between the unit and myself. You are to report to nobody else, you hear? Of course you will need to deal with this little runt' – Berger slapped the document with the back of his hand – 'and a few other spineless pricks in the Foreign Ministry. But he has a point – the propaganda value will be great, and that is worth remembering.'

Strasser nodded slowly. The task reeked of internal politics, which he disliked. The role of 'liaison officer' would mean being a whipping boy for both Berger and the Foreign Ministry. He could see why such a Legion was being formed, but he couldn't see the British going for it. Failure would be the likely outcome and then he, Strasser, would be back to the Front. But he had to show Berger that he was willing. If he refused he would find himself freezing his balls off in a marsh outside Kiev by the end of next week.

'As you say, sir,' began Strasser, 'the propaganda value will be great. I would consider it an honour to help establish a new Legion. When do I start?'

'Now. Hand over your existing work to Esser – he will be able to manage – and then tomorrow morning I want you to begin. Of course I shall be wanting weekly progress reports.'

'Of course.'

Berger then lifted up the file and slammed it down in front of Strasser.

'Some bedtime reading for you. Background, profiles and all that crap. Now you can go.'

Strasser stood up and saluted, but Berger was already looking at the next file. As the new officer in charge of the British SS reached the door, Berger called out to him.

'Hauptsturmführer!'

Strasser turned round.

'Sir?'

'Don't fuck this up. You're a good man, so I don't expect you to. But I could really live without a fuck-up right now.'

'Yes, sir,' Strasser replied and saluted once more. Leni had better be free this evening.

* * *

He wondered what the time was. He knew that he had been captured in the early morning, and then questioned and beaten up a few hours later. He must have drifted in and out of sleep for another few hours, after which he had woken up and untwisted his testicle. He had slept again, and now he was lying in a stupor. He guessed it was late that same evening, but for all he knew he could have been out for a fortnight.

He felt desperately thirsty – the last time he had had anything to drink was just before they had attacked the arms dump. The back of his throat hurt when he swallowed and his tongue felt like a piece of dried meat. He didn't have an appetite, but the lack of sustenance he knew would soon make him tired and weak, and more vulnerable under interrogation. He dimly recalled the senior officer ordering him to be deprived of food and drink, but he couldn't remember if that was a dream. Had Anna gone, or was she still going, through all this? She would be tougher than him. The thought gave Lockhart strength.

He tried to feel optimistic. His testicles, although still sore, were feeling a lot better. His nose must be broken, but that didn't bother him – countless friends had done the same in rugby matches, so he had merely joined a rather unexclusive club. Apart from a few other bruises, he was more or less fine. That he was being kept in solitary confinement probably meant that he wasn't going to be shot, or at least not yet. There was still hope – all that remained was how well he would do under torture.

Lockhart guessed that the senior officer was Dietrich. Manoli had described him, although Lockhart did not need a description. Dietrich's cruelty was enough to identify him, and he assumed that the shots he heard were the reprisals being carried out. How many men had died because of their botched raid? Was it Lockhart's fault? He had known that Dietrich would carry out such an action, so didn't that make him culpable? Between him and Manoli's men, they must have killed at least five Germans, and in return fifty Cretans would have been shot. Was that what he was here to do – to make widows and orphans? Because he was bloody good at it. Perhaps it would have been better if he had taken the suicide pill on the boat. But they all knew the risks. They couldn't let the threat of reprisals stop them from resisting. It was a high price, but they couldn't just let the Germans rule without any opposition.

He heard voices approaching. It sounded like Dietrich and that bastard Fasshauer. He sat up, not wanting them to see him curled up. The bolt slid back and the door opened to reveal the unmistakable silhouette of Dietrich, the backs of his hands pressed against his hips. It made him look slightly effeminate and spoiled the effect of authority that he had presumably hoped to create. Behind him stood Fasshauer. Arsehole. How satisfying it would be to kick the hell out of him, to watch him scream and beg.

A light came on in the cell. Lockhart instinctively shut his eyes and then opened them slightly. The two men walked in slowly, looking down at him with a mixture of menace and curiosity. Lockhart stared up into Dietrich's eyes, which crinkled into what passed for a friendly smile.

'And how are you this evening?' Dietrich asked, his voice full of mock pity.

Lockhart coughed.

'I'm sorry,' said Dietrich. 'What was that?'

Lockhart held his stare. 'All the better for seeing you, Herr Oberst.'

Dietrich turned to Fasshauer.

'He seems to have learned a little respect since this morning. Well done, Gunther!'

But instead of smiling, Fasshauer looked puzzled.

'I'm very impressed he knows your rank, sir; normally these peasants don't have any idea.'

Lockhart cursed to himself. He was being too clever. Just act the dumb peasant, that was all he had to do. He also knew that if he registered any reaction to their conversations in German, he would have a lot of explaining to do.

Dietrich leant down.

'How did you know I was an oberstleutnant?'

'Because you were called it earlier.'

'When?'

'This morning, when you came to see me this morning.'

'What sharp little ears you have.'

With that Dietrich started twisting Lockhart's left ear. Lockhart did his best not to scream out, although he couldn't help wincing. Dietrich was almost lifting him up.

'Perhaps we should cut them off, to stop you listening. But as you're not going to be around for much longer, it hardly seems worth the effort.'

Dietrich released his grip and Lockhart slumped back to the floor. His ear felt raw and livid, but he knew this was merely a warm-up.

'So then,' Dietrich continued, 'you seem to be a lot brighter than the average peasant. I think you're some sort of leader, and you're going to tell me all about it. Perhaps it may interest you to know that we managed to kill two of your friends as they were escaping from the fuel dump. The others will be here shortly, so as you can see, your little band has been truly defeated.'

Niko and Christos were dead and it was entirely his fault. Poor bastards. He suspected that Dietrich was bluffing about the others. Lockhart continued looking at the floor – he didn't want Dietrich to see a flicker of emotion.

'So are you going to say anything?'

It would be better if he told Dietrich something, just to buy himself time and to save himself from any further beatings.

'What do you want to know?'

'That's more like it! You could begin by telling us where you are from, something you were reluctant to tell us this morning.'

Lockhart knew that if he mentioned any village, it would be burnt down by tomorrow night. He decided to make one up.

'I'm from Cleftika.'

'And where the fuck is Cleftika? I've never heard of it.'

'It's to the far east, near Sitia. It's a very small place.'

'So what are you doing over here?'

'I came here to raid the arms dump.'

'You came all the way here to do that?'

'Yes.'

'I don't believe you, but we can come to that later. What's your name anyway?'

'Yanni.'

'Yanni what?'

'Yanni Marinaki.'

Yanni Marinaki was actually the name of a long-gone archaeologist, but they weren't to know that.

'Got any family, Yanni?'

'No.'

'What happened to them?'

'They died.'

'How?'

'They were killed.'

'By who?'

'You.'

'Me?'

'No, you, the Germans.'

'We killed *all* your family? You must come from a pretty bad bunch. It's just as well we caught you. Why did we kill your family?'

'They were in their house when the whole village was burnt down.'

'And why was the village burnt down?'

'I don't know.'

'When did this happen?'

'In the summer.'

'And since then you have been on the run, no doubt swearing revenge on us.'

Lockhart nodded. It was nice of Dietrich to complete his alibi.

'And how did you end up with that gang of idiots?'

'I came across them in the mountains.'

'Where exactly?'

'I don't know.'

Dietrich paused.

'Don't tell me that you don't know, Yanni, otherwise you'll get another kicking.'

'I swear I don't know – I was just wandering around, and I came across these *andartes*, who asked me to join them.'

'Tell me where, Yanni. This is your last chance.'

Lockhart didn't want to mention a location for fear that it really did contain *andartes*. He would just have to take a kicking.

'I really don't know.'

Dietrich breathed sharply in and out through his nose.

'Come on, Gunther, let's see if you can help him to remember.'

Fasshauer grinned and walked over to Lockhart. He bent down and whispered in Lockhart's ear, as he had done that morning.

'So where would you like it this tiime – your balls or your face?'

Lockhart drew his legs up to his chest and shut his eyes. He knew the only way he would get through this was to take his mind somewhere else, to disconnect it from the agonies he was about to feel.

'I've had a change of plan. I think we'll start with your fingers this time.'

Lockhart snapped open his eyes to see Fasshauer remove a pair of pliers from his breast pocket. Would he be able to bear this? He desperately wanted to save himself the pain, to tell them everything – the hideouts, the identities, even about the training camp at Arisaig. But he knew that he couldn't do that – there could be no pain on earth that would make him tell these two about all that. Fuck them. He could live without a finger or two. He shut his eyes again – he did not want to see the pleasure Fasshauer was getting from this.

He found himself being thrust on to the floor and a boot standing on his left forearm. Cold metal sharply gripped the little finger on his left hand and pulled it back. He suppressed a scream through clenched teeth.

'Now then, Yanni,' Dietrich began. 'Are you going to tell us where you found your friends?'

Lockhart ignored the question and began to pray. He thought of Anna and Amy and wanted to cry, but he stopped himself. The pliers grew tighter and his finger was being bent to just before breaking point.

'Come on, Yanni, tell us.'

He was so tempted, but he knew he couldn't. Dietrich nodded at Fasshauer and the junior officer pulled hard on the pliers. The finger broke with a gristly crack, pain pumping from Lockhart's hand to his brain with a ferocity and venom that he didn't think was possible. He screamed high and loud and could dimly detect the sound of laughter.

'Christ!' he bellowed.

Dietrich and Fasshauer stopped laughing. Lockhart had said the word in English.

*   *   *

The two officers looked at each other.

'What was that?' asked Dietrich. 'It sounded like English.'

'I think it was,' Fasshauer replied. 'I'm sure he said "Christ".'

Dietrich chewed his bottom lip. He had been certain this captive was unusual, and now he had proof. Just one little word had uncovered a cowardly English spy. How many more idiots like this were running around the mountains, causing him trouble? There was only one way to find out. He crouched next to Lockhart, who was moaning softly. Dietrich cleared his throat.

'So then, you're not really a "Yanni", are you? You're probably a "Geoffrey" or a "Nigel".'

Dietrich pronounced the names to make them sound absurd. The prisoner continued to look away. Had he even realised that Dietrich had spoken in English? He must have done.

'Come on, my friend,' Dietrich continued in a mock-soothing tone. 'You nearly had us fooled, but you can give up now. Don't pretend that you're some sort of peasant – your moustache isn't big enough. If you don't tell us everything, I'm going to break one of your fingers every hour. If that doesn't work, I'll then smash a kneecap. And then the other one. Perhaps then I'll move on to your arms. Maybe cut off an ear. Anyhow, you're not going to die for a long time now. And if you do tell me what I need to know, then I might let you live. Nod if you understand me.'

* * *

Lockhart was barely listening. His brain was occupied by pain, nausea and, worst of all, guilt. He knew he had sworn in English, and all he wanted to do was to end it, to somehow let himself slip away. But he knew he had to find the strength to face more agonies, not to let down the organisation and his comrades. If he ever met Anna and Amy in this, or another life, he would be able to embrace them as an honourable man, and not as a betrayer of secrets.

As his thoughts stumbled around, he could make out occasional phrases in English coming from Dietrich's mouth.

'Don't pretend . . . smash a kneecap . . . Nod if you understand . . .'

He looked up at Dietrich and nodded.

'I understand,' he husked.

He saw Dietrich smile.

'Good! Now shall we start again? What language shall we speak? It would be useful if you spoke German.'

'I don't mind,' said Lockhart in German. 'But can I have some water? I can hardly speak.'

It was true. Lockhart's throat was so dry that speech was becoming impossible.

'You can, and you may even have some food as well.'

Dietrich nodded to Fasshauer.

'Guard!' Fasshauer shouted.

A breathless young soldier appeared at the door.

'Yes, sir?'

'Get the prisoner some food and water.'

'Yes, sir!'

He must live, for the sake of his family. Anna would cling and fight and be strong, because she would want to see him and Amy again. He had to do the same, to keep his side of the bargain, to show her that he would endure anything to see her again, to show her that he was her equal. It would be harder to stay alive, too easy now just to let go, to give up. To do so would be a waste. Fuck Dietrich. He could break all his fingers and do whatever his sick brain liked.

Lockhart's mind went back to his finger. It was swelling alarmingly and the pain was changing from a stabbing to a throbbing. The nausea was worsening, and he retched violently, as though he was trying to turn his stomach inside out. The sound brought Dietrich and Fasshauer back into the room. Dietrich observed his captive with scorn.

'So you are at last beginning to feel sick then?' he asked. 'I hope you're not going to bring up the food that you are about to be given. That would be most ungrateful.'

Fasshauer laughed.

'I think he would even if he was feeling well,' he observed.

Dietrich smiled and then let the smile fade from his eyes. He crouched down and spoke into Lockhart's ear.

'I know you're a spy, and you know full well I can have you shot. It wouldn't even break the Geneva Convention, so it would be legal! But let's just say that I'm feeling generous, and let's just say that you're feeling generous too and feel like giving me some information. In return, I could get that finger of yours dressed up. And if you were very clever and generous, you could perhaps help me, and I would help you. Who knows? Perhaps you might even live a little longer.'

Lockhart stayed silent, taking it all in. Dietrich continued.

'I think you know what I'm saying. I'm sure you'd rather stay alive, and if I'm going to be honest, I'd rather you stayed alive too. You're fun to have around, and you could be very useful to me. So why don't you eat some food and have a think, eh? Of course, if you don't want to help me, then I'll leave you in the oberleutnant's hands.'

Lockhart looked up at him. Dietrich's eyes were wide open, and he was breathing heavily through his nose. Lockhart did his best to register no emotion, and he held Dietrich's inquisitive stare. The German was almost willing him with his eyes to work for him, to betray the Cretans and the SOE, to betray his country. There was no way Lockhart could do that; there was no way he could become a traitor. If that was the only way to live, then he would rather die. Anna would expect it of him.

As Lockhart opened his mouth, Dietrich's expression turned to that of near-desperate expectation.

'May I sleep on it?' Lockhart asked. He wanted to buy himself some time. Perhaps he could turn this offer to his advantage, but at the moment he couldn't think. He was tired, hungry and still in great pain.

Dietrich's face fell. But then the prisoner had a point – it was getting late and it had been a long day.

'You may, but so long as you tell me your real name.'

There was nothing to lose. In fact, it might even buy him some goodwill, whet Dietrich's appetite.

'My name is Lockhart. Captain John Lockhart.'

Whatever it was, it wasn't sleep that Lockhart got that night. Instead, it was a type of disturbed and fearful drifting, caused by nervousness and exhaustion. His body ached for rest and yet his mind kept churning over the same thought. Its ramifications both troubled and delighted him, gave him comfort and threw him back down.

It would be a tremendous risk. Losing his life was one thing, but others might lose theirs. What had he to gain? Everything. Anna, Amy and an escape from torture and imminent death. It gave him a slim chance of growing old in that often-imagined armchair by the fire. But his decision would hazard the lives of those he hoped to save. What right did he have to risk them for his sake? None, but what if it worked? Surely Anna would want him to do what he had in mind? Surely she would see that if there was an opportunity for them to be reunited, then it should be taken?

He thought of Theseus, who had come to Crete to save fourteen young Athenians from being murdered every nine years by the Minotaur. Theseus had risked his life to kill Minos's beast, thought Lockhart, risked his life to save his people, his family. He could have stayed in Athens and rested on his laurels. Would Theseus have posed as a traitor to save his family? Like Theseus, Lockhart had come to Crete to stop others from dying, and he must do the same.

Loyalty to family, loyalty to country. He had never doubted either of them, but if one of them had to give, then he knew which one it would be. He would rather die a true husband than a true patriot.

'Good morning, Captain Lockhart.'

It was Dietrich, staring down with that same expression of expectation and contempt. Lockhart pushed himself up off the floor and slumped back against the wall. Even that slight movement made him breathless.

'So,' Dietrich continued, 'are you going to help me? Or are you going to die instead?'

Lockhart smiled faintly at Dietrich's ludicrous succinctness.

'Yes, I will help you.'

Equal doses of relief and guilt flooded Lockhart's veins. Dietrich looked delighted, like a small boy.

'Good! And in return, I shall keep my side of the promise. You can have your finger seen to.'

'I'd like to make a deal with you, Herr Oberst.'

Dietrich started back.

'A deal, Captain? What sort of deal?'

Lockhart inhaled deeply.

'I have a wife.'

'Yes . . .'

'A wife who I love very much.'

'Carry on.'

'And I have a child, who I also love very much. I'd like to see them both again.'

'I don't see how I can help.'

'You can, Herr Oberst.'

'I am confused – what do you want me to do? Fly over to England and bring them back here for a little holiday?'

'My wife is in Belgium.'

'Belgium?'

'Yes, in Vught, one of your many concentration camps, Herr Oberst. She was in Holland when you captured it, and she never made it back to Britain.'

'And how do you know she's been imprisoned?'

'There are . . . channels.'

'And why?'

'She'd gone there to help her family. But when you invaded, she started working on an underground newspaper. I understand she wrote quite a few articles scoffing at your Nazi theories about being a "master race".'

Dietrich stood silent for a few moments.

'And so now she's a captive, in Vught you say? I've never heard of it. What do you want me to do?'

'I'd like you to free her.'

Dietrich's eyes widened at the preposterous request.

'You know I can't do that.'

'I'm sure you could. I would do anything to help you if you freed her, or at least made her safe. Even a word that she was still alive would be enough.'

'You'd do anything?'

'Yes.'

'You'd turn traitor – become an informer – in return for your wife's life? I don't believe you.'

'She's more important to me than anything else.'

Dietrich stood silent for at least a minute. Lockhart looked intently at the floor.

'You mean it? You'd really become an informer?' Dietrich asked eventually.

'I really do.'

'I'll need to cable Berlin to confirm your story. You realise that this will take a few days?'

'I can imagine.'

'In the mean time, you can stay in the sanatorium. If your story is a lie, I will shoot you myself.'

Lockhart nodded. Inwardly, he felt uplifted by the thought of a clean bed and a wash. His finger would be cared for and he would be on the mend. But at what price? He wouldn't tell Dietrich about SOE or his training. Instead, he would tell him that he was only sent here because he knew the island. As far as Dietrich was concerned, he would just be a regular soldier working undercover. That would seem plausible – Dietrich would believe it when he was told about the work at Knossos.

More problematic was what to tell Dietrich about the *andartes*. He couldn't betray Manoli and his men. But the truth could easily be twisted. The landing beach could be changed; the locations of the hideouts could be kept vague. And as Lockhart did not know Manoli's whereabouts, he wouldn't be able to tell Dietrich anyway. The men's indentities could be restricted to first names – that was pretty much the truth too. Lockhart could say that they operated on that basis in case of interrogation. He would have to deny that he knew what villages they came from for the same reason. Surely Dietrich would understand that any sort of resistance group worked on a need-to-know principle?

Lockhart anticipated that Dietrich would find much of his supposed ignorance hard to swallow, but he was counting on the German's keenness to have an informer, and an English agent to boot. Dietrich was merely playing the oldest trick in the espionage book: work for us or we'll kill you. It had worked before, and Lockhart was hoping that Dietrich's greed and vanity would make it work again. And in return, Lockhart would have bought Anna's life.

For Lockhart, the sanatorium was like a hotel. His finger was put in a cast and a Wehrmacht medic dressed the myriad cuts and bruises. His testicles were given the all-clear, although there was little that could be done for his nose. He was shocked when he saw it in the mirror – crooked and still swollen. He looked like a thug, but he could have looked a lot worse.

He slept through much of that first day. The last bed he had been in was at Tara. That had been two weeks ago, but it seemed longer. Tara, the castle of ancient Irish kings, whose name had been appropriated by Dickie for their house in Cairo. One of the Billys had found it – a slightly decrepit mansion in the smart Zamalek area. It even had a ballroom. SOE had requisitioned it for use as an 'operations centre', but in truth, it had become a venue for some great parties.

Seven of them lived there, Lockhart being the most recent addition. He had arrived early one evening, the jacaranda in full gaudy bloom, the wide tree-lined street quiet and secluded from the manic bustle of the city. A mongrel ran down the steps and licked his hand as a precursor for a cheeky attempt at stealing his small suitcase. Abdul the houseboy came down to shoo him away, telling Lockhart in pidgin English that he must not worry about Pixie, Pixie always like that with new people, Pixie very naughty.

Abdul led him through the cool, dark hallway. The marble floors were in need of a polish, but this was far grander than Lockhart had dared hope for. He had expected to be slumming it in some sweltering hut – a far cry from the bedroom Abdul was showing him into. Oil paintings hung on the walls; the furniture was a medley of Middle Eastern styles, ornately carved, some pieces inlaid with exquisite marquetry. Lockhart couldn't help but cackle when he saw the magnificent four-poster.

'This is really for me?' he asked Abdul.

'Oh yes, Mr Lockhart, this is smallest room.'

'Where are the others?'

'Drinks.'

'Excellent! Where are drinks?'

'In the drawing room, of course! You come down now?'

'You bet, Abdul. Lead on!'

The drawing room was grand, but it was a grandeur that had withered, the rugs a little threadbare, the chairs and sofas faded and tatty. The Persian wall hangings were in good shape, although those nearest to the large windows that overlooked the garden were almost bleached. The room's six occupants, Lockhart's fellow agents, looked for all the world as though they were taking cocktails in a drawing room in Wiltshire.

'Aha! It's the new boy! Come in, come *in*!'

They stood up as Lockhart walked in, with Pixie reappearing from under a table, yapping away excitedly.

'Don't worry about Pixie, she's an excitable little rogue. Hello, I'm Dickie – you must be the legendary Lockhart. We've heard about your power station in France; you must tell us about it over dinner – we're all a little jealous.'

'Thanks,' said Lockhart, somewhat embarrassed. 'You've got a bit of a reputation yourself.'

Aged twenty-five, Dickie was already an SOE old-timer, having spent at least a year in Crete. He exploded with charm, his toothy smile always present under a rakish moustache.

'Christ, not *that* type of reputation, I hope! Anyway, some introductions. We've got two Billys – Billy Mackintosh and Billy Farson – and one Alex and one David, which leaves us with one very delectable Natasha, who you must call Countess. Got it?'

Lockhart shook each of their hands in turn. They were friendly and gregarious, like a large happy family, the sort of family that Lockhart had always wished for, right down to the idiotic and lovable canine.

Lockhart found that the days dragged, with interminable meetings down at SOE headquarters at Rustum Buildings – 'the Spy House' as the taxi drivers called it – but the evenings were a different matter. Lockhart found himself amassing a huge bar bill at Shepheards, and even a quiet night at Tara would involve some drunken use of the ballroom.

Apart from briefings down at headquarters, the inhabitants of Tara got most of their news about the war from *The Egyptian Gazette*. It described itself as 'as complete and well informed a newspaper as it has ever been', which led Lockhart to surmise that it had last appeared on papyrus. Nevertheless, it was from that paper that they learned about the Allied bombing of Europe and the Russian successes on the Eastern Front. The liberation of Sicily also provided much cheer, along with the German evacuation of Sardinia and Corsica. Plainly the war was going the Allies' way, and there was much talk in Tara about the nature of the Second Front, which was predicted to be only a few months away.

Dickie and Lockhart had proved to be peas in a pod. Both were classicists, although Dickie was mainly self-taught, having wandered throughout Europe for a few years after dropping out of school. Both loved drinking, and Dickie's alcoholic bouts usually saw him end up in the arms of some beauty. However, his charms were lost on the dark and mysterious Natasha, who appeared to have rather more time for Billy Farson, a tall and athletic Old Etonian. Natasha was a Polish aristocrat who had made her way through the Balkans and found refuge in Cairo. But nobody knew her role in SOE, not even Dickie.

'All I know about her is that that smooth bastard Billy's got her in the bag,' Dickie moaned when Lockhart enquired.

The few months at Tara reminded Lockhart of a

summer at Oxford. There was a lot of work, but there was a lot of fun, a lot of innocence. They played cards out on the verandah, or would hire a dhow and go down the Nile. They even went racing at the Gezira Sporting Club, Lockhart taking home over a thousand piastres, much to Dickie's annoyance. The winnings were blown on dinner at Shepheards on Lockhart's last night, the most expensive evening he had ever forgotten.

Tara had been a magical place, Lockhart thought, all the more so from his present vantage point. But it had lacked Anna, and at times he had felt guilty when he had enjoyed himself a little too much. He had been careful never to flirt, no matter how liquid an evening had become, but there had been no shortage of female attention. He would have hated himself if he had sought solace in the bed of a stranger, however tempting the prospect. Dickie had encouraged him, told him it would do him some good, but Dickie was a little young in some respects, a little naive. He would be coming back to Crete soon, Lockhart remembered. He wondered whether, being unmarried, Dickie would find it easier to face death.

He knew Dietrich was buttering him up, spoiling his new star pupil. The food was palatable, and he was even given a bottle of German beer with his dinner. There had been no questioning and no visits from Dietrich or Fasshauer. He was alone, apart from a medical orderly who came to see him every hour or so. He thought of escape but knew it would be fruitless – he had noticed two guards had been posted at the entrance, and his window was barred.

This was the lull. Soon he would need every portion of physical and mental energy to beat Dietrich at this game. If he failed, then Anna would undoubtedly be killed. But Lockhart knew this was the only way they could both stay alive. He would tell Manoli exactly what had happened, and together they could spend months leading Dietrich and his men up the wrong trails. Lockhart knew that he would have to give the appearance of betraying the *andartes*. A few supply drops would have to be compromised, a few ambushes supposedly rumbled, but it wouldn't take long for Dietrich to demand some blood.

That was Lockhart's Achilles heel – how was he going to supply Dietrich with captives? He couldn't just call his bluff and hand over a few suspected collaborators as the Cretans did from time to time. No, some real *andartes* would have to get captured, but he knew that was impossible. Nobody would volunteer – it would be suicide. He would just have to deal with that problem when it came to it. Until then, he would feed Dietrich with a lot of bogus information and give him the occasional nugget of gold to keep him happy. The *andartes* should benefit overall, as through Lockhart they could ensure the Germans were distracted when they most wanted them to be.

The questioning started in earnest the next day, although this time it was without violence. Fasshauer, sitting next to Lockhart's bed, seemed almost apologetic and contrite. No doubt Dietrich had ordered him to wear kid gloves. Lockhart was careful not to surrender information too readily, and occasionally he allowed Fasshauer to threaten him with a return to the cells or another broken finger.

Fasshauer appeared to accept Lockhart's story that he was a regular soldier. He was less convinced by Lockhart's ignorance of the *andartes*, saying that he would have to do better. By and large, Lockhart stated the obvious, things that the Germans probably already knew or had surmised. Yes, there was a transmitter, but it was always moved around. Who looked after it? Lockhart had no idea, all he knew was the codename 'Minotaur' – a complete lie, but Fasshauer was scribbling it all down. How many *andartes* were there? Thousands, replied Lockhart, another lie. Better to exaggerate, get them worried. How often were parachute drops carried out? No idea, Oberleutnant, I'm not supposed to know. When was the next drop? Again, no idea. Who was the leader of the band he was with? Lockhart was prepared for that, and used another fictitious codename – 'Theseus'. Were you in contact with any of the Cretan members of the dig at Knossos? No. How about Manoli Pentaris, didn't he work with you at Knossos? He did, but Lockhart hadn't seen him since he left Crete ten years ago. And they had had no contact since? Apart from the odd letter before the war, none at all – why, what had Manoli done? He was a leading terrorist, replied Fasshauer. Lockhart acted surprised, saying that he thought Manoli was more interested in girls than guns.

The questioning about Manoli shook Lockhart. The Germans obviously had a relatively capable network of informers. When – if – he saw Manoli again, he would have to ensure that Manoli let nobody else know about Lockhart's double-dealing. If an informer found that Lockhart was attempting to dupe the Germans, he would be done for, as would Anna. Fool, Lockhart, fool. This game was too dangerous and far too complex. But there was no going back now. If he killed himself, then the Germans would be sure to let the *andartes* know that Lockhart had told all and was preparing to be an informer. He didn't want to leave such a reputation over Anna and Amy's heads. He had to find Manoli, at the very least to tell him what had happened.

Nevertheless, Lockhart slept better that evening, his mind having been put partially at rest by the appearance of another bottle of beer with his supper. Fasshauer had seemed pleased with him, and even Dietrich had passed by and enquired after Lockhart's health in an avuncular way. No, he had no news about his wife, but surely Lockhart knew that German bureaucracy was probably the same as British bureaucracy? Slow, inefficient, unreliable. He would let Lockhart know as soon as he did, and only then would he be 'released' back to the *andartes*.

Lockhart was woken by Fasshauer at seven o'clock the next morning.

'Get up, Lockhart. The oberstleutnant wants you.'

Fasshauer's tone had reverted to one of menace. Gone was the near-friendliness of yesterday and back was the voice of the torturer. Lockhart eased himself out of bed. Despite his nakedness, Fasshauer continued to observe him closely – perhaps he was going to give out another kicking, or maybe he was a queer.

After Lockhart had put his peasant clothes back on, Fasshauer motioned him out of the room, through the ward and into the raw morning light. Lockhart realised that he hadn't been out in daylight in three days. The fresh air and light felt good, and it lifted him. They were walking over a parade ground, and to the right he could see the prison block. It looked harmless from the outside and innocent of its cruelties. Lockhart knew this short walk was a valuable opportunity to gather information about the barracks. The only Cretans who had seen this much were dead ones. He started memorising the layout, the positions of the guards, the number of trucks.

But he had little time to do so. Fasshauer had noticed that he was slowing down, and grabbed him by the elbow and shoved him forward.

'Move it, you arsehole.'

Something had riled him. Knowing Fasshauer the little he did, Lockhart suspected he had been deprived of some violent little task. He knew that if Fasshauer had had his way, he would have been exterminated a couple of days ago. Fasshauer plainly thought of himself as being Dietrich's intellectual superior, and Lockhart could tell that the younger man had to exercise a lot of restraint. Could Fasshauer's bad mood be good news for him? Was Dietrich really going to allow him to leave?

They were now entering the office block, and they had to wait while a guard checked Fasshauer's papers. Fasshauer snapped at the young NCO.

'Come on, you fucking idiot, you know who I am.'

'Of course, sir, but I have orders . . .'

'Yes, yes. Come on, let me through.'

Practically pushing the guard to one side, Fasshauer propelled Lockhart through to a large flagstoned corridor with whitewashed walls. Various NCOs and officers walked past, all saluting Fasshauer with a mixture of fear and curiosity at this strange couple. It must have been unusual to see an officer frogmarching a prisoner without an NCO. Evidently Dietrich wanted Lockhart to have minimal contact with his men.

The corridor took a right turn, and they walked down a passage that flanked a courtyard, in the centre of which stood a disused fountain. A monastery, thought Lockhart, grimacing – trust the Germans to have hijacked a monastery. They approached a large door, which Fasshauer rudely opened with little ceremony. This had to be Dietrich's office.

Dietrich's batman stood to attention behind his desk.

'Can I go straight in?' asked Fasshauer.

'Yes, sir, he's expecting you.'

The batman opened the door and Fasshauer pushed Lockhart so hard that he stumbled and fell in front of Dietrich's desk. As he got up, Dietrich jokingly admonished Fasshauer.

'Be careful with our new friend, Gunther. He is going to be very useful for us.'

Fasshauer nodded back with a reluctant grunt of agreement.

112

Dietrich lit a cigarette and scrutinised Lockhart through the blue haze. Lockhart was becoming accustomed to Dietrich's long stares, and he found them less threatening. Finally, the German spoke.

'It seems as though your story is true, Captain Lockhart.'

Lockhart stood transfixed. Anna was alive! He knew she must have been. She would never allow herself to die without a struggle.

'Well, aren't you going to say anything?' Dietrich asked.

'An . . . Anna?' stammered Lockhart. 'You're sure she's alive?'

'Indeed she is. Although she is not in Vught; she is currently being held as a political prisoner in Germany. She is being well looked after.'

Dietrich told him the name of the prison camp. He had never heard of it, but if it was like others that he *had* heard of, then it was a miracle that Anna was alive. Back in Cairo, Lockhart had read reports that claimed the conditions in such camps were subhuman - murderous even. And just before he had left, he had read of a speech Churchill had made in the Commons, stating that the Nazis were systematically murdering the Jews, the Gypsies, the mentally ill, the politically hostile - any enemy - in such camps. Lockhart tried to stop himself picturing Anna's emaciated corpse, her eyes permanently frozen in a wasted face. Could she really be still alive?

'You do not look very happy, Lockhart.'

It was Dietrich, again in his avuncular tone. Lockhart cleared his throat.

'It's just that I had heard that these camps . . .'

'That's all nonsense,' said Dietrich. 'She'll be all right. Anyway, it's the Jews who get the tough time. She may have to work hard, but that's good for the soul, eh?'

'Quite.'

'Come on, Lockhart – cheer up! When the war is over, you will see her again. Perhaps you'll end up in the same cell!'

Lockhart smiled weakly, and then the obvious occurred to him.

'Can I write to her?'

Dietrich's smile vanished.

'Of course you fucking can't! That would be a terrible breach of security, her knowing you had been captured. Besides, I'm not some fucking post office. Who the hell do you think I am?'

Lockhart stayed silent.

'It's time you started to earn your right to live,' said Dietrich in a more measured tone, 'since I've kept my side of the deal. You see, Lockhart, I am a man of honour, and if you do not prove to be one too – if you betray me – then I only have to cable my friends in the SS, and – well, I don't need to tell you. Understand?'

Lockhart nodded.

'And I'll probably burn down a couple of villages too. So you see, Lockhart, you really do have to help me. Fasshauer here will be your liaison man and you will report to him at least once a fortnight. You can discuss the details with him after this.'

Dietrich stood up.

'I'm not going to salute you, Lockhart, but I almost find myself respecting you. Many informers are butchered by the Cretans, so you will have to be careful, very, very careful. In a way, Fasshauer and I are your only friends on this island – remember that. So goodbye, Lockhart, and good luck.'

Dietrich leant over the desk and held out his hand.

Even as he was shaking it, this small gesture caused Lockhart more pain than any torture ever could.

That night, Lockhart found himself refusing a cigarette from a guard in the back of a truck. They were climbing out of Rethimno, heading for a barren stretch of country where he was to be dropped off unnoticed. He was sandwiched between two guards, and on the bench opposite sat Fasshauer, cradling an MP40 sub-machine gun, its safety catch off. With the way the truck was lurching and jolting, Lockhart expected a few rounds in his chest at any moment. No doubt that would please Fasshauer, who would tell Dietrich that Lockhart had tried to overpower a guard. Fasshauer cleared his throat.

'So, Lockhart, you're clear about our arrangements?'

The idiot had been over them repeatedly.

'Yes, Gunther my friend, quite clear,' Lockhart replied brazenly, knowing that with Dietrich's protection he could revert to his normal cockiness. 'I'm to meet you at the Fournare cave outside Patsos at midnight in exactly one week's time. And if I'm not there then my wife dies and a few villages get burned down.'

Fasshauer looked quietly enraged, but nodded in the darkness.

'Good,' he muttered.

They carried on in silence for another ten minutes. Lockhart was feeling mildly elated at the prospect of freedom, or a semblance of it. All Fasshauer would tell him was that he was going to be dropped off somewhere between the monastery at Veniou and the village of Apostoli. The Germans had it in their heads that the area was thick with *andartes*, and that Lockhart should have no problems re-establishing contact. The lorry would slow down for a bend, and Lockhart would jump out the back.

What Lockhart hadn't told Dietrich and Fasshauer was that he knew the area well. Apostoli was on the fringes of the Ida range, and he, Anna and Worstead had walked a lot round there during that far-gone summer. Lockhart would head for Zeus's Cave in the side of Mount Ida, which he knew to be a semi-permanent hideout. Despite the cold, and with any luck, there should be some *andartes* there. They might know where Manoli was, if indeed he was still alive. As the crow flew, it was only eight miles from Apostoli, but with the twisting mountain paths, Lockhart knew it to be nearer to sixteen – sixteen tough miles of icy paths and little shelter. Still, he thought, it was better than having a Hun kick your balls in for breakfast.

The road was getting steeper, and the truck slowed down to little faster than running pace. Lockhart looked up at Fasshauer.

'Get ready, Lockhart, we're nearly there.'

Lockhart checked himself over. There was little to check. He had no gun, no food, not even a knife. Fasshauer had secured him a stinking and raggedy sheepskin coat from one of the prisoners, which gave some protection. The temperature must have dropped by nearly ten degrees since they had left the coastal climate of Rethimno.

He looked out the back of the truck. It was a clear night, which meant that he would have no trouble orientating himself. He would cut through to Kasteli, which was about an hour or two east, and there bed down in one of its two churches. He would save the slog to Ida for tomorrow – he risked getting both exhausted and lost if he tried it overnight.

'Get up.'

Fasshauer motioned him towards the back of the truck with the MP40. Lockhart did as he was ordered, and went over and sat on the tailgate, his legs dangling over the edge. He heard the lorry changing gear as it slowed to a walk, bracing itself for the next climb.

'Out!' barked Fasshauer. 'Get out!'

Lockhart jumped on to the road. As he stumbled, something told him that Fasshauer was going to open fire, and he started running towards some boulders over to the left. The coldness of the air entering his lungs shocked him, but he sprinted as hard as he could. But there were no shots. As he reached the boulders, he turned to see the lorry continue to lumber up the road, its engine straining and belching with the effort. It then rounded a hairpin, and was gone.

Silence. As he caught his breath, Lockhart looked around. On the other side of the road lay a drop of about fifty feet, and then a space of a few hundred feet until the ground rose up as the Ida range proper began. The space was densely vegetated with gorse and thyme. Somewhere in there lay the track to Kasteli, along which he had walked before, one August day ten years ago.

Anna often referred to Worstead as 'the wheezing windbag'. Even though she didn't say it to his face, Lockhart thought it a little harsh. But she had a point – he constantly complained about the heat, the basic conditions at the site, the food, and especially his inability to seduce any of the Cretan girls.

'It's all right for you,' he would say to Lockhart. 'You're not a tubby carrot-top like me.'

And then Lockhart would have to say:

'Oh come on, Andrew, I'm sure there are plenty of girls here who would like you.'

'I doubt it very much.'

'You should try a bit harder.'

'I do.'

'No you don't – you spend too much time drinking with men.'

'But I like doing that. What's wrong with that?'

And so on. Such conversations would invariably end with Lockhart saying that Worstead couldn't just expect a girl to fall into his lap, and with Worstead saying that it was all right for Lockhart as he was good-looking and rich.

Worstead's moan that August day was about the steepness of the route from the Arkadi monastery to

Kasteli. Lockhart's long-distance running and Anna's long legs ensured that Worstead lagged behind as they made their way over Mount Tsones. Although he had lost some weight over the past few weeks, Worstead was finding the going tough.

'Couldn't we have gone round this bloody mountain?' he shouted up at Lockhart.

'No way,' replied Lockhart, pausing to catch his breath. 'That would have taken too long – I want to be in Kasteli before dark. Besides, there'll be a great view from the top.'

'View or no view, I'm sodding knackered.'

'It's not *that* bad, Andrew – you'll make it.'

'I'll probably have a heart attack and then you'll have to carry me.'

Anna laughed.

'You're always about to have a heart attack,' she said. 'You said you were going to have one when we went for a swim in that lake.'

'I'm not joking, I can feel it pounding away like fury.'

'You're serious?' she asked.

'Of course I bloody am. You should have told me it was going to be like this.'

'Oh come off it.'

'No, you come off it. Can't you go at my pace?'

'Perhaps if you sped up,' said Anna, 'you'd get a bit fitter.'

'Oh thank you very much, Miss Perfect. What a pleasant ramble this is turning out to be.'

'Oh stop it you two,' Lockhart intervened. 'This

bickering's getting just a little dull. All right, Andrew, we'll go a big slower, but I don't want to be caught here after dark.'

Anna glowered at him.

'Why do we have to slow down for him?' she asked.

'I thought we wanted to go as a group.'

Anna's eyes widened.

'I seem to remember that was your idea.'

'No – you said you didn't mind. Remember?'

'I hardly had any choice.'

'Oh come on – what's the problem?'

'That he's here for a start. And that you'd rather listen to him than to me.'

Lockhart tilted his face skyward.

'That's not what I meant – it's obvious that Andrew can't go any faster.'

Anna shook her head, her mouth forming into a sarcastic smile.

'I am still here, you know,' Worstead shouted up, but they ignored him.

'What?' Lockhart asked Anna. 'What?'

'Forget it. You two carry on at your own pace. I'm going on ahead.'

'Don't be ridiculous. We can all go together.'

But Anna was already marching off. Lockhart ran after her.

'Don't be like this – it's boring.'

'Not as boring as walking at Fatty's pace.'

'You're totally overreacting.'

'And you were being condescending to me – "I don't

want to hear this bickering" – you sound like a bloody teacher.'

'That's not what I said.'

'Well – it was along those lines.'

'Anyway, don't call him Fatty.'

'Stop being so self-righteous. It doesn't suit you.'

Lockhart stopped walking. As Anna carried on, he shouted after her.

'Well at least I don't behave like a spoiled brat!'

Anna turned round and flashed another sarcastic smile.

'Sometimes I'm glad I'm single,' puffed Worstead as he drew level with Lockhart.

Lockhart grinned as he marched through the night. That was their first row, and like the many to come, it blew over quickly. They had apologised to each other that night, as they shared a small bed in a shepherd's cottage, Worstead snoring on the floor at the other end of the room. That was the first time that Anna had touched him, and he had come after she had only stroked him a few times. She had then started to giggle, which started Lockhart off. Their laughter woke Worstead, who had shown much indignation that his beauty sleep had been disturbed.

The vegetation on the path to Kasteli was thicker than ten years ago. Perhaps that shouldn't have surprised him, but Lockhart had expected it to be the same. He wondered whether the place had changed, whether that room in that little cottage was still there. Lockhart remembered it being a typical Cretan village – whitewashed houses, goats wandering the dirty streets, children running around, old men sitting underneath trees, their faces lined with decades of sun and labour. All the women seemed to do was to shout at the children and goats, and sweep the paths at the front of their cottages. They had stayed for a few days, witnessing the return of the shepherds early on the Saturday night, and joining them in what passed for a bar to drink raki and retsina. Lockhart and Worstead were in their element, although Anna had found the lecherous curiosity a little hard to bear.

Kasteli had been a place of life and innocence, and not the blackened ruin that Lockhart was now walking into. He had known something was wrong before he could even see the village – menace hung like foul breath in the cold air. With his eyes streaming, he started running around the rubble and burnt timbers, looking for – what? If he was looking for the past, there were only stinking and charred tokens of it. All that remained were signs of death and horror. One of the few walls was pockmarked with an uneven line of bullet holes at chest height. The Church of St Demetrios in the centre of the town was still standing, but it was a shell. The roof had collapsed, and the interior was a pile of burnt rubble. The air smelt strange, slightly sweet and yet mixed with an odour of rotten cheese.

Lockhart saw a child's shoe sticking out of the detritus. He picked it up, and with it came a small leg up to the knee. In the moonlight, Lockhart could see a writhing body of agitated maggots fall out of the stump. He dropped the leg, his stomach starting to spasm. He vomited until his insides ached and burned. For minutes afterwards, he stood with his hands on his knees, spitting the bile and mucus out of his mouth. He tried taking deep, calm breaths through his nose, but he caught that smell of decay, and retched again. There was nothing to come up, and he felt his stomach and throat burning with the spasms. Covering his face, he ran out, tripping over the rubble.

The Germans must have massacred most of the villagers in that church. Manoli had told him what had happened elsewhere. After the rapes and the executions, they would lock the population in the church, and then throw grenades through the windows. Sometimes a flame-thrower was used, or machine-gunners casually stood at the windows and raked the pews. The only reason why anybody had known of such actions was that occasionally a child had survived by lying under his or her dead mother.

For the next hour, Lockhart staggered around the corpse of Kasteli. He was beyond tears, and instead entered a limbo of shocked stupor. Where exactly he walked during the rest of that night, he never knew. Neither was he able to remember lying down in the shepherds' shelter, but that was where he woke up at dawn a few hours later, shivering and hungry.

As he walked to Mount Ida that day, Lockhart recalled his father's words, spoken some time after Lockhart's mother had died: 'The path of maturity is not a smooth hill, but instead a series of roughly hewn steps. Some are small and easy, but others are vast and tricky. But climb them you must, for when you stop, you die.' He and Richard hadn't understood them then, but Lockhart found now that it seemed to be grief that gave him the ability to climb those steps.

He had climbed many, but he didn't know if he had matured, or merely become more hollow. Mother's death when he was five; father's when he was twenty-three; Anna's disappearance; Richard's death in North Africa last year – was that what he was here to do? Was he merely destined to climb his way through sadness just to experience more of it? Every step made his life before seem frivolous, shallow. That made him feel worse, not more mature. Life had always been about him, John, not really about anybody else. Yes, there were people he loved and cared for, but was that for his sake or for theirs? And before he could put things right, they went and bloody died or disappeared. He had to see Anna again, to apologise for the fact that he had never loved her deeply enough, not because he hadn't wanted to, but because he was too selfish to know how. But he knew now. Had it needed all these deaths – these slaughters – to tell him that? Perhaps. Their deaths had made him better, but that wasn't why they died. They died because – there were no real reasons, just prosaic ones like illness, heart attacks and war, bloody war.

He arrived at Mount Ida at ten o'clock that night. He walked into the cave and collapsed at the feet of two young *andartes*. After twelve hours of heaving himself through snow, and suffering from hunger and exposure, Lockhart had exhausted himself. He was a husk – empty of any sustenance or joy, almost unable to speak. 'Find Manoli,' he said, and then he let blackness overwhelm him.

* * *

Manoli arrived two days later. Lockhart was taking a siesta, and had woken to find the big man talking quietly to three other *andartes* at the far end of the cave. The very sight of his old friend brought a huge smile to Lockhart's face, although his joy was tempered by what he would have to tell him.

'Manoli!'

Manoli crawled over and clutched Lockhart's shoulders, kissing him on both cheeks.

'My dear friend,' Manoli said. 'You do not know how happy this makes me. I had prayed for your return, and even promised I would remain chaste until the day I married if you turned up alive.'

'In that case I'd have thought you would have wished me dead.'

Manoli mock-sighed.

'I know, but it is the poor women of Crete who will be more deprived.'

'I think they'll be delighted – they need a rest, I expect.'

The two men laughed, but a little too loudly and a little too much. They paused, and stayed silent until Manoli asked:

'Who bandaged up your finger?'

Lockhart looked directly at Manoli.

'What's the time?'he asked.

Manoli shrugged.

'It must be about five o'clock.'

'It's not cocktail hour yet, but I'm going to make an exception. Is there any raki here?'

'Gregori!' Manoli shouted. 'Bring over some raki!'

Little Gregori did as he was told, and was then shooed away by Manoli.

Lockhart took a big swig, coughed, and then swigged again.

'You must keep this a secret, Manoli.'

The Cretan looked back, his face creased in puzzlement. Lockhart resolved to hit Manoli with the straight truth.

'The Germans think they've enlisted me as an informer.'

'What?'

'I have done a deal with Dietrich: I will act as informer in return for my life and Anna's.'

'You've done what?' Manoli shouted.

'Shush!'

'You? A collaborator! For my brother's killer! I don't believe it! Why?'

'Calm down, Manoli! I'm not really going to be a bloody collaborator! If I was, I wouldn't be telling you, would I?'

'I still can't be—'

'Please, just shut up for a few minutes while I explain.'

Manoli quietened down.

'All right, tell me the story then.'

'Good,' said Lockhart. 'I'll start from when we were at the arms dump.'

Lockhart told Manoli the full story. The beatings, the interrogation and the deal – he left nothing out. Afterwards, Manoli simply stared at the ground.

'So what are you going to give this Fasshauer on . . . when is it?'

'I have to see him on Sunday night,' Lockhart replied. 'What's the day today?'

'It's Wednesday.'

'Is there anything coming up we can distract them from?'

'The obvious thing is the parachute drop on Monday night.'

'Where's that?'

Manoli paused, looking at Lockhart suspiciously.

'Manoli! I'm not a real bloody traitor!'

'So why are you so keen to know?'

'So I can tell Fasshauer that it's somewhere else.'

Manoli chewed his lip.

'All right. It's up at Arkadi.'

An image of Anna walking through the monastery flashed up, but before he started to wallow, Lockhart collected himself.

'Good, so all I have to do now is to tell Fasshauer it's over at Asigonia or somewhere, and Dietrich will send his goons to the wrong place.'

'And what happens when they find nothing there?'

'I'll tell them I was misinformed, or that the plan had changed. I'll have to give them something eventually, but let's worry about that when we come to it.'

'We, John, we?'

'Sorry?'

'I don't know if I want to be part of this.'

'Why not?'

'It's too dangerous.'

'Manoli!'

'How do I know that you aren't really a traitor?'

Lockhart was stunned. Did Manoli really think that?

'For Pete's sake, I'm bloody well not! Do you really think I would betray you? I'd rather kill myself. Look, Manoli – if we can make this work, it buys us all a chance. If anybody has to be sacrificed, then of course it had better be me – this is my plan after all – but Christ! I'm no bloody traitor! I never would be. And if I thought I was going to be, then I would shoot myself without any hesitation.'

Manoli sat in silence.

'Come on, Manoli,' Lockhart implored. 'Just give it a chance. If it doesn't work, then I'll do the decent thing, but let's just give it a go. What do you say?'

Manoli looked up.

'I have to think about this. I'm not going to give you an answer now. Tomorrow, I'll tell you tomorrow.'

'All right. I suppose that's fair.'

'Just don't force me, John. This is my island, not yours, and these are my men. Your last plan lost us Niko and Christos and the rest of us only just managed to escape.'

'I'm sorry, Manoli.'

'I'm not asking you to be sorry. I know we must take risks – but just remember the consequences.'

The two men sat in silence. Lockhart was inwardly kicking himself – he had been too pushy with Manoli. Idiot, Lockhart. Anna always had a go at him about this, his habit of expecting things to go his own way. She said it was the outcome of having a laissez-faire father and no mother.

'I'm sorry. I don't want to push you into anything, Manoli. Perhaps my plan is absurd and far too risky. But I don't want to blackmail you by saying that I'll kill myself if you don't want any part of it. I'll just disappear. I'll get off the island. Try to get back to Cairo.'

'And when you disappear, the Germans will kill Anna.'

'Perhaps.'

'They've got you by the balls.'

Lockhart laughed gently at Manoli's use of idiom.

'It's better than being dead.'

More silence. Lockhart decided to change the subject.

'I came through Kasteli on the way here. Do you know why that happened?'

'Sure. It's because we shot that officer on the side of the road.'

There was little conversation as the five of them ate the few remaining scraps of goat that night. Lockhart drank the best part of a bottle of raki, and went to sleep knowing that he had just climbed the biggest step of his life.

He woke with the type of hangover he would get at Oxford. He stared numbly at the roof of the cave, remembering a different world, an innocent world in which the biggest treachery on offer was taking another chap's girl out for a sly dinner in Thame. Not that he had done that – he would never have cheated on Anna. Although she had stayed in Greece until after Lockhart had graduated, despite many temptations he had remained true.

It had suited him – having a girlfriend in Oxford would have curtailed his drinking and gambling exploits. It was more convenient, at that time, to have one who existed on paper. He had felt guilty for having this attitude, but once again Anna's frankness, expressed when he had visited her in Athens one spring vac, had disarmed his worries. 'I wouldn't want you hanging around here either,' she had said, and Lockhart had gone back to Oxford with a clear conscience.

Some of his friends doubted that she existed, especially two of his closest ones – Phil Howard and Edward 'The Test Tube' Barham, so called because he spent most of his time in the chemistry lab. Reluctantly, Lockhart had to produce some letters from Anna as evidence, but the intimate nature of their contents had Phil and The Test Tube billing and cooing.

Both Phil and The Test Tube had ended up at Dunkirk. Phil had made it back, but Edward had been taken prisoner. Poor bugger, Lockhart thought, he had been in Spangenburg POW camp for three years, three long years without his test tubes and Bunsen burners.

He sat up, his head throbbing. It must have been early morning, although Gregori was awake, smoking. There was no sign of Manoli.

'Gregori!' Lockhart whispered loudly.

Little Gregori turned round. He looked shifty, but then it was of Lockhart's opinion that Cretans often did.

'Where's Manoli?'

'He went out with Vangeli to check the snares.'

Lockhart lay back down, relieved. At first he had feared that Manoli had abandoned him. It was hard to tell what decision the Cretan would reach, although Lockhart resolved to accept whatever Manoli came up with. As he had said, it was his island, these were his people. Lockhart was the hired help, borrowed from a nation that had not served the Cretans well during the invasion. He was part of the payback – not exactly a great deal so far. He shut his eyes and let himself go back to sleep. His hangover demanded it.

'Am I always destined to be your alarm clock?'

Lockhart opened his eyes. It was Manoli, almost on top of him, shaking him awake.

'Sorry,' Lockhart yawned. 'What time is it?'

'It's about nine o'clock. We've got a couple of rabbits for breakfast.'

The last time he had rabbit was at the Randolph in the June just before the war. It had been their third wedding anniversary – the last one they'd had together.

'I don't suppose you've got some sautéed potatoes to go with it?'

'No, but we've got some more raki if you want it.'

'Christ, no,' Lockhart drawled, although his hangover had abated.

They were making small talk, ducking the big issue. Lockhart didn't want to ask him, not wanting to appear pushy again. They avoided the subject through breakfast, until Lockhart got up and announced he was stepping outside to relieve himself.

'Wait a moment,' said Manoli. 'I'll come and join you.'

They walked out into the snow, making their way to some large boulders that formed an ideal sheltered spot for defecating.

'It's getting colder,' said Lockhart.

'Don't you want to know my decision?' asked Manoli.

Lockhart stopped walking.

'Look, I'm sorry. I know what I've done seems—'

'I'll go along with it.'

'You're sure?'

'You know me well enough. When I make a decision, I stick to it.'

'Thank you, Manoli.'

'There's no need. But I've had an idea.'

'Oh yes?'

'The only people who know about this are Dietrich and Fasshauer – correct?'

'I think so – yes.'

'Well then – if we killed them, you'd be free, wouldn't you? The deal would be off, and Anna would be safe.'

Lockhart paused.

'But if the SS heard that Dietrich had been killed, they might kill her anyway.'

'They might. But they may never find out. It's got to be worth the risk.'

'Maybe,' Lockhart replied, although he was deep in thought.

They made their way to the boulders.

'Now,' said Manoli, imitating an English gentleman, 'if you'll excuse me – I'm going to take a shit.'

*   *   *

Lockhart relieved himself and walked briskly back to the cave. Gregori and Vangeli were both holding their hands up to the dying fire. Lockhart sat next to them and did the same.

'Is there any more wood?' he asked.

'Very little,' replied Gregori. 'We'll have to find some more when it gets dark.'

Lockhart shivered. It was going to be cold sitting around in the cave all day. At least they had a few blankets – they would just have to huddle under those. He got up to fetch one. As he did so, a rifle shot rang out.

For a second, Lockhart froze. He looked down at Gregori and Vangeli, who looked back at him blankly. And then a whole fusillade opened up, coming from behind and above the cave. Lockhart ran to the back and picked up Manoli's Marlin. He checked the magazine and returned, pulling back the cocking handle. Vangeli and Gregori were still transfixed.

'Come on!' Lockhart urged. 'Get over here!'

The two *andartes* reluctantly crawled over to Lockhart. They looked terrified, their rifles shaking.

Lockhart stuck his head over the lip of the cave. Running towards them, holding up his breeches with his left hand, was Manoli. More shots were fired, kicking up chunks of snow around Manoli's ankles. There was little Lockhart could do apart from urge him on.

'Faster, Manoli!' he screamed. 'Faster!'

The Cretan was only fifteen yards away, but the snow

and his loose breeches were hampering him. He looked up at Lockhart, his eyes wide with terror.

'Run, Manoli, run!'

The first bullet that hit him smashed into the back of his right shoulder. It knocked him flat into the snow, which quickly started to go pink, and then red. He lay still as another two rounds narrowly missed him, then looked up at Lockhart, his face contorted with pain.

The second bullet punched into the base of his spine. Manoli screamed. With each intake of breath, he got louder and more desperate. He knew he was dying.

Without thinking, Lockhart started to get up. Gregori pulled him back down.

'It's too dangerous!'

Lockhart turned to face him, tears in his eyes.

'I can't just bloody stay here!'

He looked up again. Manoli was still looking at him, but the pain had been replaced by hate. Blood was pouring out of his mouth.

'You . . . you,' Manoli gasped. 'You . . . traitor.'

'No, Manoli!' Lockhart screamed back. 'No!'

And then Manoli's head shattered. Fragments of his skull and brain kicked up in a beige and red mist and then scattered into the snow. Lockhart continued screaming, just repeating that one word, 'No!' He tried getting up again, and it required both Gregori and Vangeli to restrain him. Lockhart fired the best part of the magazine into the air.

'You bastards! You sodding fucking bastards! I'll fucking kill you!'

The two *andartes* held their grip on Lockhart until they felt his body go limp. Lockhart buried his face in his hands and sobbed. He had killed his friend – it was his fault.

'Captain Lockhart!'

Lockhart didn't notice Fasshauer's voice at first.

'Captain Lockhart!'

It was coming from above the cave.

'Lockhart! If you don't leave the cave immediately, we'll blow you out with grenades! Do you hear me?'

Lockhart didn't reply.

'Do you hear me? Once more, if you don't leave, you'll be blown up! Come out with your hands up!'

Lockhart turned to Gregori and Vangeli.

'We've got no choice.'

They nodded. Together the three men stood up, and walked out of the cave, away from Manoli's body.

'Just shoot me, Fasshauer!' Lockhart shouted. He turned to look up the mountain, and there was Fasshauer, thirty yards above them, crouching behind a rock.

'I don't want to shoot you, my friend! You've been a great help by allowing us to follow you here!'

Lockhart let his head drop on to his chest. The one person he hated more than Fasshauer was himself.

October 1949

'We all know about your father.'

'What do you know?'

'He was a *traitor*. A *coward*.'

'No he wasn't!'

'Oh yes he was!'

'No he wasn't!'

'He should have been *hanged*, hanged in the Tower.'

Amy had heard this before, but it was getting worse, unbearable. She didn't dare tell the teachers about it, because she knew she mustn't snitch, mustn't tell on the older girls. Once, she had hit a girl who had said things about him, but that had got her into trouble, so now the only thing she could do was to find somewhere quiet where she could cry on her own.

She had been told that a traitor was somebody who fought against his own country, and that traitors were the worst type of people in the world. Some of the girls said that if your father was a traitor, then that made you one as well. She didn't believe that, any more than she believed that Daddy was a traitor. Her father was a brave man, and he didn't fight for the Germans, he fought for the British.

But if that was what the older girls said, then maybe they were right. She would never tell anybody at home about her doubts, because she was afraid of what they might say. It was hard to get away from the fact that the only people who said Daddy wasn't a traitor were those back home. Everybody here thought otherwise. So what was *she* supposed to think? She didn't know, but she told herself that when she was a grown-up, she would find out, prove to the world that her father was in fact a hero, a father to be proud of.

They would stop teasing her then.

* * *

January 1938

He's got them really worked up.

'And so I ask you all,' he shouts into the microphone, 'to embrace the Germans not as our enemies, but as our brothers! They, like us, have suffered for too long the scourge of Jewry in their society – those tumid Shylocks out to rob the helpless and the poor, sticking their long snouts into everybody's trough except their own. They are a putrescent boil on the face of decency – a boil that must be lanced for the good of all!'

Huge cheers from the crowd. There must be at least four hundred of them, all crammed into this hall down in Maidstone. The Leader is away, so he is speaking instead. The honour! To speak in place of the Leader! His Eileen was so proud.

'In Germany, that process has begun. Their brave Führer is smashing the menace of Jewry, and has shown us the way forward. Smash up their shops! Smash up their homes! Send them anywhere, anywhere but back here! It is time for us to take our lead from the strong German people, and declare ourselves to be what we are: strong too, and above all, PURE. The poison coursing through the Jews' filthy veins shall not taint our blood. No! They are a sub-species, and their presence among us brings us down to their level. We are better than that! Far, far better!'

More cheers. He looks down at the front rows, which are reserved for the local hierarchy. Fine men, one and all, wearing their black shirts emblazoned with the party's lightning flash. He is dressed the same, except for the black boots he bought last week, which add an extra dimension of authority.

'Let there be no doubt in your minds that the British people are a great people, who will soon realise that ours is the only way forward. Imagine a Europe without borders, a Europe that need never fight itself again, for the Great War was in fact a civil war, brother against brother. And now imagine Africa as the Empire, serving Europe with its raw materials. Imagine the streets clean of Jews and Communists, all packed off to Russia where they belong. Wouldn't that be paradise, gentlemen? Wouldn't that be a place fit for heroes, a Europe fit for our sons? I tell you now that such a paradise is getting ever nearer, cleansed of scum and troglodytes, a paradise where purity and strength are our watchwords. Let us rid ourselves of the dangers of international finance and the tyranny of Marxism. There is another way, and it is a right way, and it is OUR way! It is a glorious path to freedom and dignity . . .'

But shouts are coming from the back of the hall. A scuffle is breaking out, and he can make out a couple of blackshirts doing over a young thug with a beard. Everybody turns round, ignoring his speech. The scuffle gets rowdier, as does the shouting. There is little doubt that Bolsheviks have infiltrated the meeting! Time to fight them with words too.

'See here, gentlemen, the actions of the Communist . . .'

A few heads turn back to face him.

'. . . intent on violence and terror to disrupt our show of patriotism. We came to this town in peace and we intend to leave in peace. But if we are attacked, then we will show that Fascism is above all STRONG . . .'

But shout as loud as he can, the scuffle is turning into a fight. There must be at least fifty filthy Commies amongst them, intent on causing trouble. Well, they'll get it all right;

they'll get it where it hurts. He steps down from the stage – he'll show them that a man like him leads from the front, that he is more than a speaker.

He runs to where a couple of Bolshies are kicking a helpless blackshirt on the floor. He slides his truncheon out of his pocket, and with his left hand grabs the shoulder of a Bolshie and turns him round.

'Have this, you bastard!' he shouts, and swings the truncheon into the Bolshie's face. Without the embedded nails, the truncheon might have just broken his nose, but with them, the damage is a lot worse. He must have got the bugger in the right eye as well, because blood is pouring out of it. The man brings his hands to his face and starts screaming – good. More and more blood, dribbling through the cracks between his fingers and down his arms. He kicks the Bolshie in the groin for good measure, whereupon he collapses.

The Commie's mate stops kicking the blackshirt. He looks stunned at the ferocity of the attack and readies himself, his fists raised in front of him. Stupid fucker – thinks he's so brave, such a little fighter. The truth is, no Communist can fight, they're just a bunch of yellow nancy- and Jew-boys and this one will prove no exception.

He smashes one of those puny fists with the truncheon. He sees the skin over the knuckles split open and more Bolshie blood gets spilt. But this one's a little tougher than he expects, and still he comes forward, shouting some nonsense at the top of his lungs. But before he can throw a punch with the remaining good fist, he gets a kick in his little Jew balls. He bends double, and then crack! Up comes knee under chin, snapping his head back. That sends him to the floor all right.

He helps the blackshirt off the floor. He looks as though he has a broken nose and no doubt he'll have a few broken ribs. He might need some new teeth too.

'Come on, my friend,' he says gently. 'Up you get.'

'Thank you, sir,' the blackshirt splutters through his bloody mouth. 'You're a hero, sir.'

That makes his chest swell, but he does not want to show it. A hero, eh? How about that?

'You are the hero, my friend, taking on those two Jews. Come on, let's get you to an ambulance.'

They come in peace, but they bring their own ambulances. They cannot rely on the hospitals; instead they take their wounded back to a ward in London, staffed by loyal wives and sisters. A state within a state, that's what they are. And soon their state will replace the state.

The fighting is breaking up, as the Bolshies who can do so are now running. As he helps the blackshirt into the ambulance, he hears the familiar sound of police whistles. Too late again, fools! He lets the truncheon drop by his side. No one will have seen him use it, or at least no one will say they have. The Bolshies wouldn't dare, stupid scum.

They came in peace and now they're leaving with another glorious victory under their silver belts. The Leader will be pleased.

Chapter Three

December 1943

IT HAD TAKEN a lot of doing, but Strasser had wangled himself an office on the Potsdamer Strasse – far enough away from the SS-Hauptamt to give him the privacy required. Since he had seen Berger last week, he had spent much of his time waging war on red tape and deflecting Max's inquistions. Even Leni had asked him what he was now doing, her curiosity aroused by his slight irritability. He had snapped back, telling her it was none of her business, and that she was just a whore and had better get on with her job. Upset, she went to her task, and Strasser apologised afterwards. He couldn't help it – he liked her too much. He had offered her more money than normal, but she had refused, saying that his apology was worth more than any amount of reichsmarks.

Strasser looked at his desk. Piles and piles of paper,

from just about every department in the Reich. He had skimmed through or ignored most of them, trying to keep the job simple. All he had to do was enlist thirty Englishmen, train them, and then his job was done. He wasn't going to put his heart into it, but then he wasn't going to fail.

It would be tough. The impression he had got from Hillen-Ziegfeld's letter was that there were at least twenty or so members of the Legion of St George, but in fact there were only six. Four were committed fascists; three of them had even been members of the British Union of Fascists. Reading between the lines, Strasser guessed that the other two were rather more opportunistic and had enlisted to get out of their stalags. He couldn't just bully them as he had done with recruits in the Das Reich division, otherwise they would want to go straight back to their camps. Lightness of touch. That would be hard, especially in the SS.

He looked at his watch. Ten past nine – they should be here in the next twenty minutes. They were coming up from the camp at Genshagen, a few miles south-west of Berlin – it would be the first time he had met them. No doubt they would think this was going to be a jolly in Berlin, but Strasser was determined today's meeting was to be productive. There were practicalities to sort out – uniforms, accommodation, even the name of the unit.

As an aide-memoire, Strasser had assembled brief biographies of the recruits. He looked over them, refreshing himself before their subjects' arrival. He cursed his handwriting – he should have typed them up, but he knew that finding a typewriter would be almost as hard as finding an office.

> Butcher, Matthew Halley
> b. Chiswick, 29 August 1919
> German mother, English father
> London BUF. Came to Germany in July '39 to seek work. Joined Waffen-SS. In training and garrison roles until May '41 whereupon he joined the Death's Head Oranienburg Guard Battalion at Krakow. Unterscharführer November '41. Transferred to Russian front February '43. Wounded by shrapnel in both legs. Awarded Wound Badge in Silver. Recuperated in Holland, but transferred at the request of Hillen-Ziegfeld and the England Committee to Genshagen staff in September this year.

At least they had a real soldier, thought Strasser. This man Butcher looked capable, and had served the SS bravely. The next one also looked of some use.

> Catchpole, Ray Nicholas
> b. London, 15 June 1912
> English mother, father unknown (Jew?)
> New Zealand Expeditionary Force. Served in Africa and Greece, captured April '41. Rank: corporal. Imprisoned Stalag XVIIId. Approached Gestapo as a 'White Russian',

volunteering to fight the Bolsheviks. Approach declined, but acted as camp interpreter. Sent to Genshagen June this year. Has broadcast propaganda for the Concordia Bureau.

It was good to have another NCO, but what was this man's motive? Like many, perhaps he thought the Germans were going to win. Strasser had him down as a sycophant, and suspected that his loyalty wouldn't stretch far if the Germans started losing. He turned the page.

Lee, Julian
b. Aylesbury, 4 March 1909
English parents
Graduate of London University. Studied classics and archaeology. Worked in Greece and Italy. 2nd Lt. in Oxfordshire and Buckinghamshire Light Infantry. Reduced to private in October '39 for impregnating his CO's daughter. Son born in March '40. Refused leave. Captured May '40 near Dunkirk. Interned in Stalag XXb. Enlisted in Legion April '43, transferred to Genshagen in June.

A bitter man, thought Strasser, but who wouldn't be? This was someone who hated his system for perhaps the strongest reason of all: love. Promising, but he couldn't make him an officer over men like Butcher and Catchpole. That would cause too much resentment, promoting a private over two NCOs. Lee would need some special attention.

Maclaren, Charles
b. Liverpool, 18 June 1915
English parents
Pharmacist. District secretary of Liverpool
BUF. Royal Army Medical Corps, March '40.
Promoted straight to sergeant. Captured at
Wormhoudt, Belgium, on 31 May '40. Stalag
XXId at Schildberg – pharmacist at camp
hospital until September '43. Volunteers to join
SS – sent to Genshagen on 1 October.

Maclaren looked a good mixture – he was both a fascist
and had a useful qualification. As a sergeant, he would
almost certainly want to be the senior NCO, but Strasser
felt that Butcher, of an equivalent rank and with his
fighting experience and SS training, would be far better
suited. He could already see the potential squabbles. He
would have to stamp them out before they got out of
hand.

Marston, Albert Vincent
b. Weston-Super-Mare, 17 January 1920
English parents
Merchant seaman. Served on ship SS *Empire
Ranger* sunk off Norway by the Luftwaffe on
28 March '42. Taken prisoner and interned at
Marlag/Milag at Westertimke near Bremen.
Persuaded to go to Genshagen by Frederick
LEWIS (where now?) and brought into unit by
Butcher in October.

Pugh, Thomas Mervyn Edward
b. London, 24 April 1910
English father, American mother
Graduated in English literature and history,
Birkbeck College, London. Married Eileen Bates
April 1930. Joined London BUF in '34 as a
speaker and administrative officer. Arrested
September '37 for instigating riot – charge
dropped for lack of evidence. Germany August
'39. Broadcasts for Concordia Bureau. Associate
of John Amery. Approached by Hillen-Ziegfeld
in May '43 and transferred to Genshagen to
work as recruiter and interpreter in June.

Here was the ideologue. He was bound to have ideas
above his station, especially as he had been recruited
directly by the Foreign Office. But he would be good for
indoctrinating any new recruits into National Socialism.
As for Marston, he appeared young and malleable, a good
foot soldier perhaps. With his contacts amongst the
deckhands at the Merchant Navy camp, he might be able
to go back there and recruit.

Strasser heard the sound of a truck outside. He went to
the window and opened it, letting a rush of cold morning
air into the room. Coughing, he looked down three floors
to see a small truck pull up and disgorge six men dressed
in civilian clothes. They were accompanied by an armed
SS sturmmann and a Wehrmacht private – that would be
their interpreter, Wilhelm Richter. Strasser wouldn't need
Richter of course – Richter was there to see off any

inquisitive policeman who heard a batch of Englishmen walking down a Berlin street. He could hear the men laughing and joking as they made their way to the entrance. So they did think it was a jolly.

Strasser shut the window. Walking over to the flimsy table and chairs at the other end of the office, he could have sworn that it was colder in than out. There was a grate in the office, but no wood, coke, anything. He was tempted to burn some of those nonsensical Foreign Office files, but thought better of it. He sat at the head of the table, neatly positioning some paper and a pencil in front of him. He straightened his tie and smoothed down his tunic. He waited, his eyes closed.

After a couple of minutes, he heard voices and footsteps. There was a knock on the door.

'Yes!'

The door opened, and in stepped the six men and Richter. They sauntered in, nodding casually at Strasser, and continued talking to each other.

'Who the fuck do you think you are?' asked Strasser. He spoke in English, his voice calm, measured.

The men went silent. Strasser continued in the same authoritative monotone.

'Get the fuck out, come in again, one at a fucking time. I want each one of you to salute me, stating your name and date of birth. If you show any such disrespect again, then you'll all be off to a punishment camp. Now – out! Richter – you stay here and sit next to me.'

Like chastised schoolboys, the men sheepishly left the room. The first to re-enter was Butcher, who announced himself in German and with an immaculate Heil Hitler.

'Much better, Butcher,' said Strasser. 'Although I had expected you to show an example.'

'I apologise, Hauptsturmführer . . .'

'Just sit down.'

Pugh and Catchpole came in next, both giving Nazi salutes. Marston and Lee merely stood to attention, but Strasser let that go – they were not yet in the SS. As he expected, Maclaren also gave a full Heil Hitler.

Strasser looked slowly round the table, sizing them up. They mostly looked like scum, useless scum skimmed off the surface. He breathed out theatrically, and pinching his pencil so it stood upright on the table, let his thumb and forefinger slide slowly down it. When they reached the bottom, he lifted the pencil up, and turned the top end down to the table, whereupon he tapped it down again and repeated the process. He did this at least thirty or forty times, the silence only broken by the rhythmic tapping and the occasional nervous cough.

'Right,' Strasser eventually began, 'I am Hauptsturm-führer Carl Strasser, and I am your officer in charge. You will report directly to me. Is that understood?'

A low murmur went round the table.

'Good. I'd also like you to remember one thing above all else. You are each here because we want you here. That is a great, great privilege. So, if any of you give me a reason, no matter how small, to throw you out, then I'll do so. You will go straight to a punishment camp, which will not be pleasant at this time of year. You can forget about going back to your original camps. I hardly think your fellow countrymen will welcome you back with big smiles. Is that also understood?'

Another low murmur of assent.

'Good. Now, to business. Oh yes, and another thing – everybody speaks through me. You are effectively back at school. So, hand up if you want to talk. I see from your files that you've all been to school, so I'm sure you know how it works.'

The men smiled nervously.

'So,' continued Strasser, 'the first thing is the name of the unit. At present you're to be known as "the Legion of St George" – any problems with that?'

The men stayed silent.

'Well?' asked Strasser.

A hand went up. It was Butcher's.

'Yes, Unterscharführer?'

Butcher coughed.

'Some of us feel, Herr Hauptsturmführer, that it sounds a little too . . . religious. It sounds like we're a band of nuns tending to the sick.'

Everybody laughed, including Strasser. Butcher looked taken aback at the laughter – he had not intended his comment as a joke. He didn't look like a natural comedian: his face was thin and sallow, and his eyes were deep-set beneath thick eyebrows. His black hair was greased back, showing a pronounced widow's peak.

'But surely St George is England's great hero?' asked Strasser. 'Surely many Englishmen would rally around him?'

Lee raised his hand. Strasser nodded.

'That's partly the problem,' Lee began. 'You'd only get Englishmen. The Scots, Welsh and Irish would never fight for St George.'

Strasser chewed his lip – it was a good point.

'Well then,' he said, 'why don't we call it . . . the British Legion? That would keep in well with our other foreign legions. After all, we have a French Legion—'

But Strasser was interrupted by the group all starting to speak as one.

'Quiet!' he shouted. 'This really is like school! One at a time.'

It was Lee who caught his eye.

'I'm afraid that there already is a British Legion – it's a veterans' group from the last war.'

'I see,' said Strasser. 'Hardly appropriate. Any other suggestions?'

The room went quiet again, until Marston tentatively put up his hand. He looked like a boy, thought Strasser, with his gawky, slightly mischievous face and large eyes.

'I was reading *Signal* the other day, and in it I saw that the Danes have an SS legion called the Freikorps Danmark. Couldn't we call our legion something like that?'

'What? Freikorps Gross Britannien?'

'I was thinking, sir,' replied Marston, 'of something like "the British Free Corps".'

Strasser pondered it. There was no doubt, it did sound good.

'What does everyone else think?'

The table nodded, each man looking at the others for guidance.

'Good!' exclaimed Strasser. 'Well done, Marston. Subject to higher approval, we'll go with your name. The British Free Corps it is.'

In the truck on the way back to Rethimno, Lockhart sat in a daze. His hands were tied behind him, which meant that he could not steady himself as the vehicle blundered over the rough Cretan roads. One pothole was so bad that he was tossed on to the floor at the feet of the grinning Fasshauer.

'You might as well stay there!' the German laughed, the two guards joining in.

Lockhart swore under his breath. The metal runners dug into his ribs, the pain magnified by each jolt. It was all he deserved. Every time he shut his eyes, the vision of Manoli's head disintegrating played in front of him. And now he felt extra guilt for Vangeli and Gregori, who were in the other truck, en route to their graves. He wanted to cry, like he had done when Mother had died, his father's awkward hands clutching the five-year-old Lockhart's snivelling face to his chest. But he couldn't cry, not in front of Fasshauer.

It took four hours to reach Rethimno. As the truck pulled into the parade ground early that afternoon, Lockhart saw Dietrich waiting for them. Standing next to him were two civilians, wearing long black leather coats and snap-brim hats. Gestapo. He had been taught about them at Arisaig, how no agent could hope to survive an encounter with the Reich's secret police. They even had the legal right to beat confessions out of their prisoners. So, finally, this really would be the end. He would be taken off to another cell by fat men in leather coats, where the tortures would be more brutal, the deprivations and abuse horrific. He had made a shambles of everything and now the Fates were to punish him for it. The situation was so dire, he could have laughed – fear was now replaced by an almost comic sense of resignation.

Grinning slightly, Lockhart looked at a perplexed Fasshauer.

'Stay where you are,' the German said, and jumped out the back.

Lockhart watched as Fasshauer walked over to his commanding officer, saluted him, and was introduced to the two Gestapo men. The conversation was inaudible, until he heard Fasshauer shout:

'You must be joking! He's far too valuable for us just to give him . . .'

But then Dietrich was already quietening the young man down, and the conversation carried on for another minute until Fasshauer shouted over to the truck:

'Bring the prisoner here!'

The two guards bundled Lockhart to the back of the truck and pushed him out so hard that he nearly fell flat. Desperate to impress Dietrich, they made great play of roughly shoving their prisoner over the few yards.

'Untie his hands!' ordered Dietrich.

Lockhart felt a bayonet sawing vigorously between his wrists, and briefly thought that he might be killed there and then by some idiot private accidentally slicing up his veins. When the rope came off, he found it difficult to move his arms in front of him, so cramped and stiff were his shoulders.

'Welcome back, Captain,' smiled Dietrich. 'I'm glad to see you're safe and well. Many congratulations, although I am sorry that I didn't quite trust you enough not to have you followed. No hard feelings, I hope?'

Lockhart smiled sarcastically back. Dietrich's bogus chivalry was absurd – he was clearly trying to show the Gestapo what gentlemen the Wehrmacht were.

'I'm so glad. Unfortunately our friendship must end here, as these two gentlemen from the Gestapo would like to take you in for questioning. Believe me, Captain, I tried as hard as I could, but they were most insistent that they become your new guardians.'

Lockhart continued with his insincere smile. Part of him relished the fact that Dietrich had been overruled by these two *policemen*. His attempts to make light of it were pathetic, childish even.

'So it's goodbye, Lockhart,' said Dietrich, holding out his hand. 'I wish you the very best of luck.'

Lockhart loosened some phlegm at the back of his throat, and spat solidly in Dietrich's face. The Gestapo men and Fasshauer made a grab for the insolent prisoner, but Dietrich was there first, punching Lockhart in the jaw.

As he was marched, beaten and kicked towards the Gestapo's car, he knew that a handshake would have hurt a lot more.

* * *

'HERAKLION 65 km' read the sign. Lockhart knew the town well from his summer at Knossos. He also remembered the road, which followed the coast and then cut inland to Crete's capital. The journey would take two hours, two hours of more discomfort, wedged between the two Gestapo officers. They spoke neither to Lockhart nor to each other, simply staring ahead as the car's shadow started to lengthen in front of them.

He had often come down this road with Anna. During a break in the digs they would disappear as quickly as possible, despite Worstead's complaints of abandonment, and find a village beside the sea where they could rent a room. Afterwards, they would take a dip in the sea to cool off. Once, Anna had taken off Lockhart's shorts when they were swimming, and had run back towards the dunes with them. At least twenty Cretans had seen him streaking across the beach until he had caught up with her, rugby-tackling her to the ground.

They reached the imposing Canea gate on the south side of Heraklion by five o'clock. Their progress was slowed by a churning mixture of Cretans carting produce and Germans attempting to direct them. Lockhart recalled that everything had moved much more smoothly ten years ago. Curious faces looked in through the windows, and still the Gestapo officers stayed coolly silent. The bustle and the noise reminded him of Cairo, as did the smell of drains.

It took fifteen minutes to reach the Platia Venizelou, Heraklion's main square. Every building of note carried a swastika flag, flapping lazily in the mild early-evening breeze. The square too was crowded, although mostly with German officers, making their way to the many bars around the fountain. Apart from the 'guests', little had changed in the past decade. He and Worstead had spent many drunken evenings here, which often incurred Anna's wrath. Lockhart would defend himself by saying that he was on holiday, and Anna would tell him that wasn't an excuse to behave boorishly.

The car pulled up to an archway at the end of the square – the entrance to the old town hall, Lockhart recalled. His heart began to quicken. How could he ever have expected that one day the Heraklion town hall would cause him such fear? He longed for Anna, and, closing his eyes, prayed that he would see her again, and for the strength to endure what was about to happen.

However, there was no torture – only questions, insistent questions. He would remember little of the next seventy-two hours. The interrogation was certainly insistent, but there was nothing in it that Lockhart had not already been asked by Dietrich and Fasshauer. His inquisitor made much of 'the deal' and whether Lockhart would continue to co-operate in the future. Lockhart replied that that would depend on whether they could guarantee Anna's safety. It would be looked into, said his inquisitor.

After the first few hours, delirious and finally over-whelmed by thirst and hunger, Lockhart had collapsed. They had tried to revive him, but it was impossible. At first they thought he was dead, but there was a pulse, and they took their prisoner's emaciated form to a damp cell, where they poured water through his cracked lips. After that had woken him, they had given him a bowl of cold stew and a blanket. He had begged for another blanket, and to his surprise they obliged. They didn't want him to die, he had thought – there was still hope. It was the beginning of a two-day pattern of interrogation punctuated by small amounts of sleep and food.

On his third morning, the two Gestapo officers who had picked him up from Rethimno entered his room. They threw an unmarked Wehrmacht tunic and a pair of grey breeches on to the bed. A pair of boots was dropped on the floor. Lockhart noticed that the laces had been removed.

'Get dressed – you're going.'

'Where?' asked Lockhart.

'Berlin.'

Because they refused to tell him their names, Lockhart christened his Gestapo escorts Tweedledum and Tweedledee. Assuming that they were not allowed to kill him, he took the liberty of insolently addressing them by their nicknames. It appeared that they had read little or no Lewis Carroll, and looked nonplussed whenever he used the names on the week-long trip to Berlin.

It started easily enough, with a two-hour flight in a Junkers 52 from Heraklion to Athens. Lockhart guessed the plane was a veteran of the paratroop invasion in May 1941, as it still carried the scars of battle, with patches of canvas covering a score of bullet holes. Although short, the flight was freezing, and the Wehrmacht tunic provided little protection. Tweedledum kindly secured him an army greatcoat in Athens, which caused Tweedledee some annoyance. It was the nearest the pair got to an argument, but Tweedledum said the train would be cold, and he didn't think it would be wise if Lockhart fell ill, as it would only cause them more hassle.

Tweedledum was right – the train was little better than the plane, often stopping for hours while a vast Balkan snowdrift was cleared, or because the Wehrmacht were mopping up a band of partisans. Their route took them from Athens to Skopje and then on to Belgrade, where they changed trains. The journey up to this point brought back many memories of the same journey taken with Worstead ten years ago, although much of that innocent trip had been spent in an alcoholic haze in the dining car. Apart from into his reminiscences, Lockhart had no chance of escape, as one of his escorts always stayed awake. They even made him use the lavatory with the door open, which Lockhart reasoned was more unpleasant for them than it was for him.

They did not stay long in Belgrade; a train to Vienna was leaving two hours after their arrival. Lockhart noticed the swastikas were multiplying, appearing on buildings, passengers' arms, even on flagpoles in people's gardens. Tweedledum and Tweedledee began to grow more relaxed as they approached the Austrian capital, although Lockhart felt the opposite. All that gave him cheer were the first signs of bomb damage, but it looked nugatory compared to what he had witnessed in the Blitz. They spent that night in Vienna, Lockhart having to endure a cell in the

Gestapo headquarters, although he was given both blankets and food. By the next evening they were in Prague, where they changed for their final train, which took them through the night to Berlin.

Lockhart noticed the devastation as soon as he woke up. He was becoming an expert at sleeping on the hard wooden seats, although some part of his body was always knocked in the middle of the night by either Tweedledum or Tweedledee. As he rubbed his sore neck with one hand, he wiped the condensation off the window to reveal a scene of snow-covered chaos.

The train was passing through the suburbs, where around a quarter of every street had been bombed out. Families gathered around makeshift braziers in the rubble, while others rooted through the mess for any surviving possessions. Just like London, thought Lockhart. Other passengers were also frantically wiping away at the glass, and were passing shocked comment to their neighbours.

So much for Hitler's promise that Berlin would never be bombed. He expected his fellow passengers were thinking it too, but they wouldn't dare express such views in public. Tweedledum and Tweedledee were also looking, their hitherto motionless faces registering a hint of concern.

'So how does it feel to get a taste of your own medicine?' asked Lockhart.

'What?' replied Tweedledee, still distracted by the view from the window.

'I asked – how does it feel to get a taste of your own medicine?'

Tweedledee scowled at him.

'This is nothing compared to what we've done to your cities,' he replied.

'How do you know?'

'I've seen the newsreels and photographs – they never lie.'

'Is that so? Well, if your Luftwaffe is so successful, how come they can't stop us coming through?'

A pause.

'We're winning the war elsewhere.'

'Where?'

'Last month we took two Greek islands, and we're driving you back out of Italy.'

'Not true, my friend – you're the ones being kicked out, not us. And let's not forget what the Russians are doing to you. I'd heard they'd retaken Kiev. And how about the seventeen U-boats we sank last month? And now you've got all this bomb damage . . .'

Tweedledum turned from the window.

'Shut it,' he ordered menacingly.

Lockhart did so, but with a smile – the moral victory had been his. He looked through the window again. So this was it, the heart of the great Third Reich, a crippled black-and-white world, the omnipresent red swastika banners like drops of blood in the snow. Up till now, Berlin had seemed a mythical place, a place so evil and otherworldly that it didn't seem to exist. And yet here he was, entering what for many back home was a city of the imagination, no more real to them than Troy, or Knossos for that matter.

Although he hadn't expected lines of goose-stepping troops and cheering crowds, Lockhart felt their absence. The city just seemed so ordinary, like a city in Britain, albeit with different architecture. But the smokestacks, the roads, the flats and little houses, the nativity scenes in bombed-out shop windows – all these were the same. What made this place so evil? Lockhart looked at the passengers. What made them want to take over the world? What was it that these people lacked?

The conductor entered the carriage – even he was wearing a swastika.

'What time do we arrive at Anhalter Bahnhof?' asked Tweedledum, showing his pass.

'Haven't you heard?' the conductor replied.

'No – what?'

'Anhalter was completely destroyed nearly three weeks ago – we're coming into Lichterfelde instead. We should be there in ten minutes.'

Lockhart smiled as the two Gestapo men exchanged concerned glances. Suddenly the train came to a violent halt.

'What's going on?'

The conductor didn't answer Tweedledum's question. Instead, he wiped the window.

'What is it?'

The conductor started back – his face had lit up.

'The Führersonderzug!' he exclaimed. 'It's coming right past us!'

The words had the immediate effect of causing the passengers to scramble over to the right side of the carriage.

'Can you see him?' people were asking – even Tweedledee and Tweedledum were caught up in the excitement. It was not every day that Hitler's special train went past.

Lockhart looked through the window and saw the dark violet carriages fifty feet away, slowly trundling in the other direction. The windows were large, and underneath them, running the length of each carriage, were two white stripes. He could see the occasional face, but many of the windows had blinds pulled down. Was Hitler himself really behind one of them? Lockhart felt helpless – to be this close to him, and yet unable to do anything.

He counted the carriages – there were ten, with platforms containing quadruple AA guns at either end. Two streamlined locomotives hauled the train, their sooty smoke partly obscuring the view. In the unlikely event of him getting back to Britain, somebody would want such information. There must be plans somewhere in Whitehall to kill Hitler, but Lockhart had never had access to them. Someone at his club had told him that the top brass wanted to keep the Führer alive, as he was a usefully inept military commander. That had been at the end of January, just after Stalingrad had been won. Perhaps the brass had a point, but it seemed too arch. Kill Hitler, and surely the madness would end, or at least abate? They couldn't all be maniacs like him. But that same someone had added that killing Hitler ran the risk of making him a martyr, rejuvenating Nazi fanaticism.

The Führersonderzug had now gone, but the joy on the faces of the passengers remained. The women looked the most ecstatic, in a state of rapture. Everybody was smiling, even Tweedledum and Tweedledee. Would it be the same in England, Lockhart thought, if a train with Churchill on it had gone past? He had to admit that it would, and yet . . . This was different. When people cheered for Churchill or the King, it was out of respect and reverence, but on these faces it looked more like adulation. The entire population was like a teenage girl admiring someone's big brother. They reminded Lockhart of Lizzie Potts, the housekeeper's daughter, who would swoon over Richard when he came back from Marlborough for the holidays. Was the German population really so unsophisticated? 'A feudal society with capitalism and modern technology' – that was how Anna had described it. She was right, and now she was a victim of it. These people, right here on this train, these were the people who had put her away, taken away his Anna. He hated them for it – the whole lot of them.

The train jerked forward, and crawled the rest of the way into Lichterfelde. Tweedledee snapped a pair of handcuffs on to Lockhart's wrists. They were too tight, and Lockhart complained, but he was ignored. As he was pushed on to the huge smoke-filled platform, he wondered if that was the last time in his life he would take a train.

'You appear to love your wife very much, Captain Lockhart.'

'Of course I do, don't you?'

'Forgive me, but I do not have a wife.'

'There's a surprise.'

The comment was ignored.

'It's my understanding that you're willing to help us if we keep her alive. Yes?'

A pause.

'Yes.'

'That's quite something, putting your wife before your country. You wouldn't catch a German doing that – that's why we'll win, because we're more brutal than you.'

'You haven't had a very good year for a side that's supposed to be—'

'Temporary setbacks. We are regrouping and soon Moscow will be in our hands. And then England will finally be invaded. A pity. Bolshevism is the real enemy, not each other. The Russians and the Jews are the real scum in this war, not the English and the Americans.'

'That's kind of you to say so.'

'It's the truth, Lockhart.'

Another pause.

'I hear that your wife was captured in Holland in 1941. She was part of an underground printing press, publishing nonsense and sedition. Why was she doing this?'

'She's never been one to hide her opinions.'

'Even if they are lies? Even if they are dangerous?'

'She's a very headstrong woman.'

'So it would seem. And now she is in a camp wearing a nice red triangle on her chest. That means she is a political prisoner – her opinions have no place in the Reich. You know she was lucky not to be shot? I hope her luck lasts . . . you understand me, Lockhart?'

'Yes.'

'So, if you don't help, well, I wouldn't like to say . . .'

'How do I know she's really alive?'

'You have to trust me.'

Lockhart stared at his latest inquisitor, sitting behind his desk in a sumptuous office in Gestapo headquarters on Prinz Albrechtstrasse. The face was anything but trustworthy – deep, dark eyes that occasionally looked up, and a small, thin-lipped mouth. The hair was short, nearly shaven, which accentuated his already large ears. He was wearing a well-cut black double-breasted suit, a swastika armband around the left arm. The face, Lockhart was told, belonged to none other than Heinrich Müller, head of the Gestapo. Lockhart had heard of him – but he remembered the intelligence file on him was thin. Müller had successfully shunned the limelight, watching and planning, slowly rising through the ranks. He had taken over from Göring's man, Rudolf Diels, in 1934, and had survived the shake-up after the assassination of Heydrich in June 1942. There was little else in the dossier, not even a photograph.

'Could I write to her?'

'No.'

'Could she at least write to me?'

Müller looked up briefly.

'If it'll make you more co-operative.'

'It might.'

'Don't push your luck, Lockhart. I could have both of you shot tomorrow morning. I have far more important things to do than worry about you. If you act up, you could even watch her being raped and tortured. How about that, eh?'

Lockhart clenched and unclenched his fists by his sides. The fucking bastard. He wanted to kill Müller, right there and then. He could grab the letter knife from his desk and stick it in his badly shaven neck before the guard had time to react. Wouldn't killing him partly make up for his mistakes? Another scalp, after Heydrich, for SOE? And then he thought of Anna – he would be signing both of their death sentences, not just his. Besides, chop this Müller's head off and another would grow in its place. No, if he was going to make this double-cross work, then he would need to make the risk worth it. The stakes were too high just to play at killing overblown functionaries. What difference had Heydrich's death made? None. Lockhart took a deep breath and spoke.

'It would make me more co-operative, yes.'

'Good. I shall see what can be arranged. Now go.'

The letter arrived three days later. Lockhart's new residence was a cell in the Columbia-Haus, a monolithic five-storey edifice that had once been a concentration camp. Much of the building was empty, but a few cells remained in use – an overflow for headquarters. He had been given a minimum amount of food, but he counted himself lucky when he looked at the stains on the walls. The letter had arrived with his breakfast of stale rolls and even staler water. He had ignored the food and torn open the envelope, on to which his name and rank had been typed. The letter too was typed, which aroused his suspicion.

15 December

My dearest dearest John,
I heard two hours ago that you are alive, and I have
been in tears of joy ever since – what a beacon of
hope in this dark place! So many questions to ask you!
How are you? How is Amy? Where were you captured?
Where are you now? Are you hurt? Oh my darling, I
am so relieved. I am told that you cannot write to me,
but I must not be greedy – just the news that you are
alive gives me so much STRENGTH. Things here are
not so bad, but for the Jews it is much worse. We have
enough food, and I have even managed to grow a few
vegetables! I am not allowed to say more as I am
dictating this. I cannot actually write for security
reasons – whatever they may be! – but that I can
communicate with you gives me so much hope. I love
you so dearly, and am missing you and Amy dreadfully.
    Yours as always,
    Anna
    XXXXX

Lockhart read it four times, tears in his eyes. It sounded
like Anna, but it was not as forceful as her. But then she
would have changed after three years in a camp – her
confidence replaced by desperation. Nevertheless, the tone
was similar, and besides, how would the Germans know
their daughter was called Amy? He had never told them.
That would have been proof enough if it wasn't for the
fact that the letter was typed.

'For security reasons'. What possible reasons were they? The most likely was that the letter was a fake, and somehow the Germans had found out about Amy, although God knows how. But the vast part of him wanted it to be genuine. Maybe it was typed because her handwriting might reveal a deterioration in her health. Or perhaps the Gestapo thought that Anna could conceal some sort of code in her script that would be eradicated when typed out.

He clutched the letter to his chest. It *had* to be her. Otherwise all his bungled actions up to now were pointless. He knew that he was trying to convince himself that it was true, but he couldn't stop himself. What options did he have? To tell Müller that he thought it was a fake, and no, he wasn't going to co-operate? He might as well hang himself, and Anna too.

For a while, maybe as long as fifteen minutes, Lockhart did not notice the knocking coming from the cell to his right. Lying on his mattress, encased in a shell made from his thoughts, brooding, rereading the letter, his subconscious put the sound down to water pipes expanding, or perhaps the noise of a rat stuck in a cavity.

But the noise was more logical than that, more insistent, so that its urgent tapping broke through, cracking his shell. Lockhart sat up and put his ear to the wall. He held his breath, listening to the welcome sound of human contact. The knocking was muffled, but he could clearly make it out – three taps followed by a pause, and then another three taps.

Excitedly, he knocked back, using the knuckle of his right index finger. But the wall was hard and rough, and he doubted that the recipient would hear it. In vain, he looked around the cell for a hard object, but as he well knew, there was none. His boots. He would use them, alternating between the two every few minutes, so as to spare one foot from being the sole victim of the freezing temperature in the cell.

Lockhart gave a boot heel three hard knocks against the wall in response. He listened for a reply: tap – tap – tap it came, and then again, louder, TAP – TAP – TAP. As he knocked, Lockhart wondered how they were going to communicate. Morse code? Or the quadratic alphabet? This was a universal system Lockhart had been taught at Arisaig, far simpler than Morse, in which the alphabet was arranged into a five-by-five grid of twenty-five letters. The letter A thus required one tap to signify that it was in row one, and another tap to signify that it was in column one, while F, being in row two, column one, required two taps followed by one tap. And then what of language? Lockhart decided to start with German.

He stopped tapping and waited for next door to do likewise. After a minute or so, Lockhart resumed, this time slowly, trying hard to visualise the letters of the German alphabet and where they would appear on the grid. He knocked out only one word, then repeated it, nervously hoping that it would be understood:

WHO

There was no reply. Damn. Perhaps the quadratic system wasn't so universal. It looked as if Lockhart was going to have to summon up his Morse code. Just as he was ruing the fact that he hadn't paid more attention in the signals classes at Arisaig, he heard a tapping. It was slow, but it appeared to make sense.

M...I...C...O...L...A...S

Micolas? He must have meant 'Nicolas'.

NICOLAS, tapped Lockhart.

YES YOU, came the reply.

JOHN

ENGLAND

YES YOU

RUSSIA

Russia. Who the hell was this?

WHY YOU HERE, Lockhart tapped.

He listened, but the wall stayed silent. Nicolas had evidently not liked the question, found it too intrusive. Perhaps he was fearful that Lockhart was in fact a Gestapo man posing as a prisoner, attempting to extract information by guile rather than by straightforward torture. He would need to reassure him.

ME BRITISH OFFICER

Again, nothing.

CAPTURED IN CRETE

Still silence. Lockhart gave up and lay back on the mattress. Who was Nicolas? Was he an agent? Was he even Gestapo? The thought troubled Lockhart, but he dismissed it. The Gestapo, if they suspected he was holding back, would want to torture him first, not play clever little games of knocking on walls. That would be a last resort for them. No, this Nicolas had to be an agent of some sort, not just because that was what Lockhart wanted to believe, but because it was simply more believable. But why was he not knocking back? Lockhart tried again, if only as something to do.

HOW LONG YOU BEEN HERE

Nothing. With a sigh, Lockhart put his boot back on and got up. He did some stretches and press-ups, his body still stiff after a week of having to sit tight on the train. He jogged on the spot, counting out each step, trying to work out how many would make up the equivalent of a mile-long run. Two thousand? Three thousand? Well, there was nothing else to do, he thought, so he might as well keep on running, imagining himself sprinting out of the cell, down the corridors, out the gate, along the streets, and all the way to Anna, to save her – if indeed the letter was real and she was still alive. He imagined them running together, back to England, back home to Amy, to live the decently simple family life that they had always wanted. Even as Lockhart fantasised, concocting this idyll, part of him knew that the possibility of regaining the past was hopelessly romantic, absurd even. But it *had* to be tried, especially if there was a chance, no matter how small.

Just then, he heard the knocking again. He rushed to the mattress and pressed his right ear against the wall. The tapping was faster than before, and Lockhart had to do his frantic best to work out what it meant. Nicolas was obviously excited, and had seemingly decided to trust this 'John' from England.

. . . REE WEEKS BUT NOT MUCH LONGER

Lockhart took off a boot, and replied.

WHAT WILL HAPPEN

There was a pause, and then came the word that Lockhart had expected and feared:

SHOT

There was something definite about the way Nicolas had tapped out the word – there was defiance in him, bravery. For a while, Lockhart's boot hovered against the wall. He wanted to say something, but he didn't know what to say. All he could think of was:

SORRY

It felt pathetic, but what else could he tap? There was another pause. He imagined that Nicolas might have broken down, would be weeping, but his response suggested that he was very much together.

LOOKING FORWARD TO IT

Lockhart started back from the wall. Looking forward to it? What had they done to him? He tapped out:

YOU MEAN IT

Nicolas tapped back immediately.

YES YES

WHY

TORTURE

Lockhart shut his eyes, trying to stop himself envisaging what they had done to Nicolas. He didn't want to know – it wouldn't help him. Instead, he decided to ask Nicolas once more why he was here.

WHY YOU HERE

There was a silence again. Nicolas was being cagey. Lockhart tapped again.

PLEASE

After a minute, Nicolas tapped back, much more quietly this time, as if he was afraid of being overheard.

GRU

Lockhart breathed out – it was as he had suspected. The GRU was the Chief Intelligence Directorate of the General Staff in Moscow – the Soviet equivalent of MI6. Nicolas was an agent all right. And if he was an agent, then he would know something worth knowing – something that Lockhart wanted to find out. But before Lockhart could tap back, Nicolas had restarted.

AND YOU

Lockhart knew that he had to pay back Nicolas's trust, but there was no way he was going to reveal the existence of SOE, not even to an ally. There were plenty of people he couldn't tell in London – high-up people – never mind a doomed Russian agent in a cell in Berlin.

ARMY, Lockhart tapped.

CAN I TRUST YOU

YES, Lockhart rapped. So his hunch was right – Nicolas *did* know something, the knowledge of which had probably got him locked up.

A pause.

ARE YOU GOING TO GET OUT OF HERE

I HOPE SO, Lockhart knocked back.

HA HA

Lockhart didn't reply.

WE LEAVE IN COFFINS, tapped Nicolas.

Surely he was playing with him now, teasing him?

I LEAVE ON FOOT

HOW, asked Nicolas.

I MADE A DEAL

Nicolas's tapping came back quickly and incorrectly.

WHAV SORT DEBL

Lockhart took a deep breath. He would have to trust Nicolas. He couldn't be Gestapo. If they had wanted to use a fake prisoner to get information out of him, they would have made them share a cell, and not have bothered with this unreliable and laborious tapping process.

I PRETEND TO HELP THEM

HELP

MY WIFE PRISONER

Lockhart could imagine Nicolas's face. His eyes would be bulging in disbelief at what the wall was telling him. He would be lifting his boot, or whatever it was he was tapping with, and then lowering it again, unable to decide what to knock first.

WHERE WIFE

IN A CAMP

Lockhart waited, listening to the sound of his own breathing. Come on, he urged, come on, Nicolas, tell me what it is you know.

YOU MAD

YES, knocked Lockhart, humouring him.

OR CLEVER

Lockhart left it. He was getting frustrated, angry that Nicolas was keeping him dangling. He would ask him point blank, and then leave it.

WHAT DO YOU WANT TO TELL ME

He dropped his boot on the floor and lay back down. His arm was beginning to ache, as was his brain, which was getting mildly irritated at having to visualise the German alphabet on a grid. It was time to do some more exercise – some sit-ups. He clasped his hands behind his head, and with a slight grunt heaved himself up and let himself back down slowly, feeling his stomach muscles tense. He would do a hundred, if possible, and then tap through to Nicolas again.

But Nicolas stopped him on his thirtieth sit-up. Lockhart missed the first few letters, but the message was clear.

. . . Y HAVE A NEW WEAPON

Lockhart picked his boot off the floor and knocked back.

WHAT WEAPON

NERVE GAS

NAME

SARIN

SARIN, Lockhart confirmed.

YES VERY DEADLY

HOW

KILL MILLIONS

Lockhart swallowed. This had to be fantasy.

HOW, he tapped again.

DON'T K . . .

But Lockhart interrupted him. He wanted to check Nicolas's claim.

MILLIONS, he tapped.

YES GERMANS COULD WIN WAR

HOW YOU KNOW

FROM A SOURCE

WMO, tapped Lockhart in a hurry, meaning 'who'.

Nicolas paused, and then:

CANT SAY

That was fair enough, thought Lockhart, but he needed to know, and told Nicolas as much.

NO came back.

MORE ABOUT GAS, knocked Lockhart.

THIS ALL I KNOW

DO GERMANS KNOW YOU KNOW

NO

GRU

NO BECAUSE CAPTURED

TELL ME MORE

And then Nicolas went quiet again. At first, Lockhart thought he was being reticent, but the reason soon became evident, for Nicolas must have heard the echoing sounds of heavy footsteps a few seconds before Lockhart. He pressed his ear even harder to the wall, in case Nicolas tried to quietly tap something out. But all he could hear were voices and laughter, until, very faintly:

M

The voices were louder now, loud enough for Lockhart to make out the words 'Russian filth'. Was this Nicolas's execution squad? Then came:

I, followed by:

T

The squad was so close that he could hear the sound of keys chinking together.

T

That was to be the last letter, because through the wall, Lockhart heard the sound of Nicolas's cell door being opened.

'Out!' shouted a crude voice.

For a few moments, there was a muffled quiet, then the sound of the cell door being shut, and once again the footsteps, slower this time, their noise clacking and reverberating against the sides of the corridor. Lockhart wanted to run to his own door, and shout out some words of encouragement to Nicolas, but it would be pointless, and might even serve to put him in a similar situation. Instead, he listened to the sound dwindle, until the corridor lay guiltily silent.

Lockhart turned his head to the wall, now robbed of its voice. Perhaps the voice would return, but he doubted it. He clenched his right fist and repeatedly hit the wall with its side, allowing the roughness of the stone to scratch and graze him.

MITT. What – or who – was Mitt? Perhaps it was the beginning of a word – Mitt . . . something. Was it the name of Nicolas's source? He could be anybody – an official, an SS officer – but whoever he was, if indeed he was the source, he knew something that he couldn't keep quiet, something so dreadful that his conscience was troubled enough to tell a Russian agent about it. And that something was, apparently, a gas that could kill millions.

Or maybe it was lies, the fantasy that Lockhart had initially felt it to be. But why make up such a story? And the name – sarin – sounded too specific to have been made up by a partially insane, torture-racked Russian agent. Gas had been used in the last war, so why not in this? And technology would have moved on a lot since 1918 – perhaps it was possible that the Germans had formulated some horrific chemical that could eradicate the populations of whole towns, whole cities. Lockhart breathed out. There were too many questions: Where was it? How was it to be used? Had it already been used?

The answer to one question, however, was now clearer than before: he had to continue. It wasn't just for Anna and Amy, but for – Christ, was it *really* true? – the whole war effort, the whole of Europe. It seemed ridiculous. It occurred to him that he might be floating on a giant swell of lies – his family could be dead, and sarin could simply be the product of a lunatic imagination. But then the whole war was the product of a lunatic imagination. Anything was possible. What didn't seem so, thought Lockhart, was how he was going to find out more and how he was going to tell the Allies. There *would* be a way, but right here, right now, his options felt just a little limited. He smiled wryly at his own understatement.

Exhausted, Lockhart drifted into a half-sleep. Although his body demanded it, something kept him from going fully to sleep. *Mitt.* No, it wasn't possible, he told himself. It was just hope talking, cruel hope.

A few hours later, the sound of boots once more invaded the still corridor. Lockhart felt his pulse quicken as he heard the rattle of keys unlocking the cell door. Müller entered, now wearing the black uniform of an SS gruppenführer – three white braid oak leaves on each collar, a Knights Cross at his neck.

'Good afternoon, Lockhart – you have had a letter from your wife, I understand?'

'I have.'

'Is she well?'

'So it would appear.'

'You don't sound very happy about it.'

'That's because I'm not sure if it's genuine.'

'And why do you think that?'

'Because it's typed.'

'Well of course it's typed!'

'Why?'

'The SS are not in the habit of giving prisoners pencils or pens. They make very good weapons.'

Lockhart paused. Annoyingly, the explanation made sense.

'You would be surprised,' Müller continued, 'how many of our guards have been killed by the most innocent of items. It was at Theresienstadt, I think, where a guard was murdered by having a small bar of soap forced down his throat. Imprisonment makes men very inventive!'

Müller laughed – it was a dry, husky laugh. Evidently methods of killing were of some humorous fascination to him. Lockhart nodded quietly.

'So – now do you feel that the letter is genuine?'

'It looks like it,' Lockhart replied reluctantly.

'Good. And I assume that you are willing to co-operate?'

'What did you have in mind?'

'I'm not going to tell you yet. Guard! Come in and handcuff the prisoner!'

* * *

Once again, Lockhart found himself wedged between two Gestapo officers in the back of a car. They were driving out of Berlin – Lockhart guessed southwards – and passing through many bomb-damaged streets. The passers-by looked gaunt and malnourished, their misery no doubt increased by the fact that Christmas was only a few days away – it was hardly a time for celebration. Teenage girls stood on street corners rattling collection tins, but nobody appeared to put any money into them.

In the suburbs, the damage became lighter, although as they ran parallel to a railway line, Lockhart saw the occasional bombed-out goods shed. He smiled, glad that the Germans were experiencing the same horrors that they had meted out to Britain three years ago.

After an hour, they were in open, flat countryside. The furrows of ploughed fields were visible through a layer of snow, and the whitened pine trees reminded Lockhart of winter up at Arisaig. He had spent Christmas there last year, a bittersweet affair. Many of the men were missing their families, but the camaraderie helped to make up for it. They had even gorged themselves on fresh salmon, poached from the nearby loch by a couple of Dutch resistance fighters. Their method had been unorthodox: a stick of dynamite thrown a few yards out had stunned nearly every fish within a hundred yards. Lockhart had feigned outrage at this theft, but was more than happy to share in the spoils.

Life at Arisaig now seemed almost as mythical as life at Tara. Hidden in the north-west of Scotland, the house had been requisitioned by SOE at the beginning of 1941. On cold days – which were common – Arisaig was a severe place. Dark brown, with small windows, it could be bleak and charmless, but when the sun came out, the view thirty miles out to sea was spectacular and liberating.

Lockhart remembered being driven down the wooded drive for the first time. It had reminded him of his first day at his prep school, sitting in the back of a taxi from the local station, even clutching the same small suitcase. The same nerves had come back too, although they had disappeared after a few hours – there was little time to sit and brood at Arisaig. Lockhart had welcomed the distraction – Whitehall had provided him with too many dull moments in which he could sink into a funk.

The training was tough, and he found that his regular runs around St James's Park had kept him in good enough shape. After just a few weeks, he had started to master the skills of unarmed combat, laying explosives and living off the land. With some exceptions, there was an air of amateurism about the place that Lockhart enjoyed. Apart from the odd policeman drafted in from the tough streets of places such as Glasgow and Shanghai, the tutors were an assortment of scientists and academics, all of whom were prostituting their particular skills and experience for the benefit of SOE. Very few had been in the services. In fact, Lockhart's more or less honorific rank of captain, gained from working in military intelligence in Whitehall, made him one of the few officers. But when his fellow trainees had found that he wasn't a real soldier, they quickly scoffed at his rank. He took it in good cheer – in truth, he had felt a bit of a fraud when he wore the uniform around London.

The pines were getting more numerous, and soon they were driving through thick forest. They had to stop for ten minutes to let a Wehrmacht convoy go past. From his position in the back seat, all Lockhart could make out were the huge wheels of the trucks – there were at least fifty of them. It must have been the best part of an army going past, probably on their way to Berlin to help with clearing up.

A few miles into the forest, they turned left down a dirt track. Soon the trees cleared, and the car stopped at a large wood and barbed-wire gate. Lockhart leaned forward and peered through the windscreen: it was the gate to a prison camp. Two guards were approaching the car, both being dragged by a couple of urgent Alsatians. Bloody dogs, thought Lockhart, it was because of one of them that he was here now.

The sign above the gate read 'Sonder Trennung 517 – Stalag IIId'. This was a prison camp for NCOs, Lockhart thought, as officers were kept in oflags. 'Sonder Trennung' meant 'special detachment' – what was so special about this place? As they drove through the gate, he saw that the camp was small. Four large wooden huts surrounded a small field, but the car was approaching a larger building, the size of a typical English church, Lockhart mused. The car drew to a halt in front of it, and he was asked to step out. It made a pleasant change from the normal push.

As he got out of the car, Lockhart noticed the camp was nearly silent. He had expected to see a few men kicking a ball around, but it was deserted except for the sentries patrolling the perimeter fence. The quiet was broken by the appearance of a bulky SS NCO jauntily coming down the steps.

'Hello, Captain Lockhart,' he shouted in an American accent. 'Welcome to Genshagen holiday camp!'

Lockhart stayed silent, looking at the man. He was huge – at least six feet four, and immensely broad, about the same size as Manoli. The thought made him wince. His curly hair was a dirty blond, and he had a ruddy, clean-shaven face. He looked friendly enough.

'Remove the prisoner's cuffs,' he ordered the Gestapo officers.

One of them did so, barely concealing his distaste at being bossed around.

'Do you need any refreshments?'

The Gestapo men shook their heads and walked back to their car.

The big man looked back at Lockhart.

'Not very friendly, don't you think?'

Lockhart was nonplussed.

'No – not particularly.'

'Sorry – let me introduce myself. I'm Sonderführer Oskar Lange – one of the men in charge here.'

'You're American?'

'Hell, no! I'm German through and through. I sound like a Yank because I used to work over there – as a longshoreman in New York.'

Lockhart nodded.

'You call this place a holiday camp?'

'That's right. Allied prisoners who behave themselves can come here for a break. The food's better for a start, and there are a lot more privileges.'

'Such as?'

'All these questions, Lockhart! Come on – let's go inside, it's far too cold! Anyway, there are some people I'd like you to meet.'

They walked up the steps.

'This building is the headquarters – it contains the barracks and my offices.'

He paused halfway up the steps and turned round.

'And that building over there,' he said proudly, pointing at one of the four large huts, 'is the concert hall.'

'Concert hall?'

'Oh yes – we may be small, but it's all here. Do you play anything?'

'The piano – badly.'

'That's better than most! Anyway, that building there is the wash house and canteen, and the other two huts are for the two hundred or so holiday-makers we have here.'

'Two hundred? Where are they all?'

'Oh, they're all inside – we didn't want them to see you coming!'

'Why not?'

'More and more questions! Come on, inside!'

They stepped into a long, dimly lit corridor. As they walked, Lockhart couldn't help but warm to this man Lange. He was the friendliest German he had met, and his charm seemed genuine. This was obviously a camp where Allied prisoners were being buttered up for something, and Lange was plainly the man to do it.

Lange opened a door marked with his name, and ushered Lockhart in.

'Here we go, my friend, this is my huge office, and in it are two very important gentlemen who are dying to meet you.'

The office was anything but huge, but it was at least warm – heated by a furnace in the corner. Lange's two other guests sat on either side of it. One was an SS officer, young, blue-eyed, but with a drawn face. The other was dressed like an English gentleman, wearing a green tweed suit and brown brogues. His hair was Brylcreemed back and he had a drinker's face. They both stood up at Lockhart's entrance.

'Captain Lockhart,' began Lange, 'may I present to you Herr Arnold Hillen-Ziegfeld of the Foreign Ministry, and Hauptsturmführer Carl Strasser of the SS-Hauptamt.'

Strasser saluted with a Heil Hitler, and Hillen-Ziegfeld shook Lockhart's hand.

'How do you do,' said Hillen-Ziegfeld. His voice sounded absurd – he was evidently trying to speak in an upper-class English accent. Lockhart smirked a little.

'Very well, thank you,' he replied, making his voice as ridiculously pukka as possible. As he spoke, he could spot Strasser sizing him up, those blue eyes staring straight into him. Strasser looked as though he knew Lockhart was taking the mickey.

'Well, why don't you sit down?' said Lange. 'We've got lots to talk about. And I expect you're hungry too.' With a flourish, Lange removed a cloth from his desk to reveal a plate full of cheese, cold meats and bread.

'Please chow down – there's more than enough for all of us.'

Lockhart was indeed hungry, but he didn't want to look desperate – it would seem weak. Whoever Strasser was, he didn't want to find himself being judged badly by him. He sat opposite the others, Lange having brought his desk chair over to the furnace.

'Right, shall we begin?' said Lange. 'Perhaps Herr Hillen-Ziegfeld can explain why you're here.'

Hillen-Ziegfeld cleared his throat and started speaking in his faux-English accent.

'Captain Lockhart. You're here because we want you to perform a duty for us. We understand that you have a wife held captive here in Germany, and that in return for her safety you are willing to ... shall we say, *assist* in some way.'

Lockhart folded his arms and nodded slightly.

'Before I tell you exactly what it is we would like you to do,' continued Hillen-Ziegfeld, 'first I should give you some background. As you are probably aware, it has long been the belief, held by the Führer downwards, that England and Germany do not need to be enemies. We are both Aryan peoples, advanced, intelligent and lovers of freedom.'

Lockhart snorted.

'Yes, Captain Lockhart, freedom. For in comparison to the true enemy, Russia, both of our countries are very free indeed. The Bolsheviks, with their savage ways, are the real opponents of European peace. There is little doubt that Communism, aided by a Jewish plutocracy, threatens to overwhelm us all, and then how free would we be?'

Hillen-Ziegfeld cleared his throat.

'Part of my job at the Foreign Ministry is to sit on the England Committee. Our task is to find Englishmen who also believe in the menace of Communism and would like to join us in our struggle to smash it down.'

'What is it exactly you want me to do?' asked Lockhart.

'Please do not be so impatient,' replied Hillen-Ziegfeld. 'I am coming to that. So far, we have managed to recruit some of your fellow countrymen to make broadcasts, warning the British people of the dangers of Communism.'

'Lord Haw-Haw and those others? But they're just a load of traitors.'

'I would suggest to you that they are not. They are merely doing their duty as good Europeans and lovers of freedom. But some of your fellow countrymen have chosen to go one step further and have actually chosen to fight the Russians.'

It wasn't usual for Lockhart to be rendered speechless, but this news, if true, knocked the wind out of him. Before he could collect his thoughts, Hillen-Ziegfeld continued.

'You look surprised, Captain Lockhart. You have heard of a man called John Amery?'

'Yes, I have. He's another one of your broadcasters, isn't he? Not only that, he's the son of a cabinet minister.'

'That's right – Leopold Amery, the secretary of state for India. I find it interesting that a man like John Amery,' from such good stock, should be active in wanting to fight the Russians, don't you?'

'Every family has its rotten apple.'

'I hardly think John Amery is a rotten apple. He is a brave man.'

Lockhart snorted again.

'Why do you keep laughing, Lockhart? Do you not see it as bravery when a man chooses to go against his entire nation because of the strength of his beliefs?'

'I think he's a coward. He only joined you because the war was going your way.'

'He's not an opportunist, Lockhart. He genuinely believes that the Soviets are evil, and is ashamed by his – and your – country's alliance with them. I'm sure time will prove him right.'

'I'm not saying that Stalin is the ideal bedfellow, but we need him – and he needs us – if we are to beat you.'

'Such naivety, Lockhart! Can't you see that in the unlikely event he does beat us, he will turn on you next? Europe will turn red, not only with Communism, but with blood.'

Strasser interrupted.

'I do not think this ideological conversation is going anywhere. If Captain Lockhart does not wish to help, then he knows the consequences. I see little point in trying to persuade him, when he is already predisposed to working with us.'

Strasser too spoke with a slight American accent, although it sounded more Ivy League than Lange's. There was no doubting his natural authority, which had stopped the aerated Hillen-Ziegfeld dead in his tracks.

Hillen-Ziegfeld looked flustered.

'You were talking about John Amery,' said Strasser.

'Oh yes!' said Hillen-Ziegfeld. 'John Amery. Well, Lockhart, even if you do not approve of his views, you will soon find yourself working to promote a scheme of his, a project that is beginning to gather a great number of followers – brave fighting men like yourself.'

Lockhart raised his eyebrows.

'Really?'

'Yes, Lockhart, really. The project is called the British Free Corps. It is a unit of the SS staffed entirely by Englishmen dedicated to the destruction of Communism.'

Again Lockhart was speechless. Could this be so? He found it hard to imagine a single Englishman joining the SS.

'You look surprised, Lockhart.'

'I am. How many men have joined up?'

'Several, and soon there will be many more.'

'And where are they all?'

'They are here, here in this camp.'

'What sort of men are they? Where are they from?'

'You'll find out when you meet them.'

'And what do you want me to do?'

'We want you to be the unit's commanding officer.'

Lockhart stayed silent, taking a deep breath through his nose. He reached for a piece of bratwurst, aware of the three pairs of eyes scrutinising him. He chewed the meat, and pulled the rind out of his pursed mouth.

'Let's get this straight,' he said, finishing his mouthful, 'you would like me to be an SS officer, leading a unit staffed by traitors. And would you expect me to fight?'

'That is the purpose of the Waffen-SS,' said Strasser dryly.

'Against the English?'

'No, we would not ask you to do that,' Strasser continued. 'You would fight against the Russians.'

'And when would we go into action?'

'As soon as the unit reaches a strength of thirty. That is a direct order from the Führer.'

'If I joined, that would make me a traitor. I would be taking up arms against an ally of the Crown. If I was caught, I would be hanged, assuming that the Russian front didn't do for me first.'

'Your conscience is your own problem, Lockhart. All I can tell you is that by joining the BFC, you will guarantee your wife's safety. It's that simple. If I was in your boots, I'd do the same thing.'

The other men nodded.

'Come on, old boy,' said Hillen-Ziegfeld. 'You know—'

'Don't "old boy" me,' snapped Lockhart.

Strasser and Lange chuckled a little. It was clear that they had a similar antipathy towards the bureaucrat.

Lange piped up.

'May I make a suggestion?'

The question was addressed to Strasser, who nodded.

'I think maybe we should leave Captain Lockhart for a few minutes to collect his thoughts. He is clearly in some sort of turmoil, and I think he needs a little time to himself.'

Lange stood up, and walked over to his desk. He took a piece of paper out of a drawer, and slid it, along with a pen, over the desk in Lockhart's direction.

'When we're outside,' he said, 'have a look at this. It's just a form. No pressure.'

Strasser and Hillen-Ziegfeld stood up.

'Good idea, Oskar,' said Strasser. 'Let's stretch our legs.'

Lange locked the drawer and looked up at Lockhart.

'Don't treat me like an idiot and try to steal anything or jump out of the window – all right?'

'Sure,' said Lockhart.

The three men left the room, Lange patting Lockhart on the shoulder as he did so. Lockhart waited until he heard their voices fade down the corridor, and then leant over and picked up the piece of paper. It contained only one sentence:

I . . . . being a British subject consider it my duty to offer my services in the Common European struggle against Communism, and hereby apply to enlist in the British Free Corps.

Signature . . . .

It looked so innocent, framed like that. But then that was its intention. Lockhart put the paper down and walked to the window. It was dark outside. Maybe he should treat Lange like an idiot and try to escape. He turned his head to the door and then looked back out at the shadowy figures of the pine trees. He could be through the window, over the fence and running through them in a minute, free from this hateful situation. At least if he was shot he wouldn't die a traitor. They would probably shoot Anna as well. They'd be together then – perhaps that was the only way they could be reunited. Lockhart wondered whether Anna, from where she was, could see any trees. Doubtful, he thought.

But this was too good an opportunity. The Germans were handing him a chance, small though it was, to investigate the possibility of whether sarin existed; to establish whether Nicolas's warnings should be heeded. He would now have to act the role of traitor in full, knowing that the Germans would make great propaganda out of having an English officer joining them. When the news got back, he would be as vilified as those buggers Haw-Haw and Amery. Perhaps Cairo and Baker Street already thought he was a traitor. What would they think of him at Tara?

Although, to actually join the Waffen-SS . . . There was plenty of information about their massacres of POWs and their treatment of Jews in Poland and elsewhere. The SS even ran the concentration camps, but nobody truly believed the stories starting to come out of them. A chill ran down his spine as he pictured a starving Anna in a camp. He *had* to save her, and so many others, but in doing so, did he have to join their tormentors? It looked like it. If he died a traitor, then too bad – at least he would have a clear conscience before his God.

Lockhart walked over to the desk and picked up the pen. His hand was shaking so uncontrollably he had to put it back down. He sat and took several deep breaths, which made him feel faint. He let it pass, and then stood up and once more took the pen. He poised the nib above the sheet, but found that he could go no further. Rationally, he knew he should sign, but his instincts, his background, his whole sense of self stopped him doing it. It would be like signing his own death sentence. No. He couldn't sign – for what was he really going to achieve? The idea that he could discover anything about one of the most closely guarded of Nazi secrets was risible. He threw down the pen.

The door opened, and in stepped the odd threesome. Lange came in first and looked at the table. He grimaced when he saw that the sheet of paper lay unsigned. He shared the expression with Strasser and Hillen-Ziegfeld, who in turn looked at the paper. Lange breathed out slowly. Lockhart sat looking at the floor, preparing for the inevitable chastisement. Strasser walked over to the window, his hands clasped behind his back.

'So,' Strasser began, slowly, deliberately, 'you are refusing to sign the paper.'

'I am,' said Lockhart.

'May I ask why?'

'Because I don't wish to be a traitor to my King and country. I would have thought that was pretty obvious.'

'But if it was that obvious, then you would never have got as far as this, would you?'

'What?'

'Well, you have certainly been flirting with the idea of helping us. So why stop now?'

'Because I'm not a traitor.'

'So you'd rather your no doubt pretty wife died? You'd put your King above your wife? Yes? Is that right?'

'It's not that simple and you know it.'

'No, Captain Lockhart, I do not.'

'Of course you do. Especially you, with your SS oath to your Führer. I thought you lot were more than happy to put your leader before your family.'

The room went silent. Hillen-Ziegfeld cleared his throat to speak, but after a fierce look from Strasser, he thought better of it and looked back down.

Strasser turned round to address his compatriots.

'This has been a waste of time. Lock him up overnight and let's shoot him in the morning. In fact, I'll do it myself. After that, send orders for his wife to be executed.'

The others nodded as Strasser turned to Lockhart.

'I'm not going to allow you the luxury of dying with your wife. But you will be able to spend the night imagining her being taken from the line-up tomorrow. One of my SS comrades will inform her that you have been shot. I expect she will cry and pull her hair – that's what they normally seem to do. But she won't have any hair, will she? It will have been shaved off! And then – well, I don't know how – she too will be killed, perhaps with a shot to the back of the head. The bullet will come out the front of her face, taking her brains and maybe one of her eyes with it . . .'

Lockhart could take no more. He jumped up and grabbed Strasser by the throat, trying to squeeze the life out of the murdering bastard. He felt hands unsuccessfully trying to tear him away, but he had been seized by a ferocious energy. As his thumbs dug deeper into Strasser's windpipe, the two men crashed around the room, knocking over the desk and chairs, colliding with the furnace. And then everything went black, as the handle of Lange's pistol connected with the back of Lockhart's head.

Lange brought Strasser a brandy after the unconscious Lockhart had been dragged away.

'How are you feeling, Hauptsturmführer?' Lange asked.

Strasser didn't reply until he had taken the drink and drained it.

'Fine,' he said, putting the glass down.

'Another?'

'No.'

In truth, Strasser was feeling a little stunned and battered. The old wound in his right thigh was aching horribly, but he wasn't going to let on to these two, especially to that little worm Hillen-Ziegfeld, who was sitting – shaking – in silence. The ferocity and strength of Lockhart's attack had caught Strasser off guard. Well, it was hardly surprising – perhaps he had been a little too explicit in his threat. He touched his throat. It felt grazed and raw, but nothing really, nothing compared to the pain of that shrapnel being dug out of his leg.

'What do you want to do with him?'

Strasser coughed, the spasm causing him some pain.

'As I said, we'll shoot him.'

But before Lange could reply, Hillen-Ziegfeld piped up:

'No, Hauptsturmführer, I absolutely insist that you do not do that!'

'Oh? And why?'

'Because we need an officer – don't you see what a coup that would be?'

'My orders are to lead this unit,' said Strasser. 'Recruiting is your fucking job. Thanks to you, Ziegfeld, today has been a complete waste of time. This is an SS operation now, and it will be run according to how I see fit, not in the schoolgirl way that you civil servants like to run things. And that means Lockhart will be shot! Do you understand? He is of no use to anybody – in fact, he's a fucking liability.'

'But . . .'

'No. There's nothing more to say, Ziegfeld.'

Hillen-Ziegfeld stood up and puffed out his little chest.

'I really must protest!' he shouted, his voice high-pitched and trembling.

'Protest all you like,' said Strasser, waving him away with his hand. 'I'm going to get something to eat. What time's dinner in this place, Lange?'

Lange looked at his watch.

'In about an hour.'

'Good. In that case, I'm going to go to my room for a wash and I'll meet you later in the mess.'

As Strasser stood up, Hillen-Ziegfeld started to speak. But Strasser stopped him.

'I don't want to hear it. If you have a problem, tell Berger, not me.'

With that, Strasser opened the door and walked out,

leaving behind a gasping civil servant and a smirking sonderführer.

Strasser walked to his room, musing over Lockhart. He found the British officer intriguing and, despite the tussle, likeable. He was intelligent and appeared principled – it seemed unlikely that he was ever going to turn traitor. Men did the most stupid things because of women, thought Strasser, but betray their country – no way, at least not in his book. Perhaps he was too much of a cold fish, as Leni had once told him, but he couldn't see himself going down the same path as Lockhart had nearly gone down, even if he was in love. He had come close to love, but that was at university with a girl called Hilde, though in retrospect he regarded that as little more than an innocent crush.

He studied his neck in the mirror. It looked badly bruised, damn it. He had also sustained a small cut above his left eye – that must have happened when they fell against the side of the desk. It worried him that Lockhart had got the best of the fight before Lange stepped in. It was a lesson, a warning. Time to get back to those rigorous morning exercises. Working in the Hauptamt had not exactly made him flabby, but he certainly knew that he could be fitter, a lot fitter. Maybe a spot of boxing as well – that was good for reflexes rendered docile by a small smoke-filled office and Berlin life.

Strasser washed his face and patted it dry, leaving some specks of blood on his towel. He removed his tunic and dusted it down – Lange's office floor could do with a clean. He brushed the grime from the back of his breeches, and then inspected his boots. They looked a little scuffed, not exhibiting their usual brilliant shine. He would get an orderly to polish them up overnight. He kicked them off and decided to lie on the bed for a few minutes. It had been a long day, and he could do with a catnap - a habit he had picked up on the Russian front.

He thought of Lockhart in his cell. He would probably still be unconscious, the fool, although Strasser had to admit that he had done the honourable thing. He would have to be shot, whatever Hillen-Ziegfeld said. Nevertheless, part of him didn't want that. He wanted to know more about this man who had had the wit to stay alive this far. Still, it was too bad - he couldn't just let a British prisoner get away with attacking him. Anyway, he was a spy, and spies got shot, just as they did in Britain. He would do it himself, first thing in the morning. There was always a possibility, he supposed, that Lockhart would change his mind, but the chance of that was negligible. No, Lockhart was a man who knew he had taken things too far, and had realised that it was time to die.

Strasser awoke with a start. He looked at his watch - he had been asleep for over an hour. He was late for dinner - not that it mattered. Groggily he put on his tunic and boots, brushed his hair, and went over to the mess. He found Lange sitting on his own, greedily tucking into a bowl of soup.

'What's it like?' asked Strasser, sitting down.

'Shit,' said Lange. 'But I need all the food I can get. There's a lot of me to feed.'

Strasser smiled a little.

'Where's our Foreign Office functionary?'

'He's been trying to get through to Berlin for the past hour or so,' said Lange in between slurps. 'He's gone mad, you know, jumping up and down, saying that Lockhart mustn't be shot.'

'Too bad.'

'Quite. Anyway, I doubt he'll get through – the lines are probably down as usual.'

'He could drive there.'

'Good luck to him! In this weather and with minimal headlamps – forget it!'

A private brought over a bowl of soup and some unappetising-looking bread. Strasser took a spoonful of the liquid and immediately spat it out.

'God almighty!' he exclaimed. 'What the hell is this?'

Lange laughed.

'I told you it was shit!'

'Yes, but I didn't think you were being literal.'

'I'll have it then.'

'Not a chance,' said Strasser. 'I'm starving.'

The men sat in near silence for a while, exchanging the odd unappreciative comment on Genshagen cuisine.

'Do you want to see Lockhart again tonight, Hauptsturmführer?' Lange asked.

Strasser chewed it over with some of the stale bread.

'I don't see any point.'

'You're right. A shame he didn't agree to join up – I rather liked him.'

'So did I,' said Strasser. 'So did I.'

Another silence.

'Lange?' said Strasser, looking up from his bowl, straight into Lange's eyes.

'Yes?'

'Let's do it at half past seven tomorrow morning. Hopefully Ziegfeld will still be asleep.'

Lange smiled.

'How many men do you want?'

Strasser shrugged, unconcerned.

'Oh, I don't mind. Four should do it. Three live rounds, one blank.'

Lange nodded, and then lifted his bowl to drain it with a slurp that Strasser found uncouth and mildly irritating.

Another cell, his coldest yet. Through the small barred window he could see that it was twilight. There was no bed, just a rough wooden floor, from which a splinter dug into his hand as he pushed himself up. His head was throbbing unbearably – the back of it felt puffy and bruised, but his hair was not matted, which meant that it hadn't been cut. He felt sick and took several deep breaths, which did a little to help.

So this, finally, was his last night. And it would be Anna's too, not that she knew it. He let his head slump forward. Was this for the best? Was this really the best thing for Amy, to make her an orphan? No, but there was no choice. He winced as he recalled Strasser's description of Anna's execution. His Anna, lying in a frozen pool of blood. That face that he had kissed so many times, that had spoken comforting words, that he had gazed into deeply when they had married; that face that had looked both tired and proud after Amy's birth, and which would shortly be reduced to a mass of blood and sinew, butchered for no other reason than his not playing a game with some people who spoke a different language.

A game. Yes, that was what it was. Just a sodding playground game on a ridiculously large scale, an evil scale. Couldn't he just treat it as that, play along with them? He could avoid their deaths by putting on a uniform and acting a part, playing the game. He thought of MacNeice again, his *Autumn Journal*, written just before the war. He had read them in Cairo; Dickie had had a copy.

> All we can do at most
> Is press an anxious ear against the keyhole
> To hear the future breathing . . .

And now he and Anna had no future. There was no breathing behind the keyhole, just a couple of gunshots and then a permanent silence.

At last, thought Strasser, it was finally a clear morning. About time. The past few had been obliterated by near-blizzards, but this was a fine one, beautiful even. Through his window, he could see the wintry sun beginning its ascent over the pine trees, causing the snow to glow a deep orange. He never got bored of snow, even after Russia, although many of his comrades had vowed to emigrate to hotter climes after the war. There was something pure about it, something clean and hygienic. He could never leave Germany, never leave its northern climate. Strasser treasured his four seasons, and he liked them to be distinct and correct. A farmer – maybe that was what he'd be. He needed to stay outside, adopt a simple existence. There was strength and freedom in that, living off the land.

He pulled on his boots. They had been cleaned overnight, and they looked immaculate. He would ask Lange who it had been and would go out of his way to thank him, stand him a drink in the mess, because he was feeling generous today, full of bonhomie. Such a mood was rare for Strasser, who was normally much more reserved, taciturn even. But the fine morning had made him feel likewise, and he was ready to get out and lead a full day.

There was real coffee for breakfast, which made him feel even better.

'You're in a good mood this morning,' said Lange. 'If you don't mind me saying.'

'Not at all, Oskar! It's a lovely crisp morning – exhilarating! I want to get out there straight away.'

'Aren't you forgetting something?' asked Lange, eyeing Strasser with some suspicion.

Strasser waved his hand.

'No, Oskar, I'm not. Is everything ready?'

'Yes.'

'Good. And Ziegfeld? Did he manage to get through to Berlin last night?'

'No. Just as I thought, the lines were down.'

'So he didn't try driving there?'

Lange shook his head.

'And . . . he's still asleep?' Strasser asked.

Lange nodded, with the trace of a smile.

'Like a lamb,' he said. 'Sleeping off the best part of a bottle of schnapps.'

'Good! I don't want him bleating around. Perhaps the shots will wake him up!'

Strasser put down his cup of coffee, rubbed his hands together, and then stood up.

'Come on, Oskar! Let's get this over with and then we can enjoy our day. Have you ever seen a firing squad in action?'

'No.'

'Well, they're not so bad. Unless of course your guards are bad shots, and I have to finish him off myself,' said Strasser, patting his holster.

Lange swallowed.

The cell door was swung open violently. Three privates and a rottenführer entered the cell, their expressions impassive.

'Good morning,' said Lockhart, breezily, as if this was just another morning; as if his visitors were there to serve him a cooked breakfast rather than to shoot him. He thought he detected a slight awkwardness, especially in the face of the youngest private, who was unable to look him in the eye.

'Up!' said the rottenführer.

Lockhart stood, doing his best to conceal his shaking legs. He knew that he would be dead in fifteen minutes, his life extinguished, and Anna's too. But that could be changed, that could be avoided. He could replace that dread silence, breathe some life back into their future by playing the game. And he didn't have to play it just for his little family; he could play it for everybody else too. He could *play* the traitor, strut on the fragile boards of treachery, while all the time plotting against the enemy. If what Nicolas had told him about the sarin was true, then he had to follow it up, act upon it, and to do that, he *had* to stay alive. He could win too, he could bloody well win. He wasn't going to lose, and he certainly wasn't going to die. He was cleverer than them, more cunning. He had made mistakes up till now, bad mistakes, but now he was going to be faultless, put in a performance that would fool them all, until he emerged as the victor.

Sod Strasser and the rest of them. Let them think they had won, while all the time he drew up his plan. He wasn't going to throw away his life now, just because he'd refused to sign a scrap of paper. The paper meant nothing – they could rule his body but not his mind. One day, when he had won, he would see Anna and Amy again, tell them what he had done for them, and what he had done for the country. And if he died, well, he would have put up a fight, not just been dragged out of here to be shot, watching his last breaths in the cold air. He owed it to everybody, especially to Manoli, to continue the fight.

Strasser and Lange walked out into the morning air. Strasser breathed in deeply, savouring the sharp sensation of his lungs inflating with crisp coldness. Last night's snow crunched under their feet as they made their way to the front gate. Against Strasser's initial wishes, Lange had insisted that Lockhart should be shot outside the camp, in the woods, away from his 'holidaymakers'. Strasser had capitulated, agreeing with Lange's assertion that the POWs in Genshagen would hardly regard the place as a holiday camp if they witnessed one of their countrymen being executed.

The guards at the gate saluted them.

'Has the prisoner already been taken through?' Lange asked one of them.

'Yes, sir! About five minutes ago.'

'Right on time,' said Strasser. 'Well done, Oskar – your men are not disappointing me. That reminds me . . .'

'Yes?'

'Who was the man who polished my boots? He did a first-rate job – I'd like to thank him.'

'A young schütze by the name of Schmidt.'

'Well, please tell him to come and see me.'

'I will.'

'Are you all right, Oskar? You seem a little *sotto*, not your normal booming self.'

'I suppose I am a little apprehensive.'

'That's natural. But I hope you don't think it's wrong,

Oskar. Lockhart is a spy – remember that. I'm sure the British would do the same.'

'Yes. I'm sure you're right, Hauptsturmführer.'

Strasser patted Lange on the back.

'Good. And after this is over, we can see how the unit is getting along this morning.'

'Yes, sir. Good idea.'

'Oh yes – and when the lines are back up, remind me that I must phone through about his wife.'

Lockhart hadn't expected to be led into the woods. He had thought he would be shot in the camp, against a wall somewhere, but the woods – that was a surprise. Not that it mattered where he died. All it showed was that the Germans wanted to keep his death secret, sweep it under the carpet.

His hands had been crudely tied behind his back. However, he was neither pushed nor shoved, but allowed to walk at his own pace, as if the four men leading him to his death wanted to show some pittance of respect. It was a lovely morning, Lockhart thought as they walked in silence. The low sunlight was piercing through the trees, casting out orange rays. A perfect morning for a run, he thought, or to run away.

He felt unusually calm. He couldn't work out whether that was because he had gone beyond fear, or whether he really didn't think he was about to die. He liked the pines, imagined that he might see Anna walking through them, walking along with Amy clinging to her hand. Perhaps he would see them both very soon, coming through the winter light, collecting pine cones.

There was no way he could die. There were too many reasons to be alive. He thought of Scylla berating the departing Minos:

'Where are you going?' she cried. 'You whom I have preferred to my country and to my own father?'

He couldn't just go. He had to stay.

By the time Strasser and Lange arrived in the clearing, Lockhart had already been tied to a small tree. The squad had assembled a few yards away from him, their backs turned, a column of cigarette smoke rising gently from their huddle. They stood to attention when they spotted the two officers, throwing their cigarettes to the ground.

'All right, line up,' Strasser barked.

As the men did so, Strasser and Lange went over to Lockhart.

Strasser had seen many men in this position before, but none had looked the same as Lockhart. Most were terrified, and others defiant, but none looked this . . . *at ease.*

'Do you have any last requests, Lockhart?' asked Strasser. 'A cigarette, perhaps?'

Lockhart shook his head slowly. Strasser could see that he was looking at the bruise on his neck, causing, to Strasser's annoyance, a smile to appear on Lockhart's face.

'How's your neck, Hauptsturmführer?' Lockhart asked.

Such insolence, thought Strasser, although it was almost admirable.

'My neck is a little painful, Captain Lockhart,' he replied. 'Thank you for asking.'

'That's quite all right.'

Strasser grinned.

'You're not without a sense of humour,' he said. 'Lange here and I think it's a shame you're not going to co-operate – we could have had some fun!'

'What sort of fun would that be, I wonder? Murdering POWs in the middle of forests?'

Strasser narrowed his eyes.

'Goodbye, Captain Lockhart,' he said brusquely, and then turned on his heel.

Lockhart watched Strasser walk away. A small victory, but he had rattled him. He couldn't help it, couldn't help but put one over on this sadist, because now Strasser could do no more. He waited until the German reached his men, and only then did he decide to shout out.

'Hauptsturmführer!'

He watched Strasser turn towards him.

'Yes, Captain Lockhart? Do you wish to say something?'

'Yes, I do.'

'What then?'

From somewhere far off, a rook cawed.

'I'll join your corps. If it saves my wife's life, I'll join it.'

Strasser paused.

'I'm afraid it's a little late for that!' he replied.

Lockhart nearly collapsed under the weight of Strasser's response. Surely he couldn't shoot him now, not when he had volunteered?

'I'm sorry,' said Lockhart, 'but I understood—'

'You understood wrong. It's too late.'

Strasser turned to the squad.

'Ready!' he shouted.

Lockhart instinctively shut his eyes, feeling his heart throbbing absurdly hard. He wanted to scream, to drown out the reality of what was about to happen to him, the sheer horror of the knowledge that these were his last seconds. He saw Anna. He saw Amy. He saw the pine cones.

Because his eyes were shut, he didn't see Lange run over to Strasser. But when it occurred to him that he had not heard any further command, he opened his eyes and saw the two men talking heatedly. In addition, he noticed that the soldiers had lowered their rifles. He couldn't hear what they were saying, but he could guess – Lange was no doubt insisting that he should be spared, telling Strasser that now Lockhart had volunteered, he should not be shot.

After a minute's conversation, Strasser came over, his eyes looking straight at him. He drew up, his face no more than inches away. He looked livid. Lockhart knew why, and even when he felt the sharp smack of Strasser's fist against the side of his face, he loved the pain because it was sensation, a sensation that meant he was alive, *alive*, Goddammit.

Even as Strasser led the men out of the woods, he began to wonder what had brought about Lockhart's change of heart. Either he had misread him, and Lockhart really was the snivelling, treacherous type, or maybe he had some other reason, some reason that Strasser would do his best to find out. Just before he reached the camp, it occurred to him that Lockhart could have been playing with them all along. For the time being, he would keep his thoughts to himself. His own counsel, he reckoned, was usually the wisest.

He signed the form with his eyes closed. Even though this was an act, he didn't want to see his hand inscribing the mark of his treason. If he didn't see it, then it didn't really exist. Childish, but emotionally useful. He threw the pen back down, some ink splattering over the bottom of the form.

He ignored them as they looked at the declaration, gathering around it like schoolboys looking at naughty pictures.

'Excellent, Lockhart!' boomed Lange.

'I knew you'd see sense,' said Hillen-Ziegfeld, who had been summoned by Lange.

Strasser stayed angrily silent and walked over to Lockhart.

'You realise that now you have signed that paper you are a member of the Waffen-SS?'

'I do.'

'This means that you will take orders from and report directly to me. Your rank will be decided shortly, but it will probably be the same as mine – SS-Hauptsturmführer. I shall of course be the senior officer.'

Lockhart swallowed. He now had a name for his part.

'In the mean time, I do not yet wish to introduce you to your men. I would like to spend the next few days over Christmas acquainting you with the practices of the Waffen-SS. My intention is to present you to the others as a fait accompli. We will spend our time here in this building, and you will not be allowed to leave it – is that clear?'

'Yes.'

'I will also need to carry out an in-depth interview with you, about your background and so on and so forth.'

Lockhart's eyes widened.

'Naturally, this report will be kept secret, just for our records, you understand.'

'Naturally.'

He had better think up some more lies, quickly. He would tell as much of the truth as possible, but he would omit any reference to SOE and Whitehall. Strasser seemed crafty, but Lockhart hoped that he would not see any need to grill him now that he had joined up.

After the past few weeks of living in cells and on trains, a bed with sheets and blankets seemed the greatest luxury. The camp doctor even saw fit to remove the cast on his little finger and apply a small field dressing. He slept better and better each night, gradually growing accustomed to his membership of the SS. It didn't seem real – after all, he was just sitting around in a wooden hut in the middle of a forest, talking to Strasser about Winchester and Oxford. His would-be executioner was even opening up, telling Lockhart a little about his days as a student.

It appeared that the two men shared a love of gambling,

a habit that had got both of them into financial difficulties as students. Lockhart had accrued a lot of poker debts at Oxford, and his father had had to bail him out. It was the first time he had raised his voice at Lockhart, saying that despite the wealth the boys had inherited from their late mother – her father had made a fortune on the railways – it was an insult to her memory to have her money used in this way. Lockhart hadn't gambled again until his father had died; since then, each time he had visited White's he'd felt a twinge of guilt. Strasser had been less lucky, and had had to wait tables in the evenings to cover his debts. He would never gamble again, he said, as the SS frowned on it. Lockhart tried to tempt him to a game of backgammon, saying they could make a set from cardboard and buttons, but Strasser had refused even that.

Christmas Eve was a raucous affair, sitting with Lange and Strasser in the mess for a traditional dinner of carp, weisswurst and sauerkraut, washed down with vast quantities of pilsner. The alcohol had made Lockhart relax somewhat, and he reluctantly found Lange's humour and Strasser's sophistication engaging. However, in the morning he suffered, along with his hangover, a sense of guilt. He had nearly enjoyed himself, and he recalled that he had even hummed a verse from the 'Horst Wessel Song'.

> Flag high, ranks closed,
> The SA marches with silent solid steps.
> Comrades shot by the red front and reaction
>   march in spirit with us in our ranks.

Did humming along to that, even though he was doing it for appearances, make him a traitor? On the surface it did. But he knew he was acting. If he was going to make this deception work, then he had better look wholehearted. But he hadn't toasted Hitler, and had stayed sitting, scowling. Strasser had let it go, but he knew that the German had filed it away somewhere in his brain, ready to use it one day.

Early one morning, between Christmas and New Year, Strasser burst into Lockhart's room. He looked unusually fired up.

'I have some good news for you, Lockhart.'

'Yes?' yawned Lockhart, sitting up.

'The unit officially comes into existence on New Year's Day. I will introduce you to your men on New Year's Eve – it will be a double celebration . . .'

Lockhart did his best to look excited. It was hard to act this early in the morning. Strasser continued.

'. . . and I am expecting a consignment of uniforms to arrive before then.'

'Uniforms?'

'Yes – full SS uniforms with the BFC insignia on them.'

'*Insignia*? What insignia?'

'You will see!'

No longer Anna, but 10678, tattooed on the underside of the left forearm. The tattooist's needle had hurt, but not as much as the beatings that came later, the daily dispensations of casual brutality. The sharp smack of the whip; the crude pain from the hobnailed boot; the savage pistol-whipping – the pain was quotidian and merciless. Pain for breakfast, lunch and supper, although of course there were no such meals. Instead, the numbers received a foul and watery concoction twice a day, accompanied by some mouldy bread. If she was lucky, 10678 would get near to the end of the queue, and would be doled out some of the solids that had sunk to the bottom of the big serving drum. But if she got too near the end, she would miss out altogether, and would starve until six o'clock that evening. And nobody would share with 10678, for it was every number for herself.

She was shutting down; her brain, her limbs, her womb – all were petrified through starvation, exhaustion and fear. And when she wasn't thinking about food, or the lice, or the cold, 10678 remembered that in another time, another place, she had a husband and a daughter. She recalled the daughter being a pretty little thing, with brown hair like her father, who was a warm, funny and kind man.

Sometimes, an image of this mythical family would come out through the fog. It might be of him, driving their sports car very fast from Oxford up to London, her hand permanently resting on his left thigh. Or it could be of when she gave birth, those hours of struggle in that room in the Radcliffe. Or their wedding day, staring at him directly through her veil, their eyes locked together, occasionally glancing at the small globe of sweat making its way down the side of his face. At night, she would fantasise that she would hear from him, maybe receive a letter, some sort of sign. Deep down, 10678 knew it was pointless, but she was still strong enough to hope. She also knew that she wasn't so much living in hope as dying in it.

They all wanted a sign, the women here. Her former bedmate, a Gypsy girl called Mila, had dreamed every night that she had been reunited with her husband, and every morning, when she awoke, she would cry and scream. 10678 had been sympathetic at first, but the girl's regular hysterics soon wore her down. And then, one day, Mila had disappeared. 10678 tried hard not to feel relieved, such was the nature of the place – it brought out your worst side, and it could become your only side. Mila's disappearance meant that 10678 had the bed to herself for a few nights, and for that she was grateful, but she would rather have had Mila and the sleepless nights back, because she hated the fact that the price of comfort was another's life. That disturbed her, kept her awake more than Mila ever could.

Over the next two days, Strasser taught Lockhart about the SS training routine. It was similar to that of the British Army, although there was a greater emphasis on political 'education' as Strasser called it – 'indoctrination', thought Lockhart, but kept his mouth shut. Lockhart learned that recruits were woken at six o'clock for an hour's gymnastics before breakfast. The morning could be taken up by weapons training, the recruits learning how to strip and assemble a whole variety of weapons, or it could involve infantry training, in which skills such as bayonet practice and unarmed combat would be taught. After a good lunch, there was a 'make and mend' session, in which recruits would have to clean the barracks and their boots and uniforms, as well as attending to any other chores. The afternoon was filled with further physical exercise – a route march or a cross-country run in full kit. In the evening, the recruits had time to themselves. Normally they would read, play cards, or listen to the radio, although they were encouraged to play chess. Some would have earned a pass to go into the local town, where they had to be on their best behaviour – drunkenness was not tolerated in the SS, Strasser reminded Lockhart.

There were at least three political lectures given per week. These often covered the policies of the Nazi Party, and lectures on racial superiority were frequently given. Jews, Slavs, Gypsies, Communists and even Freemasons were all regarded as *Untermenschen*, and SS men were taught that they were superior in every way. In short, said Strasser, the SS were not just front-line troops, but missionaries of a new world order. Lockhart asked if Strasser believed in it all, especially as the SS was even taking so-called *Untermenschen*, such as the Ukrainians, into its divisions. Strasser said that what he thought was of no consequence. But did Strasser expect him, Lockhart, to believe in all this claptrap? No, said Strasser, he did not, but he added that the BFC's men would receive the same lectures, in addition to their daily German language classes. They were perhaps a little more amenable, he told Lockhart.

*   *   *

The last day of 1943 began in the way Lockhart was starting to consider routine. A wash and a shave, and then on with the old Wehrmacht tunic and trousers he had been given in Crete. Breakfast with Strasser and Lange followed, and then some exercises in an area away from the glare of the other prisoners, who Lockhart had caught glimpses of from time to time. At around noon, it had started to snow, and he made his way in, not looking forward to the inevitably cold shower. As he walked down the corridor, he heard brisk footsteps behind him.

'Lockhart! There you are!'

It was Strasser.

'Yes?'

'Follow me – I have something for you.'

Strasser led him to Lockhart's own room. There, hanging on a hook, was the uniform of an SS officer.

'Your uniform, Hauptsturmführer Lockhart,' announced Strasser, with an air of satisfied formality.

Lockhart looked at it. It was field grey, similar to Strasser's, who had swapped back from his light blue tunic. But the insignia were different. Around the left cuff was a band, on which was embroidered in Germanic script, 'British Free Corps'. Further up the forearm was the Union Jack in the shape of a shield. On the upper arm was positioned the spread eagle of the SS. The left collar tab bore the three pips and single line that denoted the rank, but the right tab, instead of showing the SS runes, bore three lions, as on the royal standard. The breeches were hanging beneath it, and on the floor was a pair of brilliantly polished black boots. An officer's cap, bearing the death's-head badge, and a belt were also hanging on the hook.

'When do you want me to wear it?'

'From now on, of course!'

'Can I have a shower first?'

'By all means – and then come and see me.'

Lockhart had his shower. Despite how cold it was, he wanted to stay under it for ever, to permanently delay wearing that uniform, a uniform that signified so much evil. See it as a costume, he told himself, a prop, all part of his dangerous act.

He walked slowly back to his room and lay on the bed, staring at it. There was something powerful about it, something magnetic that held his gaze. He had witnessed the effect of such uniforms in the newsreels, but now he was about to wear one, become a part of it, even if his motives were hostile. But this SS uniform – the same uniform proudly worn by so many maniacs and murderers – bore a Union Jack and the three lions. It was an insult to King and country.

A knock on the door.

'Are you ready?'

It was Strasser.

'Not yet. Give me five minutes.'

'All right. But hurry.'

Lockhart swung his legs out of bed. Finally, some underclothes had been provided, and he put them on. He pulled the breeches down from the hanger and stepped into them – the material felt rough, but a little less itchy

than his Cretan crap-catchers. He then pulled on the
boots, sitting on the edge of the bed. They were a little
large – he would need some more socks. So far, if an
Englishman walked in, he could not be accused of wearing
an SS uniform. The next stage would seal it.

He lifted the hanger off the hook and removed the
tunic. It felt heavy and would be warm, which would be
about its only benefit. He slid his right arm in, and then
the left, once again feeling the fabric's coarseness. His
hands shook as he did up the five buttons. It fitted well,
and he fixed the belt around the waist. He had lost a lot of
weight since he had landed in Crete, and he had to buckle
the belt at its tightest position.

He sat back down on the bed and put his head in his
hands. This was like the hour before some great stage
performance – the same nerves, but magnified many,
many times. As it so often did, his mind turned to Anna
and Amy. He would be ashamed if they saw him now –
their husband and father wearing the uniform of a butcher.
But he was wearing it for them and perhaps so many
others – Anna would understand that. He sniffed deeply
and collected himself.

Without any more reflection, he stood up, put on the
cap, and walked down the corridor towards Strasser's
office. An NCO walked past and saluted him, causing
Lockhart to salute back – a knee-jerk reaction only, he told
himself. He knocked on the door.

'Come in, Hauptsturmführer!'

Lockhart walked in, feeling self-conscious at having to
parade himself.

The Traitor

Strasser looked him up and down, a thin smile on his lips.

'It looks a lot smarter than mine! What do you think of the insignia? Smart, huh?'

'Oh yes, very smart.'

'Don't you like your new uniform?'

'Not much.' Surly – like an adolescent.

'Don't disappoint me, Lockhart.'

'I won't. But I'd like to ask you for one thing.'

'Yes?'

'Please, Strasser, please don't ever try to enthuse me into the wonders of your glorious SS. You know that I am only doing this for my wife – I'm not some fascist. I dislike this uniform and what it represents, but I will play along with this scheme for her sake. I can see what you are trying to do, and I will help you, but just remember that in my heart I am still a British officer, not a Nazi one.'

Strasser stuck out his bottom lip in a pensive sneer. He looked down at his desk and then back at Lockhart.

'Isn't it ironic,' he said eventually, 'that just by wearing that uniform you seem to have acquired an authority that you lacked before?'

'Oh, what crap!'

'Really?'

'You know it is.'

Strasser raised his eyebrows playfully.

'Whatever you say, Hauptsturmführer Lockhart. I will go along with your request not to "enthuse" you, as you put it. But I will ask you for a favour in return. You and I must maintain our special relationship, and in order to do

219

that, you must not speak as you have just done in front of anybody else. You can be honest with me, so long as you promise to maintain our united front. Is that clear?'

Lockhart shrugged in acknowledgement.

'Good. Now let's get some lunch. I want to show off my new comrade. And later, at seven o'clock, we shall meet your men.'

As they walked to the mess, looking for all the world like old comrades, Lockhart reflected that Strasser's observation had been spot on.

'A schnapps before you meet your men?'

They were in Lange's little office. He had quite clearly been drinking all day, and looked a little unsteady.

'Yes – thank you,' said Lockhart.

'Why not?' said Strasser.

Lange poured a couple of healthy measures.

'To you, Hauptsturmführers Strasser and Lockhart, and to the success of the British Free Corps!'

'Thank you, Oskar,' said Strasser, and drained his glass.

Lockhart drained his too, hesitantly acknowledging the toast.

'Another?' asked Lange.

Just as Lockhart was offering his glass forward, Strasser said, 'No, Oskar, we must go and see the men.'

Lange looked a little crestfallen.

'Come on, Oskar,' said Strasser. 'There will be plenty more later.'

'Ach – you're right. Fine – I'm coming.'

* * *

They walked out into the night. It was snowing, and Lockhart felt the cold under his tunic. He rubbed his hands together.

'I'll see if I can get you a coat and some gloves,' said Strasser.

'I'd appreciate that,' Lockhart replied, genuinely grateful. It must have been ten below.

'An officer should always have a coat!' said Lange, a little too boisterously.

The guard at the gate to the prisoners' part of the camp saluted them keenly. They all saluted back, Lockhart half-heartedly.

'Well done, Hauptsturmführer,' said Strasser under his breath.

Lockhart ignored the patronising comment.

'By the way,' he said, 'you still haven't told me how many men have enlisted.'

'So far, we have eight . . .'

'Eight!'

'. . . and more will come shortly.'

'Eight?!'

Lockhart's voice went up an octave. He stopped and addressed Strasser directly, pointing his finger at his chest.

'This is ridiculous! You can't call eight men a corps – it's not even a bloody football team!'

Strasser stayed calm.

'I know, Lockhart, I know, but we are actively looking for more. With you on board, I'm sure many more will join.'

Lockhart let his hand drop to his side.

'You didn't tell me anything about recruiting.'

'That's because you didn't ask. Anyway, we're nearly at their quarters – we can continue this conversation tomorrow. And before I forget – I've told them you've joined up because you think the Allies are going to lose the war.'

Lange led the way up the steps to a sectioned-off part of one of the two large prisoner huts. He opened the door, candlelight spilling on to the snow-covered steps. He could hear English voices, evidently already fuelled by drink. As the three men stepped into the crude dormitory, the revellers stood to attention.

'Men,' said Strasser, 'I would like to present your new officer-in-charge, Hauptsturmführer John Lockhart. Hauptsturmführer Lockhart will be . . .'

But Lockhart was no longer listening. Instead, he was looking straight at the flushed and shocked face of Andrew Worstead.

August 1939

It's time to leave, time to get out of England, away from this rotten state corrupted by Jews and Commies. It's time to embrace a new life, a life where they will be free to speak their minds, in a place where their views will be respected. But time is against them and they must hurry. He knows it will be war soon – everybody knows it will be war soon – and as far as he's concerned, he wants to help fight it somewhere else.

They're living in Earls Court now, not Tooting. The money's tight, and so they're in a grubby little basement flat – Eileen hates it, but she knows it's not for long. One day, he tells her, one day they will have the run of every building in London, for they will come back as heroes, back to claim what is rightfully theirs. The Leader will see to it, don't you worry, my love, for the Leader is a good man, and he will make sure that their loyalty is rewarded. But for now, there is only one place for them, and that is Berlin.

It is the busiest day he can remember: winding up bank accounts, dismantling and disposing of his revolver – how he would love to take it! – saying goodbye to some of his old friends, settling the rent and doing the packing. And then Eileen puts a spanner in the works by saying that maybe they should go to Dublin instead. Not on your Nelly, he tells her. They'll be much safer in Berlin – they could be kidnapped from Dublin, but from Berlin, no way. He has contacts there, he knows people, high-up people – Berlin is the place to be, the centre of the civilised world. She's still reluctant, but that's too bad. It will be his decision, and his alone. If she doesn't want to come, she can stay here, weeping into her mother's apron down in Sussex.

They don't sleep that night, and the next morning they get up early and take a taxi to Victoria. A small panic as Eileen nearly forgets her passport – he thinks she's done it on purpose, but she swears she hasn't.

At the station, he's looking around for them, waiting for a hand on his shoulder, waiting for a 'Stop!' There's no queue at the ticket office, and they walk straight up and order two tickets for the boat train.

'Through to where, sir?' asks the bearded functionary behind the small window.

He coughs.

'I'm sorry, sir?'

'Berlin. Through to Berlin.'

The man looks taken aback.

'Berlin, you say? You're quite sure?'

'Yes, dammit! Just give me two tickets for Berlin.'

'Very well, sir. Single or return?'

He's already thought about this. Asking for a single will look too suspicious, and even though he can scarcely afford the return, he knows he must buy it.

'Return, of course!'

'Quite, sir. You wouldn't want to stay there, would you?'

He smiles nervously as Eileen grips his arm.

'Oh no – I'll be coming back all right. Hopefully we won't be there for long.'

September 1958

'I came up with your father in '32. A good chap, I thought – a little on the wild side, but great fun. Sharp too, although come to think of it, he was a rotten card player, despite what he thought. I remember comprehensively fleecing him during our first term.'

Amy smiled. Now up at Oxford herself, she was sitting in the study of one of her father's contemporaries, a classics don called Ian Massey.

'And no, I'm not one of those who subscribes to the

theory that he was a traitor. I don't think he had a treacherous bone in his body. He was nothing like those buggers Amery and Joyce. They were cut from a completely different cloth. Amery was a fool and a tearaway, and Joyce was a nasty little Jew-hating fascist. Your father was a decent man – I don't think he was capable of committing a single dishonourable act, let alone betraying his country.'

Since Amy had started at Oxford, she had sought out as many people as possible who had known her father. The picture that Massey was painting was a familiar one – everybody had testified to her father's decency and charm, finding it inconceivable that he should be thought of as one of the war's most despicable traitors.

'The problem I have, Professor Massey,' she began, 'is whether I should just accept that my father was a traitor, and get on with my life, or whether I should fight against that, and end up making my life a misery. After all, it is possible that he *was* a traitor. How should I know any better? He left when I was six.'

Massey took a long draw from his pipe.

'Of course it's possible,' he said. 'But why him? Men from our generation, our background, would never have considered treachery. Yes, he wore an SS uniform, but I can't believe that he didn't have his reasons. Perhaps he took Forster's words to heart, and decided that he would be better off betraying his country than a friend.'

Another draw, and then Massey leaned forward.

'But Miss Lockhart, you *must* find out. The truth is fundamental. Truth is one of the things we fought for. You owe it to your father – and to your family – to discover what happened, even if it hurts. You may be living on a false inheritance. You must not accept that! It would be too easy to give in to consensus. For heaven's sake, please do not let the opinion of the mob rule your heart.'

Amy swallowed. She hadn't expected such a speech.

'Do you think that all men should have a drop of treason in their veins?' she asked.

'Rebecca West?'

'Yes.'

Another draw.

'If by that she means that we citizens should keep questioning our country, challenging our leaders, then yes, yes we should have a drop or two. Maybe even a whole pint! They stopped questioning in Germany, and look what happened. And you must question too – otherwise it wasn't worth me losing this.'

Massey rolled up his left trouser leg to reveal a wooden leg.

'Made out of oak. They tell me it'll last longer than the one I've still got!'

Chapter Four

January–February 1944

IF SHE WAS being honest with herself, sometimes she enjoyed it. But those times were rare, very rare, and mostly it disgusted her. Few asked how she was, or even cared what she might be feeling. She would just smile, get on with the job, and think of 'the higher cause'. She may have lost her dignity, but she was doing her bit to win the war, riding up and down on the groins of Wehrmacht generals as she was doing now.

At least this one didn't want to be tied up. It was normally the SS officers who wanted that, along with a bit of humiliation. It was ironic – the SS would treat her with contempt and then pay her to treat them likewise. And after they had finished, they never left anything extra, not even a little present. At least the Wehrmacht were gentlemen of sorts – this one here had even brought her some real coffee.

But she enjoyed it with Carl. He was only one who seemed interested in her, made more remarkable by his membership of the SS. It wasn't that he did anything different, he just did it with a different tone, a different air. He visited often, and they both knew that they liked each other. But Carl was careful – he *never* talked about what he did, and neither did she want him to. Instead, they talked about what every other Berliner talked about – last night's air raid, the shortages, the worst winter in years . . .

But the last time he had been ratty, and he had rebuked her for asking what was wrong. It was the first time he had treated like her a whore, shoving her head down to his lap. She had felt like sobbing as they made love, but afterwards he had apologised and kissed her all over. Nobody had done that since Paul, at university back in Dresden. She remembered smiling to herself, thinking that they were like a normal couple, patching up a row with physical tenderness.

He had tried leaving more money, but she had told him that would make her feel more of a whore. Just leave half, she had said, the half she had to give to Kitty; the rest was on the house. They laughed, and Carl said that he had to go, and gave her a playful smack on the bottom. She tried to kiss him, but he had put his cap back on, and she knew that meant he was in a different mode. He had allowed himself an affectionate smile, and she blew him a kiss as he walked out. He had scratched the back of his neck. Was that an acknowledgement or a refusal? Carl was difficult to read.

She looked down at her latest client. He seemed to be

enjoying himself, not that she could really feel anything. He was overweight like many of them, but she had been with fatter. In his day, this one might have been good-looking, but those looks had gone with the ravages of staff-officer indulgence and war. His hands shot up to grip her breasts, and she reminded herself to give out a little moan of appreciation, watching as his mouth contorted into a moistly lecherous grin. She grinned back, willing him to hurry up. She leant down to whisper into his ear.

'Look in the mirror, look in the mirror.'

They both turned their heads to the wall near the bed, upon which hung a large gilt-framed mirror. Seeing the reflection usually brought matters to a close, and this occasion was to prove no exception. She found that soldiers, accustomed to a visual diet of violence, when faced with the sight of a twenty-two-year-old woman straddling their bodies, would climax within several seconds. And if that didn't work, then she would use the oldest trick in the prostitute's book – for which her leather opera gloves were a hygienic boon. It was repellent, but less so than going on for hours.

As the general grunted and shuddered, she stared at herself in the mirror. This time last year she had been at Dresden, studying law. And now she was a prostitute in Berlin, a stooge for the SD – the internal security service. Her job was to wheedle indiscretions out of her clients, which she would then have to type up by the next morning. Throwaway remarks about how badly the war was going; comments against the Führer (which were getting more frequent); military gossip – all these were precious nuggets to those back at SD headquarters on Prinz Albrechtstrasse.

And talk they did. Brimming with an expensive potion of champagne, brandy and sex, the officers blurted out the type of secrets that caused some of them to lose their heads. Hitler had reinstated the axe as the Reich's preferred means of capital punishment, and Leni knew, even as they spoke, that some of her clients would be enjoying their last bout of sex before the chop. She had felt sorry for one of them – a junior officer who had told her how much he hated the Nazis, how he had half a mind to shoot 'good old Adolf' the next time he was near him.

But she hated them too, much, much more than her headless young major, who had been arrested as soon as she had handed in her report. He hadn't been violated and abused every day. He hadn't had to live with the shame, the knowledge that you were no longer the person you had wished yourself to be. She should have been Leni the lawyer, not Leni the hooker. Her only comfort was that she was doing it for the best reason of all – not really for that 'higher cause', but for the life of her father.

'Leni?'

She didn't notice the general's voice at first. She must have been staring at the mirror for too long. He would want to go now, thank God.

'You looked as though you were miles away!'

She lifted herself off him, putting on her practised smile.

'Not at all, Kurt, far from it,' she purred. 'I was just thinking how much I love watching myself on top of you.'

The general nodded his head in polite acknowledgement, as though he had performed some small service for her, such as opening a door. Fool.

'And I can't wait to try some of that delicious coffee you've brought me.'

'It's the best,' he said as he got up. 'You deserve it.'

Leni lay back on the bed, smiling back up at him coquettishly, although the true nature of her expression was relief. Now was the time, in this supposedly post-coital glow, in which she gleaned most of her information. But tonight she couldn't be bothered. It was getting near one o'clock, and she would still have to type up her two other clients from this evening. They would be angry with her, she knew it, but it was too bad.

No, perhaps she had better give it a try. She turned herself on to her stomach, and let her head and arms dangle over the side of the bed.

'So when will I see you again?'

'Not as soon as I would wish.'

'Oh?'

'Maybe many months.'

'Where are you going?'

'I can't tell you that, my little Leni.'

'Will you bring me back some more coffee, though?'

'They don't have much coffee where I'm going.'

'Is that a clue?'

The general's face turned sour. He crouched down in front of her, the rolls of his stomach just inches from her face. Grabbing her chin, he yanked her head up to face him.

'You're a good fuck, and that's how it stays. What I do, or who I am, is no business of yours, understood?'

Leni did her best to nod. She wasn't scared – she rarely was. Having seen these men having an orgasm, she found it impossible to take them seriously.

'Sure,' she said, 'sure. It was just an innocent question.'

'There are no innocent questions, young lady.'

He let go of her chin. She carried on staring at the floor while the general continued to dress. At least she had tried. He had probably suspected that the place was an SD outfit, but that wasn't going to stop him sampling its delights. Kitty's had a reputation for being the best in Berlin.

'Right,' said the general, now dressed, 'I'm leaving now.'

She looked up, a teasing grin on her face.

'Not even a kiss goodbye for your little Leni?'

He looked embarrassed. Good – she had got the upper hand again. Instead, he bent forward and clicked his heels together.

'Goodbye, Fräulein.'

Fuck his formality. He couldn't just screw her and then pretend they had spent the last half-hour making social chit-chat at a reception. She didn't lift her head up, only her hand, as if to wave him goodbye and dismiss him at the same time.

She lay like that for many minutes, just gazing at the pattern on the Persian rug, following its swirls. Mother and Father had a similar rug, although not as sumptuous as this one. Her twin brother Heinrich used to lie on it, using its patterns as a bizarre road system for his wooden cars. He hated it when she joined in, as she would want to make the cars have hideous crashes, sometimes damaging their fragile frames.

Poor Heinrich, gentle Heinrich, dear Heinrich. She used to love to tease him, saying that he was the girl and she was the boy. And at eighteen, when he had gone off to fight in France, she had been jealous, saying that he would be a hopeless soldier; she would be a better one – much stronger, much braver. But all that came back from France was a 2nd Class Iron Cross and a swastika flag. Gentle Heinrich had actually been very brave Heinrich, knocking out two French machine-gun emplacements until a third one had claimed him. They put the medal in a glass box, and hung it next to Father's 2nd Class Iron Cross from the first war. At one point during the tears, Father had worked out that Heinrich must have won his medal about five miles from where he had won his.

And so, until November 1942, they were the average German family, with their share of loss and hardships. Leni had started her law course at Dresden, and was seeing Paul. Father carried on working as a civil servant, and Mother did voluntary work to help with the war effort. And then came the visit they had long feared, their guilty little secret that they had kept well hidden to allow Heinrich to join the army and Leni to become a student. Their war-hero father, who had fought so bravely for the Fatherland, was in fact nothing more than a Jew.

For the Gestapo, the knock on the door was at a surprisingly sociable hour – nine o'clock on a Sunday morning. As soon as Father had opened the door, he knew that he had been denounced. It wasn't worth wondering who had done it; it could have been anybody – even family members were betraying each other. He was taken to the cells, where he spent a week with little food or water, and was beaten so badly that his left eyeball was dislocated. It had then got infected, and had to be removed in hospital.

He was lucky. Apart from his eye, the only other thing he lost was his job. He hadn't been sent to the camps because of his Iron Cross, but even that wasn't a guarantee. He was allowed back home, although he had to report to the Gestapo at four o'clock every day. And because the tram conductors wouldn't let him on, he would have to walk there, a four-kilometre gauntlet of abuse, spit and blows. Within three weeks, Father's spirit had been broken. The light in his eyes, which had stayed burning even after the death of Heinrich, vanished. He would sit in front of their empty fireplace, his remaining eye fixed on the Iron Crosses and a picture of Heinrich.

It didn't surprise Leni that Paul ended their relationship – she had always suspected he was a bit spineless. Neither did it surprise her that the great amount of attention she normally received from other men disappeared, replaced with the whispers of '*Jude*'. And no longer was she asked to sign up to all those Nazi *Mädchen* groups, the ones who had been so desperate to have her join because of her great figure and looks. Never mind that she wasn't actually a Jew, but then she wasn't going to deny who her father was, wasn't going to pretend that he wasn't a part of her. It was they who were making her into a Jew, not her family.

What did surprise her was the arrival of the SD. Mother

had screamed at the two officers, dressed in black SS uniforms, when they took Leni away. That had earned her a punch, and words to the effect that where Leni was going was better than living with a bitch who had soiled the *Volk* by marrying a filthy Jew. Leni had cried too, and had felt a little scared, but she knew she wasn't being taken to a camp. They would have taken Father first, and besides, she didn't think the SD had anything to do with the camps.

Instead she was taken on a hellish five-hundred-kilometre, two-night train journey to a small hotel outside Stuttgart, where she found herself sharing a room with a girl called Heidi from Bohemia. Over the next two days, around fifty other young women joined them. They had come from all over the Greater Reich, all attractive and, it soon appeared to Leni, intelligent. Nobody knew why they were there, and the guards and hotel staff were not forthcoming. The consensus was that as all of them were in some kind of trouble, they were presumably being groomed for a task that might serve as atonement.

On the third morning, a tall thirty-year-old man wearing the uniform of an SS untersturmführer walked into the dining room during breakfast. The room went quiet as the officer walked slowly along the tables, and Leni noticed that many of the girls flinched as the uniform passed directly behind them. The officer stopped at the picture of the Führer that hung above the buffet table, saluted it with a stiff Heil Hitler, and turned to address them.

'Ladies,' he began, a little too loudly, 'ladies, you are here because there is a vital task we want you to perform for the Reich. You have been selected because you possess characteristics that are rare and therefore extremely useful for your Führer and the Fatherland. However, I should tell you that everything that takes place here is absolutely secret. If any of you talk about it, then you will all – all – be sent to a concentration camp.'

He allowed himself to look down at their faces, all of which were registering some form of shock, except that of Leni, who raised her eyebrows at him mockingly. He looked away. Pathetic. She had always suspected that most of these SS men were little more than their uniforms, and this one seemed especially hollow. He cleared his throat before continuing.

'Over the next week, myself and a team of experts will be assessing you to see whether you match up to the rigorous standards required for the task. I am afraid that only twenty of you will be selected . . .'

This caused a murmur throughout the room. The officer lifted his hand to silence them.

'The other thirty have nothing to fear. They will be sent back home, where they will be put under twenty-four-hour surveillance. Believe me, that is no fun, and you will earn far more freedom if you are selected. The tests will be hard, and I expect you all to try your best for the good of your Fatherland. You should be honoured even to have got this fair, but I regret only the very best will be chosen. Are there any questions?'

Although the girls started to speak all at once, it was Leni whose voice carried above the din.

'What is this task? There seems little point in taking all these tests if we don't know what they're for!'

'I regret, Fräulein, that only the twenty lucky girls who have been selected will find out what the task is.'

'Lucky?' Leni came back in a flash. 'Lucky?'

The officer looked exasperated.

'Yes, Fräulein – lucky. It will be a privilege to serve the Reich in the way we intend. And of course, Fräulein Steiner, those problems you have at home will be alleviated if you make it through to the last twenty. That goes for all of you.'

That caused Leni, as well as the others, to shut up. It wasn't so much the threat, but the fact that he knew who she was.

'Yes, girls, for this is your way to help yourselves. If you succeed, we shall turn a blind eye,' he said, pointedly looking at Leni, 'to any indiscretions that you or your families may have committed. Any other questions?'

The girls stayed quiet. Like Leni, they were all reflecting on their problems back home, each knowing that they had little choice but to co-operate. Bastards, she thought, especially this one for joking about Father's eye.

'Good. One final thing. My name is Untersturmführer Schwarz. I shall be here for the duration of the tests, so please feel free to contact me about any problems you have, large or small. Enjoy the rest of your breakfast!'

What a shit, thought Leni as Schwarz walked out, what a shit, acting the kindly uncle, the benevolent schoolmaster. He was as bad as his uniform indicated. Leni wanted to shout at him, to tell him what she thought, but she knew that would see her father in Theresienstadt before the day was out. Neither could she share her thoughts with the others, because one of their number was bound to be an informer. Leni looked around – many of the girls were crying slightly, including Heidi, who was sitting next to her. She brought Heidi's head to rest on her shoulder, and, gently stroking her hair, whispered words of encouragement to her.

Schwarz was right: the tests were hard. It seemed that the SD had assembled every leader in his or her field to assess them. A professor of English from Berlin University grilled Leni in that language for two hours, asking her questions about her family and her childhood. The head of Stuttgart's medical school carried out a thorough investigation of her physique, even asking her questions about her sexual background. A female psychiatrist spent an inordinate amount of time trying to establish whether Leni had any mental difficulties, any hang-ups, any dysfunctions.

It came as little surprise that Leni was picked for the last twenty. Schwarz told her that she was 'outstandingly qualified' for the task, although she would have to learn to temper her rebellious streak. She never got the chance to say goodbye to Heidi, because those who had failed were immediately spirited away. She often wondered what had happened to Heidi, who had seemed too fragile for the task. Had she really gone back to Bohemia, allowed to live a near-normal life? Or was she now in a concentration camp? Leni knew the answer – it was only optimism that kept her asking.

At six o'clock the next morning, the remaining girls were picked up by a sealed truck, which took them two hundred kilometres to the alpine town of Sonthofen, just north of the Austrian border. There, they were installed in an *Ordensburg*, a training school for SS cadets and future Nazi leaders. This *Ordensburg* was a 'castle' built in the Teutonic style in 1934, and was one of four such establishments in Germany. The presence of so many young women caused some excitement, although Schwarz did his best to keep them separate from the male cadets.

Over the next two months, Leni was trained in a wide variety of activities. For the first time in her life, she handled firearms, which she took to well after some initial apprehension. Although not the best, she was a more than competent shot, as well as showing a natural skill in unarmed combat. They were also taught how to code and decode messages, and were given lessons in National Socialism, economics, the war, first aid, as well as learning how to drive all manner of vehicles.

But despite the glamour and range of these topics, it was becoming clear to Leni and the other girls that there was a growing emphasis on topics such as sexual health, cosmetics, seduction and conversation. It was Leni's nature to be direct, and thus she put it straight to Schwarz over soup one evening.

'So, Karl,' she said, adopting an intimacy that infuriated the untersturmführer, 'are we going to have to screw some people at some point?'

Schwarz put down his spoon, and looked around the table. The other girls had also stopped eating.

'Because that's what all this is about, isn't it, Karl?' Leni continued, enjoying her audience. 'You want us to become whores, don't you? All this training in guns, and learning how to spot a Romanian officer's uniform and the rest is just rubbish, isn't it? Why else would we have all these lectures on venereal diseases and learning how to make the perfect cocktail? We're just going to become SD whores—'

'Shut up!' barked Schwarz. 'That's enough!'

Leni stopped, remembering her father.

'Have you finished?' asked Schwarz.

Leni nodded.

Schwarz took a deep breath.

'All agents, male or female, have to undertake activities they may find distasteful. And yes, that often includes sex. For sex is the most powerful weapon in the female agent's armoury, and it can achieve far more than long and expensive surveillance. You will become some of the most valuable tools in the protection of the Reich, for many of you will be posted to establishments frequented by senior Wehrmacht and SS officers. It is important that the SD knows what men at this level are thinking, and it is essential to the war effort if we weed out those who are starting to, shall we say, question their allegiances.'

Schwarz paused, taking in the mood of the table. It was silent and a little stunned. The girls had suspected that sex would be part of the task, but not to the extent that Schwarz was outlining. Leni caught Schwarz's eye.

'Yes, Leni?' Schwarz asked wearily. She might be a pain, he thought, but she would be brilliant. What man wouldn't be captivated by her long brown hair and defiant, pouting mouth? And as for her figure, well, that had been the talk of his fellow officers here at the *Ordensburg* for the past eight weeks.

'So you *do* want us to work as prostitutes?'

'Yes, Leni, we do, and that is final. I don't need to tell you what will happen if you don't help. You're all too far in just to turn round and go back to your mothers and fathers.'

Nobody, not even Leni, finished their soup.

She looked up from the swirls on the Persian rug. There was a knocking on the bedroom door, accompanied by Waltraut the maid's insistent exhortations for her to open up. She looked over at the clock on top of the chest of drawers. It was quarter past one. Surely not another client at this time? It wasn't as if it was Friday or Saturday night. She got up, yawned, and put on her silk robe.

'Yes, Waltraut?' she asked, as she opened the door.

'It's Hauptsturmführer Strasser here to see you, Fräulein Leni. He says he hopes it's not too late.'

Leni broke out into a big smile. Carl. Her lovely Carl. If it had been anybody else she would have had him shooed away, but not Carl.

'Tell him to come up in ten minutes. And then sort out the room while I have a wash.'

Any tiredness disappeared as she walked down the corridor to the bathroom. She hadn't heard from Carl in a month, and now here he was, turning up in the middle of the night. It was unlike him to be so random, a thought which troubled her as she ran a shallow bath. She removed her gloves, and stepped into the lukewarm water. At least it wasn't cold, which it always was in her flat. A regular hot bath was one of the few luxuries, along with good food and wine, that made working at Kitty's bearable. She knew that there were some women in Berlin who had prostituted themselves just to earn some scraps for their children – in comparison Leni felt lucky, very lucky. In fact, she might even have put on a little weight since leaving Sonthofen. She looked down at her stomach, and pinched it – there was very little fat, but she had definitely been thinner back in Dresden.

She splashed herself all over with a sponge, concentrating on her breasts and vagina. She and Heinrich used to joke about such a bath – a 'whore's bath' – when the water supplies ran low back home. The force of the irony never stopped hurting, especially when she had up to five such baths a day. She got out and briskly towelled herself dry.

Strasser was already sitting on the edge of her bed, his boots off, and swigging from a bottle of champagne. His uniform, normally so well pressed, looked crumpled, and she could smell that he had been drinking heavily. His state somewhat dented her enthusiasm.

'Hello, Carl,' she ventured tentatively. 'I thought we had New Year's Eve a couple of days ago!'

He looked up, his eyes glazed and watery. He smiled broadly.

'I'm drunk, Leni,' he slurred. 'Very, very drunk.'

'I didn't think you got drunk.'

'No, but tonight I am. It's all Max's fault – he said he would try to get me drunk and he succeeds to have appeared.'

Leni laughed.

'Appears to have succeeded, you mean.'

'That's what I said.'

'You nearly did. Here, give me the bottle. It looks as though I've got some catching up to do.'

Strasser stretched out his arm, waving the bottle towards her. It was a 1921 Louis Roederer – it would have cost him a fortune. She took a gulp, feeling the gently sparkling liquid slip down. She tried handing back the bottle, but Strasser was slumped forward, staring at the same spot on the carpet she had been gazing at a few minutes ago. She took another swig, and then went to stand in front of him, his forehead coming to rest just below her stomach.

As she stroked his hair with her left hand, Strasser started slowly kissing her through the silk of her robe. His kisses soon became a little more urgent, more passionate. Leni took another swig of champagne, enjoying the decadence of the moment. She felt his hands work their way through the opening of the robe and clasp her buttocks, squeezing them, drawing her towards his face. He then lowered his head, and she opened her legs slightly, enough for him to be able to kiss her between them. She looked at herself in the mirror, watching the movement of the back of Strasser's head, now buried under the silk. She smiled at herself, satisfied with the pleasure she knew she was giving someone she actually cared about.

What was it that she liked about him? Perhaps it was his calculation, his self-control. She knew she should have hated him, despised everything he and his uniform represented, yet she got the feeling that Carl was different, more *simpatico*. And even though he was drunk, he still knew what he was doing as he worked away under her robe. She ground herself into his face, feeling herself becoming genuinely aroused. The last time that had happened was when he was last here.

She opened up her robe and looked at him.

'How are you doing down there?'

He didn't so much as reply as let out a grunt.

'Fancy a drink?'

Another grunt. She poured some of the champagne over his mouth and her vagina. It felt cool and slightly sticky.

'More?'

Just as Strasser let out a further grunt, the air-raid sirens started. Leni's shoulders slumped.

'Shit.'

Strasser looked up.

'What?' he asked.

'Can't you hear them?'

He paused and then tutted.

'Just my luck,' he sighed.

'I'm sure they won't be here straight away,' she said, accompanying her words with a slight grin.

Strasser read her mind. He stood up, snatched Leni's robe down from her shoulders and started kissing her hard, his hands on her breasts. They made love quickly, crudely, Strasser bending Leni over the bed and thrusting into her eagerly. Just as they had finished, they heard the first of the bombs, landing perhaps only a couple of kilometres away. As they dressed, they giggled like a couple of teenagers who had just heard a parent knock on the door. Strasser was struggling to get his boots on.

'Hurry up, Carl!'

'I'm nearly there,' he said as he heaved.

'Just leave them here.'

'You're joking. These are my best friends.'

A bomb blast rattled the window.

'Christ, Carl! Get a move on.'

'Yes, yes.'

But still he couldn't get even the first boot on, drunkenness, tiredness and a hint of post-coital stupor rendering him uncharacteristically clumsy. Leni snatched the boot from him, then picked up the other one from the floor.

'You can put them on in the shelter. Come on!'

She grabbed Strasser by the hand and pulled him off the bed. She practically dragged him down to the shelter, where they were presented with a candlelit assortment of prostitutes and senior Wehrmacht officers in various states of undress. And in amongst them, holding court, was the glamorous middle-aged figure of Kitty, a glass of champagne in one hand, a cigarette holder in the other. She appeared unperturbed by the explosions, which were getting nearer, and instead was telling some of the officers one of her many anecdotes. She nodded over at Leni and Strasser as they came in, and carried on with her story.

They found a quiet corner of the shelter, and lay on their sides on an old mattress, a couple of blankets for cover. Strasser made some joke along the lines of how a mattress in a brothel's air-raid shelter must be *really* knackered, but most of it was drowned out by a huge blast that sent small pieces of masonry falling from the ceiling.

She felt Strasser's arm reach over her and pull her into him, pressing her back into his chest. It felt comforting, it felt affectionate. As they lay like that, she was already beginning to miss him.

'When will I see you again?' she whispered.

'Hmm?'

'When will you come again?'

'I don't know.'

She heard laughter coming from Kitty's courtiers.

'But soon, though?'

'Yes, soon. As soon as I've finished my new job.'

'What's that?'

'You shouldn't ask.'

'I know. I was just interested, that's all.'

'Of course.'

Silence. He was right, she shouldn't have asked, which was what made her all the more surprised when she heard him say:

'If you really want to know, I'm putting together a corps of British SS men. To tell you the truth, it's a complete waste of time.'

Leni's eyes snapped open in the near-darkness, watching the candlelight flickering on the walls. They would want to know that. They would certainly want to know that.

A little balder; somewhat thinner; still just as chippy – Andrew Worstead had changed only slightly since Lockhart had travelled with him back from Crete ten years ago. It was now three days after New Year's Eve, and

Lockhart had managed to collar Worstead on his own –
the rest of the men were attending a lecture in the camp
headquarters. It was four o'clock in the afternoon, already
dark, and Lockhart was absent-mindedly gazing at the thin
layer of snow building up on the window ledge. As he
watched Worstead, his hand tugging his right earlobe, get
up and walk to the window, Lockhart recalled that
moment from three nights ago.

The room had gone silent as soon as they had seen each
other. It was as though the force of their surprise had
enough energy to silence a stadium, let alone a handful of
drunken men. Lockhart remembered Strasser's voice
trailing off:

'. . . Hauptsturmführer Lockhart will be your officer in
charge, answerable directly to me . . . Lockhart? What is
it, Lockhart?'

Lockhart did speak, but his words were addressed to
Worstead.

'Andrew,' he began, 'in heaven's name . . . what . . .
what are you doing here?'

Worstead tried staring back, his eyelids flickering furiously, as if trying to negate the sight of his old companion.

'Hel . . . hello, John,' he spluttered. 'I was going to ask
you the same question.'

Worstead allowed himself a half-smile under closed
eyes, evidently regarding his reply as in some way witty.

Before Lockhart could answer Strasser had gripped him
by the elbow and walked him firmly out the door. As he
did so, he turned to Lange.

'Bring Lee along to your office – the others are to stay here until I say so. There will be no more celebrations tonight.'

Lange, a little nonplussed by the schnapps and the nature of what he had just seen, stood motionless for longer than Strasser cared for.

'Sonderführer! Do it now!'

'Yes, Hauptsturmführer!'

Strasser forced Lockhart down the steps, the two men nearly slipping on the ice. As they made their way back to the gate, Lockhart's thoughts were in a frenzy. Andrew bloody Worstead, of all people! Was he a traitor? If so, why? Lockhart couldn't remember him being a fascist. Did he really hate Britain that much? What had happened to him?

'What the hell is Andrew Worstead doing here?' he asked Strasser impatiently.

'We'll talk in Lange's office.'

'Fine, but you can let go of me, I'm not going to run away.'

Strasser did so, accompanied by a briefly muttered and uncharacteristic apology. He was clearly rattled, thought Lockhart. As they neared the main building, the sounds of New Year's Eve grew louder in the black and frozen air – marching songs washed down with laughter and an out-of-tune piano.

They reached Lange's office, which was mercifully warm. The bottle of schnapps lay open on the desk, and before he spoke, Strasser had the decency to pour them both a glass. Together, the men knocked them back, although while Strasser slammed his glass clumsily back down on the desk, Lockhart, keen to appear calm, replaced his very gently. He looked up at Strasser, who acknowledged the gesture with a wry smile.

'So, Lockhart, why don't you tell me all you know about Lee?'

'Lee?' said Lockhart. 'His real name is Worstead.'

'Worstead, Lee – I don't care!'

Lockhart was stalling. God knows what he was going to tell Strasser. What if Worstead was acting the traitor as well? He'd do well to stick to the innocuous truth, which, mercifully, was all he knew in this instance.

'You remember when I was telling you about my time in Crete?'

'Yes,' said Strasser, who began deliberately to pour just one glass of schnapps.

'Well, that was where I met Worstead. He was a fellow student on the digs. We were friendly for the two or so months we were there. When we got back to England, we saw each other a little bit, and then just drifted apart.'

'When did you last see him?'

'I suppose it would have been in the spring of 1936. Yes, that's right, just after you lot occupied the Rhineland. Must have been around March then.'

Strasser looked up to see if Lockhart was having him on. Lockhart's face stayed straight, but inwardly he was enjoying playing with the German. Strasser drained his glass, once more slamming it back down, this time defiantly, to show Lockhart that he was a man with purpose, that the first time he had slammed it down had been deliberate. There was a knock on the door.

'Yes?' shouted Strasser irritably.

'Hauptsturmführer, it is Lange, here with Lee. May we enter?'

'No! Wait there!'

'Yes, Hauptsturmführer.'

'I am going to let Mr Worstead tell you his story himself,' said Strasser, who was regaining his normal steady composure. 'It is a very interesting story, and in its way, quite sad. It is a good example of how British society is so very backward compared to the Reich.'

'I'm all ears.'

'Good,' said Strasser, missing Lockhart's cynicism. 'Good. Sonderführer!'

'Yes?' came Lange's voice.

'You may come in now!'

Lange stepped into the office. He was followed by Worstead. Lockhart tried making eye contact with his old companion, but he was merely shown a tangle of red hair as Worstead stared at the floor. Lange took a seat behind his desk, and Worstead sat on the same chair at which Lockhart had sat a few days before. The irony occurred to Lockhart as he sat next to Strasser. He crossed his legs and his arms, bracing himself for the nonsense that Worstead was bound to deliver.

'Now then, Lee, or is it Worstead?' Strasser asked.

Worstead looked up briefly. Strasser continued.

'I'd like you to tell your old friend Mr Lockhart – sorry, Hauptsturmführer Lockhart – what you told us. Your life story, as it were.'

'I'd like a cigarette,' said Worstead brusquely, looking at Strasser.

'You may,' said Strasser. 'Oskar – do you have any?'

Lange's expression brightened at Strasser's use of his first name.

'Of course, Hauptsturmführer!'

Lange offered the packet to the small gathering, and after much business of passing the only book of matches around, the room was soon filling up with the smoke of four – presumably black-market – finest Turkish cigarettes. As Strasser put the matchbook back in his pocket, Lockhart noticed that it bore the word 'Kitty's'.

'So what's Kitty's?' he asked, trying to make it sound as though he didn't care one way or another.

Strasser smiled.

'Kitty's is a place for bachelors,' he said. 'Or for men missing their wives. Who knows? I'm going there in a day or so. It's in Berlin. Perhaps I might even take you there one day. You're definitely in the right category.'

Lockhart restrained himself. It was pointless getting angry about it – he was beginning to realise that Strasser loved getting a rise out of people. Bland, be bland.

'That's a very kind offer,' he replied. 'So long as you're paying.'

'Hah! You must be joking! Kitty's costs a fortune, but it's worth every mark.'

'But I don't have any money.'

Strasser took a long drag on his cigarette.

'We shall see about that – I must sort out some form of remuneration for you.'

Lockhart swallowed. Not just the uniform, but money too. Being *paid* for what he was doing seemed much worse, much more treacherous. Just play the game, he thought, do it properly, stop beating yourself up about it – get even.

Strasser turned to Worstead.

'Now tell us your story,' he said.

Worstead mumbled towards the floor. His speech was a little slurred, presumably the result of the party from which he had been snatched.

'Er . . . I'm not sure where to begin,' he said, coughing out thick grey smoke.

Lockhart must have been looking at Worstead's back for at least five minutes. The two men had remained in silence, pondering, as the snow continued to accumulate on the window ledge. Worstead had just taken the opportunity to reveal that much of what he had gone on to say at the meeting on New Year's Eve had been bunkum. Yes, he had an illegitimate child with his CO's daughter, a girl called Beth, and yes, he had been busted to ranks for it, and yes, he was bitter, but a traitor, no way. He was hamming that up for the Germans, earning their confidence, when in fact he was gathering information, attempting to wreck the unit. And as to taking the name 'Lee', that had merely been a precaution – something he had been advised to do. Worstead said that he wanted to show everybody back home that he could be a hero, more than just a military disgrace with an illegitimate child.

He had asked about Lockhart too, about whether everything he had said on New Year's Eve had been rubbish as well. Not at all, said Lockhart; for he had told the truth, told Worstead in front of Strasser and Lange this was coercion and not genuine treachery. His only motive for joining up, he had said, was to save Anna's life. He knew she was alive, he said, because he'd even had a letter from her.

Worstead turned from the window.

'You know, John,' he said, 'I can't tell you how sorry I am to hear about Anna.'

Lockhart smiled weakly.

'Thanks, Andrew.'

'I liked her very much, even if she did have a go at me on that walk . . .'

'Like, Andrew, like; she *is* still alive.'

'Hmm?'

Worstead coughed and hacked again before resuming:

'Bloody cough. I'm supposed to have given up the gaspers – doctor's orders. Sorry, yes, of course – *like* – I do like her, you know. I was jealous of you – she's the type of woman that any man would want. Beautiful, intelligent, and an archaeologist to boot! You lucky sod, I thought. Still do, actually, still feel a bit jealous.'

'Really?'

'Oh yes. In fact I was a bit bloody jealous of your whole bloody perfect life. Not that it's perfect any more, of course; nobody's life is, not now. But when Anna came back from Greece, I suppose that's when I felt the most envious. You didn't seem to want to know me any more.'

'Oh come on, Andrew! That's not true!'

'Isn't it?'

'Of course not – we just drifted apart, that's all.'

'Really? You didn't even invite me to your wedding.'

253

'Christ – there were plenty of people I didn't invite! We had to keep the numbers down.'

'All right, John – I'm sorry. I suppose I'm a little too sensitive.'

'Don't worry about it.'

Both men fell silent, and after a few moments, they started to speak simultaneously. Lockhart insisted that Worstead went first.

'I was just going to say that it makes all the difference now that you're here. We'd make a great team, don't you think? I can be your eyes and ears amongst the men, and you'll be able to manipulate things higher up the ladder.'

Lockhart nodded slightly. This was a new, upbeat Worstead that was emerging. An apologetic Worstead, a positive Worstead even, albeit with some slight snivelling. He felt more comfortable with the old version, knew where he stood. What if Worstead really was a traitor, now briefed by Strasser within the last few days to act as Lockhart's 'chum', to find out what Lockhart's real intentions were? Or perhaps he had genuinely started to lose some of his less attractive qualities; perhaps he was truly grateful to see Lockhart again. Lockhart resolved to be cautious. There was no rush. Worstead was not yet his friend – their relationship would have to start again. After all, thought Lockhart, this was a different world, a world with new rules.

Suddenly, the door opened and in came Lange, along with a blast of freezing air.

'Strasser wants to see you,' Lange announced, looking at Lockhart.

Here was an opportunity for some fun, thought Lockhart.

'Since when did you not salute a senior officer, Sonderführer?'

Lange's eyes visibly enlarged, his mouth contorting as he attempted to restrain his shock. Such impertinence!

'I *am* your senior, aren't I?' said Lockhart.

'Yes, sir, you are.'

'Well then, a salute would be nice.'

Lange thought about it, and after a second or two clicked his heels together, stretched out his right arm, and hailed his Führer. Lockhart couldn't resist a slight smile.

'So where's my fellow hauptsturmführer then?' he asked.

They were marched out on to the parade ground, which had been covered by a crunchy layer of snow. 10678 still had her wooden clogs, having slept with them every night. Many had had theirs stolen, and then sold back by the thieves for two days' worth of food. No food for two days would be enough to kill those already near starvation. She looked down at a pair of bare feet walking next to her – they had already turned blue. She had seen it before. The woman would get frostbite, and then gangrene would start its invidious march through the body.

The *Kapos* – guards drawn from the prison population – marshalled the women into neat rows for the morning roll call. Everybody knew it was pointless, merely another way for the SS to exert discipline and to delight in a summary execution or two. The *Aufseherinnen* – the female SS supervisors – were often the most brutal, seeking to prove themselves to their male counterparts. Catch the eye of an *Aufseherin* and you might just die. There was no logic to it – death visited randomly, on the whim of either a woman who wanted to live a little longer or a woman who wanted to make more money than she would have done in a factory.

The roll call proceeded slowly. Any woman who collapsed from the cold would be led off to the 'hospital' and from there to the crematorium. Any woman who broke rank could be executed on the spot. The same applied to anybody who spoke, coughed or even sneezed. And of these, it was coughing that did for the Ukrainian woman immediately in front of her.

It had first sounded like a dry tickle, but it had got worse. A *Kapo* stormed over.

'What's the matter? Have we got ourselves a cough?' asked the *Kapo* in German. Anna could not see her face, but could detect the sarcasm.

The Ukrainian nodded. She probably did not understand a word that the *Kapo* was saying, but had hazarded a guess that it would be best to nod and not to shake her head.

'Well stop it!' the *Kapo* screamed.

The Ukrainian started backwards, almost falling on to Anna. She regained her balance and nodded once more. The *Kapo* walked away, her smug little face, held up high, looking for the approval of an SS woman. By the time she had walked five yards, the Ukrainian started coughing again.

Anna felt herself tense up. This was going to be bad.

'Didn't I tell you to stop it?' the *Kapo* yelled.

Once more a nod.

'Then stop it!'

But as she nodded, the coughing resumed. Enraged, the *Kapo* grabbed the Ukrainian by the arm and dragged her forward, pulling her to the ground. Out came the stick, and soon the large woman was shielding her head from a battery of well-aimed blows. 10678 looked at her feet. Anna wanted to reach out and help, even if she was the worst bedmate ever, but 10678 held her to the spot.

A senior *Aufseherin* rushed forward.

'What's all this?' she demanded.

The *Kapo* explained.

'Bring her forward,' the *Aufseherin* ordered.

Anna heard the large woman starting to beg for mercy as she was dragged. Not that Anna understood the words, but she had heard pleading in many languages and it had always sounded the same. The *Aufseherin* strutted over to an SS officer, and after a brief conversation, during which Anna could see them both smiling and looking at their watches, the *Aufseherin* returned to the Ukrainian, who was now attempting to clutch the feet of the *Kapo*, begging, imploring, her voice desperate and high-pitched.

The *Kapo* and the *Aufseherin* dragged their victim further away from the line-up, bringing her to a position where everybody could see what was about to take place. But Anna did not want to look – she had seen it before. She did not look at the woman's utterly anguished face, nor at the SS officer striding over, unbuttoning his holster, and taking out his pistol. But she could hear it all, especially the howl which emanated from the Ukrainian, which sounded as though it was coming from another world. She heard the officer pull the breech back, and then the silence before he pulled the trigger.

That night, even on her own, without the Ukrainian, 10678 did not sleep well. They had looked at their watches, she recalled, glanced at them, as if waiting for a train. So casual the horror, so mundane the evil, to fit one in before breakfast.

Strasser had wanted to see Lockhart about the unit's imminent move from Genshagen to Hildesheim, a town about twenty miles to the south-east of Hanover. Lockhart had seen many postcards of the place – his parents had been before the last war – and it looked, in his father's words, like a 'must-visit'.

Those words had returned when Strasser mentioned the move. Strasser had noticed Lockhart start, and had asked him if he already knew the town.

'No, but I was planning to pay it a visit before the war,' Lockhart had replied. 'Although I doubt I would have worn a German uniform to do so.'

Even Strasser had allowed himself to smile at the irony.

'You'll be housed in the St Michael Cloister,' he had said. 'It's been converted by the SS.'

The St Michael Cloister. According to his father, it was Hildesheim's finest building.

'Converted into what exactly?'

'It is now called the "Haus Germanien" – an SS Nordic study centre.'

'And what's that?'

'Its purpose, to quote the Reichsführer-SS, is "to maintain and intensify the political, economic and cultural bonds between the Reich and the other Nordic nations". It's part of the *Ahnenerbe*.'

'The what?'

'The German Ancestral Heritage Society for the Study of German Prehistory. It's a branch of the SS.'

'So it's a sort of school we're going to.'

'Something like that. The head of the Haus Germanien is a Sturmbannführer Parsch, who is also a professor of Viking history. The men will be learning all about the Aryan races, and we'll be teaching them German, as well as training them to become SS men.'

'Sounds like brainwashing to me, Carl.'

'No, not brainwashing. We think that "education" is a more sensitive – and honest – term.'

'Of course, of course.'

This was becoming the pattern of their conversations. Both men, realising the strength of the other's will, had allowed an almost light-hearted impasse to exist. Strasser knew full well that Lockhart was never going to join the SS in spirit, so he resolved to permit him his displays of cynicism. For his part, Lockhart knew that it was pointless arguing with Strasser. The German was seemingly too indoctrinated, too immersed in the supposed greatness of Nazism for Lockhart to even make a dent. But what was more salient than this unspoken, perhaps gentlemanly agreement – although Lockhart would not have admitted it as such – was the fact that Anna was a hostage. Neither of them ever forgot that.

Fellow Countrymen!

We of the British Free Corps are fighting for YOU!

We are fighting with the best of Europe's youth to preserve our European civilisation and our common cultural heritage from the menace of Jewish Communism.

MAKE NO MISTAKE ABOUT IT! Europe includes England. Should Soviet Russia ever overcome Germany and the other European countries fighting with her, nothing on this earth would save the Continent from Communism, and our own country would inevitably sooner or later succumb.

We are British. We love England and all it stands for. Most of us have fought on the battlefields of France, of Lybia, Greece, or Italy, and many of our best comrades are lying there – sacrificed in this war of Jewish revenge. We felt then that we were being lied to and betrayed. Now we know it for certain. This conflict between England and Germany is racial SUICIDE. We must UNITE and take up arms against the common enemy. We ask you to join with us in our struggle. We ask you to come into our ranks and fight shoulder to shoulder with us for Europe and for England.

Published by the British Free Corps.

Lockhart handed the pamphlet back to its author.

'So what do you think?' asked Charles Maclaren.

'You spelt "Libya" wrong,' said Lockhart, smiling at the serious little man in front of him.

Maclaren frowned and looked down at the paper.

'So what? It doesn't matter.'

'Perhaps not,' said Lockhart. 'But spelling mistakes never look very . . . *authoritative*.'

Maclaren sneered, his nostrils and top lip twitching furiously.

'So you don't think it has any authority then, do you?'

'That's not what I said.'

'But it has *some* authority, doesn't it?'

Lockhart sighed.

'Yes, Maclaren, it does indeed. I'm sure it will be a great success and have hundreds signing on the dotted line.'

'Are you having me on?'

Lockhart laughed a little.

'No! Why? Don't you think you're going to get hundreds of recruits?'

Maclaren paused, his twitching sneer making an unwelcome return.

'I'm sure we will,' he said, a touch of pride in his Liverpudlian tones.

'Well then? What are you worried about?'

'I'm *not*,' Maclaren instantly retorted, menace creeping into his voice.

Lockhart rolled his eyes skyward, if only to wind Maclaren up still further. There was something childish and petty about him that Lockhart found intensely distasteful. He was evidently one of those men who felt that life owed him more, and as a result he bore an air of permanent frustration. Neither was he shy of expressing his anti-Semitism, always ready to blame the Jews for the war. It was usually men like him, Lockhart thought, little men with persecution complexes, who felt that the Jews were the real agents of evil and destruction. It had come as no surprise to Lockhart that before the war, Maclaren had been the district secretary of the British Union of Fascists in Liverpool. He looked mischievously back at Maclaren.

'So then, Maclaren, before the war, when you were in the BUF, did you wear your black shirt in bed?'

Maclaren glared at him. Lockhart continued, relishing the opportunity to bait this absurd figure:

'I bet you even wore it under your white coat in your little pharmacy in Liverpool, all the time secretly wanting the chemist to accidentally catch a glimpse of it. Quite a thrill, was it, being a blackshirt? Beating up Jews, that sort of thing? I bet you even had to serve some of them the next day, dole out the iodine to those you had smashed up the night before. That would have annoyed you, wouldn't it?'

Maclaren's twitch was getting so violent that Lockhart nearly started laughing. When Maclaren eventually spoke, it was under great restraint.

'I would ask you, *sir*, not to talk to me in this manner. You know that I cannot reply as fully as I might like.'

'How very proper of you, Sergeant! Tell me, did you show the same respect to those whose heads you used to kick in?'

'I never beat anybody up!'

'Is that so? So how does one get to be so high up in the BUF? I thought you lot were promoted on the strength of your fists, not the strength of your arguments.'

'I'll have you know that the BUF is a perfectly proper party, which does not seek violence—'

'Oh why don't you just shut your boring fascist gob, Maclaren?'

Lockhart and Maclaren looked up to see the huge figure of Gabriel Hull standing next to them, a stein of beer in his hand. Hull continued:

'You're so full of shit, Maclaren – your lectures, your pamphlets, they're all crap. Of course we used to beat people up! Or at least that's what we did in Norfolk. Why else do you think they used someone like me as a chucker-out? I was more of a hitman than a doorman. Not that I killed anybody, mind.'

Lockhart smiled inwardly. Hull was someone he felt he might be able to trust. The son of a farmer, he had been brought up on the land before going to London to work as a professional strongman. As a result, he had a massively developed physique, which gave him the quiet confidence to tell people what he pleased. He was an ugly sod too, thought Lockhart – big ears that stuck out, and a wide mouth with a curvy top lip that resembled a shallow letter M. A tangle of short curly brown hair sat awkwardly on the top of his vast head, looking like some wire wool perched on a raw potato. Hull might have been simple, but at least he wasn't a German sympathiser. Along with his sidekick Barney Andreae, who was standing next to him, he only seemed to be in the BFC to get away from his POW camp. Both he and Andreae were keen to indulge in essential luxuries such as alcohol, cigarettes and, most importantly, the company of women.

Lockhart got up from his chair before Maclaren could respond. They had been talking for twenty minutes, and he welcomed Hull's interruption.

'Why don't I leave you gentlemen to it?' he said, grasping both men by the shoulders, 'I'm going to get myself a drink.'

He winked at Hull and Andreae, and then surveyed the crowded bar. Under the low-beamed ceilings, with their orange lights dim in the smoky, atmosphere the room was packed with SS NCOs, all of whom were jostling for the attentions of the few females. The officers enjoyed better-looking *Fräulein* at their haunts, Lockhart mused, but then it was ever thus. Earlier that evening, Strasser had insisted that Lockhart join him and some other junior officers at the Schlegels Weinstube, but Lockhart had said that it was better if he fraternised with his men, here at the Rosenstock. Strasser found Lockhart's conscientiousness hard to argue against, although Lockhart's real reason was that he could not bear to spend the evening with a group of SS officers. Better to spend it with his fellow countrymen, even if they were a bunch of renegades. It made him feel less of a traitor, although it didn't make him feel any less alone.

Lockhart made his way to the lavatories. One of the few benefits of his hauptsturmführer's uniform, especially one with a Union Jack on it, was that the NCOs cleared a path as soon as they caught sight of it. Unused to seeing an officer in the Rosenstock, many of them looked startled, some almost falling over in their desperation to get out of his way. Lockhart found the effect amusing, although he maintained an austere and cold expression that complemented the uniform. He could see why so many men wanted to join the SS, especially those who were life's victims. The clothing, the pageantry, the iconography – all of these gave the impression of a medieval order, the membership of which could transform a lowly picked-upon peasant boy into a model of chivalry. No wonder they were such fanatics, thought Lockhart. The SS gave these people a purpose they otherwise lacked. And that was especially true of some of the members of the BFC. Being in the SS made them feel big, made them feel part of the best bloody gang in the whole bloody world.

The prime example of this type was Pugh, the odious Thomas Pugh, next to whom Lockhart found himself standing at the urinal. Pugh, like Maclaren, was a member of the BUF, and had been an administrative officer at the BUF's 'Black House' on the King's Road in London. However, unlike Maclaren, Pugh was willing to admit that he had beaten up Jews and Communists, and even boasted how he had started a riot in Maidstone. He had fled to Germany just before the war, and along with others had spent his time in Berlin making broadcasts for the *Germany Calling* programme that was transmitted by the Reichsrundfunk to Britain. Pugh had been one of the first to join the BFC, and had already visited several POW camps attempting to find recruits. So far, his only two 'scalps' had been Maclaren and Catchpole, but he was confident that he would find a lot more.

Pugh and Lockhart urinated in silence. It crossed Lockhart's mind to 'accidentally' piss on Pugh's boots, but he thought better of it. Pugh finished first and walked over to the basin to wash his hands, whistling tunelessly while he did so. As Lockhart waited for him to finish, he looked at Pugh's face in the mirror. It was the type of face that hid in dark corners, eager for its prey. A large port wine stain covered most of its left side – Lockhart wondered how Pugh would have turned out had he not had it. Maybe the small eyes would have looked less shifty, maybe the eyebrows would have been less cruelly arched, the mouth not stuck in that petulant sneer.

Pugh looked in the mirror and caught Lockhart staring at him.

'What are you looking at?' Pugh asked aggressively.

'Nothing in particular,' Lockhart replied.

'You're looking at my stain, aren't you?'

Lockhart shook his head.

'Yes you are. Go on, admit it – everybody looks at it.'

'As a matter of fact, Pugh, yes I was.'

'Well, keep looking – I'm not going to stop you.'

With those words, Pugh turned round and held his face right up to Lockhart's, forcing him to examine the stain in detail.

'What do you think, eh? It's called a "naevus", if you want the medical term.'

The stain was purplish red, and it contained scores of porridge-like lumps and bumps. What a thing to be born with, thought Lockhart. But he'd be damned if he was going to show any sympathy to Pugh. There was a chap at school who'd had a port wine stain, and he hadn't seemed that miserable about it. Lockhart muscled past Pugh to get to the sink.

'I think you're very unlucky,' he said, turning on the taps.

'Unlucky? Is that all?'

'Yes. It's not as though it's doing you any harm, is it?'

'It does me a fuck of a lot of harm. You try chatting up a girl with this on your face.'

'There's no need to swear, Pugh.'

'Oh, I'm so sorry, Hauptsturmführer.'

'My real rank is that of a captain in the *British* army. This is merely a costume,' said Lockhart, pointing to his chest with his wet hands. 'Simply a means to an end. Unlike you, I'm not a real traitor.'

'Me? A traitor!'

'I don't see how you can be regarded as anything else.'

'I'm not a traitor, Mr Captain in the British army; I'm the biggest bloody patriot you're ever likely to meet.'

'So what the hell are you doing here in Germany?'

'Saving our country from the Jews! Isn't that obvious?'

Here we go, thought Lockhart, yet another rant against Jewry, Bolshevism, international finance and American rapacity, those four horsemen of the paranoiac's apocalypse. Lockhart walked over to the filthy hand towel, Pugh's hectoring speech echoing off the urinal, which was the most fitting place for it.

'Britain is being poisoned by the Semites,' said Pugh,

his voice getting louder. 'They are taking over our businesses, our banks, our culture, our very *identity*. This war was started by *them* – not the Germans – started in order for the Jews to take over after we have destroyed ourselves. We should be *with* Germany, not against them, fighting side by side against conspiratorial scum like the Jews and the Reds . . .'

'That'll do, Pugh.'

But Pugh was not to be interrupted.

'. . . because that's what the real patriots are doing, not fighting our European brothers, but *joining* them, becoming brothers in the worldwide fight against the poison of Jewishness—'

'All right,' Lockhart half shouted, 'you've made your point!'

Finally, Pugh stopped.

'You can spare me all that rot,' said Lockhart. 'I'm not one of your blackshirt bum-chums, ready to believe that the whole world is against him just because he once stubbed his toe. What's the matter with you people? Can't you see the truth for what it is? We're fighting Germany because they're trying to *enslave* Europe, not free it. Isn't that obvious? Just ask a Pole.'

Pugh stayed silent. A condescending smile came to his lips, implying that Lockhart was just a naive, an innocent. Lockhart tensed his wet fists, keen, for the first time since school, to start a fight. It was clear that Pugh was never going to believe what Lockhart told him, so why not just beat it into him? But that was their tactic, not his. Violence was the Nazi way, the way of the insecure bully, the fascist way. He would have to be more subtle if he was going to break the spell cast by their beloved Führer. Idiots. He finished drying his hands and turned back to Pugh.

'Let me make one thing clear,' he said, jabbing his finger at Pugh's chest. 'You can spout your fascist drivel as much as you want, but you'll do exactly as I say. Otherwise I'll have you sent to one of those SS punishment camps that Strasser likes talking about. Understood?'

Pugh nodded slightly, his expression still one of schoolboy defiance.

'Good,' Lockhart replied. 'Now get out.'

Pugh clicked his heels together and saluted with an immaculate Heil Hitler, all the time that same condescending smile on his lips. Lockhart had really wanted to tell him that instead of sending him to a punishment camp he would personally beat him to a pulp, but he knew that a threat like that would get back to Strasser.

He walked back into the bar, noisy with the sound of NCOs singing marching songs. Somewhere in the smoky din a piano was being played badly, about as badly as Lockhart himself could play it. Over by the bar, talking to a barmaid, were Ray Catchpole and Albert Marston, the latter seeming even younger than his twenty-four years. It was Marston's birthday tomorrow, hence the presence of all eight members of the corps here tonight. They were a sorry bunch, Lockhart thought, not a patch on the *andartes*.

Sitting at a small table in a corner was Unterscharführer Matthew Butcher, the quiet ascetic, his eyes deep-set, his face cadaverous. Unterscharführer Butcher of the Waffen-SS since 1941; the man who had boasted of throwing

Jewish women out of top-storey windows in Krakow; who claimed to have personally shot two hundred Poles and eighty Jews one day in Warsaw; the man nicknamed 'Mikado' by the members of the BFC because of his obsession with Japan – this was who Lockhart was to have as his senior NCO, to discipline the men, to act as a buffer.

Lockhart walked over to him. Butcher's thin fingers were neatly clasped around a glass of what appeared to be apple juice. As Lockhart approached the table, Butcher looked up, his eyes so dark and hidden that they looked like sockets in a skull. The corners of his mouth turned slightly upward – Lockhart supposed that was the nearest the man got to a smile.

'Have you seen Worstead this evening?' Lockhart asked. Now that Worstead's alias had been rumbled, he'd decided to revert to his real name.

'I saw him leave about ten minutes after we arrived, sir.'

'Really? Where did he go?'

'He went out the front door – looked as if he was in a bit of a hurry.'

Odd, thought Lockhart, very odd. Worstead had seemed very eager to wet his whistle this evening.

As usual, her flat felt colder than it was outside. It was four o'clock in the morning, and she had just evaded the curfew and walked back from Kitty's to find ice forming inside the windows. She was desperate for a hot bath, but the bombing had denied even Kitty's that luxury, despite the efforts of the SD to get the plumbing fixed. Kitty had stuck her neck out, yelling down a crackling line to a harassed obersturmbannführer at Prinz Albrechtstrasse, 'What would you prefer? Cold, dirty whores, or warm, clean ones? And don't tell me "warm, dirty ones" because I've already heard that four times this morning.' Kitty was right to be so angry – she knew that her girls did not perform as well when they felt dirty, soiled. Leni, like all the girls, always washed herself afterwards, and even if cold water was more or less as effective, it didn't feel that way.

Leni drew the heavy blackout curtains and turned on the solitary dim bulb that illuminated her single-room flat. The pile of washing-up in the sink; the unmade bed; the clothes rail with her meagre collection of ordinary, 'non-professional' clothes; the two pairs of shoes below that; the chipped table bearing a typewriter and some books; the single picture of Heinrich, smiling proudly in his uniform; the large cobweb that hung out of reach above the shower unit in the corner – all was just as it always was, damp and unloved. This was not her home – this was merely a refuge from Kitty's and its constant demands upon her body and her sanity.

She threw her bag on to the bed, and kicked her shoes off. Sleep was high on her list of things to do, but she had something more important to attend to, something that had been eating her up for the past two weeks. She sat down at the desk, and took a couple of sheets of flimsy paper from the drawer. She methodically inserted one into the typewriter, feeling the ratcheted rollers of the heavy machine secure the paper firmly into place. Poised to start, she decided that she needed a cigarette. She leant over to the bed and grabbed her bag, taking a packet of American cigarettes out of it – a gift from a grateful Wehrmacht oberst, if she remembered rightly. She had three left. Well, she would have one now, and another when she had finished, which would leave one for after breakfast. Or maybe *as* breakfast, she thought wryly. There was no food in this place, and she always got up too late to get anywhere near the front of the queue at the bakery.

She lit the cigarette, depositing the match in an unemptied ashtray. She let the smoke billow gently out of her mouth, allowing it to swirl around the typewriter and then up to the yellowing ceiling. It had been a fortnight since she had seen him, since they had made love and then gone down to the air-raid shelter. Fourteen days of feeling guilty for not telling them what he had told her. Thirteen nights of restless sleep, trying to put into some kind of order her feelings of personal loyalty, duty, affection, and safety, not just hers, but that of her mother and father. And now she had reached her decision, or at least she thought she had.

Resting the cigarette on the lip of the ashtray, she began to type.

Report from LS
18 January 1944

<u>SS-Hauptsturmführer Carl Strasser</u>

The above officer visited me on the night of 3/4 January. My delay in reporting the nature of his visit is owing to the size of my workload at present. Because my work is getting on top of me I have been unable to

At first, she had been too tired to notice the double entendre, but when she did, she smiled slightly. Anyway, she was usually the one on top. She ripped the sheet of paper out of the typewriter and scrunched it up. She would burn it later, she thought, inserting another sheet.

Report from LS
18 January 1944

<u>SS-Hauptsturmführer Carl Strasser</u>

The officer above visited me at Kitty's on the night of 3/4 January. So far, I have been too busy to type up my report, because of the size of my workload. I hope you will take this into account and will see fit to excuse me.

I have known Hauptsturmführer Strasser for several weeks now, and in my experience he has proved to be the most discreet of SS officers. However, on the night of the 3rd, he came to me in a state of utter intoxication.

Leni took a long drag of her cigarette. She exhaled, and then sniffed, feeling an imminent onslaught of tears. Another drag, and then another – the tobacco might not have lessened the guilt, but it made her calmer.

Hauptsturmführer Strasser and I proceeded to make love. After we had done so, we evacuated my room for the shelter on account of an air raid. It was at some point during this raid that Hauptsturmführer Strasser revealed to me that he was assembling 'a corps of British SS men'. Furthermore, he added that it was 'a complete waste of time'.

The cigarette was nearly exhausted, but pinching it gingerly between index finger and thumb, Leni managed to extract one more drag. She dropped the butt in the ashtray, letting it burn itself out.

Hauptsturmführer Strasser did not give me any more information regarding this unit, despite my probing. All I can add is that he seemed agitated and unhappy with this posting. I had noticed that he was in a similar state last month, although he was not so forthcoming at that time.

No, he certainly wasn't, she thought. He had been a complete bastard, very much the SS officer all over.

At present, I am unaware of the whereabouts of Strasser. I am under the impression that the unit is not stationed in Berlin, but the specific location is unknown to me.

I have built up a good rapport with Strasser and I

expect I shall see him again shortly. I shall attempt to make him reveal more information then.

Was there anything else? No, but no doubt she would find out more soon. She typed one final word:

Ends

She gently pulled the sheet from the typewriter, and read the text through. These few words should help save her parents back in Dresden, she thought; keep them alive, out of harm until permanent safety finally invaded. She hugged herself. God, it was cold.

Over the next few days, the unit settled into their quarters at Hildesheim. Lockhart began to feel curiously at home in the town. It had the same feel as Bath, albeit a Bath bedecked in snow and swastikas; a Bath occupied by SS men speaking every language from Serbo-Croat to Spanish; a Bath whose most beautiful buildings had been requisitioned by a regime intent on re-educating its people. The church of St Michael, in whose cloister the BFC were housed, was, as his father had said, Hildesheim's jewel. Flanked by six towers and sitting on top of a small hill, the church exuded a sense of Germanic power and austerity. Strasser had told him that its ceiling had been removed for safety, and Lockhart was therefore disappointed not to be able to see its 1,300 oak panels painted with depictions of trees in the Bible. Lockhart doubted

Strasser's reason for its absence. The imagery of the ceiling would have rested uneasily with the hundreds of items of Nazi regalia scattered around the building – the SS runes, the swastika flags, the spread eagles, the garish recruiting posters, the countless paintings of the Führer and Himmler. They were trying to create their own religion, their own monastic orders, thought Lockhart; far better for them to strip St Michael of its Christianity, using the fear of bombs as an excuse.

A lot of Lockhart's time was spent trying to control the unit. Much to his annoyance, two more men had joined, bringing the unit's strength to eleven. Both Richard Simpkin and Andrew Smith had been members of the BUF, and had come to Hildesheim via Genshagen. Simpkin, who was a lance corporal in the Royal Warwickshire Regiment, had been captured in Crete a month after the invasion, in June 1941. He looked very pasty, thought Lockhart, a complexion he soon discovered to be the result of repeated bouts of jaundice and malaria, both of which he had caught in North Africa. Smith, like Marston, had been in the Merchant Navy, and had also been imprisoned at the Milag near Bremen. Lockhart found Smith shifty and quiet, another of those pinch-faced little men who blamed the Jews for everything.

The arrival of these two meant that the BFC was becoming increasingly ideological. Lockhart found the simplicity of Hull and Andreae, both out to have as good a time as possible, refreshing compared to the hectoring natures of what he termed 'The Bonsai Hitlers'. Not that

Hull's and Andreae's actions were praiseworthy – far from it – but Lockhart felt that they were not real traitors. Neither of them seemed to have any intention of fighting, and were keener to spend the rest of the war abusing the Germans' misplaced hospitality. Constant were the complaints from members such as Pugh and Maclaren, who were distressed that Hull and Andreae kept shouting them down when they gave their lectures on Nazism and the so-called 'Jewish threat' to the world order. Lockhart was of course sympathetic to Hull and Andreae, and was in no mind to tell them to stop laying into the unit's *fascisti*. So he told Pugh and Maclaren he would 'have a word', when of course he never did.

The heckling continued; swastikas were torn down and replaced in the common room every other day; arguments and punch-ups were commonplace. Butcher, who was the senior NCO, had his work cut out keeping some semblance of discipline, constantly complaining to Lockhart and Strasser that they had recruited a bunch of idiots, and for once, although silently, Lockhart agreed with his oberscharführer. Strasser told Lockhart that any further lapses in discipline would be his responsibility, which had caused Lockhart to complain that he was not responsible for the low calibre of recruits. How was it his fault that the unit consisted of such a potent brew of men with opposing motives? Give me the right tools, Lockhart had said, and I'll do you a nice job. That had bought him some time and some space, although Lockhart knew that Strasser would not be stumped for long.

* * *

The letter annoyed him. Its tone suggested that he was being slack, lazy, when he was being nothing of the sort. Fucking Berger – he'd known this job was going to be thankless, but not as bad as this. It was an achievement in itself that the Corps numbered as many as eleven. Strasser re-read the letter. He took a deep breath, and breathed out slowly.

From: SS-Obergruppenführer Gottlob Berger, Head, SS Hauptamt
To: SS-Hauptsturmführer Carl Strasser, British Free Corps
Date: 31 January 1944
Subject: Recruitment

Strasser

I am concerned at the slow progress you are making in finding members for the British Free Corps.

Although I am glad you have found yourself a British officer, you are still far short of the desired strength of thirty that the Führer has ordered the unit to reach before it goes into action.

I insist that you redouble your efforts, and use every means at your disposal to recruit more men. There must be hundreds, perhaps thousands, of Britons languishing at our expense in POW camps who are willing to join in our cause against the subhuman scum from the east.

You must find them. Use every means necessary.

I order you to mount the recruiting drive immediately, using the best of the existing members as advertisements to the POWs. They are more likely to sign up if they see their fellow countrymen have already done so.

You will not fail.

Berger

He threw the letter back on his desk in disgust. 'You will not fail.' The past few weeks had been an endless series of phone calls, letters and telegrams. Organising a recruiting drive, on top of looking after the unit, was a lot harder than Berger seemed to think. POW camps had to be rung – who then wanted written confirmation. The Gestapo had to be informed. Photographs had to be sent to Berlin, passes to be prepared. The railway authorities notified. And the Wehrmacht, just in case. Then of course there was the SD, the RSHA, and those dolts in the police. And those were just the ones Strasser could remember. All of them needed convincing, needed proof that this wasn't some sort of joke, or a devious piece of trickery devised by the Allies. This was a civil servant's job, not his, not a *soldier*'s. Hillen-Ziegfeld ought to be doing all this, but the odious little rat had wriggled out of it.

The only thing that remotely cheered him was that his office was a little more hospitable. He had requisitioned a

piece of state-approved art from the gallery in town and
had hung it above the small fireplace. It was a cheerful
painting, showing naked and long-limbed Aryan youths
dancing around an Alpine meadow. When the war was
over, when he was living off the land, he would do that –
dance naked with a beautiful girl in a spring meadow.
Strasser smiled to himself – perhaps he was more romantic
than he thought. Who would the girl be? Leni? No – he
couldn't marry a whore, no matter how much he liked her.

On the wall opposite the painting was a magnificent
framed poster of the Führer on horseback, dressed as a
knight in armour, complete with a lance. Strasser had also
managed to get himself a better desk and chair, and now
had two phones instead of the one. But bundles of paper
lay on nearly every flat surface – he was the victim of
bureaucracy. He took another deep breath.

He looked at the small clock on his desk: five past
twelve. Lockhart was late. He had taken the unit to the
outdoor municipal baths, where they would be swimming
in their full kit, along with dummy weaponry. It caused
Strasser no little amusement to think of the valiant British
Free Corps plunging into the icy water, especially those
such as Pugh and Worstead who had had it too easy in
Berlin for too long. Berlin. He wished he was back there,
back in his office with Max and the hideous Frau Buch.
The only thing he didn't miss was the air raids. There was
a rumour going around that Hitler hardly spoke to Göring,
that he regarded the head of the Luftwaffe as a fat, drug-
addled whale and blamed him for letting the bombers
through.

There was a knock on the door.

'Come in!'

Lockhart walked in – or rather sauntered in – his hair still a little wet. Before Strasser could speak, Lockhart had beaten him to it.

'Going up in the world, Carl?'

'What?' said Strasser irritably, slightly puzzled.

'Your office – it's looking very . . . smart.'

Lockhart was teasing him – it was typical of his behaviour of late. He seemed to think he could get away with anything. Well, what Strasser was about to say would eradicate his grin.

'Sit down, Lockhart.'

Lockhart did so, drawing his chair up near the fire, but only after he had surveyed the painting with something approaching a slight sneer. For an archaeologist, Lockhart was perhaps a little bit of a philistine, thought Strasser.

'How was your swim?' asked Strasser.

'Cold,' said Lockhart, '*very* cold. Simpkin almost drowned, but Hull and I managed to fish him out.'

'Can't he swim then?'

'Oh no, he can swim all right, but he just seems to be permanently ill. I think he must have picked up something pretty vile when he was in Africa.'

Strasser shrugged. In a perfect world he wouldn't have to make do with weaklings such as Simpkin.

'So this is why you're late?'

Lockhart started slightly.

'I suppose so, yes.'

Strasser was fed up with Lockhart's near impudence. He slammed his desk hard with his hand.

'I do not expect you to be late again! Do you understand? This is the SS – not the British army!'

Lockhart narrowed his eyes. 'I'm sorry – it won't happen again.'

He said the words indifferently, flatly, as if he was an automaton. He clearly didn't mean them. For the time being, Strasser would leave it – but he would get the measure of Lockhart one day. In the mean time, he needed to talk about recruitment.

'I have a memorandum here,' he said, 'which I would like you to read.'

'Poor you, Strasser,' said Lockhart after half a minute. 'It sounds as though you're having one hell of a time.'

'I don't need your sympathy, Lockhart.'

'Sorry I offered it.'

Strasser held up his hand as a small gesture of apology. Perhaps Lockhart had been sincere.

'All right, Lockhart. Here's what you're going to do. On Monday, you, Butcher, Pugh and Worstead are going to set off on a little tour. The four of you are going to spend the next few weeks visiting your fellow countrymen, persuading them to join you. You will give lectures, explaining the origins of the BFC . . .'

Lockhart shifted in his seat, readying himself to interrupt, but Strasser was not going to let him.

'. . . handing out pamphlets, and recruiting as Berger suggests. The fact that you are an officer will make you a very good advertisement, I think. All that intelligence and charm won't hurt either.'

Strasser could see Lockhart was squirming. He looked deeply uncomfortable. Good – he could *earn* his right to live.

'What, Lockhart? What do you want to say?'

'I think it's a mad idea, a complete waste of time,' said Lockhart.

That impudence again. Strasser sat back. He'd let Lockhart say his bit, indulge him a little.

'Why's that?'

'Because nobody will take us seriously.'

'How do you know?'

'Because the British, like the Germans, aren't very good at being traitors. We tend to leave that to the French.'

'The French?'

'Isn't there some sort of French SS legion? Butcher said there was.'

'He's right – it's called the Légion des Voluntaires Français, although it's part of the Wehrmacht. They fought very bravely on the Eastern Front, which is what we should all be doing. There's talk that we in the Waffen-SS might soon take them over.'

'Lucky you.'

'I don't know what the problem is with you English. You seem to regard the Soviets as your ally, when anybody who has any sense can see that they are the real threat to peace and freedom.'

Lockhart let out a disapproving snort.

'We have only occupied countries such as France and Holland in order to save them from the menace of the Jews and the Bolsheviks. Just think what would have happened if we hadn't acted.'

Lockhart shook his head.

'If you can't persuade me,' he said, 'what chance do you think I have of persuading my countrymen, most of whom will have had comrades killed by Germans? And besides, they will have witnessed your barbarity at first hand – your executions, your burning down of villages.'

Strasser didn't speak. What did Lockhart know of anything like that? He recalled one such action in Russia. He had burned down an entire village because it was harbouring partisans – it was his duty, that was all. A small village on a great plain, just another Bolshevik nest – it needed wiping out, cleansing, even the women. Fuck. Russian women – they were tough, tougher than some of the men, their eyes cold and impassive in front of the firing squads. Strasser looked down at the desk. He gently grasped his pen between his thumb and forefinger, and repeatedly tapped it on the desk, a long pause between each tap. He didn't feel proud about what had happened back there, back on that great plain, even though he knew he should. After nearly a minute, he looked back up at Lockhart, who was starting to speak again.

'Look, Strasser, so far I've kept my side of the bargain, and you yours. And every time you have asked me to do something more, something else, you've given me that little extra. And this time, because you're asking me to do a big thing, I'd like to ask you for a big thing.'

'What?'

'I'd like to see my wife.'

Strasser sat up.

'That's out of the question!' he shouted.

'Really?'

'Absolutely!'

'Why?'

'Because it would be impossible!'

'Why? She is alive, isn't she?'

'Of course she is!'

'Then why can't I see her?'

'Because you would never get permission.'

'It's not up to you then? So who do I get permission from?'

'It is up to me, but you can't have it!'

'So you really want to go back to Russia, do you, Strasser? You really want to go and get your fucking feet frozen off, that's if you don't die first, butchered by some Commie in the snow?'

'Whether you're part of this unit or not makes no difference to me!'

'I don't believe you! You need me, Strasser, of course you bloody do, so why don't you just allow me this one little request? Christ! How much is it to ask? And you have so much to gain. Just think about it, man! I see my wife - I'll get you your remaining men. You're still here, I'm still here, my wife's still here - none of us dead, none of us on our way to Russia. Doesn't that make sense? Kill me, kill my wife, and you'll end up getting yourself killed.'

Strasser glowered back at Lockhart, who was sitting back triumphantly. 'You will not fail' echoed in his head. Lockhart was right – damn him! Damn his English arrogance.

'Come on, Strasser. Yes or no?'

'Be quiet!'

Strasser was tapping his pen once more, but this time far more quickly. He was rattled, his eyes searching around the room as though the answer was hidden somewhere in a cold corner. One day, he would kill Lockhart – it would be a pleasure, a joy to kill this . . . this know-it-all. He had been cornered by him – this was not part of the plan, not at all what he had wanted to happen. He let himself slump slightly. Screw it. Why did it matter anyway? So long as he stopped himself going back to the Front, that was all that mattered. And if Lockhart became more enthusiastic because he thought he was going to see his wife, then great – excellent, in fact. There was no earthly reason why he, Strasser, would need to keep his side of the deal. So Lockhart thought he had the better of him. Well, let him think that.

'All right,' he began. 'All right. You will be able to see your wife . . .'

Lockhart's eyes widened.

'. . . but on one condition.'

'Yes?'

'You succeed in recruiting the required number of men. This is not open for discussion.'

'Fine.'

'You have asked for a lot from me, Lockhart. This will be your final request.'

'Just so long as I see her.'

'Just so long as you recruit another nineteen men. And now you may leave.'

Lockhart stood up as Strasser looked down at his desk. 'By the way, Lockhart . . .'

'Yes?' said the Englishman, already at the door.

'I nearly forgot. Happy birthday! Would you allow me to buy you a drink this evening?'

For once, to Strasser's delight, Lockhart looked truly flabbergasted.

Lockhart might have been taken aback by Strasser's birthday salutation, but secretly he was delighted at the prospect of the recruitment drive. Finally, he had the opportunity to get in touch with Baker Street. POWs – including members of the BFC, but not Lockhart – were allowed to write letters back home, letters that were vetted by the Germans and then delivered by the Red Cross.

Lockhart was still not in a position to trust Worstead, let alone any other member of the Corps. He had desperately wanted to send a coded letter, via a member of the unit, to SOE, telling them what had happened, and more crucially, telling them about the supposed existence of sarin, but he had stopped himself. If the person to whom he entrusted the letter ratted on him, then the game would be over. Strasser would undoubtedly have Lockhart – and Anna – shot.

But at a stalag he should be able to find a trustworthy POW, a POW he might be able to recruit as a link-man, a POW untainted by any connection with a Pugh or a

Maclaren. The only problem, Lockhart thought, was finding a POW who would trust him in return. But he couldn't let that stop him, couldn't allow that to be a hindrance. The threat of sarin was too huge, and he needed to act, to clutch whatever straws blew towards him. With the absence of any further information about the gas, the best he could do for the present was to let London know about it.

That night, in his small room, Lockhart took two hours to write a letter that looked like any other from a British POW, complete with deliberate spelling mistakes:

Dear Hattie,

It's a bloody big stalag this! Richard Welsh arrived here Wednesday night, really upset and tired. Also, Will Thomas, Betty's husband! How about that? Anyway, how's Father? Still selling Mum's jam at market? We don't have fresh food here except bad eggs if the guards have left some to go manky! Life is all right, even managed to find some flowers to plant and look after! They're quite ugly little things really. I reckon daffs would grow well here – soil's excellently rich and breaks up into fine lumps of mulch. Anyway, fat chance!

Any further grumbles from Walter's dickey tummy? He's not been to our favourite quack doctor or has he stayed away this time? Poor Walt! Perhaps it's got better now I hope! Must be flipping boring sitting around with nothing to eat or drink. Please send my love when he's around next.

I hope this war might end soon, as my flippin feet are bloody well blistered because our stupid heavy boots wore thin as wafers on our grim march over here. Would give hundred pounds to cobbler Phil! Any shoes apart from my dodgey, old, sodding, damn smelly, delapidated footwear! I must complain every day to the Huns but they couldn't be slightly bothered. I wonder whether German POWs have found their guards equally tough nuts?

Please forgive constant complaning! Things well? And you and Ian doing well? We're so happy married life suits both of you and your Jimmy is coming along helthily. I miss following his progress week by week! Sitting him on my knee was one happy moment!

Take care Sis! With love, your

Lockhart deliberately left out a name. That would come courtesy of whoever it was that sent the letter. The code was simple, but it was unlikely that the German censor would have either the wit or the time to uncover the eighteen-word message contained within it:

In renegade unit British Free Corps in Hildesheim have learnt nerve gas sarin held in place starting Mitt

Lockhart folded the letter and put it in an envelope addressed to a Mrs Susan Dykes of 1 Glenilla Road, Belsize Park, London NW. The address was fictitious, but it would end up in the right place. He lay on his bed and held the unsealed envelope to his chest. Its contents, he reflected, could save the lives of millions.

March 1940

He's proud of his script – it's one of his best, he thinks. He knows that much of it is overblown, but they pay him handsomely for it, and have even given him and Eileen a smart apartment in the Kastanienallee in the Charlottenburg district. They told him a Jew once owned it, but he and his family no longer needed it. The apartment makes Eileen happy, but she still says she feels uncomfortable here. Well, too bad. Let her moan – she's not going anywhere.

The clock on the studio wall in the Reichsrundfunk indicates that it is nine minutes past seven. Young James Clark will be finishing off reading the news as part of the Germany Calling programme, and then it will be his turn. He'll have twenty minutes all to himself, twenty minutes in which he can tell the whole of Britain the truth. Not just a crowd of the curious at Hyde Park Corner, not just a hall full of loyal blackshirts, but anybody back home who can listen to a radio. Apparently, they told him, he has already earned himself quite a reputation. That made him feel proud, made him feel that he has made the right decision.

But he has his doubts. Not even here, here in the heart of fascism, is he convinced that the creed is being followed closely enough. The deal with Stalin has rattled him – why did the Führer do that, make a pact with the Bolsheviks? Others tell him that it is part of a bigger plan, that the Führer knows what he is doing, that they will just have to wait and see. He wonders about that, but in the mean time he is going to work for the wider cause, not least because there is nowhere else to work. He knows which side his bread is buttered.

The second hand sweeps steadily up to the top of the clock, and when it reaches it, a red light comes on above.

'Good evening,' he begins in a slow, low voice, not in the haranguing tones he once used at public meetings. 'Tonight I'd like to talk to you about the Jews. As many of you know, this war was started by the Jews, and I think it only right that we should avail ourselves of as much information as possible about this pernicious race of people, exposing the means by which they hope to gain world power.

'Many of you have written to me asking why it is that I dislike the Jews so much. Well, I would have thought that would have been self-evident, but in listing my reasons for my dislike of them, I will also expose their underhand practices, their devious ways. The Jew has a number of reproachable tendencies, tendencies which I will now list in brief, and then expand upon later.

'For a start, the Jew has an incapacity to avoid forming a state within a state. Do not let the Jews tell you that they have been forced into their stinking ghettos, for it is they who chose to live like that, huddled together in a mass, creating their own customs and laws, sitting like a parasite on the skin of their host society.'

He catches the eye of Manfred, his producer, through the glass partition. Manfred smiles, and gives him a thumbs-up. This is going well, he thinks, this will earn him a place in

*history. When he goes back, back to an England free of Jews,
an England cast out of the twilight and back into the bright
rays of hope, he will be a hero, one of its saviours. No traitor
am I, he thinks, merely just ahead of the game, ahead of time,
always ahead of time.*

November 1962

Her flat was crammed with papers, books, letters and
files. Friends would joke about it, telling Amy that she
should just throw the whole lot away, forget about it, get
on with her life. It was history, they said, let it go.

But she couldn't. She was determined to find out the
truth, even if her research led her to the conclusion that he
had in fact been a traitor. One way or another, she had to
find out. It was easy for her friends to tell her to drop it –
they knew who their parents were, what they had done,
how they had fought. They had that security; she didn't.
Couldn't they see that it was important? Some could. But
there were others who said that she wasn't getting very far.

The doubters had a point. Despite the time and effort,
despite all those piles of paper, she was nowhere near
finding an answer. She felt like Sisyphus, eternally pushing
his rock to the top of the hill. Just as she felt she had got
to the summit, something would snatch the rock away
from her, and throw it back down.

That something could either be secrecy, bureaucracy or
accident.

'Dear Miss Lockhart, we are sorry to inform you that

the papers you require are not available to the public . . .'

'We're sorry, but we only release such wartime correspondences to bona fide historians . . .'

'Unfortunately we suffered a fire . . .'

'Those papers will be released in 2046 . . .'

'We suspect that the papers you seek are currently held in the Soviet Union. At present, this department lacks the facilities to be able to access those papers. However, let me assure you that we are doing all we can . . .'

Every letter was a slap in the face. Who were these records for, then? What was the point of democracy? It was *her* father, not theirs. She had even written to the Russian Embassy, who were more polite than any of the British organisations she had dealt with:

Dear Miss Lockhart,

The Embassy of the Union of Soviet Socialist Republics thanks you for your enquiry concerning your father. We regret that we are unable to assist you at the present time. However, we wish you luck in your research, and if the eventuality arises in which we may be able to help you, then we shall contact you forthwith.

Yours sincerely,

Dimitri Kirov

Two days after that letter had arrived, she had received a phone call from Kirov.

'I shouldn't really be telling you this, Miss Lockhart,' he had said, 'but you should keep trying – you *must* keep trying. The records you seek do exist, and one day they will be opened. Write to us every year, pester us by all means. One day it will work.'

'But Mr Kirov . . .'

The line had then gone dead.

Amy had little idea when 'one day' would be, but she supposed it would be a long way off. She *would* keep trying, as Kirov suggested, even if the truth about her father was somewhere in a vault in the middle of Moscow.

It seemed absurd. All she wanted was a few sheets of paper, and it seemed as if the whole world was stopping her.

Chapter Five

February–April 1944

MANY OF THEM had children, and they liked talking about them.

'You should see my son, he's a real knock-out – the girls love him!'

'I hope he treats them well!'

'My son speaks five languages.'

'My daughter is the most beautiful pianist.'

'Mine plays the violin.'

'Maybe they could play together!'

And it was comments like that which ended such conversations. To talk about the future, as though it would be milk and honey, was a sin. The women didn't want to embrace such thoughts, they just wanted to keep the images of their children frozen in their heads, putting them into a kind of inner present borrowed from years long since passed.

'How about you, Anna? Do you have any children?'

'I have a small daughter,' 10678 replied.

'What's her name?'

'Amy.'

'A pretty name! How old is she?'

'Six.'

'And where is she now?'

'In England.'

'In England?'

But this was when 10678 stopped answering. Even if she got Amy back, she would have lost all those years. How many was it now? Four. 'Dada in car' echoed from the past. What words did she know now? She'd be able to run. To go to the lavatory on her own. Read and write. Have some proper friends. Ask where her mother was.

The railway carriage was nearly empty, save for a few officials wearing swastika armbands over heavy suits. Pugh and Butcher were stretched out along the uncomfortable benches, attempting to get some sleep. They had left Hildesheim at five that morning, and by now, at two o'clock, all were exhausted. Worstead was sitting opposite, doing his best to read a book on the Valkyries. Evidently the German classes were of some use then, Lockhart thought.

Lockhart looked out the window. It was flat country-side, ploughed brown and dull, and made duller by the rain. The occasional village in the distance broke the monotony, but there was little else of interest. He felt that he should keep his eyes open, take in all he could, but he too was tired. They wouldn't be arriving in Danzig until tomorrow morning, assuming that all the lines were intact and there wasn't too much military traffic. Strasser had warned him that trains could wait for hours – if not days – on end, and they could count themselves lucky if they completed the journey in around twenty-four hours.

He folded his arms, closed his eyes, and leant his head back against the seat and the side of the carriage. His left hand felt a small bump inside his tunic. It was his letter to 'Hattie', along with his pass, whose few small pages confirmed his apparent treachery. Grey, the size of a passport, and emblazoned with the SS runes on its cover, his SS *Personalausweiss* confirmed that he was six foot tall, was born in London on 2 February 1913, had *Blutgruppe* O running through his veins, and held the rank of hauptsturmführer. The small photograph of him stapled to the inside front cover had been cut into a clumsy octagon, and stamped with two spread eagles. He could barely look at it.

The other item that he had been issued with was far more welcome: a Luger. However, Strasser had forbidden him any ammunition, so the pistol was not much better than a club. Strasser had said that was just as well, as the Luger's capacity to jam meant that it made little difference whether it had bullets in it or not. Naturally, Lockhart would have preferred to have been properly armed, but it was reassuring to be carrying a gun again.

The group had three nights in Danzig before visiting their first POW camp, Stalag XXa near Thorn, a few hours south. Except for Lockhart, the men found the break an opportunity to sleep with nearly every dockside prostitute. Even the normally abstemious Butcher had struck personal gold by finding a half-Japanese girl. Lockhart was in no mood to stop them, reasoning that a sexually satisfied Pugh, Butcher and Worstead would be a little more relaxed and malleable. Lockhart was slightly surprised that Worstead cheated on Beth, but he didn't ask. It made him think there was no Beth, that the whole story had been a lie, but then he knew that many men did not see whoring as cheating, especially away from home in wartime. Even if Lockhart had been the cheating kind, however, he would hardly have been tempted by what was on offer – mostly young Polish girls beaten and abused by German sailors, emaciated and riddled with God knows what.

Danzig was a grim place, Lockhart thought. Colourless and cruel, beaten down and cold, its soul broken. Sailors everywhere, green from malnourishment, and the occasional submariner, pasty from months under the Baltic. What had once been a proud port was being raped by the war, abused and spat out. It was fucked, thought Lockhart, there was no other word for it. Its women, its buildings, its pride – all were being gruesomely fucked until they were dry and cracked. Soon it would be empty, just a churning mass of black fog, steel, concrete and flesh. And sitting on top of this industrial corpse, its fluids seeping into the gulf – the drip tray under a stained dissecting table – would be the inevitable swastika, flapping wildly in a hollow gale.

The city made Lockhart feel nervous. It felt like the future, or how he imagined it – an absence of warmth and love, no freedom, and just a waiting, a longing even, for death. The future would be modern and yet barbaric, a new type of paganism, complete with its soot-rimmed chimneys and its new tortures. The human would be a unit, a statistical unit that would work to build the heartless dark glory of the Nazi corporate state, an eyeless beast that ate its own offspring, their sinews stuck in its bloodied and worn teeth as it gorged.

But Lockhart also felt nervous because of what he had to do. He had to face the friend, dressed as he was as the enemy, and persuade the friend to join him in wearing this vile costume. Surely it was impossible? But then maybe there were more opportunist Hulls, and maybe there were a few more Pughs who had kept their fascism tucked away under straw mattresses. Perhaps the latest recruiting leaflet, this one written by Pugh, might encourage them to come forward to declare themselves.

As a result of repeated applications from British subjects from all parts of the world wishing to take part in the common European struggle against Bolshevism, authorisation has recently been given for the creation of a British volunteer unit.

The BRITISH FREE CORPS publishes herewith the following short statement of the aims and principles of the unit.

1) The British Free Corps is a thoroughly British volunteer unit conceived and created by British subjects from all parts of the Empire who have taken

up arms and pledged their lives in the common European struggle against Soviet Russia.

2) The British Free Corps condemns the war with Germany and the sacrifice of British blood in the interests of Jewry and international Finance and regards this conflict as a fundamental betrayal of the British People and British imperial interests.

3) The British Free Corps desires the establishment of peace in Europe, the development of close friendly relations between England and Germany, and the encouragement of mutual understanding and colla-boration between the two great Germanic peoples.

4) The British Free Corps will neither make war against Britain or the British Crown, nor support any action or policy detrimental to the interests of the British people.

Published by the British Free Corps

Lockhart scrunched the leaflet up and threw it on to the floor of his grubby hotel room. It was the last night before they were due to leave, and he was lying on a stinking bed, still in his uniform, staring at the exposed masonry at the top of the wall.

His mind was churning with his priorities, priorities that conflicted, priorities that shifted. First, he had to find a trustworthy NCO, someone who could pass on the letter. That was essential – London had to know about the sarin, if Nicolas was telling the truth. And in the mean time, he had to find out more about the gas. What would it be stored in? How could it be destroyed, if at all?

He needed help, needed to find an expert, but who? And where would he find him? Perhaps London could help, but he couldn't assume any assistance from that direction.

Secondly, he had to go through the motions of recruiting traitors to serve in the unit – a prospect that revolted him, but something that had to be done if he was to stay alive. The deeper he became involved in the recruitment drive, the more London would get to hear, via POWs' letters back home, of his treachery. And if London thought he was a traitor, then they wouldn't believe his message about the sarin.

But he needed to find some more men. If he was going to do something about the gas, then he had to assemble a team, a body of men who would be able to join him. Men like Hull and Andreae, men who he could rely upon to be loyal to him. If he was going to have to deal with the sarin himself, if he was going to have to track it down and destroy it, then he couldn't do it alone.

And always there, at the back of his mind, was Anna. His thoughts kept returning to her, wondering where she was, how she was, *if* she was. The thought that he might be able to see her soon was almost too good – he didn't allow himself to believe that it would happen. The notion that Strasser would be true to his word was inconceivable, but there was surely some chance of it.

It was either the church or him, but Lockhart felt hot. He guessed it was him, as he vainly inserted a finger into his stiff collar, fruitlessly attempting to cool down. He was sitting in the front pew, next to Richard and his father. His leg was jigging violently up and down.

'Keep still, brother,' said Richard. 'You'll just make it worse.'

'Make what worse?'

'Your sweat.'

'Shit. Is it really—'

'Shh! You're not supposed to say that in here.'

'Shi—'

'You nearly said it again!'

'All right, all right. Pass me a handkerchief.'

Richard produced one from his breast pocket.

'I was saving this for the ladies,' he said, before handing it over.

'Your brother, the groom, takes precedence,' said Lockhart, bending down in the pew to wipe his face out of sight of the two hundred or so members of the congregation.

'This organist, even though he's ancient, is pretty good,' said Richard.

'Is he? I wouldn't know – you know I'm rubbish at the piano.'

'Who is he?'

'All I know is that he's some sort of music professor, Saunders or something.'

'Have you seen his tails?'

Lockhart looked over to the organ. Richard was right to remark on Saunders' tails – they were filthy, covered in assorted grey and white stains, moth-holes visible from ten feet away.

'I hope whatever lurgies that lie within the evil tails of Mr Saunders do not migrate to the chaste and ivory purity of your bride's dress.'

'Stop it,' said Lockhart, struggling not to get the giggles.

An usher, one of Anna's cousins, approached them.

'They're here,' he said.

'Thanks, Bill,' said Richard.

The news knocked the schoolboyish giggling out of the two brothers. Lockhart looked at his father, who gave him a slight nod and a wink. There was a sadness in his eyes. He would have wanted Ma here today, Lockhart thought, he would have wanted her here so badly. Lockhart and Richard walked up to where the priest was standing; he gave them both a reassuring smile. Saunders stopped playing, and for a few seconds Lockhart could hear the muted sounds of shuffling and coughing coming from behind him. He felt the top of his forehead moistening, and started to worry that he would look like a sweaty wreck.

Anna looked more sensational than he could have imagined. When he first saw her, arm in arm with her father, he felt an enormous sense of calm, an instinctive – rather than a merely rational – realisation that he was doing the right thing, that this was who he had always wanted to be with. The church, the world felt still, and to him there was no noise, just the sight of her graceful approach. His leg stopped shaking, although he had to force himself to stop worrying about the drop of sweat that he could feel crawling down from his forehead.

By the time she was standing next to him, he felt completely serene. His eyes studied every part of her veiled face, and she was doing the same to him. Every few seconds, an uncharacteristic bashfulness on both their parts meant they both looked away, but it was only for a few seconds. Neither of them really sang 'Guide Me, O Thou Great Redeemer', but just mouthed the words, all the time gazing at each other. Anna's father made up for them, singing both loudly and mostly in tune.

As the train drew in to Thorn station, Lockhart noticed that they had a welcoming committee on the platform.

'Looks as though we've got the commandant himself,' he said, addressing the men, who were buttoning up their tunics and replacing their caps. Although it was noon, both Worstead and Pugh looked tired, still recovering from the excesses of the previous evening. Butcher looked alert, having shunned the company of his half-Japanese conquest and turned in early. Lockhart, typically, had slept badly, although anxiety at what the afternoon might bring negated any exhaustion. The train drew to a halt, and the men got up, Lockhart putting on his overcoat and his cap. It looked bloody cold outside, judging by the NCOs shuffling their feet and rubbing their gloveless hands.

They stepped out on to the platform. A paunchy middle-aged Wehrmacht major came forward to greet them. He had a pleasant enough face, like that of the typical jolly butcher, thought Lockhart, albeit with a huge greying Prussian moustache.

'Hauptsturmführer Lockhart?'

'That's right.'

'Major Jüttner at your service.'

Lockhart was relieved to see that Jüttner gave him a normal military salute, and not a Heil Hitler. Lockhart saluted back.

'Thank you, Major,' he said. 'And these are Oberscharführers Butcher and Worstead, and Rottenführer Pugh.'

The men saluted the major in turn, Pugh and Butcher showing off their most fanatical Heil Hitlers, as if to make up for the traditional salutes of Lockhart and Jüttner, who was indicating that they should make their way to the cars at the station entrance.

'I must say, Hauptsturmführer Lockhart, I have been looking forward to meeting the legendary members of the British Free Corps.'

'I didn't realise we were legendary, Herr Major.'

'Oh but you are! It's quite something when one learns that the British are helping us to fight the Russians.'

Lockhart practised his idiot smile.

'Well, they are the real enemy.'

'Quite so! And I must say, the leaflets you sent last week have caused quite a stir in the camp.'

'Oh yes?'

'The prisoners seem to be looking forward to meeting you very much, although I doubt that your reception will be exactly friendly.'

'I didn't expect to be welcomed with open arms.'

'They will take some convincing. I'm afraid those leaflets have been put to an unexpected use.'

'Really?'

'Apparently the prisoners have tied them together with string and hung them in the latrines.'

Lockhart was delighted, knowing that Pugh, who was following close behind, would have heard every word of their conversation. It seemed appropriate that his crude propaganda should be put to an even cruder end. Lockhart did his best to sound serious.

'I'm sorry to hear that, Herr Major.'

'Ach! Never mind! You know how inventive prisoners can be.'

'Quite. So, has there been any interest at all?'

'We have had two approaches so far – you shall meet them after your address. They're not exactly the most upstanding members of the prison community, but I would have thought you would be interested in any potential recruits for your unit.'

'Very much so. I'm sure we'll be able to whip them into shape.'

'I'm sure you will – the SS has quite a reputation for turning men against their true natures.'

Lockhart saw at once the major's deliberate ambiguity. What did he mean? Was he in some way trying to get Lockhart to open up, to reveal that he wasn't a real traitor? Or was it just a comment on the renowned brutality of the SS? Act dumb, thought Lockhart, idiot smile.

'I'm sorry, Major, I don't know what you mean.'

Jüttner laughed.

'Oh Hauptsturmführer, I think you do! But never mind. Here are the cars. You come with me, and your men will go with mine. It's about a twenty-minute drive and then we shall have some lunch, before you address the prisoners at half past two. You must be hungry, yes?'

'Starving.'

He was indeed starving, but he had no appetite. The thought of speaking to four hundred British POWs – all men and NCOs, brutalised by the toughness of the camp regime – and preaching to them of the rightness of the Nazi cause against the Russians was too much. Jüttner and two of his junior officers had been asking him questions all the way through lunch, and Lockhart had allowed his subconscious to answer. Where was he from in England? Oxford. They had heard of Oxford – a nice town? Very nice, thanks. And what did he study there? Classics. The classics, eh? So you are a very educated man, Mr . . . sorry, Hauptsturmführer Lockhart. A little? Come, come – you are too modest! More wine?

The talk was too small, infinitesimal compared to the talk he had to give in quarter of an hour. Lockhart had knocked back a couple of large glasses of the major's adequate Riesling, grateful for its calming effect. He wanted to concentrate on Jüttner's questions, hoping to distract himself, but it was no use. Instead, his mind turned to his lecture. He knew he couldn't stop now, not when he would shortly be approaching the long climb out of treachery. He would have to invest a bit more before he could get out of debt.

Jüttner looked at his watch.

'Twenty-five past two, Lockhart! I think it's time we went over to the camp theatre. Are you ready?'

Lockhart smiled back.

'Oh yes, Herr Major, as ready as I'll ever be.'

'Good!' said Jüttner, wiping his mouth clean and standing up. 'Let's go then.'

Lockhart drained a third glass of wine and got up. He felt a little drunk, but he'd rather have been comatose. He flashed Jüttner an ironic smile.

'Well, this should be fun,' he said, dusting the top of his cap.

Jüttner grinned, causing his moustache to elongate. He might have looked a bit of an ass, thought Lockhart, but his eyes hinted at a deeper perspicacity. The grin dropped and he started speaking slowly.

'I'm sure you have a good reason for putting yourself through this, Lockhart. You are certainly no National Socialist, and you are certainly not the stuff of traitors.'

'I think you're being too clever, Herr Major.'

'Clever enough to recognise a cleverer man.'

With that, Jüttner came up very close to Lockhart.

'I'm not going to ask you why, but I cannot pretend I'm not curious. I don't think you would tell me, and besides, I wouldn't want to be burdened by your secrets. If, like me, you are trying to get through this war alive – at any cost – then you are a coward. Yes, Lockhart, I am a coward. That is why I am running a POW camp rather than being on the front line – I have come to accept my nature, and that is my problem. But if your reason is more noble than self-preservation, then I wish you all the luck in the world. I would like to help you, but as I say, I am a coward. Nevertheless, I will cheer you on, and perhaps one day, if you succeed, you might tell me your reason. Yes?'

Lockhart looked back at Jüttner, astonished. That the words that might give him some extra resolve should emanate from the commandant of a POW camp was bizarre, outlandish even.

'Yes, Herr Major,' said Lockhart quietly. 'I would like to tell you one day. I hope I'll be able to.'

Jüttner nodded, looking at Lockhart's face, studying it. 'I think you will. No, I'm sure you will.'

Lockhart and Jüttner walked across the frozen parade ground to the camp theatre. Pugh, Worstead and Butcher had fallen in behind them, and the plan was for the five men to stride up the central aisle and mount the stage, whereupon Jüttner would introduce them and Lockhart would give his talk, followed by Pugh. Lockhart had told Strasser that any speech by Pugh would be counter-productive, but Strasser had enigmatically replied that it was not up to him whether Pugh spoke.

As they neared the entrance to the theatre, Lockhart developed an uncontrollable urge to go to the lavatory.

'Major,' he said, 'I'm sorry about this, but I really must take a leak.'

'What – now?' said Jüttner.

'I'm afraid so.'

'Nervous, eh?'

'Maybe.' Lockhart shrugged. 'More likely to be the wine.'

Lockhart was aware of Pugh and Butcher tutting behind him.

'Very well,' said Jüttner with a smile, 'but don't be long – the men are eager to hear you.'

'Well, you know how it is with eager crowds,' said Lockhart. 'Keep them waiting – makes them more eager.'

'That's what I'm worried about,' said Jüttner. 'You know where it is?'

'It's just round the back of your admin block, isn't it?'

'That's right.'

'I'll see you in a minute.'

Lockhart walked off quickly. He certainly was nervous, but he would be damned if he was going to talk to a mob of British soldiers on a full bladder. Besides, he needed a minute or two to himself, time to collect his thoughts, take a few deep breaths. This was going to be hell, he knew it, but he told himself to think of Nicolas, presumably now dead, but who had died hoping that the man in the next cell would be able to continue what he couldn't finish. He reached the latrine, a predictably grim wooden affair with a badly tiled floor, six cubicles, and a basic metal urinal. What was not so predictable was the presence of a POW cleaning the floor.

The two men looked at each other. The POW must have been about forty, slightly overweight, and mostly bald except for patches of hair at his temples and remarkably bushy eyebrows. He was leaning on his mop when Lockhart walked in. His uniform indicated that he was a corporal. Lockhart had half a mind to use one of the cubicles, but he refused to be intimidated by the man's stare.

He walked past the man, stood at the urinal, unbuttoned his flies, and started to urinate. He could feel the corporal's eyes on the back of his neck. At any moment, he expected a push from behind, but none came. The corporal continued mopping the floor until Lockhart had finished.

As he turned away, Lockhart found the corporal standing right behind him. A little shorter than Lockhart, he was looking at him aggressively, clutching his mop so tightly that his knuckles were white.

'Can I ask you a question?' said the corporal, his accent East End, his tone indicating that Lockhart did not have much choice.

'Certainly,' said Lockhart.

'Are you one of them fucking idiots who thinks we should be fighting against the Russkis?'

'No,' said Lockhart. 'No, I'm not.'

'Then WHY,' said the corporal, his eyes bulging now, 'why are you wearing a fucking Kraut uniform then?'

'It's not as simple as that,' said Lockhart.

'Oh isn't it? We know all about you lot, you and your bloody leaflets. You know what we do with them? We wipe our arses on them, that's what we do, wipe our bleeding arses on them.'

This was getting nowhere, thought Lockhart. He was frustrated that he couldn't tell this man the truth; he would never believe him. He tried to walk away, but the corporal put his mop handle out in front of him, blocking Lockhart's exit.

'Ah, ah, not so fast, Hauptsturm-whatever-you-are.'

'You're making a big mistake,' said Lockhart.

'Am I?'

'Yes. I'm not what you think I am.'

'And what are you then?'

Lockhart sighed. He grabbed the mop handle with both hands, and attempted to push it out of his way. But the man's grip was very strong.

'You ain't goin' nowhere,' said the corporal.

'Are you refusing to let me go, Corporal?'

'That depends. I thought we could have a little chat.'

'Oh really?' said Lockhart, raising his eyebrows in feigned amusement. 'And what would you like to chat about?'

'I'd like to know—'

Lockhart gave an almighty shove towards the corporal. At first, his effort seemed to have worked, as the corporal was knocked back a few feet. But the man's reactions were quick, and he took a swing at Lockhart's stomach with the mop. The handle connected with Lockhart's ribs, causing him to bend double in agony.

'There,' said the corporal. 'Take that, you fucking traitor!'

Lockhart felt the handle smash down on his back. The pain enraged him, and head first, like a bull, he charged at the corporal, sending them both flying into the door of a cubicle. The door smashed open, and they fell on the floor at the foot of the lavatory pan, the corporal's head narrowly missing the rim.

Lockhart now had the advantage. Pinning his assailant to the ground with the mop handle, he forced him down, securing him to the floor. He didn't want to hurt the corporal, who was now attempting to struggle free with his legs.

'Just listen to me,' said Lockhart in between grunts. 'Just stop it for a moment, I'm not going to bloody hurt you!'

The corporal spat in Lockhart's face. Lockhart didn't wipe it off, for fear that the corporal would take advantage of Lockhart lessening his grip on the mop. He would have to tell him the truth, whether the man believed him or not.

'Just stop it!' yelled Lockhart, then, under his breath, 'I'm not a traitor! I'm not a bloody traitor.'

'Oh yeah? So who are you then? Robin fucking Hood?'

'No, my name's Lockhart, John Lockhart. I'm a captain – not a German one, but an English one, understand?'

The corporal briefly stopped struggling.

'I'm not some German stooge,' Lockhart continued. 'I'm just pretending to be.'

'Bollocks,' said the corporal, groaning under Lockhart's weight.

Christ, how could he convince him?

'Listen,' said Lockhart, 'I've got something in my pocket that will prove to you that I'm not a traitor.'

'What?' said the corporal.

'Do you promise not to move if I let go?'

The corporal stared at him from under his huge eyebrows. He nodded slightly. Lockhart released his grip gently, bracing himself for the man to go against his word. He didn't, so Lockhart stood up, wincing slightly at the pain in his ribs. He reached inside his tunic pocket, and fished out the letter to 'Hattie'.

'This letter,' said Lockhart, looking straight into the corporal's eyes, 'it's vital that it gets to London.'

The corporal looked confused, his eyebrows knitting together.

'What's in it?'

Lockhart looked at the man. Could he trust him? He didn't know, but he admired his pluck, his ability to take a risk – it wasn't every POW who would willingly assault an SS officer. Just as Lockhart was about to tell him more, he heard the sound of running footsteps approaching. It was now or never, thought Lockhart; he might not get such a good chance again.

'Just take it!' he said, holding the letter out to the corporal. 'Put your name on the bottom of it and send it off. Do it!'

The corporal eyed him suspiciously.

'Please,' Lockhart begged. 'You *have* to do this.'

He pushed the letter against the man's chest.

'Take it,' Lockhart hissed.

The footsteps got closer – they were now just outside the door.

The corporal obviously found something in Lockhart's demeanour that made him trust him, because just before the door burst open, he stuffed the letter inside his tunic. Two NCOs stormed in, their rifles at the ready, a puffing Jüttner behind them.

'What's going on here then?' panted Jüttner. 'Lockhart? Are you all right?'

'Quite so,' said Lockhart, mustering as much calm as possible. 'The corporal and I were just having a little chat.'

'So why's he on the floor? Did he attack you?'

Lockhart shook his head.

'No, Herr Major, I think he must have slipped.'

Jüttner came up to Lockhart.

'Lockhart,' he said, 'you don't have to protect this man. Corporal Stafford is a bad sort, a persistent troublemaker. That's why he's on almost permanent latrine duty. Isn't that right, Stafford? And stand up!'

Stafford stood. Jüttner went up to him and slapped him round the face, hard enough to make Lockhart and the two NCOs start.

'I think,' said Jüttner, turning to Lockhart with a broad smile under his Prussian moustache, 'you've found your first potential recruit, Hauptsturmführer Lockhart. Congratulations! It looks as though, with your blessing, Stafford's punishment will be to join you in Hildesheim.'

Lockhart looked at Stafford's bewildered face.

'Sorry about that, old boy,' he said.

At last, he thought, at last he had someone he could rely on. The team was taking shape.

Lockhart could hear the hubbub of the POWs inside the theatre, obviously excited, looking forward to a break in the arduous camp routine. Jüttner had assured Lockhart and his men that they would be safe – he had positioned thirty heavily armed soldiers in and around the building, and at the slightest physical disturbance they were under orders to shoot. Lockhart was both reassured and repelled by the idea. He did not wish to have the blood of innocently protesting POWs on his hands, and told Jüttner as much. Jüttner doubted that it would come to that, but Hauptsturmführer Lockhart should prepare himself for some heavy barracking.

The guards at the door parted to let them through, and they stepped into the dim light of a simple wooden hall. The only evidence that it was a theatre was the existence of a basic wooden stage at the other end. Although it was no more than seventy or eighty feet away, to Lockhart it looked like the same in yards, because in between him and it were four hundred faces – English faces worn thin by a bad diet and hard work – turning to leer at him, to mock him.

'Here they are!' one of the faces shouted.

He kept his eyes firmly ahead, rooted to the wall at the end. As he walked down the aisle, the men erupted into a cacophony of booing, jeering, hissing and shouting. Through the noise he could make out the occasional insult.

'Fucking turncoats!'

'Traitors!'

'Fuck off back to Berlin!'

'Nazi cunts!'

'Scum!'

This was worse than he had expected. Not that he had anticipated a reverential hush, but he thought the men might have been somewhat quietened by curiosity. But instead, fists and hands were being vigorously brandished, and the odd rotten vegetable thrown. Jüttner, despite his self-confessed yellowness, walked serenely through the throng, obviously a man accustomed to dealing with unruly POWs.

They mounted the stage and sat on some flimsy folding chairs. Lockhart felt Worstead looking across at him, presumably wanting a consoling glance, but he wasn't going to give it. He kept his gaze above the heads of the men, who Jüttner was now trying to pacify. He had no wish to catch any of their eyes, although he knew he would have to when he came to speak.

'Silence!' shouted Jüttner.

The order had no immediate effect.

'Silence! Or you'll have no food for the whole of tomorrow!'

The noise was still too great for the men to hear Jüttner's words, but a few of them had picked out the word 'food' and had correctly guessed what went with it. Word was relayed from neighbour to neighbour, and soon much of the noise petered out, leaving only the occasional 'You call what we eat food?' and 'You can fucking keep it!'

'Prisoners of war!' Jüttner began. 'You are here to listen to some of your fellow countrymen, who have made the bold decision . . .'

'Stupid bloody decision!'

'Treacherous decision!'

Jüttner let the few heckles go. Three years of running POW camps had taught him that men under the threat of a day without sustenance become extremely compliant. He continued, speaking over them.

'. . . who have made the bold decision to fight for what they think is right. For they have come to see that the real enemy is not Germany, but the Communists, who stand ready to take over the whole of Europe after Germany and Britain have exhausted each other. Some of you may have read the leaflets we distributed last week . . .'

'Leaflets, my arse!'

'Literally!'

Once more Jüttner ignored the heckling and the ensuing laughter.

'. . . and have seen that a new unit has been formed to help in the fight against the Russians. It is called the British Free Corps and already hundreds of men like you have joined up . . .'

'Not like me, mate!'

'Bollocks!'

'. . . to help counter the threat of terror from the east. So, I would like to introduce you to Haupt . . . Captain John Lockhart, the unit's commanding officer, who will now tell you about what you can expect if and when you decide to join him.'

Lockhart stood up. Rattled by the hostile reception, he could feel his legs shaking uncontrollably, hoping that the bagginess of his breeches would conceal his nerves. As he walked to the front of the stage, the jeering, whistling and booing picked up, reaching an intensity that drowned out his thoughts. He felt desperately alone, and badly wanted Anna, wanted to be back home with her in Oxford, by the fire in the drawing room, with Amy playing on the floor. It would have been bad enough if he believed what he was about to say, but that he didn't, that he knew that he was telling these men a pack of lies, made it so much worse. He agreed with his present tormentors, would have been the first among them to throw a rotten potato, the first to shout these fully justified obscenities.

He stood looking at them, almost in a trance. He forced himself to think of the bigger picture, of what he had to do. He thought of the future, of the best possible world, and knew that this was the step he had to climb to get there. Was he being brave? Perhaps he was, but he felt like a fool. He'd either get a decoration round his neck or a noose. He took a deep breath, scanning the hate-filled faces of his audience, forcing himself to look at each of them in turn, trying to show them in his expression that he was in pain, that he *had* to do this, that there was a good reason.

It worked. The abuse abated, the din reverted to hubbub. The emerging quiet gave Lockhart a sense of confidence, and yes, a small feeling of power. He hadn't won any sympathy, but perhaps a little pity. Fine, if that was what it was, then fine. Whatever it took. He needed them – even the worst of them, because those were the ones he was most likely to get. And he needed them more than they could know.

'Gentlemen . . .' he began.

'More than could be said for you!'

'Gentlemen.' His voice was a little louder. 'I'm not here to tell you how marvellous Germany is, or how the Third Reich is any better than Britain. I'm not here—'

'I bloody wish you weren't an' all.'

That resulted in much laughter, at which Lockhart smiled.

'So do I, my friend,' he said, a riposte which produced a reluctantly appreciative snigger from the audience. 'So do I. And I imagine you wish you weren't here either, enduring rotten food – some of which you have been kind enough to give me . . .'

This caused another laugh, a little louder this time.

'. . . freezing your nuts off every night under some flea-infested blanket, only to wake up in the morning to have to empty the latrines or break rocks. I bet you'd rather be somewhere where you had a healthy diet. Steaks. Fresh vegetables. Beer to drink. Some freedom. Women . . .'

Prolonged catcalls.

'. . . *plenty* of women. And some money in your pocket. Because that's the alternative I'm offering you.'

'Bribery! It's fucking bribery!'

'Yes it is,' said Lockhart. He knew that Jüttner, Pugh and Butcher would be astonished by this, but as he couldn't see them, he decided to pretend they didn't exist.

'Yes, it is bribery,' he repeated. 'And why not? Seems like quite a good deal to me. You get out of here, and spend the next several months in training. The war could be over by then! Don't worry about what's on all those leaflets you've seen – that's just propaganda stuff to keep the Jerries happy. The truth is, and this is important . . .'

Lockhart noticed that the men were nearly silent.

'. . . the truth is, this is a great way of getting out of your stalag. All right, so you have to wear a German uniform, but you would never fight the British. Maybe only the Russians, and let's face it, we didn't like the Commies much before the war anyway.'

Lockhart fancied that his audience went silent for a few seconds, but he knew that it must have been only a moment until a large sergeant in the front row stood up. He must have been forty, and his face was built like a chunk of Dartmoor granite.

'Mr Lockhart. My name is Colour Sergeant Coleman. I'd like to ask you a question.'

'Yes?'

'I may be a little slow, but it's my understanding that anybody who joins the enemy during wartime is committing an act of treason. Am I right?'

Lockhart didn't flinch. He had been expecting this one. Again he rolled with the punch.

'Technically, yes. But I would vouch for any man who joined that he had done so because he was cracking up in his stalag—'

'You're the one who's bloody cracked, man!' said Coleman.

Lockhart smiled. He wished he could tell the sergeant that he hadn't cracked, that he was as sane as the next man, that right now he was fighting for Britain harder than he had ever done before. But the way he had to go about it – Christ! What were the Germans thinking? Did they really believe they could sell the idea of a British SS unit? It was as impossible and as absurd as it had been when he had first heard about it. No, it was worse than that – it was cretinous, imbecilic.

'Let me assure you, Sergeant Coleman, I am perfectly sane. As I see it – if the Germans win the war, then being a member of the British Free Corps will put you in their good books. And if they lose, then you can turn round and say that you joined up to spy on them. Or you can say you wanted to join simply to sabotage the unit. Or you just wanted a laugh. No one can *prove* you were actually committing treason, so what have you to lose?'

'Our heads!' came a shout from the back.

Bang on, thought Lockhart, but he couldn't help but feel that maybe he had won one or two over. Taking into account the two who had already come forward, as well as Stafford, five recruits would be a good haul from just one camp. It would bring him tantalisingly close.

'I'd rather risk losing my head than losing my mind, locked up here,' Lockhart replied, earning himself a few ironic 'ooohs'. Although his audience still disapproved, he had at least managed to take off their edge, chip away at their outright enmity. He decided to close, knowing that to continue would be pointless.

'And that's all I have to say . . .'

Predictably huge cheers.

'. . . so if any of you are interested, then all you have to do is approach the camp authorities after this – in confidence, of course – and we will interview you—'

A deluge of abuse and jeering swamped his remaining words. He was surprised how quickly he had got used to it, and he let it flow over him. He took his seat, noticing Pugh and Butcher glaring at him, whereas both Worstead and Jüttner were allowing traces of smiles to form. Pugh especially looked furious, but Lockhart smiled back at him. The fool didn't realise that the only way to recruit men was to appeal to their less moral side, the side of them that was hungry. But Pugh would never understand, oh no, not Tom Pugh the speaker for the BUF, the former broadcaster for German radio, venting splenetic nonsense over the crackling airwaves. He would want to harangue them with bogus politics, which was what he was now standing up to deliver. Lockhart briefly closed his eyes. Pugh's words would undo his own, perhaps turn the minds of those who were tempted by an easy life at Hildesheim, restore them to decency. He leaned back and crossed his arms, looking down at the floor as Pugh started.

'. . . I speak to you as someone who has witnessed at first hand the evil of the Jew, the insidious march of international finance upon our people . . .'

Lockhart had thought that the prisoners could get no louder, but the racket must have trebled that of Lockhart's reception. Pugh continued, his voice getting more shrill, the Hyde Park Corner fanatic, the spitting demagogue.

'. . . Only Germany recognises the true enemy – the dragon of Asiatic and Jewish bestiality . . .'

This was too much for the POWs, who stood up, pelting Pugh with their remaining rotten vegetables.

'Fuck right off!'

'Sodding Nazi!'

'Get out of here!'

'Bugger off out of it!'

The guards, sensing a riot, unslung their rifles from their shoulders, which caused the POWs to stop shouting. Jüttner walked up to Pugh and whispered in his ear, whereupon a fuming Pugh sat down, resulting in a massive cheer from the floor. Lockhart swore that Pugh's port wine stain had turned several shades darker, almost throbbing and blistering with anger.

Jüttner held up his hands to silence the men.

'Stop this! I order you now to return to your huts in good order! Any troublemakers will receive four days in solitary! Guards – get these men out of here!'

The men filed out, not in good order, but then not in a rabble either. The occasional fist was raised at them on the stage, in addition to a few predictable expletives. Within a few minutes, the theatre was empty, many of the chairs overturned, the floor covered in the recruiting leaflets that had been placed on them. For a while, the five men on the stage savoured the stillness, reflecting on the past ten minutes of mayhem, each trying to work out what it had achieved. Lockhart spoke first.

'Well, apart from your contribution, Pugh, I thought that went very well.'

Pugh threw his cap to the ground.

'You take that fucking back!' he screamed. 'How dare—'

'Now, now, Pugh, calm down. It's quite obvious that they didn't like your speech very much—'

'What? They liked yours?'

'No – I don't think they did, but it was less badly received than yours.'

'You made a mockery of our unit! You made out that it was like going for a rest cure, a bleeding holiday! The BFC has a serious purpose—'

'It may well do, Pugh, but I thought our priority was to recruit, not to spout a load of BUF claptrap about Jews and finance—'

'It's not claptrap!'

Lockhart exploded. He couldn't be bothered to argue the toss with this halfwit, this ugly piece of excrescence.

'Oh just shut your bloody face! I'm bored with your opinions, bored with your little tantrums, bored with your nasty little prejudices. You're wrong, just plain *wrong*, full of half-baked crap chucked out by Oswald Mosley. So – just – shut – up. Got it?'

Lockhart knew that Pugh would retreat, a nasty little piece of vermin that could snarl and growl, but was incapable of standing up for itself unless it was in a pack. Lockhart's outburst appeared to have shocked Jüttner, Worstead and Butcher, who sat in stunned silence, waiting for him to continue his tirade.

But he was to disappoint them. Lockhart saw that this was a chance to take a little more control, to chair the meeting as it were.

'So what did you think, Herr Major?'

Jüttner's moustache elongated once more as he smirked.

'As you say, Hauptsturmführer, I thought it went as well as could be expected.'

Lockhart had reckoned upon Jüttner's ambiguity.

'So you thought it went badly then?'

'Not particularly. Perhaps you will get a couple more out of it. Who knows? Maybe you might get as many as four.'

Lockhart was enjoying the German's sarcasm.

'That many, huh?'

'That many.'

'How about you, Andrew?' asked Lockhart, turning to Worstead. 'What did you think?'

'Fine, John, I thought you did fine.'

Worstead's face looked slightly more porcine and shifty than usual. Lockhart couldn't establish whether his expression was approving or not.

'Just fine then?'

'Well, you could hardly say you won their devoted loyalty.'

'Heavens above! Did you really think I would? What did you think would happen? That we would just prance into a POW camp dressed in SS uniforms and say to them, "Come along now, chaps – fancy a bash at the Russkis?" and they'd all sign up, eager beavers to a man?'

Worstead scratched his earlobe, his eyes darting around, looking anywhere but at Lockhart.

'No, of course not . . .'

'Why don't you try next time?'

Worstead went silent.

'Butcher? What about you?'

'I don't have an opinion, sir.'

'Well there's a surprise.'

Lockhart turned back to Jüttner.

'So – can we see the three who have already shown an interest?'

'Certainly!' Jüttner replied. 'And let's see whether you struck a chord with any of today's audience.'

In addition to a very reluctant Stafford – but a Stafford who was given no choice by either Jüttner or Lockhart – four more POWs joined the British Free Corps that day. The two who had come forward before Lockhart's address were Privates Ian Malcolm and Duncan Allan. Both were in trouble – Malcolm, an utter simpleton, had been accused of allowing a cow he was looking after to miscarry; and Allan was in hot water for owning a radio, the defunctness of which did not appear to matter to Jüttner. Both were simple men, but seemed good enough for Lockhart to feel that he might be able to rely on them. Furthermore, Malcolm was a qualified lorry driver, a skill that might well be of some use.

Two actually came forward as a result of the speeches: Lance Corporal Bob Prain and Private Geoff Nichols. Nichols was another who had been forged from the same mould as Hull – tough, ignorant and an opportunist, which suited Lockhart's purposes. Lockhart's line of a better life outside the stalag had had an effect on Nichols, whereas Prain had volunteered because he was a fascist. With a face badly pockmarked with acne scars, Prain helped to fuel Lockhart's speculation that former members of the BUF hated the world because the world had issued them with facial disfigurements. Although less vile than Pugh and Butcher, Prain had a sinister presence, something in his cold manner that Lockhart found eerie. The chances of him helping were limited.

The BFC now numbered sixteen. Of these, Lockhart reckoned that about nine might help him, provided he had the right carrot. Worstead, Catchpole, Marston, Hull, Andreae, Allan, Stafford, Malcolm and Nichols – would these be enough? Catchpole was a dark horse, and he was still not entirely sure about Worstead. Pugh, Simpkin, Smith, Maclaren and Prain would never help him, leaving the question of Butcher. Butcher was a murderer, there was no doubt about it, but he had the respect of the men, which might prove invaluable. Should he let his repellence for Butcher's past stop him from trying to use him for good? Certainly not. To do good, Lockhart thought, one sometimes had to make a pact with the devil, albeit with fingers crossed.

At the next camp, Stalag XXId at Posen, their reception was very much the same – jeering and booing, catcalls and rotten vegetables. Lockhart's speech, a little more honed, went down slightly better, and Pugh's effort was predictably shouted down. The camp theatre was identical to the one at Thorn, and even the British faces in it, sallow and bony from years of captivity, looked like those at XXa.

As they walked out of that hall, closely jostled by the ranks of men on either side, Lockhart suddenly felt a sharp pain at the top of the right side of his chest. By the time he had reached the doors, he was struggling for breath, and was feeling faint and nauseous. Stumbling and rasping like an old man, he clutched his left hand over his chest, dimly noticing that his tunic felt warm and sticky. Just as he was realising that he had been stabbed, he collapsed outside, almost unable to breathe, coughing up blood into the snow.

She hadn't seen him in weeks, and she wondered whether he had guessed. He wasn't stupid was Carl, far from it, but surely there was no way he could have found out? God knows where he was, but she missed him, even if she was betraying him. That conflict had caused her hours of agonised confusion, until she had told herself that it was her fondness that was treacherous, and not her reporting of his loose tongue. Perhaps he was just too far away to visit her, but she had expected him sooner than this.

The last three weeks of Allied bombing had been horrific. Kitty's had miraculously remained unscathed, as had Leni's flat, but getting around the city was becoming almost impossible. Unstable piles of rubble, burnt-out trams and cars, burst water mains flooding the streets, and cordons around unexploded bombs – these were the daily obstacles for Berliners trying to go about their business. Goebbels was urging them to stay strong, to stay resolute, but Leni could see in her fellow citizens' eyes that they were near breaking point, or had already broken. Even the old dear in the flat below had eaten her beloved dachshund, the cooking of which had stunk out the entire building. What could Goebbels say to people like that, people who were being forced to eat their pets, their only source of comfort, and now sustenance?

And with the bombs came an increase in appetite for sex. Leni had noticed it not just at Kitty's, but even out on the streets, in bombed-out cellars, in the ruins. It was as if danger gave people the immediate desire to reproduce, she thought, to ensure the survival of their line. But who would want to get pregnant in this mess, bring up a new life in this hell? She could acknowledge the defiance in that, the will to live, but she thought it selfish, selfish to the child, and selfish to fellow Berliners for creating another mouth to feed.

With this sexual hunger came a new type of client at Kitty's. The functionaries, the 'notional' Wehrmacht officers, the pen-pushers and cowards – these were the ones who were visiting now, aware that the war was coming to them, that it was unavoidable. They were scared, she could see it in their eyes. Not for them the priapism of the conquering hero, back from Russia and wanting his upmarket fuck. These were the limp ones, the ones who wanted to feel bigger, to feel braver, to act like the true soldier. And they were hopeless – no amount of cajoling could get them to perform. Not that she minded – she still got paid, and she still filed her reports. Every time one of them couldn't get erect, her heart jumped. It was one notch, one gruesome defiling fewer.

Until he had arrived, the evening had been fairly typical. She had started at six, and by ten o'clock she had already been with three clients. One SS-brigadeführer, who had insisted on being sodomised by her whip handle, and two young Wehrmacht majors, who had wanted to take her together, but she had refused. They had told her that they had shared the horror of the battlefield, so could they not share the haven of her bed as well? Leni had been adamant, as would any of the girls at Kitty's – it wasn't safe, and besides, the SD forbade it, as the officers were less likely to be indiscreet in front of each other.

By half past ten, Leni was back downstairs, in Kitty's salon, enjoying a glass of champagne with a bewhiskered old general, who only came for the company, his ability to fornicate long since withered. The girls liked him, not only because he made no sexual demands, but also because he represented a father figure to some of them – in fact, most of them – always asking how they were, seeing if he could help them in any way. The snob in Kitty liked him too, feeling that the General offered a little Prussian Old World elegance that was all too lacking in the petit-bourgeois upstarts from the SS and SD. The General raised the tone, and anyone who made the girls happy made her happy.

When Strasser came in just before eleven, Leni's heart had leapt as it had not done since she had started seeing Paul at university. She excused herself from the General, and walked over to Strasser, doing her best not to show too much enthusiasm in front of the others. She kissed him on his cheek, noticing how cold it was.

'Brrr!' she exclaimed. 'You're freezing!'

'I know,' Strasser replied. 'I had to walk kilometres – no cars, nothing. Berlin is a fucking mess.'

'Why don't we go upstairs and warm you up?'

Strasser grinned.

'That's an excellent idea.'

They started kissing as soon as they were up in her room. In between kisses, Leni gently asked him questions about where he had been, what he had been doing, all the time feeling wretched that part of her motive was betrayal.

'Let's not talk just now,' said Strasser.

Initially, he was clumsy, not his usual self. He seemed unrelaxed and tense, and in too much of a hurry.

'Slow down, Carl,' she whispered. 'We've got all night.'

Her exhortation had worked, and he lay back, letting her do the work. She noticed that he had lost a little weight, not that there had been a lot to lose. She left it unmentioned and started kissing him on his thighs, smelling the ghost of

331

his damp breeches that now lay over the radiator. It wasn't an unpleasant smell – slightly manly in its way. He started groaning softly when she reached his groin.

They made love twice. Carl was conscientious, she noticed, always ensuring that she too was having a good time. He had played with her while they were waiting for him to rise again, and when he plunged in for the second time, it had made her climax. It felt good, a huge release from the tension, but after he had come, and they were lying back, she was saddened by the irony that the man who had temporarily released her from anxiety was the primary cause of it.

Not that she showed her depression as they lay next to each other, sharing a Lucky Strike – a present from another grateful officer. This was the part she hated most, the part that was her real job, not just her cover.

'So then,' she exhaled, 'how have you been?'

'Hassled, overworked and overtired.'

She passed him the cigarette.

'My poor Carl!'

'Ach, it's not that bad.'

'Hassled and overworked – it sounds terrible!'

'I'm no worse off than anybody else.'

Leni paused. Now was the time to ask him.

'How's your corps of British SS men getting along?'

From the ensuing silence, Leni knew that the question had gone down badly. She dared not look at him, instead listening to the crackle of the cigarette as he took a drag. She heard him breathe the smoke forcefully up to the ceiling.

'How do you know about that?' he asked, his voice shrouded in a menace she had never heard before.

'You told me about it just after New Year's Eve. Remember? You were drunk, very drunk. We were down in the cellar because there was a raid, and you told me then.'

Another silence, another crackle, another jet of smoke.

'I did, did I?'

'Yes, you did. You told me it was a complete waste of time, or words to that effect.'

'Then I must have done.'

Leni relaxed a little. The most dangerous part was over. She had half expected him to turn over and strangle her.

'So, how's it going?' she asked. 'You don't have to tell me if you don't want to. I'll understand.'

Half of her was begging him to keep quiet, the other half itching for him to reveal all, to tell her what he had been doing. *They* had been most interested.

'Pretty much as before,' he replied, handing back a severely shortened cigarette. 'It's a nightmare, a bureaucratic nightmare.'

'Why's that?'

She regretted asking him straight away; she didn't want to ask too many questions, arouse his suspicion.

'You want to know *why* it is a bureaucratic nightmare, or *how* it is a bureaucratic nightmare?'

Typical Carl. She giggled a little, adopting a girlish air. 'You pedant! How, of course!'

'It's a bureaucratic nightmare because one way or another I have to contact every official in the Reich asking his permission to send my men around the country. I have to phone them, telegraph them, write to them, pay them, and in return they send me pieces of paper that I have to send to other people in order to get other pieces of paper. *That*, I can tell you, is a fucking nightmare. I'd rather have your job.'

She giggled again.

'I doubt that! I don't see you enjoying the charms of middle-aged Wehrmacht officers.'

Strasser nodded to himself.

'You know, I think you're right – I'd rather have my job.'

Another silence. Leni let Carl break it.

'Anyway, since you've asked, my little unit is doing quite well. I even have an officer.'

'An officer?'

'That's right. A British captain. He's a very educated man, very intelligent.'

'So why has he joined up?'

'What? Are you saying that an intelligent person wouldn't join up?'

'No! I was just wondering what would make a British officer join an SS unit.'

'I'm not going to tell you that, Leni!'

'Will you tell me if I guess?'

'No!'

His voice had once more turned harsh. She let it go. That was enough for now. She put the cigarette out in the ashtray perched on his chest.

* * *

'As far as I can tell it's a load of bollocks.'

Lockhart couldn't thank God enough that the culprit had so far remained undetected. If he had been apprehended, he would doubtless have been executed for attempting to kill an SS officer, perhaps even hanged on the parade ground, left to rot in full view of the camp population. But Worstead had told him that the commandant, despite exhaustive punishments, searches and enquiries, had drawn a blank. What Lockhart kept to himself was his clear memory of the man's face in that scrum, a young face masked with hate and malice. Was the Hauptsturmführer absolutely sure he had not seen his assailant? An identity parade, perhaps that would help? No, said Lockhart, all he could recall was the crowd and then the pain. He was sorry, but there it was.

'What's all this crap about daffs?'

His right lung, which had been punctured, had collapsed by the time he got outside the camp theatre. The commandant had been quick to realise what had happened, and had summoned the stalag's two doctors. Luckily for Lockhart, one of them, a one-eyed veteran of the Russian front, had dealt with such a wound many times before. Ripping open Lockhart's tunic, he inserted a small tube attached to an 'underwater' drain – a bottle half full of water – into the wound, allowing the excess air to be released from around the lung, the air which had caused it to collapse. Lockhart was then taken to Posen hospital, where the wound was cleaned up and sutured, leaving a new tube and drain in place. They told him that the lung would fully reinflate after a few days, although he should spend at least a fortnight convalescing.

'There ain't no bloody code in this.'

Lockhart ordered the others back to Hildesheim, although he had Stafford stay with him in Posen. It was the day after the operation, and he was still lying groggily in hospital, with little to do but reflect. That he was actually hated enough for someone to want to kill him came not as a surprise, but certainly as a shock. He knew he had done wrong, at least in the cold eyes of his would-be assassin, but he was doing if for a reason that was above reproach.

'You'd better tell me what this is about, otherwise I ain't gonna send it.'

It wasn't just for Anna and Amy. Neither was it just about sarin. Nor just for Manoli and the other *andartes*. And nor was it just for King and country, nor Oxford, nor archaeology, nor civilisation, nor revenge, no, not even just for love, because he knew that that alone wasn't enough. It was for all of those things, and also for none of them. Instead, he wanted to save as many lives as possible, to make amends, to repair the damage he had done. Atonement, he thought, he needed to atone.

'I said – sir – I ain't gonna send it unless . . . Can you hear me?'

He coughed spasmodically, his damaged lung flaring with pain. He thought of the young man's face coming towards him, the vicious little movement of the man's wrist, the flash of dull metal and his own helplessness as he was pushed on towards the theatre doors. He remembered the pain as he lay on the ice and snow outside, the seemingly distant shouts around him, and the strange sounds his chest was making, filling his head with agony and the sound of his own husky moaning. He had thought he was going to die, and he had fought hard against any temptation to give up, even then knowing that this was the true turning point, the moment at which his rehabilitation began.

'Are you all right? Shall I get one of them nurses?'

He turned slightly on to his side. The movement of the tube as he did so caused him some pain, as they had told him it would, but it was nothing compared to the experience of suffocating in the open. He took deep breaths of the sterile hospital air, looking around the room as he did so.

'Can you hear me?'

The voice was Stafford's, and Lockhart was only just beginning to register it. He must have been semi-comatose.

'Yes I can,' Lockhart croaked. 'What do you want?'

'I asked if you wanted one of them nurses.'

'No thanks, Stafford, I'm fine.'

'Good. In that case, perhaps you can tell me what this bleeding letter is about, and why you've made me stay here.'

Lockhart looked at Stafford's hands, which were clutching the letter to 'Hattie'. Shit.

'Why haven't you sent it?'

'My old mum told me never to sign something I didn't understand.'

At least the man had a sense of humour. But before he told Stafford anything, he needed to know more about him.

'What did you do before the war, Stafford?'

Stafford looked at the floor shiftily.

'It's all right,' said Lockhart, sitting up slightly. 'This isn't an interrogation – I'm just curious. I don't suppose you were as good as gold.'

Stafford laughed a little.

'Er . . . no, sir.'

'What did you do then?'

'Er . . . perhaps I may have done a little bit of thievin', sir.'

'Thieving, eh? What sort of thieving?'

Stafford shrugged.

'Well, you know how it is, sir, the odd house here and there.'

'I'm sure I don't, Stafford. Were you ever locked up?'

'Pentonville, sir. Four years. Breaking and entering.'

'How did you get caught?'

'I was shopped by someone I thought was a mate. The coppers were waiting for me, right in the middle of this rich bird's living room.'

'And what happened to this mate of yours?'

Stafford rubbed his hands together.

'I don't think I want to answer that question, sir.'

Lockhart let it go. It was none of his business. Stafford was a thief, but a thief with his own sense of honour. There was no doubt that treachery revolted him – hence his attacking Lockhart in the latrine.

'You're a good man, Stafford.'

'No one's ever told me that before!'

'Well, I think you are. I need someone to trust. Can I trust you, Stafford?'

Stafford sat up straight.

'That you can, sir.'

'Good. And I want you to trust me as well.'

Stafford paused. It was clear that Lockhart wasn't going to win him over until he had told him what was in the letter, and why he had made him stay with him.

'All right, I'll tell you why I wanted you here. I want you to help me.'

'Help you? How?'

'I need a team, Stafford, a team of decent men who can help me achieve something desperately important.'

'Do what?'

'Perhaps it's best if I told you what's in that letter.'

Stafford's reaction was predictably one of shock. Lockhart had first explained how the code worked, and together they decrypted the letter to reveal its message.

'What is this . . . this sarin gas, then?' Stafford had asked.

Lockhart had told him all he had learned from the tapping in the cell.

'And what do you intend to do about it?'

'Well,' said Lockhart, 'I can't just wait for London to get back to me. "Mitt" could be anything – a town, a camp, a factory, even the name of a company. That's going to be hard to find out, because it's bound to be a secret. In which case, I'll need to establish which department in the German bureaucratic behemoth—'

'What?'

'Sorry – it's a sort of enormous beast – I'll need to find

out which department would be responsible for it. And then I'll need to get access to that department.'

'How are you going to do that?'

'I don't know,' Lockhart replied matter-of-factly. 'But the fact that I'm now a fully fledged SS officer might help me.'

Stafford breathed out with a 'Jeezus Christ'.

'Quite,' said Lockhart. 'However, something I *can* do is to get a good body of men together. I need a team, Stafford, a bunch of decent blokes who can help me if and when I manage to find out where the sarin is, let alone how to deal with it. That's the real reason why I'm recruiting. At the moment, I'm not sure that I have enough men I can rely on. Some of the ones we've got are a real bunch of sods, although a few of them are all right – either in trouble like you, or some who've just wanted to get out of their camp.'

Stafford was silent for a moment.

'An' what do you want me to do?'

Lockhart smiled. It looked as though he had won him round.

'You can be my eyes and ears, as well as my link man. You'll be getting lots of letters from 'Hattie' soon, I hope.'

Stafford looked chuffed.

'She sounds dead classy to me, sir.'

Lockhart laughed.

'I assure you she's not. The last time I met her she had grown a moustache.'

His lung healed quickly, quicker than the doctors had predicted.

'You're in good shape,' he was told. 'Most men would have needed another week.'

Such was the legacy of his daily running and his SOE training. Before the stabbing, Lockhart could hold his breath for up to four minutes, an ability that had won him many drinks in the bar at Arisaig. Nevertheless, even though the drain had been removed after ten days, it still hurt when he breathed in sharply, and he knew that he would have to take it easy.

On the afternoon of the eleventh day, Stafford had arrived in his room, his expression anxious.

'What's the matter, Stafford?'

The corporal handed Lockhart a folded piece of paper. Lockhart opened it. It was a telegram from Strasser.

URGENT
FOR IMMEDIATE DISPATCH
From Hpt Strasser, St Michael, Hildesheim
To Hpt Lockhart, Posen Military District Hospital

Message starts

+ + + + REPORT BACK AS SOON AS POSSIBLE TO ST MICHAEL STOP RECRUITING ON HOLD STOP NOTIFY DATE OF RETURN IMMEDIATELY STOP STRASSER STOP + + + +

Message ends

2/3/44 12:18

'Shit,' said Lockhart, leaning back.

'What's the matter?'

'Shit, shit, shit, shit.'

'What, sir?'

'There's to be no more recruiting. And no more recruiting means I'm stuck with what I've got.'

He was an ugly little man, and Leni didn't like him on first sight. Still, she had her orders, and they had told her that she must work with him. Would she have to sleep with him, she asked? No, they said, keep this one away from the bedroom. He's a great catch, this one, they said, make sure you play him right. He'd approached them direct, they told her, approached them via the Swedish merchantman in Danzig. Apparently, he used to be a real Nazi, but now he had gone against them. They had treated him badly, he had told them, lied to him, put him in some punishment unit, and now he wanted to turn against them.

They met at the Café Vaterland, a huge nightclub in the centre of Berlin. It was crowded, and they took a table in the corner and talked about how they would work together. She made it clear that all information would go through her, and then onwards. He was under her command, and he must remember that, do as she said. He was prickly about that, but she insisted, saying that they could just as easily drop him, throw him to the wolves. This was the only way he had to save himself, and she was now his lifeline.

* * *

It was a small victory, but an important one. Asking Strasser to refrain from smoking for the sake of Lockhart's newly healed lung had gone down badly, but Strasser had had to concede.

'But how can my smoking harm it?' he asked, sitting behind his desk. Lockhart noticed that a portrait of Himmler had appeared on the wall.

'It makes me cough, and when I cough, it damn well hurts.'

'But you smoke yourself.'

'Not often, and not at the moment I don't.'

'All right,' said Strasser, 'I shall refrain from offending your poor lung.'

Sarcastic sod, thought Lockhart. He had half a mind to stab him in the chest, see how he liked it. Instead, he replied sincerely:

'That's much appreciated, Carl. Thank you.'

Strasser started sifting through the papers on his desk.

'Have you got another memorandum for me?' Lockhart asked.

'I have indeed. It's from Berger. You'd better read it.'

From:	SS-Obergruppenführer Gottlob Berger, Head, SS Hauptamt
To:	SS-Hauptsturmführer Carl Strasser, British Free Corps
Date:	1 March 1944
Subject:	Recruitment

Strasser,

The news of the stabbing of Hauptsturmführer Lockhart troubles me greatly.

It occurs to me that your use of existing members of the BFC to recruit POWs is ineffective, and we should instead be concentrating on coercing prisoners who are presently confined in POW punishment camps.

Therefore I see no need for your tactic of persuasion. It is clear that many of those who have joined are either in trouble, or are sympathetic to our struggle.

I order you to recall Hpt Lockhart as well as any other BFC members who are recruiting in POW camps. I do not wish to see any corpses returning to Hildesheim.

I further order you to train the unit into an effective fighting force. Any further efforts at recruiting will be made by Sturmbannführer Vivian Stranders of Section D of the Germanic Administration. He will contact you shortly.

Heil Hitler

Berger

'Who the hell is Sturmbannführer Stranders?' asked Lockhart.
  'Stranders is a piece of shit.'
  'But he sounds English.'

'He is English.'

Lockhart looked at Strasser, his eyes requesting the other man to continue.

'I don't know much about him, apart from the fact that he's a complete swine. He was brought up in Birmingham, I think, his father was some sort of music professor. He came over here in his twenties to teach English, and then he returned to fight – on your side – in the last war, in the Royal Flying Corps. Some time after that, he set up a business in Düsseldorf of all places, importing motorbikes. However, I don't know when, he was locked up in France for a while for spying. Upon his release, he came back here, setting himself up as a journalist and academic of sorts, as well as ingratiating himself with the Nazi party. He became a professor, I believe, and he's also become a German citizen. Quite a character.'

'Quite. But why do *you* find him such a shit?'

'Stranders styles himself as a so-called expert in British affairs, a position that gives him a unique opportunity to interfere and get in my way. Unlike me, he's a politician, not a soldier, and now I see that the conniving little maggot has wriggled his way into Berger's affections.'

'What can he do?'

'I'm worried that if he turns up, half the men we've recruited will want to go back to their POW camps. However, with any luck, Stranders will stay in Berlin. He likes the high life too much to come out to a backwater like this.'

'Let's hope so,' said Lockhart, meaning it.

'And as you can see from Berger's memorandum, this puts an end to your recruiting drive.'

'*Your* recruiting drive, Strasser.'

Lockhart hadn't missed the subtle ploy of blame transferral going on. Berger had referred to '*your* tactic of persuasion' in his memorandum, enshrining on paper that it was Strasser's idea, not his own. And now Strasser was doing the same to Lockhart, suggesting that the recruiting drive was the Englishman's initiative. So much for Strasser not being a politician.

'Our recruiting drive, Lockhart.'

'*Your* drive. My life on the line.'

'Whatever. Anyway, I now want to talk about training . . .'

'Haven't you forgotten something?'

'Forgotten what?'

'Our deal.'

'Deal?'

'Yes, our deal. We agreed that I would be allowed to see my wife.'

'But I recall that you had to recruit nineteen men before that would happen. And now that recruiting has been put to a halt, I'm afraid the deal's off.'

'What?'

'You heard me, Lockhart. No deal. Don't blame me, blame Berger. You read the memo.'

'That's hardly fair!'

'Life isn't fair, especially in wartime. You should know that.'

'Oh spare me the clichés, Strasser! I damn nearly got killed in Posen, and I recruited five men from one camp alone. I'd say I deserve to see her, even though I haven't hit your magic number.'

Strasser was tapping his pen on the desk. It was a habit that Lockhart was beginning to find infuriating. He didn't want to plead, but somewhere beneath Strasser's icy casing, there must lie a small pocket of warmth. He knew he had to stay calm, not get too heated.

'I'm not going to beg you, Strasser, I'm just appealing to your better nature. So I haven't reached your figure, but I'm pretty confident that I would have done had I not been called back. Look at it from my point of view. I'm the one who's kept his side of the deal – it's your side that's broken the ground rules. And in most civilised contests, the side that breaks the rules is the side that is judged to have lost. The other side is then awarded a walkover. In this instance, the walkover is my being allowed to see my wife. I can't understand why it should be such a problem.'

Strasser got up and strolled to the window, and looked out on to Hildesheim. He had clasped his hands behind his back, and was standing quite still. Lockhart could hear him breathing, taking exaggerated inhalations, as though he was trying to compose himself.

'I hear what you're saying, Lockhart,' Strasser stated matter-of-factly, still looking out the window, 'and, of course, what you say is fair. I suppose I should not be surprised that you are so keen to see your wife, but your insistence, to the point of risking your life and hers, I do find surprising. Your wife is alive and well – you have read that with your own eyes. Is that not enough?'

'So speaks a bachelor, Strasser.'

'Perhaps you're right. But I'd just like to remind you that my threat still stands. If you do not co-operate, then she will be killed.'

Strasser turned round and continued, looking Lockhart in the eye:

'Furthermore, I will also have you shot if you attempt to sabotage the progress of this unit. Any talk of plans or plots – even the scantiest of rumours – will result in your execution. I'm sure it has occurred to you to try something, mount some sort of riot, and I am telling you now that any such move would result in your death.'

Lockhart did his best not to swallow. He held Strasser's eye, trying to stare him out.

'I'm not plotting or planning anything, Strasser. You know that would be madness with my wife's life on the line. Don't you see that it's her that I am loyal to? And so long as she's all right, then I will do nothing to risk her life. After all, that's why I'm here, and not in an unmarked grave in Crete.'

Strasser averted his eyes and sat down.

'Good,' he said quietly. 'Good. I'm glad we've got that settled.'

For a while, the two men sat in silence, Strasser going through one of his stacks of paper, Lockhart looking at the measly coal fire. Strasser's warning was not surprising in itself, only surprising because he felt the need to give it. But there was still movement in Strasser, still the ability to horse-trade. There would be no harm in asking. Lockhart cleared his throat, an action that pained his lung.

'If,' he said, croaking slightly and then clearing his throat once more, 'if I knock this unit into shape, *then* can I see my wife?'

Strasser sat back and smiled.

'You don't give up, do you, Lockhart?'

'You know me.'

'So you're suggesting a new deal?'

'That's right.'

Strasser rubbed his jaw, as though appreciating a good shave.

'What do you mean exactly by "knock into shape"?'

'Get it into a condition that satisfies the high military requirements of the Waffen-SS, of course.'

Strasser looked tickled by the idea.

'All right, Lockhart. That's a deal. And I shall be the judge of whether the unit has reached the required standard.'

'Agreed.'

'And I am allowed to break the rules at any time.'

'Agreed.'

Lockhart knew he was in no position to negotiate any further.

'Good,' said Strasser. 'Those terms suit me fine.'

Strasser's grin looked so untrustworthy, so false, that Lockhart could have laughed.

'Now then,' said Strasser, 'bring your chair up and study this training schedule I have devised.'

Lockhart drew up his chair. As he did so, Strasser rifled through the papers on his desk.

'Aha!' Strasser exclaimed. 'Here it is!'

'Here's what?'

'Another letter from your wife. I'm sorry – I almost forgot!'

Strasser passed the letter over. Lockhart's hands trembled slightly as he ripped it open.

My darling,

They came today and told me I could write to you again! I hear that you are in a POW camp, and that you are doing well, behaving yourself – most un-you! The thought that you are alive takes away so much of the pain. I am praying for you, praying that you are well, praying that we will be together again. I wish you were allowed to write to me, but just the knowledge that you will be reading these words gives me SO MUCH comfort. Have you heard from Ma and Pa about Amy? Any news at all?

I was thinking of Ephesians the other day, our lesson, and the part that goes we are to be 'one flesh'. I can't tell you how much I feel that. Whatever happens to us, there will always be US.

With all my love,

Your Anna XXX

Once again, typed – Lockhart smelt a rat. But Ephesians, though. If it was a fake, then who the hell knew about Ephesians?

* * *

Weighing only 6lbs 4oz, Amy Lockhart came out easily, although her father had conformed to the stereotype of the nervous father-to-be, pacing up and down outside the delivery room.

'Congratulations Mr Lockhart,' said the nurse as she came out. 'You're the father of a baby girl.'

It was absurd, but the first thing he could think of was how much the nurse reminded him of one of Richard's uglier ex-girlfriends.

'Can I see her?'

'Not yet. We're just getting her cleaned up. We're not used to having the father around. They're normally having a drink, you know.'

'Ah. I see. Sorry about that. It's just that I have a very modern wife . . .'

'You don't have to apologise to me! Why not go to her room, and we'll bring them both over soon?'

He did as he was told. It was only when he sat down that the hugeness of the moment finally struck him.

'I don't believe it,' he said out loud. 'I'm a father. I'm actually a father!'

He stood up and looked in the mirror. Wagging a finger at himself, he addressed his reflection.

'Now listen here, young man, you've got to grow up now, take responsibility, that sort of thing . . .'

And then he stopped, thinking himself silly. Instead, he paced round the room, smacking his palm with his fist, letting out the occasional whoop of delight. He hadn't expected to be so happy. Terrified, certainly, but not happy. It was a deep happiness, a totally wholesome joy, a sense of achievement that made everything else he had done feel so trivial, so childish.

'Are you quite all right?'

It was the nurse again, giving him a teasing smile.

'Er, yes, absolutely fine, thanks.'

'Because there are a couple of people coming down the corridor to see you.'

Lockhart bolted out of the room to see Anna being wheeled in a bed, a small bundle in her arms. She looked exhausted, but, like him, Lockhart thought she looked deeply, fundamentally happy.

Neither of them knew what to say; instead Anna merely tugged down some of the swaddling to reveal their daughter's face.

'Say hello to your father, Amy Virginia Rose,' said Anna.

'Hello, Amy Virginia Rose,' said Lockhart, bending down to kiss the crown of the dark head above the screwed-up little face. 'How are you today?'

'She says it's been a fairly eventful one, John Alexander Lockhart.'

'Has it indeed, Anna Virginia Lockhart?'

'And her mother says she is so proud of her little family.'

The words brought a tear to his eye.

'Little family,' he repeated. 'I've got a little family.'

He leant over and kissed Anna, promising, like all fathers, that whatever happened, these were the only people who mattered; that there would be no price too high to ensure their safety.

*　*　*

If the next six weeks were hellish for Lockhart, they were doubly so for the men. The new training programme Strasser had devised was as tough as anything Lockhart had been put through at Arisaig. The men found the going deeply unpleasant.

The least popular part of the day was the hour-long gymnastics session at six o'clock in the morning. Although the fitter members of the unit, such as Hull, Butcher, Catchpole, Malcolm and Lockhart himself, were up to the exertions, for the first two weeks the others were a coughing and collapsing mass of physical incompetence. But they improved, because the physical trainer Strasser had unearthed – a limping veteran of the war in Africa – was fearsome and took no nonsense.

The route marches and the cross-country runs were no fun either, especially as they were made to carry full kit, including unloaded rifles and many rounds of blank ammunition. Strasser had even got hold of a heavy machine gun, a weapon that required at least two men to lift it, let alone run with it. The men, especially the fascist element, complained bitterly and often, distressed that their easy life of lectures and language classes was over.

It was during the runs and the marches that Lockhart saw the opportunity to prove himself in the eyes of the men, *his* men. His lung was in good shape, and he had quickly regained the same level of fitness he had enjoyed in Crete. Thus he was able to help the men as they sweated kilometre upon kilometre through the cold Saxon drizzle, encouraging them, coaxing them, cajoling them, and, of course, yelling at them. He also took his turn carrying the machine gun, at one point even relieving Pugh, much to Pugh's surprise.

The sessions of unarmed combat and boxing seemed relaxing in comparison. Lockhart found that the only men with whom he had any difficulty were Hull and, more surprisingly, Pugh, who Lockhart found had the vicious tactics of a seasoned street fighter. Hull, who had been a professional strongman, could take on anybody, even three at a time. His favourite trick, which won him many drinks at the Rosenstock, was to tie a rope around his neck, leaving an end on each side dangling free. He then challenged any two of the men to pull on the rope in an attempt to make him pass out. So strong were Hull's neck muscles that nobody succeeded, not even Strasser and Lockhart. Such sessions started to build up a reluctant camaraderie amongst the men, even if there was still a strong antipathy between the two camps.

Although the ideological lectures continued, many of them were replaced with classes on weaponry. The unit was taught how to use nearly every German weapon in existence, from flame-throwers to anti-tank weapons, as well as learning how to use explosives and lay mines. Their instructors were somewhat surprised by Lockhart's familiarity with most of the weapons, with which he had trained at Arisaig. He merely gave the instructors a wink, and told them not to be so nosy. He had to admit to himself that the level and intensity of training was impressive, and he could see why the Waffen-SS was such a capable fighting force, notwithstanding the belief of its soldiers that they were members of an elite – almost holy – order, who were willing to die for their Führer.

The unit was also taught basic fighting tactics, such as methods for taking machine-gun posts, setting ambushes, clearing buildings, dealing with snipers and using bayonets. In all these activities, Lockhart set an example, taking firm control of the men when they were practising such engagements. By this stage, it was becoming evident that the men were even enjoying themselves, as the effects of physical fitness combined with a sense of purpose put a sparkle into their once-tired eyes.

Nevertheless, it was not as though the unit had completely transformed. Arguments and fights still broke out, the cause usually being a difference of political opinion fanned by alcohol. It was also clear that Maclaren, Pugh, Simpkin, Smith and Prain – the fascist cell – were hardly Lockhart's biggest fans, a fact relayed to him by Worstead. Not that Lockhart needed telling, but he was grateful to Worstead, who had also told him that the others – Catchpole, Marston, Hull, Andreae, Allan, Stafford, Malcolm and Nichols – all thought the Hauptsturmführer a 'top bloke'. This was excellent news, thought Lockhart, because including Worstead, he now had a core of nine men who were showing loyalty to him. And what of Butcher? Lockhart asked Worstead. He was a mystery, said Worstead; one just couldn't tell what he was thinking inside that black-eyed skull.

The man who was outstandingly happy was of course Strasser, who was firing off memoranda twice a week to Berger, telling him that the unit was in fantastic shape, and would be a useful addition to any front line. Berger's replies were noncommittal, revealing a lack of interest that annoyed Strasser. As far as Strasser could tell, the efforts of Sturmbannführer Stranders were ineffective, and for the time being, Stranders had come nowhere near Hildesheim.

By the end of April, things were going well. The unit was approaching a level of competence that Strasser found satisfactory, and he told Lockhart that at this rate, it would not be long before he was allowed to see Anna. Strasser would not say when, despite Lockhart's insistence; only that it would be soon. Inwardly, Lockhart was delighted too – he was building up a cadre of loyal men, a team that he might be able to put to good use. What he really needed, however, was to hear from 'Hattie', but she had been stubbornly silent.

It was nearly lunchtime, but Brigadier Watkins still had another box file to get through. Marked 'Belsize', it was a collection of the past fortnight's material sent to the fictitious address in Belsize Park. The box file felt light, almost empty. Good – he would soon be able to get something to eat.

He opened the file and was relieved to see that it contained only one envelope and a small strip of paper, upon which was typed a short message.

IN RENEGADE UNIT BRITISH FREE CORPS IN HILDESHEIM HAVE LEARNT NERVE GAS SARIN HELD IN PLACE STARTING MITT

D/H 315

Watkins knew only too well the identity of D/H 315 – Lockhart. So the traitor was alive, was he? Alive and well in Germany, no less! The last he'd heard from Cairo was that the bugger was acting as some sort of German stooge in Crete. There was no way that Watkins was going to believe this tosh. It was so manifestly some Abwehr game that it did not even dignify a response.

He uncapped his fountain pen, his famous Waterman that contained only green ink. On the strip he scribbled:

N.A.R.

He then initialled this with a large 'W'. He replaced the strip in its box, shut the box, and put it on top of all the others. No action required, thought Watkins. Lunch was what was required, and straight away.

June 1941

He hears the news on the radio a few minutes after he wakes up. It is a Sunday morning, and the weather is appropriately fine in Berlin, for it is a happy day, a day that will reaffirm his faith in the Führer, make him realise that he is a genius.

'German forces have invaded Soviet Russia. In the early hours of this morning, the Luftwaffe and the Wehrmacht launched a massive offensive to rid the Russian people of the Communist tyranny . . .'

He cheers out loud.

'This calls for a celebration!' he says.

'Does it?' asks Eileen.

'Of course! This is it! The moment we have been waiting for! At last, Communism is being swept away! Don't you see? This is the beginning of the end!'

With that, he gets out of bed and starts getting dressed.

'Don't worry about making my breakfast,' he says. 'I'm going down to the Foreign Press Club – that's the place to be this morning.'

He thinks about asking her, but he doesn't want her around. Things are in a bad way between them, and he's heard that she's seeing someone else, some young army officer. He doesn't really care. She is a burden, he thinks, let the handsome officer have her. What worries him is whether he is going to find a replacement, but for the mean time he is too interested in the news.

At the Press Club, the atmosphere is electric. There are journalists from nearly every country in Europe, except England of course. They know they should be at their bureaux, but they want to be together, sharing scraps, speculating. The air is thick with excited chatter and smoke, and he notices that a few are even drinking champagne.

He looks for a familiar face, and there are plenty, but the person he wants to find is William Joyce, his fellow collaborator and rival at the Reichsrundfunk. They call him 'Lord Haw-Haw' at home, which he and Joyce find amusing, because Joyce's voice is anything but lordly. The papers at home must be referring to Joyce's predecessor, they think, Normal Baillie-Stewart, very much a 'Haw-Haw', a Sandhurst man through and through.

He finds Joyce, instantly recognisable with the huge scar on the right side of his face, running from his ear to his mouth. He is a short man, but powerful, with broad arms that he likes to keep folded. He is there with his wife, Margaret, who is pretty and has a good figure – apparently she was a dancer, even performing cabaret shows for the BUF in and around Lancashire. He's always liked Mrs Joyce – a blackshirt bride no less!

'Hello, Bill,' he says. 'Hello, Margaret.'

They greet him, Mrs Joyce very charming, Joyce very guarded, edgy as always.

'Isn't this great news?' he asks.

'Great news indeed,' says Joyce. 'I'm going to talk about it tonight.'

This is not what he wants to hear. He thinks that he should be the one addressing the British tonight, not Joyce. Why the hell have they picked him?

'What are you going to say?'

'I'm going to tell the British that now's their chance,' Joyce says. 'That it's clear that Hitler's doing the right thing, smashing the Commies once and for all. I'll tell them that it's time they came along and helped us to beat the real enemy.'

'Sounds good,' he says. 'Have you already written it?'

'I'll do so later, when there's more news.'

He smiles, concealing his jealousy. The station vets his scripts thoroughly, taking a few days to make them worse, in his opinion. But it appears that Joyce is spared such editing, that Joyce is their star boy, the one who can go on air at short notice. He remembers Joyce from BUF days – they worked at the Black House together, and even then, Joyce was one of the stars, damn him. But Joyce left the BUF because the leader wasn't extreme enough for him. He founded his own little party, the National Socialist Party, but it never got more than a hundred members.

It was a mistake talking to Joyce, but it isn't a mistake seeing Mrs Joyce. He turns his attention to her.

'And how are you, Margaret?' he asks.

'Very well, thank you. And how are you? How is Eileen?'

It is clear that Margaret isn't very well at all. Perhaps, as with him and Eileen, she and Joyce are going through a bad patch. This may be an opportunity to find a replacement for Eileen.

'I'm well – Eileen is well too.'

'Not joining us here for the celebrations?'

'Er . . . no. She's in bed still – a little poorly.'

'Do send her my best, won't you?'

'I shall.'

He notices that Joyce is ignoring them; looking around the room. Then, without even a word, he walks off, presumably to look for somebody else to talk to. Mrs Joyce looks embarrassed.

'Would you like a drink?' he asks awkwardly.

The question takes her aback, and then she looks defiant, determined.

'Do you know? I would,' she says.

The reply startles him. Normally women don't ever accept drinks off him, but Mrs Joyce can obviously see deeper than his skin.

August 1970

Apparently she was in her mid eighties, blind, and her hearing was nugatory. Amy had been warned, told that the trip to Crete might not be worth it, but she saw it as her duty to visit the mother of one of her father's fallen comrades. Her research kept coming across one name, that of Manoli Pentaris, and after two years and many letters, she had tracked down his mother. She had been living in the same village all her life, a woman who had lost not only her husband, but both her sons. One had been a priest, executed by the Germans, the other, Manoli, an archaeologist, who had become the leader of a band of partisans. He too had been killed by the invaders, shot outside his hideout on Mount Ida.

The letter from Mrs Pentaris's nephew had said that Amy might not like what she found, that she might not be well received in Crete. But Amy had written back saying that she was not responsible for the sins of her father, if indeed he had committed any. She knew that he had been captured on the island, and she said that she was willing to hear anything about her father, no matter how unpalatable. Very well, the nephew had replied, if she wanted to dig up history, then she had only herself to blame. If she wanted to visit, then fine.

The nephew had picked her up from Heraklion airport, and the drive to the small mountain village took a couple of slow hot hours. Amy found the countryside ruggedly beautiful, and could see how it would be impossible for anybody to fully conquer an island of so many hills and mountains, gorges, woods and small villages, each with their own secrets.

When they entered Mrs Pentaris's village, Amy felt wary, wary of the eyes that she knew would be looking at her from the deep black openings in the plain white houses. Everybody would know who she was. They would have been waiting for her for weeks.

'My aunt,' said the nephew, 'lives with us. There is nowhere else for her. I must tell you that she is very old, and the conversation will not be easy.'

'That's all right,' said Amy. 'And you will be happy translating?'

'No problem.'

The coolness inside the nephew's house was extremely welcome. It was around two in the afternoon, and the sun was scorchingly hot.

'Something to drink?'

'Some water, please.'

The nephew went off, and reappeared a few minutes later with a glass of water. It was warm, but refreshing all the same.

'Your wife – children – are they here?' Amy asked.

The nephew shook his head.

'No, they are away today.'

Amy nodded. Was it because she was here?

'But your aunt – she's here, yes?'

'Yes. Would you like to see her now?'

'Yes please.'

'Follow me.'

Amy walked immediately behind the nephew as they

made their way to a small terrace at the back of the house. Shaded by two orange trees, it had the most spectacular view of the valley up which they had driven. The air was still and vibrated with the sound of crickets, which somehow conspired to make it feel even more hot.

'Quite a view,' said Amy.

'Yes,' said the nephew. 'My aunt, she is over here.'

He pointed to a dark corner, tucked well into the shade. Sitting on a large canvas chair, next to a small table, was the object of her journey. Dressed in black, her lined face deep brown and leathery, she had the countenance of one who had suffered much. The nephew walked over to her and shouted in Greek in her ear:

'The woman from England is here!'

She moaned a few words back, the nephew holding his ear right next to her mouth.

'She says, "Come over!" '

Amy walked tentatively across.

'Hello, Mrs Pentaris,' said Amy. 'It is very kind of you to see me.'

The nephew translated Amy's words. Mrs Pentaris then asked him a question, the answer to which he bellowed back.

'What was that?' Amy asked.

'I'm afraid she had forgotten you were coming, Miss Lockhart. She wanted to know who you were. I told her.'

Mrs Pentaris started mumbling again. As her nephew listened, his face turned grave. When she had finished, he stood up.

'I'm sorry, Miss Lockhart.'

'What?'

'My aunt – she will not speak to you.'

'But . . . why?'

He looked uneasy.

'Please tell me,' said Amy.

'She . . . she says that she will not talk to the daughter of the man who murdered her son. I'm . . . I'm sorry.'

Amy opened her mouth, but decided to stay silent. She stared at the old woman, whose head was shaking, her blind eyes growing moist. Amy turned and walked to the terrace wall. It really was a lovely view. If only it could talk.

Chapter Six

May–June 1944

THE FIRST OF May was a public holiday in the Reich, as it was in most European countries. However, the Nazis had appropriated it as 'National Labour Day', and because the unit had been making good progress, Strasser had allowed it to observe the holiday, and had issued them with passes to join in the festivities in town. As a result, the men, with the exception of Butcher, took the opportunity to get plastered. Hull and Andreae, the ringleaders of any activity that involved alcohol, had planned a crawl of all the bars in Hildesheim, with a prize of thirty Reichsmarks to whoever could last the longest. Although Lockhart thought the idea a great one – he had done the same, and had indeed won such a competition, at Oxford – he had resolved not to tell Strasser about it, since he was worried that fights might break out. He decided that he would join in, not least because it presented a further opportunity to bond with the men, but also because it would enable him to keep an eye on them. He had no wish for the work of the past few weeks to be undone by the unit going on a drunken rampage through the town centre.

The plan was to start and finish at the Rosenstock, the unit's regular haunt. Hull had established that there were at least twelve other bars around town that they could visit, and he had gone so far as to plan a route. The rules stipulated that each man must consume a litre of beer and a double measure of schnapps in each bar. No food was allowed, which meant that the men ate as much as they could get their hands on at lunch.

The crawl kicked off at four o'clock, and started well, although the unit remained divided into its two camps. By the time they had reached the fourth bar, there were already a few dropouts – Maclaren, Marston, Simpkin and Prain – and a number of others were looking a little unsteady. Lockhart still felt sober, and by the looks of things, Worstead, Hull, Andreae, Catchpole and Allan had an equally large capacity for drink.

On their way to the fifth bar, Lockhart urgently needed to urinate. Knowing that he could not wait until they had reached the bar, a good ten minutes away through the thick crowds, he seized the opportunity to peel off down one of Hildesheim's many tight alleyways. Luckily, a few yards down on the right, he spied a semi-derelict house that would afford him the dignified cover required of an officer. It still had a front door, which was ajar.

The interior was a mess, and it appeared that the building had suffered a fairly major fire, judging by the charred ceiling timbers and the extensive water damage to the remaining furnishings. There was a privy towards the rear, and although the only part of it that remained was a hole in the ground, it was more than sufficient for Lockhart's purposes. As he neared the end of his piss, looking forward to resuming a contest he felt confident of winning, he heard a muffled scream.

At first he thought nothing of it, taking it for a noise from the crowd. He finished urinating and made his way through the wreckage towards the front door. But then he heard it again, this time louder, much clearer, and coming from upstairs. It was a woman's scream, and she was evidently in great distress. Then came a male voice:

'Shut up, bitch, or I'll break your fucking neck!'

He heard the sound of slapping and more screams, but muffled this time, as though a palm had been clamped over her mouth.

Lockhart removed his Luger from his holster. Despite what he had drunk, he felt sober enough for the adrenalin to take effect, causing his heart rate to increase massively.

'Take that, you whore!'

The voice was familiar, but he couldn't put a face to it. Even though the Luger wasn't loaded, it would prove an effective deterrent. At first, Lockhart wanted to rush up the stairs, but that might give the man too much time to react. Instead, he trod softly, avoiding the rubble and fragments of glass and timber.

GUY WALTERS

He neared the top of the flight, and could tell that the rape was taking place in a room off to the right of the small landing. He heard grunts coming from the man, and still the same chilling sounds of female pain. His mind turned briefly to Anna, praying that this had not been meted out to her, but he forced himself to return to the present. He noticed that his pistol was shaking, which he steadied by holding it in both hands and taking a few deep and silent breaths. Slowly he walked the few feet to just before the open door. One more deep breath, and in he burst, his pistol pointing into the room.

'Stop it!' he screamed at the top of his lungs.

It was a sight that he had hoped never to see. On a filthy mattress towards the back of the stinking room, a woman was on all fours, her light-blue floral dress hitched up on to her back. An old and water-stained pillowcase had been placed over her head. Over this pillowcase and around her neck was tied a belt, the end of which was being held by the man, who was penetrating her from behind. His trousers were down and his tunic was undone. The left sleeve was visible to Lockhart, and on it was a Union Jack. The skeletal face, half obscured in the darkness, was that of Matthew Butcher.

Had the Luger been loaded, Lockhart would have shot the rapist immediately. Instead, maintaining the element of surprise, he ran over to Butcher and smashed him over the head with the butt.

'Bastard!' Lockhart shouted, hitting him again. 'You fucking bastard!'

368

The blows knocked Butcher away from his victim, and off the mattress on to a charred rug. Lockhart couldn't help but notice the colour of Butcher's penis – it was red. He looked at the woman's vagina, which was bleeding heavily. He stepped over the mattress and kicked Butcher in the groin, whereupon he let out the most ear-shattering and high-pitched cry. It took all of Lockhart's self-control to stop himself from beating Butcher to death. He allowed himself one more kick, this time to Butcher's stomach, which caused him to gag, retch and then vomit. Satisfied that Butcher would remain immobile for the time being, Lockhart put his pistol back in its holster and turned his attention to the woman.

'It's all right,' he said. 'It's all right.'

He squatted in front of her, untied the belt from around her neck and removed the pillowcase. After what he had just seen, Lockhart didn't think he could grow more angry, but when he saw that the woman was in fact a girl who could be no older than fourteen, he nearly went berserk. Restraining himself, he made the girl his priority. Butcher could wait.

'Get up if you can,' he said to the girl as gently as he could. 'Here, take my hand.'

With difficulty, the girl stood up, her dress falling back down over her legs. Her underwear was still around her ankles, and she pulled it up. It looked like such an innocent everyday action, but now she was doing it to cover up the damage, using her underwear as a bandage to dress what was now a wound.

Lockhart looked down at the girl. She was pretty, with

long blonde hair, which was now matted and rancid-looking. The last half an hour, or however long ago it was that Butcher had abducted her, would change her life for ever. He wanted to hug the girl, to attempt to reassure her, but he knew that the gesture would be misinterpreted. She looked back at Lockhart, her watery blue eyes set amidst a red and swollen face.

Lockhart smiled at her. He had no idea what to say apart from:

'You're safe now, you're all right. It's finished. It's all over.'

The girl continued staring at him, her whole body trembling as if she was about to explode.

'What's your name?'

The girl didn't reply.

'Where do you live?'

Still no reply. The trembling grew more intense.

'Tell me, so I can take you back home, back to your mother and father.'

And then the girl started to scream once more, as though she was trying to expel every morsel of evil that Butcher had pumped into her. She started beating Lockhart's stomach and chest, which he allowed her to do until it actually began to hurt. He grabbed her wrists, which caused her to struggle wildly. He had to let go. Now what was he to do? He wanted to get her to safety, but he didn't want to leave Butcher, fearing that he might escape, despite the fact that he was still writhing about on the floor.

But the girl made up Lockhart's mind by running out of the room. He bolted out after her, and saw her run awkwardly down the stairs, the effects of the rape evidently impeding her. He ran after her, but stopped himself when she reached the front door. She would find refuge, someone would help her. After a few seconds of reflection, Lockhart also realised that the sight of an SS officer running after a teenage girl with blood trickling down her legs would not look good. He knew there was little more he could have done for her, but he felt helpless nevertheless.

He went back into the room to find Butcher leaning against the wall, pulling up his breeches. His tunic was covered in vomit and blood, the latter of which was pouring from his nose and a deep cut on his forehead. Lockhart wanted to kill him, beat that head into a misshapen ball of flesh, blood and bone. No punishment would be too horrendous. He had to exercise all his self-control not to mete it out – he was no thug. Instead, he would throw Butcher to the wolf that was an SS court-martial.

'You're a dead man, Butcher.'

Butcher didn't respond. His head was slumped on to his chest, and he was breathing awkwardly. Lockhart was about to ask him what the fuck he thought he had been doing, but he realised that it was crass, useless. This was probably a regular activity for him, a hobby.

'Tell me about Warsaw, Butcher.'

Butcher stopped breathing for a moment, and lifted his head up. He said nothing.

'Tell me about that day in Warsaw. The day you killed two hundred Poles and eighty Jews. Did you rape their children as well? Well? Did you?'

'I . . . I . . . never killed any Poles or Jews,' Butcher said, burbling through a mouthful of blood and mucus. 'That's all lies, that story.'

'Lies? You expect me to believe you?' Lockhart shouted, pointing to the blood-speckled mattress. 'After *this*?'

Butcher let his head fall back down.

'You're going to die for this, Butcher. I'm not going to kill you now, but I'm going to request that I command the firing squad that does so. You're fucking scum.'

'Before . . .' Butcher began, his voice a low rasp.

'Yes?'

'Before . . . before . . . you have me killed, there's . . . there's something you should know.'

'What?'

Butcher coughed up some blood.

'What, Butcher? What should I know?'

'Something imp . . . important.'

'Get to the point!'

'Your . . . your wife is dead.'

Lockhart stepped back, as if reeling from one of the blows he had just dished out. It was inconceivable, impossible, especially after the letters he had received. Butcher had to be lying, buying time. It couldn't be true – it *mustn't* be true. Nevertheless, coming as it did on top of the alcohol and adrenalin, the statement made him feel faint. It was too much for his system, imagining Anna as a corpse, executed in the way that Strasser had described in December. *She too will be killed, perhaps with a shot to the back of the head. The bullet will come out the front of her face, taking her brains and maybe one of her eyes with it.* The horrendous thought came to Lockhart that Strasser had not been describing how she might be killed, but how she *had* been killed. No. That wasn't true. The letters proved it.

He bent down and grabbed Butcher by the front of his tunic, pulling his head up towards him. Butcher's head rolled from side to side, punch drunk.

'That's not true!'

For about a minute, Lockhart knelt in front of Butcher's wheezing form, staring down at a man who had killed and raped hundreds. A couple more firm blows would finish him off, rid the world of one more evil sod that the war had given oxygen to.

'The . . . the . . .'

Once more, Butcher was mumbling.

'The letters . . .'

He stopped.

Lockhart leant down, his ear right next to Butcher's face.

'Who told you about the letters, Butcher?'

'Just . . . a rumour.'

'A *rumour*? Who told you?'

'Don't know . . . Can't remember.'

'Not good enough! Tell me, Butcher.'

'I don't know, but apparently they're . . . they're . . .'

'They're what? Tell me!'

'They're . . . they're fakes.'

'Fakes? What do you mean, they're fakes?'

There was a panicky desperation in Lockhart's voice. This was what he had subconsciously feared, but had not allowed himself to address. But his rational side kicked in, calming him with the knowledge that the letters contained references to private things – there was no way they could be forgeries. And yet why would Butcher be claiming they were? He had to be buying time – that was the most likely explanation. Perhaps he thought Lockhart was about to kill him.

'How do you know they're fakes?' shouted Lockhart directly into Butcher's ear, as loudly as if Butcher was at the bottom of a cliff. 'Who told you? Worstead?'

'No.'

'Who then?'

'Dunno. But promise . . . you . . . they're fakes.'

'You're lying, Butcher! You're bloody lying!'

'I'm . . . not . . . I swear.'

This was rubbish, thought Lockhart, pure rubbish. He cursed himself for momentarily allowing himself to believe Butcher, this pathetic scrap of shit, this murderer, this rapist. Butcher would say anything to stop Lockhart beating him up, and he was cunning enough to know which of Lockhart's nerves were the most raw.

Lockhart was now faced with the practical problem of getting Butcher out of the room. Would he be able to walk? Unlikely, but it was worth a try.

'All right, Butcher, get up!'

Butcher mumbled vaguely into the pool of bile and blood that had seeped out of his mouth.

'Up, Butcher! Get up!'

Butcher made some attempt to move, but he was evidently drifting in and out of consciousness. There was nothing else for it: Lockhart would have to drag or carry him out of here, and then find the nearest figure in uniform to help him.

The mattress. Why hadn't he thought of it before? He could put Butcher on it and slide him down the stairs. It wouldn't matter if the bastard took the odd knock as he went down – it wasn't as if he was trying to rescue him. Would it work? It was worth a go.

The method, although unorthodox, did in fact work. It did little for Butcher's condition, however, and by the time Lockhart had got the oberscharführer on to the pavement, he was out cold, but breathing. Lockhart left him lying in the doorway, next to some dog mess, which seemed singularly appropriate. But even as he hurried to find someone who could help, the dread panic that he was a widower grabbed him tightly, and stirred up his insides with an insidious churning. It was rubbish, it had to be.

Two days later, at ten o'clock in the morning, Oberscharführer Matthew Butcher was court-martialled. Sitting on either side of the head of the Haus Germanien, Sturmbannführer Parsch, were Strasser and a Danish hauptsturmführer. Butcher stayed silent throughout the proceedings. His trial was heard in camera, with Lockhart as the sole witness. After twenty minutes, Parsch ordered the death sentence to be carried out immediately.

By half past eleven, six bullets had slammed into Butcher's body. Strasser grudgingly thanked Lockhart for discovering the rape, although Lockhart got the impression that the German's annoyance that he was one man down outweighed his sense of the rightful carrying-out of justice. For his part, Lockhart was deeply frustrated that he had been unable to press Butcher for more information about the letters.

The next night, Lockhart took the opportunity to treat Worstead to a dinner at the Schlegels Weinstube. Strasser had officially confirmed Worstead as the senior NCO, and Lockhart's pretext was that his promotion was a cause for celebration. However, by the time they had finished their aperitifs, and Lockhart had toasted Worstead's good health, the conversation had moved on to Butcher.

'There is one thing that niggles me,' said Lockhart, as he ended his account, 'something that Butcher said as he was lying on the floor.'

'Go on,' said Worstead, leaning forward conspiratorially.

'I've been trying to dismiss it, but it won't go away. Butcher said that the letters from Anna were fakes, and that she was in fact dead.'

'He said *that?*'

'He said that he had heard a rumour, but couldn't remember who from.'

'How convenient!' scoffed Worstead, scratching his earlobe. 'And did he say who started this rumour?'

'No. But I was surprised that he knew about the letters at all. In fact, I rather thought it was *you* who might have told him about them.'

Worstead looked both puzzled and affronted.

'Good God, no! John, *please*. I haven't told a soul, I promise. It must have been Strasser. It wasn't me. Really.'

'That's what I thought, Andrew, but I needed to ask.'

'Sure, John, sure.'

For a minute or so, both men studied the menu and the wine list, exchanging small talk about its merits or otherwise. The waitress came over to ask what they wanted to drink, and Lockhart chose a bottle of Spätslese. Were they ready to order any food? No, not yet, give us a few more minutes. Fräulein.

'So you're absolutely sure they're real then, are you?' Worstead asked through a mouthful of thick black bread.

'What? The letters?'

Worstead nodded, reaching for more bread.

'God, yes. There's stuff in them that only she and I know about.'

'But if you knew that they *were* fakes, who would you suspect?'

Lockhart frowned a little, and then smiled.

'Well you, of course. Although it can't be you, because you weren't at our wedding, and she writes about it. So that rules you out.'

'Phew!' said Worstead, laughing a little. 'Glad I'm in the clear then!'

'You see,' said Lockhart. 'It's just as well you weren't invited!'

The abrupt change in Worstead's expression clearly signalled that yet again another remark had been taken to heart. Fortunately, the waitress arrived with the wine, and after it had been opened, tasted, poured and the waitress told to come back in a few minutes, because no, they still weren't ready to order, Worstead appeared to have let the comment go past.

'So,' said Lockhart, 'you asked me who I'd suspect. Well, I don't think I suspect anyone.'

'Shall I tell you who I'd suspect, if it was me?'

Lockhart opened his hands out to Worstead. This was ridiculous, but almost fun, an intellectual challenge.

'I'm all ears, Andrew.'

'I'd say it was Pugh.'

'Pugh?'

'That's right.'

'For Pete's sake, why Pugh?'

'Because I don't trust him.'

'That's hardly evidence.'

'Wait. He seems to have a special relationship with Strasser, almost as if he can tell Strasser what to do. You know what he was doing before he joined the unit, don't you?'

'Broadcasting, wasn't it?'

'That's right. For the Concordia Bureau in Berlin, broadcasting all sorts of nonsense over the air to be received back home. He's been doing it for years apparently, and even seems proud of it.'

'This is a long way from him faking letters from my wife.'

'Hold on. As a result of being in Berlin for so long, I get the impression Pugh has made some very powerful friends, including Hillen-Ziegfeld of course, and Vivian Stranders, who you told me Strasser had told you about. And men like them have contacts back in Britain, spies of course, who are quite capable of unearthing information about people's pasts. Do you follow me?'

'Of course I do, but it's preposterous. You think the Germans have people foraging around Britain for details of my private life? It's absurd!'

'Perhaps it is. But then ten years ago we would have found it absurd to be sitting in a restaurant in the middle of Germany dressed up as SS soldiers.'

'Fair point, but in my experience the Germans have a bad record with their spies.'

'Oh yes?'

Lockhart paused. This was going back to his work in Whitehall, in Military Intelligence.

'You'll have to forgive me, Andrew, I can't tell you much more.'

Worstead's eyes narrowed.

'Secrets?'

'Yes, Andrew – secrets. Even from you, I'm afraid.'

'No, that's quite all right. I wouldn't want to be burdened with them!'

Lockhart had expected another display of chippiness, and it came as a relief that it hadn't materialised.

'Now then,' he said, 'let's look at this menu properly. What have we got? Crikey! "Pork in a cream and apple sauce" – I can see why Strasser always comes here!'

'Quite! This menu is music to my ears.'

The sensation was almost physical. Somewhere in his head, Lockhart could feel two facts, two hitherto useless pieces of information, connecting and reacting, spurred on by the word 'music' as a catalyst. Strasser had told him that Stranders' father was a music professor. The organist at Lockhart's wedding had been a music professor called Saunders. But Lockhart hadn't been sure it *was* Saunders, because the organist, well into his eighties, had only mumbled his name.

'John? Are you all right? You look as though you've seen a ghost.'

Lockhart didn't hear him. Was it possible that Vivian Stranders' father had played at his wedding? It would be the most hateful of coincidences if Stranders had found out about the ceremony from his father, and was now relaying details of it to Pugh, so that he and Strasser might forge some letters from Anna. And if this was the case, then Anna was surely dead. Butcher, the bastard, hadn't been lying.

'John? John! You've gone white!'

Worstead had grabbed him by the forearm and was now shaking it, trying to break him out of his reverie.

'What is it, John?'

Lockhart looked up at Worstead. His stomach had knotted itself so tightly he felt he was about to vomit.

'Christ, man, what's the matter?'

Lockhart drained his wine glass, and pointed at it, indicating to Worstead that it needed refilling. He took a long deep breath through his nose – an attempt to stop himself feeling nauseous that partly succeeded. Worstead poured him another glass, half the contents of which Lockhart immediately drained.

'I think,' Lockhart began, 'you may well be right.'

'Sorry?'

'I think you're right about Pugh. And if you are, then that means Anna is dead.'

He couldn't believe that he was saying those words – four syllables that contained so much pain, more pain than the deaths of his mother, father and Richard combined. That seemed unfair to them, but it was just the way he felt.

'Why do you think I'm right?' asked Worstead.

Lockhart told him.

'But that's . . . that's preposterous,' said Worstead.

Lockhart smiled, but only with his mouth.

'You were asking me to believe a similarly large coincidence only a few minutes ago.'

'I know, but, I mean . . . are you sure? Are you sure that the organist might not have been called Saunders?'

'Sure enough to give myself one hell of a fright.'

The waitress came over. Although Lockhart didn't feel like eating, he knew that he should. They both ordered the pork, and another bottle of wine. He was going to get drunk, wash away some of the pain. Fine, it was probably escapism – a temporary suicide – but then he felt he deserved it.

They had been pleased with what she had discovered, very pleased, but now they wanted her to push him a little harder. She told them that he was very guarded, but they said that if anybody was going to find out more, it was her. They had someone else who was helping, but he couldn't get as near to Strasser as she could. Who was that someone else? she asked. You'll meet him soon, they said.

Use every trick you know, they had ordered her, use every method to bring him out. Leni, they had said, Leni, this is important, do not worry if he loses his temper or threatens you, for we will protect you. She curtly informed them that their protection was worthless, and anyway, she could look after herself. They had laughed at that, but her manner was indignant, and there was something about her forcefulness that they respected.

Leni was recalling the words as she lay next to Strasser. He was up in Berlin for a few days, enjoying some leave, and he said that he would like to go out with her one night, out on a date. It was impossible, she had replied – she never got a night off. He was surprised, and insistent, and had attempted to talk her into telling Kitty that she was ill. No way, said Leni, it wasn't worth the risk. It was a lie, of course. She did indeed want to see Carl in a non-professional way, to go out like an ordinary couple, but she had promised herself not to get close to him. It would make her betrayal of him all the harder, and for her own sake, and that of her parents, she had to resist any intimacy.

As a result of her refusal, he had made love savagely, getting back at her. He had even slapped her across the face a few times, calling her 'bitch' and 'whore', and had thrust into her as hard as he could. It had hurt, but there was something passionate about it, something heartfelt.

He obviously cared for her, and was angry that he couldn't have her in the way he wanted. It didn't upset her, because she knew he didn't mean it, that it was his way of expressing his disappointment. Besides, she had been called – and treated – a lot worse.

'Look at my hands,' she said, breaking the silence. 'They're trembling.'

She held her hands up – they were indeed shaking slightly.

Strasser reached for her left hand with his right, and gripped it. His clasp felt strong, reassuring, steadying her. He held it like that for a minute, until he brought it down to his mouth to give it the lightest kiss.

'I'm sorry,' he said, letting it go. 'It's wrong of me to expect—'

'No, don't be,' Leni interrupted. 'In a normal time, I would have gone out with you like a shot, but I just can't. I'm the one who should be sorry.'

She turned to face him.

'Perhaps one day we will be able to see each other,' she said. 'Properly. We could pretend that we had never slept together.'

'Impossible!' he said, and they both sniggered.

She stroked his nose, and then his pale eyebrows, which caused him to shut his eyes.

'That's nice,' he murmured.

Leni said nothing.

'I'll fall asleep if you're not careful,' he said, letting out a little yawn.

'Well why don't you?'

'Because Kitty will charge me a month's pay for the privilege!'

Leni feigned indignation and pinched his nose.

'I'd have hoped you'd paid double that for a night with me.'

'Ow! Let go! You'd be lucky if I gave you a couple of marks.'

Leni tweaked his nipple.

'All right, all right, you win! One mark then!'

'Right! That does it!' she exclaimed, and reached her hand down under the sheets, grabbed his penis, and yanked it hard.

'Shit! Stop that! Jesus, you'll pull it off! A year's pay! Everything!'

She loosened her grip and kissed him on the cheek.

'That's more like it,' she said.

'Thanks for giving me my cock back.'

'Mon plaisir, Herr Hauptsturmführer.'

They lay in silence for a few moments, catching their breath.

'How's your bureaucratic nightmare?' she asked, running her hand through his hair.

'Do we have to talk about that?'

'No, of course not. I just wondered, that's all. The last time you were here it sounded as though you were having a dreadful time.'

'It's better now. There's much less paperwork, and the men are more or less behaving themselves.'

'That's good.'

'It is. My British officer seems to be knocking them

into shape, as he calls it. The unit's turning out to be almost competent.'

'What's he like?'

'Who?'

'The officer.'

'He's good. But I'm keeping an eye on him, making sure he doesn't do anything stupid.'

'Stupid? What sort of stupid?'

'I don't know, but I have to make sure.'

'But how can you keep an eye on him?'

'Well I don't exactly. One of the men does.'

'One of the men?'

'Yes, someone in the unit . . . All these questions, Leni! Anyone would think you were a spy!'

Leni laughed as naturally as possible. Even though Strasser was joking, the accusation unnerved her.

'I'd make a very bad spy,' she said.

'Really? And why's that?'

'Because,' she said, rolling on top of him, 'I like men too much.'

'Surely not *all* men.'

'No, but men who know what they're doing.'

And with that, she kissed him, not a whore's kiss, but a lover's kiss. And she hated herself for it.

Lockhart couldn't concentrate. During the lunch, a semi-formal occasion one Saturday, he found himself sitting next to a somewhat drunk Sturmbannführer Parsch, the head of the Haus Germanien. Parsch was in his mid-fifties, bald, his cranium rippling with throbbing veins. He was quizzing Lockhart about the digs on Crete – which was far better than the lecture he had been expecting on the superiority of the Nordic peoples – but Lockhart's mind was filled with thoughts about Anna, about whether she was alive. Coupled with that, Stafford had told him that they still hadn't had a reply from 'Hattie', even though other members of the unit had received post from back home, from families who still thought their men were suffering the privations of POW life.

But a chance comment by Parsch snapped Lockhart out of his reverie.

'I'm surprised that you don't have something similar to the Ahnenerbe in Britain,' said Parsch, slurping noisily on a goblet of wine, a goblet that Lockhart idly reflected was in bad taste.

'What do you mean?' Lockhart asked.

'I'm surprised that there isn't a single organisation that is responsible for unearthing and examining the prehistory of your people – the Ahnenerbe is an immensely successful operation. We have even mounted expeditions to Tibet.'

'*Tibet?*'

'Quite so. One has to travel far to learn about one's racial heritage! When the war is over, there is so much learning that our two nations will be able to share.'

'Such as?'

'Well, for example, we have conducted a vast amount of research on the European peoples, and we have discovered enormous differences between them – just by measuring their skulls.'

'Skulls? Where are these skulls from?'

'Oh,' said Parsch, his voice unconcerned, 'I don't think we need concern ourselves with things like that! The Ahnenerbe has its fingers in many pies. It is like an octopus!'

Lockhart would normally have winced at the mixed metaphor, but he let it go.

'What else does it do?'

'You name it! Archaeology, medicine, all branches of science, and, recently, even weaponry!'

'Weaponry? Why weaponry?'

'Oh yes! Didn't you know there was a war on? We all have to do our bit. Why do you think that even I, a humble professor, am wearing a uniform like this? Anyway, you can assume the Ahnenerbe is concerned with most elements of life in the Reich.'

Lockhart sipped his wine thoughtfully, trying not to appear excited. Parsch had used the word 'recently'. Whatever it was that the professor had just learned, it would probably exist on paper, and that paper would be somewhere in his office. Lockhart knew that he had to take a chance. Tonight, he would pay a visit to Parsch's office. He would need a thief to help him, and he had just the man in mind.

It was four in the morning when he and Stafford approached Parsch's door. Stafford had told him that four was the best time for a burglary, because not even early risers got up that early. His chest had swollen with professional pride when Lockhart had asked him whether he would be willing to assist, telling Lockhart that there wasn't a lock in Germany that he wouldn't be able to pick.

Parsch's office was at the top of a tower, which made Lockhart uncomfortable. Their only escape route was back down the stairs, unless they fancied their chances climbing out of one of the windows and lowering themselves on to a steeply pitched roof below. Even in daylight, such a manoeuvre would be foolhardy, but at night it would be reckless in the extreme.

'Never mind.' Stafford had grinned when Lockhart had told him of the situation. 'We'll just have to make sure we don't get caught.'

'If we do,' Lockhart had replied, 'we'll be looking at something far more severe than four years in Pentonville.'

Stafford produced a few short strands of thick wire from his pocket and set to work on the lock. Lockhart looked back towards the winding stone staircase they had just climbed. As each second passed, he readied himself for the sound of footsteps echoing up it, but none came.

'How are you doing?' Lockhart whispered after a very long minute.

'Nearly there.'

Lockhart listened intently, straining his ears for even the slightest sound. Nothing. It seemed to him as though Stafford's lock-picking was making a racket, but he knew the corporal wouldn't be able to make it any quieter.

'How much longer?'

Stafford grunted.

'Can you do it?'

'It's a bit of a bugger . . . ah!'

And then a click which put a smile on both their faces.

'You little beauty,' Stafford whispered.

Lockhart turned from the staircase and joined Stafford at the door.

'Will you be able to lock it again?' he asked.

'Should be able to.'

'Good.'

Lockhart turned the handle and started to push the heavy oak door open. It creaked so loudly that he immediately stopped.

'Do it quickly,' Stafford whispered. 'Less noise.'

Lockhart took a deep breath and pushed hard. The creaking seemed loud enough to fill the entire building. Surely everybody would wake up? Lockhart brushed the concern aside and stepped into the office, his eyes trying to make out what lay in front of him. He briefly turned on a small torch, one of two that Stafford had wangled from God knows where.

'Shit,' he whispered, and turned off the torch.

'What?'

'The place is a mess! There's paper every-bloody-where. Stacks of it! Typical bloody academic.'

'Shall we go then?'

It was tempting, because Lockhart knew that they might need all night. No, five minutes, he would give it five minutes, and told Stafford as much.

'You stand guard here,' Lockhart continued, 'and let me know when my time is up.'

Stafford nodded in the darkness, while Lockhart set to work.

Recently. To Lockhart that suggested that the piece of paper would be on the desk. He walked softly over to it – a vast affair, covered in piles of paper and books. Where to begin? He turned the torch back on and held it in his mouth. The stack of paper to the right looked promising. The stack to the left was crowned by a dusty book, which suggested that the pile might not have been disturbed for weeks.

He picked up a large handful of sheets and started flicking through them. *Viking burial ground uncovered . . . Special report on the skull sizes of Russian commissars . . . Hysterectomies on Jewish twins . . .* Christ almighty, thought Lockhart, this was unbelievable, but keep looking, keep looking . . . *Effects of high-pressure chambers on ear, nose and throat . . . Some intersting new comments on Jewish bastardy . . . Haus Germanien report on Dutch SS recruits . . . Racial theory: some new pointers . . . Dear Sturmbannführer Parsch, I am looking for a position as . . . Results of medical experiments by the discredited Dr Sigmund Rascher, January 1943 . . .*

Shit. There was nothing here, thought Lockhart, or rather there was everything. In just one handful of paper he had uncovered enough evidence of Nazi insanity to make him forget where he was, to make him gasp out loud.

'What is it?'

It was Stafford.

'Nothing,' Lockhart mumbled back, the torch obscuring his speech.

He picked up another handful of papers, and kept flicking through them. Some were marked TOP SECRET, and were to do with the Haus Germanien. Others were papers of some sort or another outlining policy as regarded different races. This was madness, Lockhart kept repeating to himself, pure lunacy.

'One more minute!'

Surely not – he hadn't even scratched the surface. He decided, for no good reason, to transfer his attention to the stack on the left. He moved the dusty book and picked up some papers from underneath it. Again, the same mixture of cod science, evil science, bureaucratic requests and denials, and academic papers on Nordic prehistory. Perhaps Parsch wasn't the typical shambolic academic, and had actually filed away the really sensitive material.

'That's five minutes!'

'All right,' Lockhart mumbled.

One more handful. Just one more. He picked up a few more sheets.

'Come on, sir!'

Lockhart ignored Stafford's urgent request. Damn, damn. More of the same nonsense. He hadn't seen one thing about weaponry. What was in this lot? *The Nordic inheritance . . . Moslem members of the Waffen-SS . . . Transfer of A4 project . . . Conference agenda for 18 July 1944 . . . Notes on the subhuman tendencies of the Russian Jew . . .*

'Sir!'

Lockhart looked up.

'Let's go!'

Just as Lockhart was about to put the papers back down, his mind went back to one of them. He rifled through them once more, and extracted it: *Transfer of A4 project*. It was so bland, but look where it was from! He skimmed over the contents of what was nothing more than a short memorandum.

From: The Office of the Reichsführer-SS
MOST SECRET – Transfer of A4 project
To: Senior officers of the German Ancestral
            Heritage Society for the Study of
            German Prehistory

With immediate effect, the responsibility for the implementation of the A4 project passes to the Ahnenerbe. This marks a new direction for the organisation, but the transfer will ensure that the project is brought fully under the efficient command of the SS.

Signed

SS-Brigadeführer Hans Kammler

29 March 1944

Was this it? What else could 'a new direction' refer to? He quickly read it once more and then put it back, deciding that stealing it would be pushing his luck.

'Sir!'

'All right, I'm coming,' said Lockhart, and switched off the torch.

*   *   *

Although he had not seen much of it back in December, the Berlin Lockhart saw now in May was a noticeably different city. What he had then taken for devastation had merely been, in comparison, some light damage, for now much of the capital of the German Empire was a blasted heap of rubble. Even when there wasn't an air raid, just being in the city was perilous enough. At any moment, a building could collapse, obliterating scores of Berliners shuffling through the masonry of their past lives, attempting to salvage some shards of hope from the ruins. And it smelt, thought Lockhart, smelt of decay, human decay.

On Sturmbannführer Parsch's order, Strasser had reluctantly given Lockhart a few days' leave. Lockhart had asked Parsch if he could visit the headquarters of the Ahnenerbe, feigning an immense interest in the organisation and its archaeological work. Parsch had been delighted that Lockhart was so keen, telling him that it was a pleasure to have such a cultured English gentleman with him at the Haus Germanien, and that he must visit his old friend Dr Erich Rudolph, the deputy head of the Ahnenerbe. He would arrange an interview immediately. That was too kind, Lockhart had said. Think nothing of it! Parsch might not have expressed such a sentiment if he had known that Lockhart's real reason for the visit was an attempt to get closer to the nature of A4. It could be a red herring, have nothing to do with sarin, but then again, he couldn't believe that it was unimportant.

As he made his way to the interview, Lockhart realised that he had been cooped up for too long, his head addled with a cloying uncertainty about whether Anna was alive.

He knew that he couldn't escape from that in Berlin, but he hoped that he would at least be able to distract himself. The wreckage of the city and the suffering of its population had provided that.

For the first time, Lockhart began to feel, if not at home, neither wary nor afraid. Berlin gave him anonymity, and even if the Union Jack patch raised the occasional eyebrow, he was left alone. Worstead had been desperate to join him, but Lockhart had refused, not wishing to endure the persistent sleeve-tugging of Anna's 'wheezing windbag'. What was he going to do there? Worstead asked. Mind your own business, Lockhart had told him. Would he be all right on his own? Of course he bloody would be, he wasn't a child.

There were islands in Berlin that had remained almost unaffected by the privations of rationing and the bombardment. One such island was the Hotel Adlon, a vast white shrine to luxury near the Brandenburg Gate. Strasser had recommended it, telling him that it was worth every pfennig. Lockhart had accumulated around five hundred marks, and, intending to use them on eating well and drinking likewise, had followed Strasser's advice. Strasser had also given him a book of matches from Kitty's, insisting that he should visit the brothel, that it was an experience not to be forgotten. And if he should see a certain young courtesan by the name of Leni, would he pass on Strasser's best wishes? Lockhart, reminding Strasser that he had a wife, told him that it was unlikely he would be visiting Kitty's, but if he did, he would be sure to say hello.

* * *

'Oberführer Dr Rudolph, please.'

Lockhart showed his *Ausweiss* to the functionary at the desk. He had entered a large atrium, in the middle of which was a vast marble statue of an idealised Nordic family of four – robust of form, fine-featured, and clad in national costume. Flags showing swastikas and every variety of rune shuddered slightly.

'You have an appointment, Hauptsturmführer ... Lock ... *Lockhart*?'

The functionary was clearly a little unaccustomed to dealing with SS officers with British names. Lockhart extracted a letter from Rudolph from inside his tunic. He passed it towards the functionary with a sigh.

'I do,' he said. 'At twelve o'clock.'

The functionary picked up a phone, and exchanged a few confirmatory words with a secretary at the other end.

'All right,' he said, handing back the *Ausweiss*, 'You can go up. It's on the first floor. Up the main stairs, turn right, and it's at the end of the corridor.'

'Dr Lockhart! How good of you to come!'

Dr Rudolph greeted Lockhart as though they were old friends. Like Parsch, he was in his fifties, but he was short, overweight, and was wearing a smart blue suit, a swastika armband around his left arm. Lockhart shook his hand.

'It's very good of you to see me, Oberführer.'

Rudolph brushed the appellation aside.

'Please! Call me Doctor! When I'm with a fellow academic, I prefer to use our academic titles! Professor

Parsch tells me that your doctorate is in Minoan history – is that right?'

'Quite so. You are very well informed.'

'I am afraid I know very little about your speciality, but I'm sure we'll have plenty on it in our excellent library here. Perhaps you would care to look at it?'

'That would be most kind, Dr Rudolph.'

'I'll sort you out a reader's ticket. Anyway, come into my office – I want to hear all about you! I can't deny I'm most fascinated about how an Englishman ends up in the SS. And in return, you can ask me all about the Ahnenerbe. And later, perhaps some lunch?'

In another time, Lockhart would have found a meeting like this most congenial. A pleasant chat with a fellow academic, lunch, and then an afternoon pottering in a library – what could be better? No doubt there would be some papers in the library that would interest him greatly, but they would just have to stay unread.

He spent the next half an hour telling Rudolph how he had joined the BFC, seeing no reason to hide anything from him, because Rudolph would already have been told everything by Parsch. Besides, Lockhart wanted to cosy up to him, earn his trust. He knew that Rudolph would never tell him what A4 was, but perhaps he might let something slip. Even if today's meeting came to nothing, then at least he would have made a start.

They had lunch in Rudolph's office, and after Lockhart had been told a potted history of the Ahnenerbe, washed down with a bottle of Mosel, he summoned up the courage to ask Rudolph a slightly more sensitive question.

'I gather from Professor Parsch, Herr Doctor,' he began, 'that the organisation is even extending its reach to the most unlikely fields of research.'

Rudolph put down his coffee cup.

'And what did Professor Parsch tell you?'

Lockhart shrugged.

'Nothing much – he merely said that the Ahnenerbe was working in medicine, weaponry – all sorts of areas. I was just a little surprised, that's all.'

Rudolph scrutinised him before answering. Lockhart felt his heart begin to race. Had he overstepped the mark?

'One thing you'll learn about the Reich,' Rudolph said, 'is that organisations end up working in fields that they were never intended for. The other thing you'll need to learn, Dr Lockhart, is that you don't ask questions like that.'

Rudolph's voice had gone cold. Any sense of friendliness had evaporated.

'I'm sorry, Herr Doctor,' said Lockhart politely, inwardly cursing himself. 'I did not mean to stick my—'

Rudolph held up his hand.

'No matter,' he said, standing up. 'Forget it. Now, I have work to do, and I'm sure you are itching to look at our library – yes?'

'Yes indeed.'

By six o'clock, Lockhart had returned to the Adlon, and he decided to treat himself to a beer in the lobby bar, briefly admiring the stained-glass ceiling several floors above. He had spent three hours in the library at the Ahnenerbe headquarters, watched over constantly by a real old battleaxe of a librarian, and had found little of use. There were indeed a few papers of genuine archaeological interest, but there were none that told him anything about A4, sarin, or any other weapons for that matter. Instead, he waded through the predictable Nazi claptrap about eugenics, racial theory and countless other examples of science that had been put to evil ends. Perhaps he had come to a dead end, but he did find one piece of information that made him suspect that he hadn't.

In the SS directory, he had discovered that Hans Kammler, the signatory of the memorandum in Parsch's office, was nothing less than the head of SS construction operations. There was only a little more information about him. He had been born on 26 August 1901 and had joined the Nazi party on 1 March 1932; his SS membership number was 113619, and he had previously worked as an official in the Reich Air Ministry. So what was a man like this doing meddling with an organisation that was meant to research Germanic prehistory? Was he using the Ahnenerbe as a cover? Lockhart knew that he could speculate indefinitely. He needed someone who had access to the highest reaches of the SS, but that was a tall order. And why – for Pete's sake why – had London not got in touch with him?

As he mulled, Lockhart was people-watching, scoffing at the sartorial vulgarity of some of the women who were wafting in on the arms of their Nazi bigwigs, most of whom were considerably older than them. Lockhart supposed that many of the women were either second wives or mistresses, the first wives ditched upon their husbands' attainment of high rank or high office. 'Twas ever thus, he thought.

One of the women caught his eye. A brunette in her early twenties, elegantly dressed in a long dark green cocktail dress, she was smoking a cigarette attached to a long amber holder, and was talking intently to a man whose face Lockhart could not see. From what he could make out, the man was wearing a plain blue suit, unadorned by Nazi regalia, not even an armband. Lockhart found the woman's face captivating – not only was it beautiful, but it looked intelligent, its eyes occasionally darting around the room as she spoke.

And then her eyes met Lockhart's. For a moment, he was transfixed, unable to stop himself looking straight at her, trapped by her gaze. She smirked at him, and then turned her head back to her companion. She would have known what effect she had on men, Lockhart thought, as he found his heart starting to beat rapidly, his palms beginning to moisten. He took a long draught of beer, and then looked back at her. But she didn't look up, and he felt guilty that he had been hoping that she would. Of course, women like her didn't need to look again – they knew that one glance would be enough to ensnare, enough to ensure the attention on which they fed.

Taking advantage of an old waiter limping past, Lockhart ordered another beer as well as a schnapps. He cursed himself for wanting to look at the woman, finding it despicable that he could feel so attracted to her. It was disloyal to Anna, even if she was dead. Yet he couldn't deny that he wanted her. A part of him cried out to seduce her, to take her up to his room and make love to her.

The waiter brought over the drinks, and Lockhart signed for them. He knocked back the schnapps, and then pointedly looked in every direction but hers. He resumed his people-watching, congratulating himself that he was resisting the woman's charms. He told himself, as he had done many times before, that he was allowed to find other women attractive, that it was only natural. Anna even permitted him to flirt, a calculated act on her part that removed any thrill that he gained from the practice. But the flirting had always been set in a formal context, placed against the background of rule-laden London society.

This, however, was different, because this was another decade, another city, in the middle of a war, and rationally he knew he was more than likely to be a widower. There were no rules, so why couldn't he sleep with someone? Perhaps it would even help. His reached his hand inside the left pocket of his breeches, and took out the book of matches from Kitty's. God, it was tempting. And it was bound to be close by. In less than half an hour, he could be in the arms of a prostitute, releasing all that tension, enjoying the feel of a woman's body.

He put down his glass, and saw the woman stand up. He couldn't help but notice she had a fantastic figure. The dress fitted her exquisitely, its bias cut revealing a form that reminded Lockhart of Anna's. Go on, look at her, he told himself, you're allowed to do that; treat her as a statue. He couldn't completely deny his appreciation.

The statue walked towards Lockhart, which led him to assume that she was making for the cloakrooms that lay behind him. But after she had covered fifteen feet or so, with a walk that caused her hips to sway in a mildly provocative way, it became clear to Lockhart that she was in fact approaching him. He resisted the need to look back gauchely over his shoulder, and confidently met her eyes to confirm that he was her target. As she approached, he stood up, smoothing down the front of his tunic. He noticed that her proximity made her no less attractive, perhaps even more so. He felt his heart thumping again. Why did she want to see him? Perhaps she was a prostitute and had identified this lonely SS officer as a likely client. That, thought Lockhart, seemed more than likely.

'Hauptsturmführer Lockhart?'

Lockhart cleared his throat in surprise.

'Yes, Fräulein, but how . . .'

'My companion recognised you. He was wondering whether you would like to join us.'

'And who is your companion?' Lockhart asked, looking over to him. The man was resolutely facing the other way.

'If I told you, I don't think you would come over.'

'Why? What's wrong with him?'

She smiled a little.

'Nothing! He's just someone who wants to be your friend, but feels as though he's a little misunderstood.'

'I'm intrigued.'

'Well, why not join us?'

'I will, but can I ask what your name is?'

'My name is Leni Steiner.'

'How do you do, Fräulein Steiner.'

Smiling, Lockhart held out his hand, which Leni shook briefly.

'You do not seem to recognise my name,' she said.

'No,' said Lockhart. 'Is there any reason why I should?'

Bending slightly at the knees, Leni picked up the book of matches.

'This,' she said, handing it to Lockhart, 'is where I work. One of my clients is a certain Hauptsturmführer Strasser, who I believe you know.'

'But . . . yes, of course. He mentioned you . . .'

Lockhart looked over to the man once more, before turning to continue.

'. . . but that doesn't look like him over there.'

'I know. Did I say it would be?'

'So who is it?'

'I think it would be easier if you came over.'

There was no way Lockhart could refuse. He walked behind her, his gaze alternating between the low-cut back of her dress and her anonymous companion. For a few seconds, Leni's form won, but when they were within a few feet, Lockhart could make out the man's left ear and a small part of the side of his face. That glimpse was all the needed to establish the man's identity, for the face was red and blotchy, scarred by a port wine stain. A naevus, if he wanted the medical term. It belonged to Thomas Pugh.

Lockhart sat down slowly, looking at Pugh. Unable to control himself, he spoke his mind.

'What the fuck is this about, Pugh?'

'I'll tell you everything. Do you want another drink?'

'Yes. And then I want to know what the hell you're doing here, living it up in a place like this.'

Pugh smiled and pointed to his left lapel. In the buttonhole was a small gold swastika badge.

'I'm a fully fledged Nazi, remember? I make a lot of money from broadcasting.'

'You're a traitor, Pugh. I'll see to it that you get hanged.'

'All in good time. But first, why don't you tell me how you got along with Dr Rudolph today?'

Lockhart swallowed, hoping that Pugh wouldn't notice. So they were on to him, and they were sending Pugh as their angel of death. Well, sod them.

'Please,' said Pugh, 'let me assure you, I'm not the person you think I am.'

'Is that right? I always had you down as a top-drawer shit.'

'Please, Lockhart, I'm here to help you.'

'Help me? You?'

'Yes.'

'You *are* joking.'

'Would it help if I told you that Fräulein Steiner and I are employed by the Chief Intelligence Directorate of the General Staff in Moscow? It's perhaps easier to refer to it as the GRU. Are you familiar with it?'

Lockhart looked hard at Pugh, shocked not only by his statement, but also by its baldness. He let Pugh continue.

'Fräulein Steiner has been passing information about

her clients to them for nearly a year now. Me since February, when we were in Danzig.'

'In *Danzig*? Who did you meet?'

'You'll forgive me if I don't tell you.'

'Of course. How convenient.'

'Please, Lockhart – you have to trust me. If this was a trap, then it would be ludicrous. The Germans, if they wanted to, could kill you at the drop of a hat – there would be no need to go through all this.'

Lockhart stood up.

'Listen, Pugh. I'm not a fool. This is some sort of set-up. Do you really expect me to believe that you and she are my new best friends? What would you think if you were in my shoes?'

'Please sit down,' said Leni. '*Please*. I'd probably think the same, but you *must* trust us.'

Lockhart stayed standing.

'Why should I trust you? Just give me one good reason.'

'All right,' said Pugh, 'I will. Your friend Andrew Worstead is betraying you. He's the one writing those letters from your wife.'

'What?'

It was on Leni's suggestion that they left the lobby one by one, and made their way to Lockhart's hotel room. Lockhart was now too intrigued not to talk them, trap or no trap. For the next hour, to Lockhart's mounting astonishment, Pugh told him how he had come to Berlin just before the war, and had spent the past few years swanning around until he had been recruited, against his will, to join the BFC. For that, Pugh blamed John Amery, who he regarded as both 'a fruitcake and a fruit'.

Lockhart found it difficult to accept that Pugh had turned against fascism, especially as he had been such a committed member of the BUF before the war, and had even been an administrative officer at the Black House on the King's Road in London. But Pugh insisted that the move to Genshagen and the progress of the war, coupled with a growing sense of dissatisfaction with the Nazis, had turned him against the regime he had once so admired. Besides, he had no intention of being hanged after the war, and so had approached the Russians in Danzig. It was the GRU that had put him in touch with Leni, and he had told her all about the BFC, as well as countless other nuggets, large and small, that he had picked up over the years.

If that was all true, said a still sceptical Lockhart, then he wanted to know two things. First, how did Pugh know that Worstead was behind the letters, and second, how did he and Leni know that he had visited the Ahnenerbe?

'There are things about Worstead which you probably don't know,' said Pugh.

'Go on,' said Lockhart.

'You know he's another fairy, like Amery?'

This was a shock.

'No I didn't. How do you know?'

'Because I saw him doing it once.'

'Where, for heaven's sake?'

'Here in Berlin. In March last year. It was at a party – an orgy more like – and I saw him doing it in a toilet.'

'But Worstead was in his stalag in March last year. He joined the unit in April.'

Pugh shook his head slowly, smiling, revelling in the telling of his story and its effect on his listener.

'No he wasn't,' said Pugh. 'He's been in Berlin for ages.'

'So what about his girlfriend? His child?'

'That's all crap. Made up by Hillen-Ziegfeld and that lot.'

'All of it?'

'Well, I don't know about *all* of it. But he's even shown me some little photos, given me his sob story as he has with everyone else. Except I didn't believe it. When I met him in Genshagen in June, it was a shock to see him. I had only seen him once before, at that party. He didn't recognise me, for the simple reason that he's never seen me before. He had been too engrossed in what he was doing!'

Pugh let out a self-indulgent giggle. Lockhart's brain was in a spin. If this was all true, and the letters were from Worstead, then what were the ramifications for Anna? But before he could ask, Pugh had started up again.

'For a while, I didn't let on to Worstead that I knew he was a queer. I also suspected that he was a plant, knowing that the story about the girlfriend had to be a pack of lies. But why would it bother me? After all, at that time, I was still pro-Germany. Why did I care if Worstead was spying on us?

'But then I saw a way of making some money. When we got back from Posen, I decided to blackmail him. I told him that I would tell you that he was a nancy-boy, that he was spying on you and that he had lied to you about his past. That made him livid, I can tell you, but there was nothing he could do. The Germans usually lock their fairies up, and so they too must have blackmailed him into helping them. If his cover was blown, he would have outlived his usefulness, and I think they'd send him to a concentration camp, give him a little pink triangle to wear. At the moment, he's paying me forty marks a month, although I'm tempted to up it.'

'But why doesn't he try to stop you?'

'How can he? He can't exactly kill me, because that puts him into a real pickle. He can't tell Strasser, because he's afraid he'll end up in a concentration camp. So the poor bugger has to pay up. Poor bugger! Ha! Do you get it? He's broke and he's a queer – poor bugger!'

Another self-indulgent laugh, this one longer and louder. Lockhart thought about what Pugh had told him. Although there was no evidence, it added up. Pugh was a monster, a conceited and vulgar little shit, but he didn't have the wit to make up a story like this. Besides, there was no motive for it. But he had to keep questioning him – he still wasn't satisfied with Pugh's story.

'Worstead seems sure that the letters were being concocted by you,' he said pointedly, 'as a result of your friendship with a man called Stranders, who, coincidentally, is the son of the organist at my wedding . . .'

'Stranders!' Pugh exclaimed. 'He's no friend of mine! He's friend of Worstead's if anybody's!'

'Really?' said Lockhart.

'Oh yes,' said Pugh. 'Another Englishman of dubious sexuality. Probably one of Worstead's bum-chums – I'd put money on it.'

'Well, apparently you're friends with Stranders . . .'

'Rubbish! But carry on.'

'. . . and Worstead says that *you* and him made up the letters.'

Leni took out a cigarette, which Lockhart lit for her from the book of Kitty's matches. She offered him one, which he accepted. The smoke caused him to cough slightly, but he enjoyed the taste and the soothing effect of the nicotine.

'He's a clever friend, our Mr Worstead,' said Leni, fixing her cigarette into the amber holder.

'A lot cleverer than I thought,' said Lockhart.

'He was obviously trying to get you to do his dirty work,' she said. 'I think he thought that you would get rid of Pugh. That would solve all his problems at once. It would finish the blackmail, and would earn your trust, thereby making him a more useful agent to the Germans.'

Suddenly, Lockhart felt enraged, enraged because he had believed Worstead, enraged because he had trusted him, and enraged because Worstead had made him think that Anna was still alive.

'You're right,' said Lockhart quietly. 'You're absolutely right.'

There was a silence, which Lockhart broke.

'Do you think Strasser has anything directly to do with this?'

'Fifty-fifty,' said Pugh. 'They may have decided that he has no need to know. In fact, they've probably told him that your wife is definitely alive, in order to make his threats to you more realistic. On the other hand, he could of course know.'

At this point, Pugh looked at Leni.

'I know what you're thinking,' said Leni, 'and I'll try. I don't know when I'm seeing him again.'

There was a brief silence. Lockhart thought it time for a change of subject.

'And how did you know about my visit to the Ahnenerbe?' he asked.

'Oh, that's simple,' said Leni casually. 'I saw you – your uniform is *very* distinctive – checking in here last night, and I've been following you all day. As soon as I saw you, I summoned Pugh here.'

Lockhart felt vaguely as though he had been cheated. Leni stubbed her cigarette out, and then leant forward and spoke earnestly to him.

'But what I'd like to know,' she said, 'is what you're up to.'

He had pleaded with her not to go, but she had been adamant, absolutely insistent. She had said that she couldn't just leave her mother over in Holland, it wasn't right. What would *he* do if *he* still had a mother? He said that he would advise her to stay put. What would he know, she had said, he hadn't had a mother since he was five. A cheap shot, he replied, and she apologised. But there was no way, she said, no way she was going to leave her mother to endure a German occupation – it would kill her. They both knew what was happening out there. She had to get her out, bring her and perhaps some other members of her family back home.

The short drive to the station was spent mostly in silence. On the platform, they clutched each other tighter than they had ever done before.

'Take care,' he said. 'If it looks risky, then please – just turn round, come straight back.'

'I will,' she said, 'I promise you.'

They hugged again, tears welling up in both sets of eyes.

'Amy and I just don't want to lose our favourite woman,' said Lockhart.

'You won't – she'll be back, along with your least favourite woman.'

Lockhart chuckled a little.

'She's not *that* bad!'

'I know – I'm just teasing you.'

She broke off from their hug, and held him by the shoulders, looking him straight in the eye. Lockhart thought how beautiful she was – exquisite – and yet how intensely purposeful.

'I love you so much, Mr Lockhart.'

'I love you so much too, Mrs Lockhart.'

'You look after that daughter of ours.'

'I will. We'll be counting the days.'

'So will I. But they'll go so quickly – I'll be back before you both know it.'

As they hugged again, the train drew in, enveloping them in a cloud of steam.

'Time to go,' she sniffed.

'Try calling me tonight.'

'I'll try, but I doubt I'll get through.'

'I'll be in.'

Anna picked up her small canvas rucksack and slung it over her shoulder. They walked arm-in-arm up to the first-class compartment. Lockhart opened the door, and Anna took a step up. She turned round, and bent down slightly to kiss him, running her hand through his hair.

'I love you,' she said.

'I love you.'

'See you in a week.'

'I'll have lunch ready. I'll wangle us some roast pork.'

A whistle blew. Anna took one more step up, and Lockhart followed her, taking her face in his hands and giving her the firmest of kisses.

'Please be careful,' he said.

'It's Holland,' she said. 'Nothing ever happens there.'

They smiled, and the whistle blew again. Anna shut the door, then opened the window and leaned out, holding out her hand, which Lockhart clutched. They just looked at each other, not speaking. There was nothing more to say. The train started moving, taking her hand out of his. They waved at each other until the train was out of sight, the noise receding until both the platform and Lockhart felt empty.

* * *

After Leni had asked her question, Lockhart had excused himself to use the adjoining bathroom. He didn't need it, but instead sat down and turned over all that he had been told. Everything Pugh and Leni had said added up, but could he trust them? He still didn't like Pugh, but then sometimes one had to make alliances with those one found distasteful. Look at Britain and Russia.

And did this mean that Anna was definitely dead? He supposed so, albeit reluctantly. That bastard Worstead, he would kill him . . . No he wouldn't, but he felt like it. His anger, his pain should be channelled into tracking down the sarin, and eliminating it. And what of the A4 project and Kammler? Was that part of it? He would need help to find out, help that was just the other side of the door. He stood up and pulled the chain. Out of habit, he washed his hands. He would tell them, tell them everything he had learned.

'Let me get this right,' said Pugh. 'You mean you want to use the British Free Corps, that bunch of wastrels, to help you destroy some gas that you're not even sure exists?'

'That's right,' said Lockhart. 'It's got to be tried. I've some debts to pay. People have died because of the course I've taken, and as things stand, their sacrifice has been wasted. They didn't die for me to be sitting here in an SS uniform. No, I want the reasons for their deaths to be a lot better than that. I owe it to them to do some good. So far, they've died for John Lockhart, and I don't think that dying for John Lockhart is such a great thing until John Lockhart has done something that makes a difference.'

'How very noble,' said Pugh.

'Well, you know, Pugh, perhaps it is,' said Lockhart, 'though that's not a reason in itself. But I'm glad you think so.'

'I think it's noble,' said Leni, 'but I just don't think it's achievable.'

'I don't deny that's it's difficult.'

'First, you need to find out where this sarin is,' said Leni. 'Second, you have to get the men there. Third, you have to destroy it. And then you've got to get away. Every one of those is almost impossible in itself.'

Lockhart smiled.

'I know,' he said, 'but its chances have improved dramatically over the past two hours.'

'What are you talking about?' Pugh asked.

'I know,' said Leni. 'You want us to help you.'

For a while, Pugh and Leni sat in silence.

'No way!' said Pugh, slamming his fist on the table in front of him. 'No way! You'll get us killed!'

'Calm down!' said Leni.

'You don't have to come along, Pugh,' said Lockhart. 'All I'm asking for is a little co-operation. I doubt very much that Worstead and Maclaren will help me, or Simpkin, Smith or Prain. You can stay with them, still acting the fascist. You can keep them off my back. That would be very helpful – I'd appreciate it very much after the war.'

'What do you mean by that?'

'I mean that if we both survive, then I will make sure that your help is recognised.'

Lockhart could see Pugh chewing this over. He knew he had to appeal to Pugh's innate selfishness.

'What you're saying,' said Pugh, 'is that if I'm tried back home, you'd give evidence in my favour?'

'Yes,' said Lockhart. 'I'd tell any court how you helped me. With my evidence and that of the Russians, I'd say you had a pretty good chance of being let off.'

'I'll have to think about it.'

'Fine.'

He turned to Leni.

'How about you? Will you help?'

'I've told you,' she said, 'I don't think you can do it.'

'You're not answering my question.'

Leni looked at him defiantly.

'I risk my life every day,' she said.

'What for?' Lockhart asked.

'I would like to give you a noble reason as well, but it's more simple than that.'

'Yes?'

'I do it to save my parents. My father is a Jew, and the SD say they'll kill him unless I work at Kitty's.'

'So why do you work for the GRU?'

'For the same reason: to save my parents. When the Nazis lose, they'll be free again, as will I.'

'But you're risking their lives as well.'

'I know – but I don't see that I have any choice in the matter.'

'I'm sorry, Fräulein Steiner,' said Lockhart. 'It is selfish of me to expect you to help. You're already taking enormous risks. It's unfair to ask you to do more.'

Leni's gloved hand took Lockhart by the right forearm. She squeezed it tight, the touch initially making Lockhart feel uneasy.

'I'm not saying I'm not going to help you,' she said. 'I'm just saying I don't know how. If you can tell me that, then I'll do something.'

Lockhart didn't want her to let go of his forearm. Her grip felt comforting and intimate – two sensations he had been deprived of for years. It felt disloyal to Anna, but the lonely part of him needed that touch. When she let go as he spoke, he missed it, but he also cursed himself for missing it.

'There is something you can do,' he said.

'What?' asked Leni.

'The man I saw today at the Ahnenerbe is called Dr Erich Rudolph.'

'Rudolph!'

'You know him?'

'Not intimately, but he's been to Kitty's before.'

Leni squinted at him.

'You want me to . . .' she began.

'I'm sorry, Fräulein,' said Lockhart. 'If there's any point at which you want to withdraw your help, then I'll understand.'

'Good,' she said. 'You realise that if you had tried to force me to help you I would have refused?'

'Yes,' said Lockhart. 'And you still can refuse.'

'Careful,' she said, a slight grin causing her features to lighten. 'It's a little too tempting.'

Pugh coughed. Lockhart and Leni turned to him.

'What's the first part of your plan, then?' Pugh asked.

There was one thing Lockhart had to do before anything else, something vital without which his plan would surely fail.

'The first part I can take care of myself,' he said. 'I'm going to sort out Andrew Worstead.'

Pugh's eyes bulged.

'Are you . . . are you going to *kill* him?' he asked.

'That's not what I said,' Lockhart replied.

Even as he was denying it, Lockhart was wishing to himself that he didn't feel the way he did. In truth, he really did want to kill Worstead. The poor bugger.

The news spread quickly around the St Michael Cloister. The Allies had landed in Normandy, but it was too early to say if they had secured a beachhead. Strasser knew that the development might well cause a change in the men's attitude, so he hauled Lockhart in for a lecture. Besides, Lockhart needed trimming down – he had been somewhat impudent since he had returned from Berlin, and Strasser also resented his friendship with Parsch. Well, Lockhart would stop smiling in a moment. Strasser had some more news for him, some news that would take the spring out of his step.

'You realise,' said Strasser, 'that this changes nothing for us? Indeed, it is more than likely that the Allies will be thrown back into the Channel. It'll be Dunkirk all over again.'

'I doubt that,' said Lockhart, looking a little pleased. Well, it was hardly surprising, thought Strasser. He had felt the same in June '41 when they had invaded Russia. What a fucking mistake that was – an opinion that Strasser had kept to himself.

'I think you'll find,' Lockhart continued, 'that we're a lot better organised this time round.'

'We could speculate all day.'

'Indeed we could. There is one thing, though.'

'What now?'

'I want your absolute guarantee that if we are sent into action, we will not be fighting against British, American or Commonwealth troops.'

This sounded reasonable to Strasser. The implication of Lockhart's words also seemed to be that he was perfectly willing to fight the Russians.

'You have that guarantee – it has always been the case.'

'Thank you,' said Lockhart.

Now was the time to spring the news, the news he was sure that Lockhart would dislike.

'In fact,' said Strasser, 'there is talk that we will shortly be sent to Dresden, so you'll be well away from any of your compatriots.'

Lockhart's expression was just as Strasser had hoped.

'Dresden? Why Dresden?'

'There is an SS pioneer school there.'

'We're going to be pioneers? But we'll be little more than navvies!'

'I didn't know the English had such a low opinion of pioneers. In the Wehrmacht and the SS, they are highly regarded – they destroy minefields, clear enemy defences, man support weapons. It's a front-line role.'

'It sounds as though your pioneers are a little different to ours.'

'We like to think of them as combat engineers.'

'So they're in the thick of it then?'

Strasser smiled.

'That's right,' he said. 'Right in the thick of it.'

'The men won't like that.'

'It's your job to see that they do.'

'And when are we meant to be going?' Lockhart asked.

'I'm not sure,' said Strasser, which was the truth. 'In a few weeks, I think.'

'Next month then?'

'More than likely.'

'Does this mean that I won't get to see my wife?'

Strasser had been waiting for that. In fact, he had thought it was going to come up earlier.

'Not at all. I'm still working on it. I hope to have some good news for your shortly.'

The Rosenstock was usually quiet on Sunday nights, which was why Lockhart chose it for dinner with Worstead. He was scrutinising Worstead's face, looking for a telltale flicker as he had done with Strasser so many times before. Lockhart felt his right leg shaking underneath the table. He was tense, steeling himself for the confrontation that only he knew they were about to have. Worstead looked down at the tablecloth – he was evidently uneasy with the whole subject of Anna.

Since returning from Berlin, Lockhart had been trying
to decide how he would play this moment. Would he play
it straight, by simply accusing Worstead of what he knew?
Or would he be more subtle, laying traps for Worstead,
hoping that he would fall into them? He favoured the
former, as Worstead had proved himself to be supremely
cunning. The straight approach had the benefit of creating
a sense of shocked panic, a sense that should ensure
Worstead would not have the right mind set to wriggle
out.

The waitress arrived with their drinks – two large
beers and two large schnapps. This, thought Lockhart,
would be the last time he raised his glass to Worstead.

'Here's to you, Andrew,' he said, lifting his schnapps
glass.

Worstead looked a little surprised, and raised his glass
as well.

'Thanks, John. But why the toast?'

'Because you're going to need all the luck in the world.'

Lockhart knocked back his drink while Worstead sat
rigid in a state of bewilderment, his glass hovering between
his mouth and the table.

'What do you mean? Is something going to happen to
me?'

'That, my old friend, is up to you.'

'I'm sorry?'

'You've got something to tell me, Andrew. In fact,
you've got rather a lot to tell me.'

'Do I?'

'Yes, Andrew, you do.'

'I'm not with you.'

'That's the problem!'

Lockhart picked up his beer, and took a sip, smiling at Worstead's unintended irony.

'What are you saying?' asked Worstead, clearly agitated, slamming his schnapps glass hard down on the table.

Lockhart took a larger sip, put the beer back down, and leaned forward.

'What I'm saying, dear Andrew, is that I know you're on their side.'

'What?'

Worstead's voice had gone up half an octave, and Lockhart noticed that his hands were shaking. The colour had drained from his face.

'I'm . . . I'm sorry, John, I'm still not following you.'

'Let me make it clear then. You're a traitor, Andrew.'

'A *traitor*? Me?'

For a moment, it crossed Lockhart's mind that Pugh could have been wrong, or could even have double-crossed him, but he dismissed the idea and pressed on.

'Yes, Andrew – you. You've been working for the Germans for ages. All that stuff about Beth and the child is bunk. Nice touch about baby David being born the same day as you, by the way. One of those coincidences that only happens in real life – added a lot of realism to your story.'

Lockhart took a swig of beer.

'Aren't you going to drink, Andrew? After all, dinner's on me.'

'No I'm bloody not. Not until you explain why you're accusing me of this.'

'All right, I will. You're the one behind the letters from Anna. You're the one who's friendly with Stranders, not Pugh. You're the one who's the German stooge, spying on us all on Strasser's behalf . . .'

'But this is preposterous!'

'Is it?'

'Yes it damn well is!'

'Shh, Andrew, shush.'

'Don't you tell me to shut up!'

'I'm not – I just don't want to cause a scene.'

Worstead's entire body was shaking now. He picked up his glass of schnapps and downed it ineptly, some of the liquid dribbling down his chin.

'Who's got to you?' Worstead asked.

Lockhart said nothing. He wanted to let Worstead talk himself out.

'Come on, who? Pugh? Yes – I bet it's Pugh. The bastard. He's always hated me, and now he's poisoning your mind, John. *He's* your traitor, not me. God – when I get my hands on him, I'm going to . . . going to wring his bloody neck. Bastard. John, you have to believe me, *please*, I'm no traitor. Can't you see they're trying to set us against each other? Divide and rule, don't you see? Oh, they're very clever indeed, but we'll get them back, oh yes, there's no doubt about that. You and me, John. Great team, we're a great team.'

It was time for Lockhart to drop his bombshell.

'How come you're feeling so short at the moment?' he asked.

'What?'

'Someone told me that you're feeling skint at the moment. I only wondered why.'

'What's this got to do with anything?'

'I'm interested, that's all.'

Worstead smiled weakly.

'Too many whores,' he said.

Lockhart raised an eyebrow.

'Really?'

'There's this great new Hungarian tart in town called—'

'Blackmail, Andrew. She's called blackmail, and she's the most expensive tart on the street.'

Worstead slumped back, the action causing his jowls to wobble slightly. He opened his mouth, but no words came out, merely a strangled croak.

'Do you want to tell me about it, Andrew?'

Worstead shook his head rapidly.

'In that case,' Lockhart continued, 'why don't I tell you what I know and you can correct me if it's wrong? Is that all right with you?'

Once more, Worstead remained speechless.

'Good,' said Lockhart.

He took a mouthful of beer. Worstead's reaction had showed that he was guilty as hell, he thought. He had him now.

'Pugh is blackmailing you, isn't he? Forty marks a month, I gather. He's blackmailing you because of something he saw in Berlin a long time ago. I don't blame you for what it was, but I blame you for allowing the Germans to make use of you.

'It's all right, Andrew, you don't have to lie to me any more. I expect you've been lying all your life. Lying to me in Crete about your bad luck with the ladies, when all the time you were probably fancying the shepherd boys. For all I know it's why you joined the army – all those men.'

'Just . . . just . . . stop!'

'No, Andrew, I won't. I want to know why you're doing it. I want to know why you're betraying your country; why you're betraying an old friend. There are plenty like you – I saw it at school – and those who continued with it after school kept it quiet, but it wasn't enough to turn them into traitors.'

'Perhaps it is,' said Worstead.

He was crying now, tears wetting his cheeks. Lockhart looked at him. The poor bugger. It wasn't funny any more, but pathetic, sad.

'Is it really?' Lockhart asked.

Worstead took his napkin and blew his nose into it. The tears were really flowing now.

'Oh yes!'

'Why, Andrew? Tell me why.'

'You've no bloody idea what it's like. You'll *never* know what it's like. You're so lucky, John, so damn fucking lucky. You don't know how it feels to be hiding something all your life, hiding something so important, so big. It tears you apart. I never told a soul, and all the time I hated the system that meant that I couldn't. I hated everybody, everything, hated Britain – bloody uptight Britain. And I hated you, you especially.'

'Me?'

423

'Yes – you, and Anna.'

'Why us?'

'Because you had it all. Brains, looks, money, each other – all the things that I knew I'd never have. And you looked down on me, thought I was a joke figure, the "wheezing windbag", I heard that . . .'

'We were just children . . .'

'It makes no difference. It hurts more the younger you are.'

'I am sorry, Andrew, but—'

'Don't apologise! It's all . . .'

As Worstead drew breath to continue, the waitress appeared.

'Are you . . . are you . . .' she began, a little disconcerted by the sight of Worstead. 'Would you like to order?'

'No thank you, Fräulein,' said Lockhart. 'Perhaps you could come back in a few minutes?'

She nodded, gave Worstead one more vexed look, and then turned on her heel.

'All right, Andrew,' said Lockhart. 'Carry on.'

Worstead didn't speak.

'What happened, Andrew? How did you get here? What's the truth? You might as well tell me. Were you in the army at all?'

'I was. But I was never an officer – I didn't make the grade. So I joined the ranks – there was nothing else for me to do. I did all right – I even made corporal, you know.'

'That's good.'

'Is it?'

'Yes, it is.'

'If you say so.'

'So where were you captured?'

'In Belgium – on the way to Dunkirk. And yes, I was sent to a POW camp. That's where things went wrong.'

'Yes?'

'I ... I ... got into trouble.'

'What sort of trouble?'

'I think you can guess.'

Lockhart nodded.

'Sure. Carry on.'

'Anyway, as a result, I was beaten up, ostracised. I had nowhere to turn, until I was offered a way out by the commandant, who must have heard from one of his ferrets that I was having a tough time.'

'What did he say?'

'He said I could leave, go and work in Berlin.'

'What sort of work?'

'It sounded easy. A bit of translating for a radio station. I jumped at it, not least because I was being offered a life away from the camp. You don't know how unbearable it was, John. It was terrifying . . .'

'All right. And what happened in Berlin?'

'At first, I had a good time. There were lots of parties, and very little work. It turned out that there wasn't much translating to be done, and what the Germans really wanted me to do was to write and broadcast propaganda. At first I refused, but they pointed out that I had no choice. Would I like to go back to the stalag, they asked? Or, worse, would I like to go to a concentration camp? I had to help them, John, otherwise I'd be dead by now.'

'And how about the Corps? When did you join?'

'I went to Genshagen in June. Again, I had no choice.'

'And what's your mission here? What are you supposed to be doing for them?'

Worstead looked up at Lockhart warily.

'Come on, Andrew! Spit it out!'

'All right. I'm . . . I'm their plant. I'm here to keep an eye on things, report to Strasser about how it's going. I'm even meant to report back to Berlin about how Strasser is doing.'

'Who in Berlin? Stranders?'

Worstead's eyes bulged. Lockhart pressed home his advantage.

'It's him you cook the letters up with, isn't it?'

Worstead took his beer glass and drained half of it.

'Tell me, Andrew! I need to know! Did you forge the letters?'

Worstead's head slumped down. He mumbled.

'What's that?' asked Lockhart.

'I didn't forge them,' said Worstead. 'It was Stranders. He asked me all about you and Anna, but it was him who did the actual forgeries. He did the first one on his own, the one you got when you were in Berlin.'

Lockhart did his best not to shout.

'For Christ's sake, Andrew! Why did you help him? Why?'

'Because . . . because I had to. They would have *killed* me, John, don't you see that? As soon as Strasser reported back to Berlin that I knew you, they told me I had to help.'

Worstead started sobbing once more. It was time for the big question.

'Andrew. Look at me. *Look at me.* I need to know if Anna is alive.'

But Worstead didn't look up.

'Tell me,' said Lockhart. 'Tell me honestly.'

'Stranders . . . told me she was dead. That's why we were doing the forgeries.'

'And did you believe him?'

'Yes . . . yes, I did.'

'And you've spent all this time playing with me, lying to me, deceiving me. And why? Just to save your skin! Just because you couldn't hack it in a prison camp! You even had the nerve to try and frame Pugh, get me to kill him, to do your dirty work! You're a coward, Andrew, a bloody coward.'

Lockhart stood up. He couldn't bear to be with Worstead, who was snivelling like a young boy. He wanted to be anywhere but here, somewhere he could indulge in his own grief, for he was now certain Anna was dead. Why else would they forge the letters? If she was alive, then why wouldn't they just let her write to him? No, she had to be dead. He looked at Worstead, wanting to knock him senseless, beat him up in the way that he had done to Butcher. Part of him felt sorry for Worstead, but it was not a large part. There were plenty of homosexuals around – not all of them became traitors. He despised Worstead's cowardice, hated his duplicity.

He knew he couldn't leave Worstead here. He would take him back to St Michael, and tell him to shut up, to act as before. He wasn't going to kill him – he wasn't even going to touch him – but he was going to put him on ice. If Lockhart did anything to Worstead, then he himself would get it in the neck – it would simply not be worth it. He would have his revenge, but it would be served cold.

'Come on, Andrew, get up.'

'I'd rather stay here.'

'I said get up!'

Worstead reluctantly pushed himself up from the table and stood with his head bowed. Lockhart removed some marks from his wallet and placed them in the ashtray, and then took Worstead firmly by the elbow. As they left the restaurant, a few heads turned, including that of their waitress.

'He's feeling a little unwell,' Lockhart said to her. 'I've left some money on the table.'

They stepped on to the street, which was dark from the blackout, and almost silent, bar the sound of a distant dog.

'What are you going to do with me, John?'

'Nothing, precisely nothing. We're going to go back to the barracks and pretend nothing has happened.'

'Are you going to tell Strasser?'

'No. Why? Does he know about the letters?'

Worstead shook his head.

'He hasn't a clue,' he said. 'I think he thinks that your wife is still alive.'

So Strasser had not been lying to him. It came as an almost irrelevant relief.

'Why didn't they tell him?' Lockhart asked.

'I don't bloody know!'

Perhaps Pugh had been right. They had not told Strasser because he had no need to know – his threats might not have sounded so convincing had he known the truth.

'What I'd like you to do,' said Lockhart, 'is to keep your mouth shut. Do you understand?'

'Y . . . yes.'

'I'll kill you if you say a word about this.'

They walked for fifty yards without speaking, Lockhart maintaining his grip on Worstead's left elbow. As they reached a corner, he felt Worstead reach inside his tunic with his right hand.

'What are you doing?' Lockhart asked.

'Getting a cigarette.'

Something stirred in Lockhart's head, but it didn't stir quickly enough. Perhaps it was because he was off the ball, thinking about Anna. He'd always thought of Worstead as a smoker, but then he remembered that he hadn't seen him smoking for a long time. There could only be one thing he was getting out of his tunic.

Before Lockhart had a chance to stop him, Worstead had pulled out a small revolver. He broke free from Lockhart's grip and turned to face him the muzzle pointing shakily at Lockhart's chest. Stay calm, Lockhart told himself, think of what you were taught at Arisaig. Keep your eye on the gun. He did so, watching the metallic

shine of the muzzle in the moonlight, bracing himself to
knock it out of Worstead's hand.

'What are you doing, Andrew?'

Worstead didn't reply.

'Put it down, Andrew – this isn't going to help.'

Keep using his Christian name. Be intimate. Above all,
lie.

'Andrew – nothing's going to happen to you. I'll make
sure of it. I promise I won't tell a soul. I'll even get Pugh
off your back.'

Worstead's hand was getting increasingly unsteady.

'There's nothing you can do,' he said. 'Nothing.'

'What do you mean? Of course I can. I can protect
you.'

'No you can't. Nothing can protect me.'

'Stick it out, Andrew – you'll be all right. Please, just
put the gun away.'

'No! Now you know what it's like, John. To be under
threat the whole time. To face death.'

'What do you want, Andrew? What do you want?'

'All I want,' Worstead said slowly, his eyes staring like
those of a madman, 'is to feel what it's like to wield power
before I die. It's a strange feeling, you know, watching you,
knowing that I hold your life in my hands. Now I can see
why people like it. The sense of power. It's rather fun. You
have that power, don't you, John? Those men in the unit
– some of them practically love you, do you know that?
Why is that, I wonder? What is it that men like about you
and hate about me? Is it because I'm queer? It can't just be
that, can it?'

Worstead put the gun to his mouth. But before Lockhart could even shout out, let alone reach forward to stop him, he had pulled the trigger. His head jerked back violently, and fragments of bone and brain burst out of his skull. His body crumpled to the ground, rendered lifeless in less than a second.

Lockhart stood motionless for almost a minute, staring down at Worstead's corpse. Blood was oozing from his head, flowing into a dark syrupy puddle between the cobbles. The poor bugger. But the bloody idiot. Lockhart felt a mixture of contempt and sympathy as he watched the puddle get larger, creeping guiltily away from its owner.

He bent down, grabbed Worstead's tunic and attempted to lift him. It was impossible, for even though Worstead was lighter than he had been ten years ago, he was still bloody heavy. There was no way that Lockhart would be able to carry him. He would have to find some help. He'd go back to the Rosenstock – there were some NCOs there.

The sound of running caused Lockhart to turn round. There, at the end of the road, were a couple of figures sprinting towards him. Lockhart squinted in the dim moonlight – judging by their caps, they looked like civilian policemen. One of them blew his whistle.

'Halt!' the other shouted.

Lockhart stood up, grateful that help had come so quickly.

The policemen came up to him, panting heavily.

'I'm glad you've come,' said Lockhart.

'We heard a shot,' one of them said.

Lockhart looked at their faces – they were the faces of officialdom, faces that made him realise that this wasn't going to be straightforward. They studied Worstead's corpse.

'He just . . . he just shot himself,' said Lockhart.

'That's your story, Hauptsturmführer.'

'No – wait a minute. I'm telling you the truth . . .'

'You can have your say at the station. In the mean time, you're under arrest.'

'What? Under *arrest*? Do you really think I would kill someone in the middle of the road? Get your hands off me!'

But it was no use complaining or struggling, for even as Lockhart spoke, the policemen had wrenched back his arms and tightly attached a pair of handcuffs.

February 1973

'I wish, Amy, you'd just let it go.'

'But don't you see that I can't?'

'Of course you can! Your father wouldn't have wanted you to carry on like this. It's causing you too much pain, and it's really not doing you any good. Look at where it's got you. Nowhere! A roomful of crumbling papers and books, none of which are of any help. The past is just that, Amy – the past.'

She and Hugh rarely argued, but the one topic that was guaranteed to get them both aerated was that of her father. They had been engaged for six months, and the pressures of their forthcoming wedding had made them both a little more tense than usual. This row had started because Hugh had wanted them to slip away for a quiet weekend together, but Amy had declined, saying that she had some newly released files to look over, and this weekend would be the only chance she would have over the next few months.

'I'm sorry, Hugh, but I promised myself that I would find out the truth. I can't give up, not now.'

'And meanwhile your life – your fiancé even – gets put on hold, while you fruitlessly search through a load of old files. You won't find the truth in them, Amy!'

'I've *got* to try.'

'For what exactly? For the future? For us? It makes no difference to us. I'll love you whether your father was a traitor or not. And I'm not going to love you any more just because you find out that he wasn't. Can't you get that into your head? Please listen to me!'

She knew that part of what he said made sense, but it would be impossible to go away this weekend knowing that the truth might be sitting in her study.

'Please, Amy. Let's just go to Shropshire, as we had planned. The files aren't going to go away. You can wait another three days, can't you?'

'I might not have the time. Work's very busy at the moment.'

'It always is. But I don't see why I should be the one who suffers, why it's my time that should be eaten up.'

Amy sighed.

'All right, all right – you win. But so long as you don't mind me staying up late next week and being a rotten fiancée for a few days.'

It was worth it just to see his smile. He came over and hugged her.

'Oh thank you, darling, thank you. It'll be so nice to be together without everyone else fussing about.'

Amy smiled. It would be nice, and she did need the break.

But even as they were hugging, she was wondering whether she could slip a file or two into their suitcase without him noticing.

Chapter Seven

HE WAS LOCKED up in the civilian police station. The cells were freezing, and Lockhart struggled to keep warm under the predictably feeble blanket that he had been issued. But even if it had been less cold, he wouldn't have slept. The matter of his incarceration did not concern him, as he was certain that no court-martial would believe him to be stupid enough to kill someone in the middle of the street and then wait next to the body.

All he was able to think about was Anna, and the last time he had seen her, the last time he now knew he would ever see her. He almost felt angry with her, angry that she had risked her neck, angry that she had been so head-strong. It was selfish of her to have deprived a daughter of a mother and a husband of a wife. Her mother would have been all right, Lockhart had thought. Indeed, she was probably still alive.

And then he cried, because he had lost her, because he had let her go, because he was feeling angry with her. It was *his* fault – he should never have allowed it. She had done what she had thought was right, and it was unfair to her memory to lambast her for that.

He recalled the day when he had heard about the invasion. It had been 10 May, the Friday after Anna had left. She had sent a telegram the day before, saying that everything was going according to plan, and that she and her mother would be leaving on Friday. Lockhart had been in the flat in Pimlico, listening to the Home Service during breakfast.

'Germany has invaded the Netherlands. Nazi paratroopers are reported to have seized several frontier towns early this morning . . .'

He had felt sick, unable to finish his toast. Not stopping to turn off the wireless or find his keys, Lockhart ran out of the flat and down to Belgrave Road, where he hailed a rare taxi. Five minutes later, it had deposited him outside the office in Whitehall. He was panicking, he knew he was, but the only place to find out more was at the office. He hadn't told his colleagues about Anna's mission – they would certainly have stopped her, and he knew that Anna would have hated him for eternity if he had thrown the book at her.

He spent all morning on the phone, but nobody could help. Many had more important matters to attend to, as Lockhart had anticipated. The line to the Dutch Embassy in Portman Square appeared to have failed. Some in the Foreign Office were rude, telling him that he was a fool to let his wife go in the first place. It was impossible to send a telegram, as every telegraph office he tried told him that services had been suspended. He even posted a letter, out of sheer desperation, knowing that it would never make it across the Channel.

As the day wore on, Lockhart knew his attempts were futile, and with that growing awareness of futility, he felt increasingly desperate. He managed to annoy nearly every department in Whitehall, as well as every military contact he had ever made. By six o'clock, reports indicated that Holland would be overrun during the weekend, such was the speed of the German advance. It would be impossible for Anna to get out – everybody else would be heading west, and with an infirm mother, her progress would be further hampered.

But there was a chance she might get out, a hope that Lockhart had clung to over the next few days. He had barely slept, trying to work out if there was something he had forgotten. He regularly thought of trying to get to Holland, but he knew that it would be fruitless, if not impossible. He telephoned the house in Oxford every hour, asking Amy's nanny if there were any telegrams. Each time she told him that none had arrived, he felt a little more hollow, more gouged out. After a week, he knew he had lost her.

As Lockhart lay in his cell, he knew that the hollowing process had been completed. Now that he knew she was dead, he felt like a husk. He did his best not to imagine the way in which she had died, but he couldn't help it. His subconscious kept replacing Worstead's face with Anna's. In his mind, it was her blood seeping on to the cobbles, her brains that had been blasted out of the top of her head. Part of him died that night, but what remained was strong enough to continue, strong enough to fight on.

Strasser entered his cell at five thirty in the morning.

'Tell me what happened,' he said.

What Lockhart proceeded to tell Strasser was true, but not the whole truth. He told him that they'd had a few drinks at the Rosenstock, during which Worstead had told him that he was unhappy being a member of the BFC, that he was sick of being a traitor, and that he knew he would never see Beth and his son again. They had left the Rosenstock without having eaten, and when they were out on the street, Worstead pulled out a gun and shot himself.

'Just like that?' Strasser asked.

'That's right,' said Lockhart. 'It happened very suddenly. I didn't have time to stop him. I had no idea he was so down, so depressed.'

'Neither had I,' said Strasser.

'So, what's going to happen to me?'

Strasser paused.

'Things aren't looking good for you, Lockhart.'

'What?'

'There's a waitress.'

'Yes?'

'A waitress at the Rosenstock.'

'What about her?'

'She says that you dragged Worstead out of the bar after you'd had an argument. She also says that you looked as though you meant to harm him, that you were threatening him.'

'Jesus Christ! We weren't having an argument, although I don't deny our voices were raised. Worstead was bloody upset, and I was trying to calm him down – he was almost hysterical. I decided to call dinner off, and yes, somewhat against his wishes, I took him out by his arm. But the idea that I looked as though I meant to harm him is pure bunk. Besides, it's not even evidence.'

'Well, it's enough to make them hunt for more.'

'What?'

'I'm afraid they don't believe your story.'

'This is absurd. Do they really think I would hang about next to somebody I had just shot? Can't you do something, Strasser?'

'I'm sorry. I can't.'

'Of course you can! *You* must believe me – go and tell them that they're wasting their time.'

'I don't know what I believe.'

'So you're going to do nothing?'

'Yes. Because nothing is all I can do.'

'Leni!'

'Yes?'

It was Waltraut, the maid, outside her door.

'It's a telegram for you.'

Leni looked at the clock next to the bed, the one she had looked at so many times as she had been with so many men. It was five o'clock in the afternoon, and, rarely for a Monday, she had already had one client, a Rumanian sturmbannführer who had been mercifully quick. She got out of bed and put on her silk robe. Telegrams were not uncommon. They were usually from regulars expressing gratitude for 'a wonderful time, my little Leni', or informing her that she could expect the sender at the end of next week, and would she keep the bed warm for him?

She opened the door, and Waltraut handed her the telegram.

'I expect it's from another admirer,' said Waltraut. 'You get so many more telegrams than the others.'

Leni smiled.

'Thank you, Waltraut.'

'Do you need anything else?'

'No. No, I don't think so.'

Leni ripped open the envelope and removed the telegram. Before she unfolded it, she noticed that Waltraut was still standing there, obviously nosy about the contents of the message.

'*Thank you*, Waltraut.'

'Sorry, *madam*.'

Leni shut the door. The poor old dear – she loved to gossip. She let herself fall back down on the bed, and sighing, opened the telegram. Which general was this one from?

But it wasn't from any General. It was from Pugh.

The Traitor

+++ Starts

Our friend is trapped and dying to get out STOP
Summon your boyfriend immediately STOP Ask him
to let our friend go free STOP Use all your charms
because our friend is desperate STOP

Ends + + +
12:34
12.6

She knew what it meant. She rushed to the door, and hurriedly pulled it open.

'Waltraut!' she shouted down the corridor.

No sign. She ran out of her room.

'Waltraut!'

She turned a corner, where she found Waltraut looking at her quizzically.

'Yes, my dear?'

'Is Kitty here?'

'No, I think she's out shopping.'

'For how long?'

'I don't know.'

'Does her phone still work? The one in her office?' Leni asked.

'I think so.'

'Good.'

'Must be quite an admirer, this one,' said Waltraut with a wink.

*   *   *

'How did you get hold of me here?' Strasser asked. 'How did you get the number?'

'I have my ways,' Leni said. 'I meet a lot of influential people in my line of work.'

Strasser laughed.

'I don't doubt it! Anyway, what do you want?'

'I'd like to see you,' she purred down the line. 'I'd like to see my Carl very much indeed.'

'When?'

'Tonight – I'd like to see you tonight.'

'But . . . but that's impossible.'

'Come on, Carl. We won't be at Kitty's. It would be just you and me. We could stay at a hotel . . .'

'I just can't. Something's happened here . . .'

'It'll be my only free night for ages. There might not be another chance. Come on, Carl, this is what you said you wanted – a night together like a normal couple.'

'Shit!'

'Language, Carl!'

'Sorry, I wasn't swearing at you, just at myself.'

'Please, Carl. We could be together *all night*. Just think of it. You could pour champagne all over my—'

'Leni! It's out of the question. I'm needed here.'

'You're also needed *here*.'

'I can't just leave, not at such short notice! Are you sure you're not free at the weekend?'

'Weekends are my busiest time.'

'Shit!'

'*Language!*'

'Sorry.'

'I don't mind how late you come.'

'Really? Even if it's very late?'

'I sleep during the day – remember?'

'Of course.'

Strasser paused.

'Carl?' she asked. 'Are you still there?'

'Yes, yes – I'm just thinking.'

'Thinking what?'

'I'm thinking that I could come. I know there's a troop train coming through later, on its way to Berlin. I could get on that . . .'

'Excellent!'

'I'd get in at about one in the morning, though.'

'Perfect.'

'Where shall I meet you?'

'Meet me at the Adlon.'

'The Adlon? But that costs a—'

'I'm paying.'

'But . . .'

'Don't worry, Carl – I have plenty of money. I'll be in Room 38.'

'How come you've already got a room? How could you have been sure I would come?'

'I knew you would, Carl. See you later.'

The phone went dead in Strasser's ear.

Kitty had not believed her when she said she was feeling unwell, but as it was a Monday, she had let it go. Kitty knew that the girls needed breaks more often than the SD allowed, and feigning illness was usually the only way they could get some time off.

'So who's the lucky young man?' she had asked with a smirk.

'No, Kitty, I promise you, I'm feeling terrible.'

Kitty winked at her.

'Of course, my darling. Why don't you come back tomorrow when you're feeling better?'

'I will. I think I just need a night to myself.'

'All right. Off you go then.'

In truth, Leni really could have done with a night on her own. She was exhausted by the nature of her work, by the anxiety about whether she would be caught, and by worrying about her parents. And now this. She wondered what had happened to Lockhart to get him locked up. Perhaps he had killed Worstead? Surely not – it would get him into too much trouble.

She liked Lockhart. When the GRU had got back to her, telling her that she and Pugh must work with him, she had not found the prospect unattractive. Pugh had bristled at it, but she reminded him that he had no choice, he was in too deep. There was something charming and gentlemanly about Lockhart, something polished, but not overly so. She liked his love for his wife – a rare display of decency. And he was handsome – he must have had a lot of admirers back in England, she thought. What was Anna like, Leni wondered, what sort of woman was she? Pugh had told her she was also an archaeologist, an academic like Lockhart. At first, she had imagined a frumpy, plain girl with glasses, but then judging by Lockhart's looks, his wife must be good-looking as well. Or *was* good-looking, Leni thought; there was no way she could be alive, not after four years in a camp, no way.

She reached the Adlon at seven o'clock. The lobby was already teeming with high-ranking Nazis. As she walked through them, the only conversation she could make out was about the landings in Normandy. From what she could gather, the Allies had already taken a few key towns, and had landed hundreds of thousands of men on the beaches. The talk in the lobby that night sounded bullish, Leni thought, but she wondered how many of those who were talking big were already planning their escape routes, arranging their new identities and new futures. If she survived, she had resolved to help track those men down, using her intimate knowledge of so many of them to get her revenge. They would regret fucking her, regret writing her off as just another whore.

'Hello, Ulrich.'

Leni had reached the reception desk. Ulrich was her favourite receptionist. He must have been about eighty, but he was spry and fit – even his moustache was in good shape. He reminded Leni a little of her father, before his spirit was crushed that day by the Gestapo.

'Hello, Fräulein Hoffman! How nice to see you!'

Ulrich turned to get her key.

'No messages for you, I'm afraid.'

He handed her the key for Room 38.

'Thank you, Ulrich.'

She smiled sweetly at him. It was her genuine smile, not

the smile she gave clients, which they all thought was her real one, the idiots.

The room was a godsend. The money to pay for it came from the GRU, who had decided a few weeks ago that she needed a base away from both Kitty's and her flat. 'Fräulein Hoffman' tried not to come here too often, in case she was noticed, but it was hard to stay away from the luxuriousness of the bedroom, which contained a huge four-poster bed with a good firm mattress. What made it even more tempting was the large bathtub, into which she was now running hot water, as well as adding some salts.

She undressed and got in the bath, briefly debated whether she would wash her hair, and then plunged her head under the water. She would need to look her best tonight. She had already worked out how she was going to play it with Carl. As Pugh had said, it would require her to use all her charms, but she had decided to play it a lot tougher than that. It would be unfair to trick Carl any longer – it was time he was compromised. There was no other way it was going to work, and besides, it might even help Lockhart.

The knock on the door came a little sooner than she had expected. She had spent the past few hours waiting, reading magazines, preparing herself.

'Hello?'

'It's Carl.'

'Just coming.'

She checked herself in the mirror. She was wearing her silk robe, under which she had on a basque and a pair of stockings. They all liked this look, she thought, especially Carl. She thought it looked ridiculous, especially with the high heels, but then there was nothing about the male sexual appetite that surprised her any more. She felt the neck of the champagne bottle – good, it was still cold. There was a large plate of cold meats and pickles next to it – she had guessed Carl would be hungry after his train ride.

She opened the door, and there was Strasser, looking a little unkempt.

'Why, you look as though you've just spent half the night on a troop train.'

'Hell on wheels,' said Strasser, before checking her up and down. 'But well worth it.'

She reached forward and grabbed him by the belt and pulled him into the room. Then she kissed him hard, and pushed herself into him.

'It's good to see you again,' she said.

'Thank you for persuading me to come.'

'You had no choice!'

'I know. You were very persuasive.'

Leni let go and walked into the room.

'Why don't you open that bottle of champagne?' she asked. 'And there's some food for you – I didn't know whether you would have got the chance to eat this evening.'

'You're right – I didn't. But first, I'd like to eat something else.'

Strasser smirked.

'Be my guest,' she said, and turned her back on him.

She walked over to the bed, knowing that Strasser

would be admiring her behind. It was his mouth she felt first, kissing the back of her neck. And then his hands on her breasts, caressing them roughly at first, and then pinching her nipples through the silk of her robe and the lace of her basque. She pressed her buttocks into his groin, feeling him getting hard.

Strasser didn't say a word as Leni bent over the bed. Instead, she could hear him unbuttoning his breeches, and then the sound of them falling to the floor. She felt his hands on her buttocks, squeezing them, and then hitching up her robe. He pulled her panties to one side, and then forced himself inside her, gripping the fronts of her thighs, slamming her body on to his groin.

Within no longer than two or three minutes, he had come. Leni was glad. Now that he had done so, he would be more relaxed, more malleable. Besides, she couldn't have faced a long-drawn-out session – it would have made her feel too guilty.

'I couldn't stop myself,' he said.

'It doesn't matter,' she smiled. 'We've got all night. That was just an aperitif.'

Strasser laughed.

'Talking of aperitifs,' he said, 'I might open that champagne.'

'Please do . . . By the way – would you like a bath?'

'Why? Do I need one?'

Leni nodded slowly and coquettishly.

'Just a little hint of troop train.'

'I'm sorry . . .'

'Don't be. I'll run it for you.'

Leni walked into the bathroom and turned on the taps. She prayed to God that there was still some hot water. She held her hand under the tap for what felt like an age, but eventually it came, scaldingly hot, hissing and burbling.

'Do you want some bath salts in it?' she shouted through.

'Yes!'

She put in a healthy dose – that would make him even more relaxed. She went back into the bedroom to find Carl standing naked next to the table, piling meat into his mouth.

'You look starving!'

'I am,' he said with his mouth full. 'Sorry, here's your champagne.'

He passed her a glass, and she raised it to him.

'Here's to our boys in Normandy,' she said.

Strasser looked surprised – he had expected Leni to toast something a little more intimate, a little more flippant perhaps.

'Our boys in Normandy,' he said. 'And those in the east.'

'Those in the east,' said Leni, and took a mouthful.

Strasser picked up a piece of ham.

'This is delicious!' he said.

'Good. I'm glad you like it.'

'How can you afford to stay in a place like this anyway?'

'Some of my rather more high-ranking clients can be very generous.'

'Extremely generous. So who's this on? Whose generosity am I abusing tonight?'

'Oh, a crusty old Wehrmacht general you've probably never heard of.'

'Try me. What's his name?'

Leni walked over and kissed him.

'Now, my darling Carl, you don't think I'm going to tell you that, do you?'

Strasser smiled awkwardly.

'I think your bath may be ready,' said Leni. 'I'll come and sit with you. Perhaps I could help you wash?'

'That would be wonderful,' he said. 'I don't think I've been washed by somebody else since . . . since my mother.'

Leni giggled.

'This will be very different from your mother's baths!'

'I hope so!'

Leni led Strasser into the bathroom. He stepped into the bath and lay back, letting the hot water wash over him.

'This is a great bath,' he said, closing his eyes.

'Let me wash your chest.'

Leni rolled up the sleeves of her robe, and took a bar of soap from the tray. It smelt of lavender, the type of detail that made the Adlon so expensive. She worked up a lather, and soaped Strasser's chest. He groaned with pleasure.

'That feels so good.'

Leni rinsed her hands in the bath water, and playfully gave his penis a tug. As she stood up, she gave him a kiss on the forehead.

'I've just got to get something from the other room,' she said.

'Go ahead,' said Strasser drowsily, his eyes shut.

Strasser thought he was in heaven. The problems with the unit felt a long way away. He wanted to lie here for the next year, washing off the grime of the war. He grinned to himself. How many other SS officers were getting their chests washed by whores as good-looking as Leni? None, he wagered. It just showed, he thought, that money was not the only thing that talked. He let his entire head submerge and held his breath, listening to the amplified sound of Leni's high heels on the bathroom floor as she walked back in. After a few seconds, he came back up, and took a deep breath. Because he kept his eyes closed, he couldn't see that Leni was pointing his P38 right at the chest she had just washed.

There had been rumours going around the camp, very vague rumours, that the Allies had landed in France. A railway worker had told somebody who had come in on a transport that there had been a huge invasion, and that the war would be over within a few weeks. Many believed the rumours, but not 10678, who knew that rumours, especially those that contained hope, were not to be believed. In her experience, it was only the bad ones that held any truth.

But these rumours were different. They kept coming round, not dying off after a few days. The Allies had made great breakthroughs; they had taken lots of towns; they were marching on Paris; Berlin would fall by Christmas. They were persistent, and yet still she did not believe them. Why are you such a cynic? she was asked. It must be true they said, no smoke without fire.

She only started to believe them when the Germans started to deny them. At the head count one morning, an officer told them that the stories of an Allied invasion were nonsense. Anybody who was caught spreading such a rumour would be shot. And even if there was an invasion, the officer continued, the English and Americans would get no further than the beaches. That proved it, she thought. But she wasn't going to share her opinion with anybody. She had survived for too long to risk her neck, not now, not when the end was in sight.

Perhaps he was with them. Perhaps he was fighting his way towards her, coming to save her. Her white knight, charging through the fields of northern Europe to rescue his true love and carry her off. She knew it was absurd, stupidly romantic, but she wallowed in it for a while, allowing herself a rare few moments of fantasy. The rumour *had* given her hope, and with it a sense of freedom, a freedom inside her head to live in a world that seemed magically normal, a world with a husband and child.

10678 looked out the window of the hut. It was a lovely evening, she thought. The sun was still catching the tops of the pine trees that stood in freedom on the other side of the wire. A light wind was tickling through them, causing their needles to ripple. Behind them, the sky was a deep blue, reminding her of a summer many years ago, the summer when she had first met him.

She shut her eyes. In her mind, she could walk through the trees, feeling the soft bounce of the dead needles beneath her feet, picking up the occasional pine cone to take back home. When she got out of here, she would take lots of the cones with her, and she and Amy would paint them. She would then arrange them into a pile, and would tell Amy that the pile represented her father, her father who was never going to come back.

She opened her eyes. The wind had stopped blowing through the pines, and now they were quite still. It seemed that everybody was dead. If it wasn't for Amy, then she would join them. She would walk out of the hut, go over to the electrified wire and climb over it. She would cross the dead ground, and go into the wood, collecting her cones. There would be no rush, because they wouldn't see her, wouldn't be able to kill her. How could they touch her, when she too was already dead?

Strasser grinned and opened his eyes. What he saw made him sit up violently, causing a wave of water to wash over the side of the bath.

'What the fuck are you doing?'

'Pointing your gun at you, Carl.'

'I can see that! Is this a game? Just what—'

'Quiet, Carl,' said Leni soothingly. 'We don't want to wake up the rest of the hotel, do we?'

Strasser looked into Leni's eyes.

'Is this what all you whores do?' he asked.

'Do what?'

'Rob their clients.'

Leni smiled.

'I'm not going to rob you, Carl.'

'So why are you pointing the gun at me?'

'Because I want you to help me.'

'Help you do what?'

'All in good time, Carl, all in good time. First of all I'd like to explain a few things.'

'Go ahead.'

'And I don't want you to shout again, either. Because if you do, I shall turn on the hot tap and leave it running. And if you try to get out of the bath, I shall shoot you.'

Strasser could not believe his senses.

'Leni? Is this a joke? Come on, stop it – it's not funny.'

'It's not a joke.'

Leni pulled back the hammer of the P38 with her thumb. She was pleased to see that this small action caused Strasser to swallow.

'You're a lucky boy, Carl.'

Strasser shook his head slightly. Lucky was the last thing he felt.

'You don't believe me, but I promise you that you are. If I hadn't liked you so much, you'd have died months ago. There's no need to look so puzzled, Carl. I'm sure you can guess what I'm going to say.'

Once more, a small shake of the head. The bath water rippled slightly.

'I'm *very* disappointed, Carl. Have a guess.'

'I . . . I just don't know.'

Leni tutted.

'All right – I'll put you out of your misery. I'm a spy, Carl, a spy for the SD. It's my job to report on all those naughty boys who don't keep their traps shut. And do you know what happens to naughty boys who talk too much?'

This time, Strasser nodded. Leni would never have imagined that he could look so surprised.

'What happens, Carl?'

'I . . . I expect they disappear.'

'That's right. They disappear. For ever.'

Strasser knew exactly what that meant. He had once heard from Max, back at the Hauptamt, about a fellow hauptsturmführer who had been in trouble with the SD. Apparently, the first the man's wife had heard about his fate was a bill for 746 Reichsmarks and 60 Reichspfennigs. The figure, Max had told him, had been broken down: 300 Reichsmarks were put down as 'Fee for Death Penalty'; 158 Reichsmarks and 18 Reichspfennigs were for the 'Cost of Execution (Beheading)'. Strasser had not believed it, had not wanted to believe it, but Max had assured him it was true.

'But . . . but what about me?' Strasser asked.

'What about you?'

'Have you told anybody . . .'

'No, Carl – I haven't. Now can you see why you're such a lucky boy?'

Another nod, this time far more enthusiastic.

'But why didn't you tell anybody?'

'Because I like you,' said Leni.

'Yes?'

'And I didn't want to see you beheaded.'

Strasser's eyes enlarged considerably.

'Well,' said Leni, 'aren't you going to thank me?'

'*Thank you*. Really, thank you.'

'Good. I'm glad my little concession to you has been appreciated.'

Strasser stayed silent.

'So you see,' Leni continued, 'that you are now effectively in my debt.'

'Yes, of course. What would you . . .'

'What would I like you to do?'

'Yes,' said Strasser keenly. 'Whatever it is – I'll do it.'

'You mean that?'

'God, yes.'

'Good. And you realise what will happen if you don't help me?'

'What?'

'I'll tell the SD that you talk too much.'

'What do you want me to do, Leni? Do you want money? I don't have much . . .'

'I don't want money, Carl. If I wanted money, do you think I'd have chosen you? A mere hauptsturmführer?'

'I suppose not.'

'What I want is something far more important to me than money.'

'What is it?'

'I want you to release Hauptsturmführer Lockhart from prison.'

Strasser clutched the sides of the bath as if he was trying to get up.

'Lockhart? But . . .'

'That's right,' said Leni.

'But how do you know about Lockhart? What's he got to do with you?'

'Neither of those things are any of your business.'
'But it's impossible! I don't have the authority . . .'
Leni turned on the hot tap.
'Leni!' shouted Strasser. 'You must believe me!'
Leni put a finger to her lips.
'Shh, Carl, shh.'
'But you must understand, I can't help you!'
Leni looked down at the bath.
'There's room for a lot more hot water, isn't there?'
'Anything else, Leni, I'd do! But this I can't. I promise!'
Leni stood up and pointed the gun at Strasser's face.
'Lie back,' she ordered.
Strasser did as he was told.
'But Leni . . .'
'Shut up! The water's going to get very hot soon, and then you're going to have to make your mind up. Stay in it and get burnt. Or jump out and get shot. Or of course there is a third option, and that's for you to do as you're told.'

Strasser could feel the hot water making its way up the bath. At the moment, it was bearable, but he knew that in a few minutes, even with the water overflowing, it would be almost boiling. What he hadn't counted on was Leni turning the tap on to full. After half a minute, he felt his feet beginning to get scalded.

'Christ, Leni! Turn it off!'

Leni's reply was to bring the gun closer to his face. The heat was now on his legs – within seconds it would be enveloping his groin.

'Leni!'

She pressed the gun against his forehead. He could feel his genitals starting to burn, the intensity of the heat more painful than he could ever have imagined.

'I'll do it!' he shouted.

'Do what?' said Leni.

'Get Lockhart out! Fuck! Please, Leni, turn off the water!'

Leni took the gun away from his head and turned off the hot tap.

'The cold!'

'Not yet,' said Leni. 'Not until you promise me one more thing.'

'Anything! What?'

'You do anything that Lockhart says.'

All Strasser could think about was the ferocity of the heat on his legs and genitals. A small part of his brain, a minuscule part that was not concerned with pain, was curious, but his priority was to listen to his body, to get rid of the agony.

'Fuck! Yes! All right! Whatever you say!'

'Say it!' barked Leni.

'Say what?'

'Say you'll obey Lockhart!'

Strasser's pause resulted in Leni reaching for the hot tap again.

'I'll obey him!' said Strasser. 'I'll do whatever he says!'

Leni smiled. This time she turned the cold tap.

'What a good boy you are,' she said, passing Strasser a towel.

'And by the way,' she added, 'don't think of doing

anything stupid. If anything happens to me, you'll be the first person they'll come to.'

Strasser nodded once more. As the cold water crept up his body, he began to wonder how on earth Leni and Lockhart could have anything to do with each other.

The key turned in the lock at around eight in the morning. Lockhart assumed it was the guards bringing some excuse for breakfast, and declined to look round. He had been staring at the cell wall next to the bed for nearly three hours, contemplating his next move. He still could not believe that he might face a court-martial, and he had been going over what he would say to defend himself. But interrupting those thoughts was a constant stream of images of Anna and Amy, images as visible as the stonework in front of his eyes. The more he tried to shake them off, the guiltier he felt for doing so, a vicious circle that would have resulted in tears if he'd had any left.

'Lockhart!'

It was Strasser's voice. Lockhart rolled over to face him.

'Yes?'

'I'm here to set you free.'

Lockhart sat upright. The sudden movement and the relief made him feel light-headed.

'But I thought they were looking for more evidence . . .'

'Not any more. I've convinced them that the charge is ridiculous.'

Lockhart stood up.

'Well, you're not such a bad bloke after all. Thank you very much.'

Strasser smiled weakly. Lockhart thought he looked washed out, an absolute wreck.

'Christ, Carl, what the hell were you up to last night?'

'Securing your release.'

'What did you have to do?'

'We need to talk about that.'

'Really?'

'Yes.'

Lockhart ran his hand through his hair and buttoned up his tunic.

'What's there to talk about?' he asked. 'Presumably you just told them that it would be ridiculous of me to stand in the middle of the road next to somebody I had just shot . . .'

'I'm afraid it's rather more complicated than that.'

Strasser looked shifty, thought Lockhart, uncharacteristically incapable of making eye contact.

'I see,' said Lockhart. 'There's some sort of quid pro quo then, is there?'

'Shall we go back to my office?'

'I'd prefer to have a wash and something to eat first.'

'You can do that later.'

Strasser poured out two cups of coffee, real coffee.

'So what is it?' asked Lockhart, blowing on the surface of the almost black liquid. 'Why so cagey?'

Strasser was slumped at his desk. He had got back from Berlin at seven this morning, and felt terrible. After leaving that bitch Leni's, he had made his way to the Zoo station, where he had tried – and failed – to sleep on a bench. He had spent the small hours trying to work out if there was anything he could do to escape Leni's threats. There was nothing. The SD was too powerful, its tentacles too far-reaching to attempt to outwit it. It occurred to him that he should kill her, but that would be barbaric. He had done enough killing in Russia, had seen too much death. He couldn't just go back to the Adlon and coldly murder her.

What puzzled Strasser most was how Lockhart and Leni knew each other. Did Lockhart work for the SD as well? No – that was ridiculous, impossible. So what did that leave? That they were both spies for the Allies? Could that be so? Had Lockhart tricked him all along – had his entire treachery been a charade, merely using the unit as a way to get deep inside the Fatherland? And how was Leni involved? A British agent also?

So intense were his thoughts that Strasser nearly forgot to get off the train at Hildesheim. He felt trapped, wretched. If Leni and Lockhart did work for the Allies, then by assisting them he would become a traitor himself. Not a fake traitor like Lockhart, but a *real* one. Images of being caught, tortured and executed flooded his exhausted brain. He had survived too long now for that to happen.

He supposed that he could tell the SS what was going on, but there would be a risk in doing that, a terrible risk. He would be more than just reprimanded for allowing Leni to dupe him – he would doubtless be shot along with her and Lockhart. The SD wouldn't be merciful just because he had blown the whistle. He would be tainted, soiled, and they wouldn't want to keep him alive. And what then? Who would they send the bill to? His old father? Bastards.

His legs, and not his mind, carried him to the police station. He was on automatic as he spoke to the duty officer, telling him that as Hauptsturmführer Lockhart was in the Waffen-SS, he would need to be disciplined by the Waffen-SS, and that it was not the job of the criminal police to deal with him. The duty officer was reluctant at first, but Strasser put the fear of God into him, telling him, that he would get him sent to a concentration camp for disobeying the order of an SS officer. It worked.

Strasser coughed before he answered Lockhart's question. It was not a good cough, the type that dislodges something, but a wheezing cough, the type that feeds on itself, making life unbearable.

'You should see the medic,' said Lockhart. 'That sounds nasty.'

Strasser waved off the suggestion.

'So what's the matter?' Lockhart asked.

'Everything's the bloody matter,' said Strasser.

He watched Lockhart take a nonchalant sip of coffee.

'Especially you,' Strasser continued, 'and especially this fucking unit! I was fine until this came along, doing just fine at the Hauptamt, pen-pushing, glad to be away from the Russian front. And now, thanks to you lot, it looks as though I'll be going back there.'

'Oh?'

'If I'm lucky! That's if I'm not shot first.'

'*What?*'

'You heard me.'

'But why . . .'

'I think you know.'

'I'm sorry, Strasser, but I don't.'

'Yes you do.'

'I do?'

'Stop acting the innocent! You and that bitch in Berlin are blackmailing me, and I want to know why!'

Strasser studied Lockhart's face, but the Englishman was expressionless. Another sip of coffee.

'I'm sorry, Strasser, but—'

'I told you! Stop acting dumb! I want to know the truth!'

'I've got no idea what you're talking about.'

Enraged, Strasser knocked his coffee cup on to the floor.

'Stop lying! You know full well who she works for!'

'All right, Strasser, yes I do know who Leni works for.'

'Who then? Who do you think?'

'She works for me, Carl.'

Strasser sat up. How was this possible?

'For you?'

'That's right.'

'But . . . but how?'

'I don't think I need to tell you that. All you need to know is that things are going to change.'

'Change? How?'

'Well, for a start, I'm no longer going to take orders from you.'

Strasser tried speaking, but his cough got the better of him. For the next half a minute, he hacked violently, until at last he managed to speak. This was monstrous, appalling. He wasn't going to take this . . . this arrogance. He knew how to shut Lockhart up.

'I'll have your wife shot for that!'

Lockhart shook his head calmly.

'No you won't, because she's already dead, as I'm sure you know.'

This was news to Strasser. He had been told the woman was alive. She would probably be little more than a skeleton, but she would be alive all the same.

'Dead?'

'Now you're the one acting the innocent.'

'But she's in a camp!' Strasser protested.

'No, Strasser, she isn't anywhere. She's dead. Just dead. Killed by you for being in the wrong place at the wrong time. A crime in your book.'

'What makes you think . . .' Strasser began.

'What makes me think that she's dead? The letters are forgeries, Strasser, something else I'm sure you're aware of, cooked up by your little friends in Berlin, and of course our very own Mr Worstead, your late informer.'

'*Worstead* wrote them?'

'Don't expect me to believe that you don't know anything about this. I won't buy it.'

'I assure you, Lockhart, that if she is dead, then *I* have been lied to. I was told that your wife was alive, and that the letters were from her.'

As far as Strasser was concerned, this was the truth.

'Where did they come from?'

'They were sent from Berlin.'

'But from where exactly?'

'From the Germanic Administration.'

'That's where Stranders works, isn't it?'

'That's right.'

Strasser watched Lockhart stand up and walk to the window. He felt like a pawn, caught between Lockhart and his superiors in Berlin. He had been misled by everyone, even those on his own side, and for what? For the success of this ridiculous unit? What a joke. The unit had created an opportunity for someone of Lockhart's intelligence, and he had grasped it successfully. All the time, those idiots in Berlin had been playing their little games, and all it was doing was losing them the war. It was farcical. What had happened to them? The Reich was surely dying, starting to decay.

'You realise that you're trapped, don't you?' Lockhart asked, still staring out the window.

Strasser coughed. Lockhart was merely stating the obvious.

'Now that you know my wife is dead,' Lockhart continued, 'you've nothing to threaten me with. I suppose you could kill me, but when Leni hears about that, she'll report your little indiscretions. That would be the end of you, Strasser, not just your career, but your life. They'd shoot you. So it wouldn't be worth doing that. And you can't really report what's gone on, for the same reason. Whichever way you move, one of us will be waiting.'

'That bitch,' murmured Strasser under his breath. He felt resigned, broken.

'I'm sorry?'

'Nothing. So what do you want me to do, Lockhart? If you're now in control, why not give me an order?'

Lockhart turned from the window and smiled at him.

'It's very good of you to be so co-operative,' he said. 'I was expecting you to be a lot more difficult than this.'

Strasser coughed again.

'I'd like things to continue as they are for the time being,' said Lockhart. 'When we're in public, I shall continue to obey you. I will tell the men nothing about this. I even want you to carry on with your preparations for our move to Dresden, although I have no intention of allowing myself or any of the men to go there. You are to give me free rein to come and go as I please, and when the time comes, I want you to be as biddable as possible.'

Strasser could barely speak.

'What . . . what do you mean, "when the time comes"?'

'When the time comes for me to carry out what it is I mean to carry out. That's all you need to know, Carl.'

'But this is—'

'Intolerable? Ridiculous?'

Lockhart stood in front of Strasser's desk, and leant his fists on it.

'I know this is a lot to take in,' he said, 'but you have little choice. And this is just the beginning. Over the next few weeks, I'm going to ask you for favours that really will seem truly ridiculous, and you'll do them. Otherwise - well - you know what I'll do.'

'What sort of favours?'

'All sorts, Carl, all sorts. I'll be needing equipment, documentation, transport – just about anything you can think of. But in the mean time, you can just sit tight and carry on as normal.'

'So you're planning to escape? Is that what you're doing?'

Lockhart merely grinned. He stood up from the table and walked to the door.

'Where are you going?' asked Strasser.

'I'm going to have a bath, and then I'm going to bed.' Lockhart turned the handle.

'Wait!' shouted Strasser, although it came out as a croak.

But Lockhart ignored him, walked out, and slammed the door shut. The waft of air sent a pile of papers on to the floor. Strasser couldn't be bothered to pick them up. They could just stay there for ever for all he cared.

Such was the acting ability of Lockhart and Strasser that only the most perceptive man would have recognised the sea change in their relationship. However, as none of the thirteen remaining members of the unit were that perceptive, it seemed to them that the hierarchy remained the same, albeit that Catchpole had now become the senior NCO. Lockhart was unsure about Catchpole, but Pugh had assured him that he was enough of an opportunist to do as he was told when presented with the right sort of carrot.

Naturally, much of the talk was about the demise of Worstead. Strasser had thought it a good idea for Lockhart to address the men, to quash the inevitable rumours that would start up. Lockhart agreed, but only on the condition that Strasser also made a speech, stating that the authorities had fully absolved Lockhart, and that Worstead had been mentally unstable, which was the truth as far as he was concerned. The men accepted this – it appeared that most of them had thought that Worstead was a crank, and that it was only going to be a matter of time before, in Hull's words, 'the bugger did himself in'.

In fact, the men were more concerned with the move to Dresden. To them, it smacked of a step closer to action, something on which they were not keen. Lockhart was firm, and said that the unit had little choice in the matter. Furthermore, he added that if anyone was caught trying to escape, they would be court-martialled and shot, and he, Lockhart, would personally command the firing squad. This threat caused a collective gasp, which was precisely the effect Lockhart had intended. He knew that he had to make the prospect of Dresden sound as unpleasant as possible, in order for the alternative to seem a little less so.

In private, Strasser had expressed a kind of shocked admiration for Lockhart's iron fist, but also bewilderment. Lockhart had had to restrain himself from patting Strasser on the back, telling him that if he was a good boy he would find out sooner or later what was going on, but he thought better of it. He had tried his luck with Strasser, and it had paid off, but he knew that he could just as easily force the very harassed Strasser to commit some uncharacteristically thoughtless act. Ironically, Lockhart showed Strasser more respect now that he had the upper hand.

Such was the nature of wielding power, thought Lockhart; something that Worstead would never have been able to comprehend.

Lockhart was musing on that as he sat on the train. It was Saturday morning, and he was heading into Berlin to see Leni. Pugh had wanted to join him, but Lockhart had insisted that he remain in Hildesheim, to keep an eye on the men. Pugh had given him an arch look, but Lockhart somewhat brusquely told him that he could erase any doubts he might have about Lockhart's continuing fidelity to his late wife.

But, regrettably, there was some truth in Pugh's suspicions. Although Lockhart had no intention of sleeping with Leni, he couldn't deny that he very much wanted to. The flesh was willing, Lockhart thought, but his spirit was thankfully weak. He resolved that the least he could do was to keep any drinking to a minimum in her presence. For now, he had to shut parts of himself down, to become even more hollow than he already felt. His biggest fear was that he would not succeed, that before long he would break down.

He knew that if any one thing was going to be the catalyst for such a collapse, it would be the attention of another woman. And the woman most likely to fill such a devastating role was the woman he would be seeing that afternoon, who could help him in a way that nobody else could. As the train drew into Berlin, Lockhart found himself, for the first time in his life, sincerely cursing the existence of feminine beauty.

* * *

Lockhart arrived at Leni's flat shortly after two o'clock. He was half an hour late – the small street map he had of Berlin was barely representative of the bombed-out maze the city was becoming. Leni's block was lucky to have survived – much of her street consisted of rubble, the remnants of domesticity being picked over by skeletal dogs and rats. What Lockhart found most bizarre was the presence of a smartly dressed old woman, making her way through the spoil, balancing herself with a parasol and a handbag. The woman smiled at Lockhart as she passed him, evidently finding something friendly about his face. Lockhart smiled back, wondering where the woman was going, why she was looking so smart.

The flat was more poky and dismal than he had imagined. He had it in his head that she would be living in an elegant apartment, which would have suited her more than the grimy single-bulbed room he was walking into.

'I'm sorry – it's not the Adlon.'

'That's quite all right,' said Lockhart. 'Anyway, the Adlon's far too public.'

Leni walked to the window and looked down to the road.

'Are you sure you weren't followed?' she asked.

'Yes,' said Lockhart.

'I hope so,' said Leni. 'You know they don't just use men in leather coats?'

'I don't doubt it,' said Lockhart.

Leni turned from the window and looked at him. Her expression was both fierce and alluring. She looked so out of place, thought Lockhart. She should be on a stage, in a film, anywhere but here, in this seedy room in this nervous city.

'What time is he arriving?' Lockhart asked.

Leni looked at her watch.

'He should be here within half an hour.'

'Excellent,' said Lockhart, sitting on the edge of Leni's small bed. 'And thank you. I mean it.'

'Don't thank me yet,' said Leni, walking to her desk.

She picked up a packet of Camel cigarettes and offered one to Lockhart, who declined it. Leni lit her cigarette.

'And how have you convinced him to come here?'

'He thinks he's getting it for free. Well, that's what happened the last time he came here.'

They remained in silence for a minute or so, listening to the sounds of the city. It felt like a lazy spring afternoon, thought Lockhart, the type of warm afternoon you would skive off doing any work, kick your shoes off, and lie in bed, reading the newspaper. It was the type of afternoon for . . . Lockhart stopped himself. It was too easy to think about making love with Leni in front of him. He cleared his throat.

'I'm sorry,' said Leni. 'Would you like anything?'

'No, no,' said Lockhart. 'Maybe just a glass of water if you have one.'

Leni wedged the cigarette in the corner of her mouth and walked over to the sink. Lockhart noticed that the washing-up was piled right up to the tap, the tap that Leni was now turning and out of which nothing was coming.

'Damn,' muttered Leni quietly. 'There's a surprise.'

'A good excuse not to do the washing-up,' said Lockhart.

'My thoughts exactly.'

Leni crossed the floor and stood in front of Lockhart, looking down at him. She took a drag of her cigarette, lifted her head and blew the smoke towards the ceiling, then looked back down. Lockhart didn't know where to rest his eyes. What he did know was that he wanted to put his arms around her hips, press her stomach towards his face, feel her hands running through his hair.

'Are you nervous?' she asked.

'No,' said Lockhart, lying.

'You look it,' she said, placing her hand on his left cheek.

Her hand felt slightly cool, but it also felt soft. He wanted to hold it there, clasp its reassuring gentleness against him. But, too quickly it seemed, it had gone, her fingertips lingering a little on his chin. He wanted to tell her that he felt guilty, ashamed that he was attracted to her; that he was worried that she would rob him of his stability. He thought of Anna, and he felt close to tears. Dead or alive, this was unfair on her.

'I suppose . . .' he began, but his voice trailed off.

'What do you suppose?'

Lockhart sighed.

'Nothing,' he said. 'It's nothing.'

'I think I can guess,' said Leni.

Lockhart looked up at her, examining her smiling eyes.

'You can?'

'Yes,' she said, grinning slightly. 'I don't want to make you feel uncomfortable.'

'Thank you,' said Lockhart glassily.

Leni went to her desk and stubbed her cigarette out on an already huge pile of butts.

'Your gun,' she said. 'Is it loaded?'

Her tone was now businesslike, crisply efficient.

'No, no it's not.'

'That's a shame.'

'I don't need bullets to kill someone,' said Lockhart.

That made her pause.

'And . . . and what do you want to do with him?' she asked.

Lockhart stood up.

'First I'll be nice to him. If that doesn't work, then we'll just have to play it by ear. I don't really want to beat him up, but if it comes to it, then I don't see any alternative. There's too much at stake.'

Leni exhaled.

'All right, but for heaven's sake, keep it quiet – I have neighbours.'

Lockhart looked out the window. Three floors below, the street was nearly empty, save for a small suited man waddling clumsily through the rubble. Lockhart started humming 'Rudolph the Red-Nosed Reindeer'.

'What are you humming?'

Lockhart stopped.

'I think our friend is here,' he said.

Leni rushed to the window and looked down.

'Shit! He's early!'

'Do you have anything to tie him up with?'

'The only thing I have,' she said, opening a desk drawer, 'are these.'

She held up a pair of stout handcuffs, letting them swing on the end of her index finger.

'Christ. Where did you get them?'

'Kitty's,' she said, throwing them at Lockhart.

'Of course,' he said, catching them.

He put them in his pocket.

'Is there a key?'

'That's in the drawer too.'

'Good. When he arrives, get him on the bed. As soon as he sounds sufficiently relaxed, I'll make myself known.'

Both their heads turned towards the door at the same time. The sound of shuffling footsteps and panting could be heard.

'He's on the final landing,' Leni whispered. 'Hide in the shower!'

Lockhart did so, noticing that the shower could not have been used in ages. There was a huge cobweb suspended above his head, in the middle of which was a fat spider. It must have been the best-fed creature in Berlin, he thought.

Lockhart heard a knock, followed by Leni's footsteps and the sound of the door being unbolted.

'Ah, Leni!'

'Erich!'

The sound of a kiss.

'It's a long way up your stairs. I'm pooped!'

'I'm sorry,' said Leni. Lockhart thought she sounded a little edgy.

'Ach! No matter! Here, I've brought you this!'

'For me, Erich? Really, there was no need.'

'Let's get it open! I could do with a drink after that climb.'

Leni's footsteps made their way to her sink. A cupboard opened and some glasses chinked together.

'Pass it here!' said Rudolph. 'That's a man's job!'

Lockhart smiled. Such gallantry. He listened to the sound of the cork leaving the bottle and two glasses being poured out. Rudolph drank greedily.

'You know, Leni my dear, you do not need to live in a place like this!'

'Oh, I'm not here very often. I'm at Kitty's most of the time.'

'I could get you a new place! There are plenty of empty flats in Berlin, despite what people think. I could get you one - so long as you didn't mind that it had been lived in by some filthy Jew!'

'Not at all, Erich, but really - it's very sweet of you . . .'

'Think nothing of it! I have some good friends in the housing administration. By next week, you will have a flat fit for a princess!'

'That's too kind of you, Erich.'

Lockhart heard the sound of a glass being put down, and then a kiss, a longer kiss this time. For a moment, he felt jealous, indignant.

'Why don't you sit down?' Leni purred. 'Sit down next to me on the bed.'

A fat chortle, and then the sound of more embracing. Silently, Lockhart unbuttoned his holster and slid out his

Luger. He drew the shower curtain back slowly, to reveal the sight of Leni wrapped around Rudolph. Lockhart stepped out of the cubicle, into the room proper, watching Leni's hands work their way over Rudolph's chest, her mouth locked on to his. It was time to set her free. Lockhart coughed.

The reaction was instant. Leni sprang off Rudolph's obese body and stood up. Rudolph jerked round to look at the source of the cough. Before he could speak, Lockhart was next to the bed, his hand over Rudolph's slimy mouth, his gun pressed to the man's sweaty left temple.

'Hello again, Dr Rudolph,' said Lockhart quietly. 'Do not attempt to struggle. Do not attempt to cry out. Do not do *anything* unless I say you can.'

Lockhart looked into Rudolph's large brown eyes. They had opened wider than Lockhart had ever thought possible.

'Nod if you understand me.'

Rudolph nodded.

'Good,' said Lockhart. 'Now I'm going to remove my hand. When I do so, I expect you to stay silent. Is that understood?'

Rudolph nodded.

Lockhart cautiously removed his hand, ready to clamp it back down if Rudolph uttered so much as a whimper. He kept the Luger in place.

'Well done, Rudolph,' he said. 'Well done.'

Rudolph nodded again. He looked terrified. With his left hand, Lockhart removed the handcuffs from his pocket.

'Now then, Rudolph – I want you to put both your hands through the bars behind you, and then clasp them together. All right?'

Another nod. Rudolph did as he was told. Lockhart held the cuffs up to Leni.

'Put these on,' he said.

Leni walked round to the other side of the bed and applied the handcuffs with what Lockhart felt to be almost indecent professionalism.

'Ow!' Rudolph moaned.

Lockhart's hand was immediately reapplied.

'Just you keep quiet, Rudolph! I don't care if they hurt. You'll have them off soon enough if you tell me what I want to know. Now nod.'

Rudolph obeyed. Lockhart took his hand away, even more slowly than before.

'I wouldn't mind a glass of Dr Rudolph's wine,' said Lockhart.

Leni shrugged. She seemed surprised.

'Sure,' she said. 'I'll get you a glass.'

'Now then, Dr Rudolph, all I want to do is to ask you a few questions. I'm afraid my visit to you the other day whetted my appetite somewhat. If you answer to my satisfaction, I shall let you go. If you don't, then I will not let you go. Simple, eh? If you choose never to answer, then I am afraid you will leave me with only one option.'

At this point, Lockhart forced the Luger's muzzle sharply into Rudolph's temple. The German yelped slightly. Lockhart eased the gun back.

'Here's your wine,' said Leni.

'Thank you,' said Lockhart, taking a considered sip. 'Hmm! Not bad – Mosel. Isn't this the same one we had in your office?'

Rudolph nodded again. Leni sat at her desk and lit a cigarette.

'Before I start,' said Lockhart, 'I want to make it clear that you are to answer my questions as quickly and as efficiently as possible. I do NOT expect to be asked any questions. Clear?'

More vigorous nodding. Lockhart took a larger sip of the wine.

'All right, Dr Rudolph. Here comes my first question. The A4 project. Tell me what you know about that.'

Rudolph didn't speak. Instead, he shook his head in shock, his jowls wobbling.

'Come on, Rudolph,' said Lockhart. 'Don't tell me you don't know *anything*. It's an Ahnenerbe project – you must know all about it.'

'I d . . . don't,' Rudolph stammered. 'I swear it!'

Lockhart gripped Rudolph roughly by his tie and the front of his shirt. He twisted the fabric and simultaneously cocked the Luger.

'I don't believe you,' he snarled.

Rudolph started to gasp for air.

'I'll let you go when you want to say something.'

Rudolph tried nodding his head, causing Lockhart to loosen his grip.

'All I know,' Rudolph began, catching his breath, 'is that . . . is that it's very important.'

'More,' said Lockhart. 'More.'

'I don't know—'

Before Rudolph could continue, Lockhart was once again strangling him.

'No more lies, Rudolph, no more fucking lies!'

Lockhart twisted the shirt and tie so tightly that Rudolph started to go bright red, his legs kicking violently.

'It . . . it . . .' he groaned.

'What?' said Lockhart, untwisting the fabric.

Rudolph panted rapidly for a few seconds.

'Yes?' said Lockhart.

'It's a rocket-building programme.'

'Rockets?'

Rudolph didn't reply until Lockhart had grabbed his shirt again.

'Yes, rockets.'

'What sort of rockets?'

Rudolph looked at him, his eyes pleading.

'I can't tell you any more. Please!'

Lockhart debated briefly whether or not to continue with the rough treatment. Rudolph was a coward, and the best way to treat cowards was to frighten them. He took the Luger away from Rudolph's temple and pointed it at his mouth. If only the poor fool knew that it had no ammunition.

'If you start screaming,' said Lockhart, 'you'll die. Now tell me about these rockets. Where are they being aimed?'

'L . . . London.'

'London? Did you say London? When?'

'In . . . in . . . the next few weeks!'

'When exactly?'

'I don't know! It's not exactly my department! There's a special committee, it's got nothing to do with me!'

Lockhart jammed the Luger between Rudolph's eyes.

'You *must* know more. Why not tell me about a gas called sarin? Has *that* got anything to do with the rockets?'

The colour drained out of Rudolph's face.

'How . . . how did you know about that?'

'I take it that's a yes?'

Rudolph nodded slightly.

'Let's get this straight! The sarin is going on these rockets?'

Another small nod. Lockhart was ecstatic – his hunch that there was a link had been proved right.

'Where are the rockets? Come on, Rudolph! This is your last chance!'

Rudolph started to blub.

'I really s . . . swear to you, I don't kn . . . know where they are.'

It would have made little difference if Rudolph had known, because at the very moment he was expressing his ignorance, Leni's front door slammed open. Lockhart turned to see three men burst in, all dressed in SS uniform. Within a second, he found himself the target of three quivering machine guns.

'Put down your weapon!'

Lockhart paused.

'I said put it down!'

Lockhart did as he was told, letting the Luger drop on to the bed beside Rudolph. The command was being issued by a youngish obersturmführer. Lockhart noticed that the lozenge on the man's left arm bore the letters 'SD'. The internal security service, or maybe even the Gestapo. Lockhart was as good as dead.

'Fräulein Steiner,' said the obersturmführer, bowing a little in mock civility, 'my dear little Leni – you seem to have got a little out of your depth.'

'Hello, Schwarz,' said Leni. 'I haven't seen you since Sonthofen.'

'That's right,' said Schwarz. 'You were quite the star pupil, although now it looks as though you've gone off the rails.'

'Congratulations on your promotion,' said Leni sarcastically.

Lockhart sized up the situation. It was a little less than hopeless. On either side of Schwarz, the two NCOs still had their guns levelled at him. One move by him and they would be bound to fire. But if he didn't do anything, then he could see himself being tortured to death over the next few weeks. There was nothing to lose.

'I must say,' said Schwarz, 'we wondered what Dr Rudolph was doing coming to your flat on his own. We've been following him for the past week. And who is your handsome friend here?'

Neither Leni nor Lockhart replied.

'Take off his handcuffs!' Schwarz barked.

Lockhart could hear Leni opening the drawer.

'Not so fast, Fräulein Steiner! What's in there?'

'The key, of course.'

Schwarz turned to nod at the NCO to his right.

'Go and get the key.'

The NCO made his way past the bed and over to the desk.

'Keep your hands up!' Schwarz shouted at Leni.

The NCO was scrabbling through the drawer.

'There's no key here, Obersturmführer!'

'Are you sure?'

'Certainly, sir!'

Schwarz pointed his gun at Leni.

'I'll give you three seconds to hand over the key or I'll shoot you here and now.'

This was it, thought Lockhart. Now, when there was only one gun trained on him.

'One . . .'

The NCO to Schwarz's left was also looking over at Leni. Who to attack first? Schwarz or the NCO? He just had to hope that Leni would use his action as a cue for her to do likewise.

'Two . . .'

'I'm sorry, I don't know where it is,' Leni was saying. He would attack Schwarz first, get Leni out of danger. He would push Schwarz into the other NCO, rugby-tackle him – there was no other way. He knew that he needed to be as aggressive as possible, but with a cool head. This would be a fight to the death.

'Three . . .'

With his heart thumping and hands outstretched, Lockhart jumped up from the bed as fast as humanly possible. Before Schwarz had time to react, Lockhart's right shoulder had connected with him, his arms around his waist.

The impact sent Schwarz into the NCO, knocking all three of them to the ground. They were now in a heap, with Lockhart on top. Lockhart raised his right fist and smashed it with all his force into Schwarz's face again and again. Schwarz screamed in agony as his nose broke, the sound of which was all too familiar to Lockhart from Crete. Blood streamed from it. The gun, thought Lockhart, he needed to get the gun.

Schwarz's machine gun was sandwiched between them. Meanwhile, the other NCO was struggling to get up from beneath them both. And what of Leni's NCO? No time to think about that – he just had to hope Leni was doing something. If he got a bullet in his back – well, at least he had tried. He had to get the gun before the NCO could break free. He reached down and tried to wrestle it away, but Schwarz's grip was too strong. With all his might, he head-butted Schwarz in the face. There was no scream, just a sickening crunch of bone and sinew. Schwarz's grip relaxed. Lockhart grabbed the gun and pointed it clumsily at the NCO, who had nearly got free. There was nothing else for it – he had to fire.

The sound of the gun in the enclosed space felt loud enough to burst his eardrums, but Lockhart's attention was focused on the NCO. His head had shattered, sending a spray of bone and tissue over the floor and wall. Lockhart rolled off the unconscious Schwarz and turned to Leni.

She was struggling with the second NCO and getting the worst of it. But at least she had tried – had she not done so, they would both be dead. Lockhart raised his gun and calmly took aim at the German's thigh. He squeezed the trigger gently, punching half a dozen rounds into the NCO's side. The man's face grimaced, contorted in agony, and he fell back behind the bed, taking Leni on to the floor with him. He started to scream unbearably loudly.

Lockhart ran round and pulled Leni out of his clutches. She was splattered in the man's blood, and she had a black eye. He pushed her behind him, and stood over the NCO, who was clearly dying. It would be unfair to let him suffer, thought Lockhart. He wasn't the monster they were. He pulled the trigger and fired one round into the left of the man's chest. The sound stopped immediately.

The room went quiet. Lockhart and Leni stood in a state of shock amid the reek of gun smoke and death. Lockhart stared at the second NCO, at his face, set in an expression of utmost pain. The pool of blood seeping from him reminded him of Worstead lying on the cobbles.

'Rudolph!'

At first, Lockhart didn't register Leni's shout.

'Rudolph! Lockhart, look! He's not moving!'

Lockhart shook himself out of his reverie.

'What?'

'Rudolph's not moving!'

Lockhart turned to the bed. Rudolph had turned slightly blue.

'Christ!' said Lockhart, dropping the machine gun. 'He's had a bloody heart attack!'

Lockhart put his head to Rudolph's chest – nothing. He then checked for a pulse at the wrist. Again, there was nothing. He opened Rudolph's mouth and looked to see if his airway was blocked. It wasn't.

'Shit!' said Lockhart, thumping the mattress. 'Shit! Shit!'

For the next few minutes, Lockhart tried to revive Rudolph, but he knew it was no good. It wasn't that he cared about the man, just what was in his brain. Where were the rockets?

'Where are the bloody rockets?' he shouted at Rudolph's corpse. 'You bastard! Where are the bloody rockets?'

He felt Leni's hand tug his arm.

'He's dead – leave him.'

Lockhart climbed off the bed.

'I suppose we'd better get out of here,' he said.

'What about him?' asked Leni, nodding towards Schwarz.

'Damn.'

Lockhart checked him over – he was still breathing.

'What are you going to do?' asked Leni.

'Well, we can't leave him. I'll have to shoot him.'

The idea of killing a man in cold blood revolted Lockhart. Did he have a choice? No. He turned back to the bed.

'Pass me the machine . . .'

Leni already had the machine gun in her hands and was walking over to him. Lockhart held out his hand, but she did not pass him the weapon.

'Please move,' she said.

'Leni! No!'

'Move,' she insisted.

Leni's eyes were alight. Her expression told him that she was not to be argued with, that her mind was made up. Lockhart stepped back.

'Go on,' he said quietly.

Leni stood over Schwarz, the barrel of the gun pointing at his chest.

'This,' she said, 'is on behalf of my parents.'

With that, she fired. Schwarz's body flinched and shuddered and then lay still. The recoil from the gun knocked Leni back so hard that Lockhart thought she was about to fall, but she regained her balance.

'Right,' she said. 'Let's go.'

'Hold on,' said Lockhart. 'There's something I need to retrieve from the late Obersturmführer Schwarz.'

Lockhart removed Schwarz's Luger from its holster, emptied it of its bullets, and put them in his pocket. Just as Leni was taking a coat from the cupboard, the piercing wail of an air-raid siren started.

'Christ,' said Lockhart. 'It never rains but it pours.'

'What?' said Leni, putting the coat on.

'Just an English expression. Have you got an air-raid shelter here?'

'No – but there's one down the street.'

'Well let's go then.'

Leni pointed towards the four corpses.

'And them?'

'Leave them,' said Lockhart. 'We've got to go!'

He grabbed Leni by the wrist and pulled her towards him.

'You won't be coming back here,' he said. 'Is there anything you need to take?'

Leni stared at him.

'I've got some money.'

'Well get it and let's go!'

Leni ran to the desk and pulled out a drawer. Attached to the back of it was a brown envelope, out of which she extracted a sizeable roll of Reichsmarks.

'All right,' she said. 'I'm ready.'

Together, they ran out of the door, Leni locking it behind her, and then down the stairs, far more quickly than any of Leni's elderly neighbours. When they reached the first floor, they came across the same smartly dressed old woman Lockhart had seen earlier. She was lying on the floor, clearly in some distress.

'What's the matter, Fräulein?' asked Lockhart.

'I tripped,' she said, her voice husky. 'I think I've sprained my ankle.'

'Come on then,' said Lockhart. 'Let's get you up!'

Ignoring her protestations, Lockhart bent down and picked her up. She was absurdly light.

'Thank you, sir,' she kept saying as he carried her down the remaining stairs. 'Thank you, sir.'

Out in the street, a panicking stream of Berliners were making their way towards the shelter. From above, Lockhart heard the throbbing sound of large aircraft engines. He looked up, and in between the gaps in the light cloud, he could see vast bombers overhead.

'Flying Fortresses!' he shouted at Leni.

'I know!' she shouted back. 'Americans!'

Carrying the old woman with difficulty, Lockhart stumbled awkwardly through the rubble. Leni followed him. The sound of the aircraft reminded him of the Blitz, the bass sound of the engines causing a sense of dread to course through his body.

'Where's this bloody shelter?'

'Not far!' Leni shouted. 'Just fifty or so metres down . . .'

Her last few words were drowned out by a massive explosion. The shock wave knocked them to the ground, Lockhart falling on top of the old woman. Darkness came over them in the form of a thick cloud of acrid dust. For what seemed like hours he lay there, covering the old woman.

Silence, except somewhere a child was screaming. Lockhart looked down at the old woman – she was still alive, thank God, just petrified.

'Are you all right?' he was shouting at her, suddenly aware that his voice sounded distant, his hearing temporarily muffled.

The woman didn't reply, just shivered violently. She had gone into shock. He had to get her to the shelter – someone would be able to help her there. Slowly he got to his knees, and looked round for Leni. She had fallen two yards behind him, and was covered in a layer of grey dust.

'Leni!'

She didn't move.

'Leni!'

Lockhart got to his feet and staggered over to her.

'Leni!'

He turned her over and shook her violently. Her eyes flickered open.

'Leni!' Can you hear me?'

He brushed the dust off her face with his hand.

'Yes,' she croaked.

'Are you all right? Are you hurt?'

'I . . . I don't think so.'

'Can you get up?'

'I'll try.'

With Lockhart's assistance, Leni managed to stand. She swayed slightly, like a drunk. Lockhart checked her over – she now had a few more scratches and cuts to add to those she had received in the fight, but she looked all right. She started laughing.

'What's so funny?' Lockhart asked.

'You look like a statue!'

Lockhart looked down at himself. His uniform had turned entirely grey.

'So I do! So do you in fact! Christ, that was close! Where did it land?'

Together they turned to look back up the street. Lockhart couldn't believe it.

'Am I right in thinking . . .' he began.

'Yes,' Leni interrupted. 'Yes you are! I don't believe it!' She smiled at him.

'You know,' she said, 'I never liked that flat.'

Almost a year and a half had passed before he heard any news of her. Between the collapse of Holland in May 1940 and the day when he received the phone call in November 1941, Lockhart had woken every morning under the assumption that Anna might have been killed in the German advance. But throughout the course of each day, he tried to convince himself that she had survived, and that it was impossible for her to send out any news. Some days he succeeded in this attempt, and almost slept normally, but the majority of the nights were broken by his sudden awaking in the small hours. His subconscious told him that she had to be dead, that she would have found a way to let him and Amy know that she was still with them, that the fact that she hadn't could only mean one thing.

Lockhart entrusted Amy to Anna's sister Elspeth a month after Anna's disappearance. He was spending nearly every day up in London, and was finding it increasingly difficult to find any time – or petrol – to get back to Oxford. There was no room in the flat in Pimlico for a child and a nanny, so the only option was to let Amy grow up with her cousins. Anna's sister had two children, both a little older than Amy, and as they lived in South Kensington, Lockhart was in fact able to see Amy more often than he would have done had she been back in Oxford.

He buried himself in his work at the Ministry. Although much of it was boring and routine, it proved a good distraction. Had his colleagues known him better, they would have remarked that he had become more with-drawn, more introverted. As it was, his charm and good nature – even at a low ebb – were far in excess of the level of those two qualities displayed by the somewhat dusty types that normally inhabited the corridors of the Ministry.

The call came one morning in the middle of November. It had just been announced that the *Ark Royal* had sunk near Gibraltar, and everybody's spirits, including Lockhart's, were especially low. He had slept particularly badly the night before, and he answered the phone in the office with a yawned hello.

'Charming!' said the voice at the end of the line. 'That's no way to treat a friend with some very good news.'

It was Nick, a contemporary of Lockhart's at Oxford, who now worked for SIS, liaising with Resistance groups on the continent. Lockhart had been badgering him every week for news about Anna, and so far Nick had always disappointed him. But here he was, saying that he had good news. It was enough to instantly dispel any feelings of weariness.

'Yes?' said Lockhart, his tone impatient, suggesting that Nick should wait no longer.

'Well, it's good news and bad news. We think she's alive.'

'How . . . how do you know?'

'This is where the bad news comes in. We also think she's being held in Vught concentration camp in Belgium.'

'What?'

'It appears that Anna has been helping to run an underground press for the past several months. It was raided over a fortnight ago, and she was among those who got arrested. I'm sorry, John.'

'But . . . are you sure it's her?'

'As eggs is eggs.'

'How come you hadn't heard about this press before?'

'Please, John, you know we're not perfect.'

'What else do you know? How do you *know* it's her?'

'One of our agents over there was told that an Englishwoman was arrested, a woman called Anna. It *has* to be her, John – I can't see how it couldn't be.'

Lockhart didn't say anything. This was both the best and the worst news possible. That she was alive should have given him the greatest sense of joy since Amy was born, but instead he felt utterly dispirited. The words 'concentration camp' cut into him, twisted in his gut, causing him to feel panicky.

'John? John? Are you still there?'

'Yes. Yes I am. What do we know about Vught?'

'Not very much, I'm afraid. It's a pretty small place, mostly political prisoners, as well as criminals.'

'Jews?'

'We don't think so. They go east.'

Another pause.

'I'm sorry, John. That's pretty much all we know.'

Lockhart breathed in and out heavily.

'Nothing else?'

'Sorry.'

'Is there any way I could get in touch with her?'

'There might be.'

'That sounds like a no, Nick.'

It was Nick's turn to stay silent.

'Do you think it's worth a try?' asked Lockhart.

'Perhaps we could try something. I can't talk about it over the phone.'

'Yes, of course.'

'I'm sorry, John – I've got to go.'

'You around for dinner this week? I owe you. My shout – at the club.'

'Next week's better.'

'Tuesday?'

'Tuesday's good.'

'Eight o'clock?'

'Fine – I'll see you then.'

'Bye, Nick.'

'Bye, and I'm sorry once again. If I hear any more, I'll let you know.'

'Thanks.'

The line went dead. Lockhart kept the receiver held up to his ear, allowing the crackling, purring sound to soothe him. After a couple of minutes, he put it back down, absent-mindedly missing the cradle. He looked at his watch – ten past eleven. He got up, walked to the door, and took his greatcoat off the hook. If they wanted to court-martial him for getting drunk on duty, then fine, but nothing was going to stop him. He knew it was pointless – pathetic even – but he had to escape, just for a few hours. For the moment, the reality was too dreadful to face in a small sober office.

August 1974

In a perfect world, Amy said to herself, she would have known the truth before Louise was born. There would have been something neat about that. She could have closed one door before opening another, left that part of her life behind, as Hugh had so often asked her to do. Of course Louise was a joy, and her priorities changed as soon as she first held her.

But she knew, even then, that one day Louise would ask her about her grandfather. And what would she be able to tell her? That he was a traitor? That he was the only British officer to have joined the SS, the most hated and feared organisation of this – or any – century? That he was a member of the organisation that carried out the Holocaust? She would have to tell Louise the truth as it stood, because that would be the truth she would hear in the outside world. She wouldn't be able to lie to her.

What haunted Amy most was the possibility that the accepted truth was in fact a huge lie. She knew that in her heart that Louise did not have a traitor for a grandfather. Her priorities might have changed, but her enthusiasm for clearing her father's memory had doubled. There was now someone else who needed to know, another generation that was owed the truth.

Chapter Eight

THAT EVENING, 'FRÄULEIN HOFFMAN' booked into a
seedy guesthouse on the outskirts of Hildesheim, using a
forged identity card supplied by the GRU. She and
Lockhart had decided that to continue as normal would
be madness; that to go back to Kitty's would be as good as
suicide. They just had to hope that the SD assumed that
she and the arrest party had perished as a result of the air
raid. It would take weeks before their bullet-riddled corpses
were discovered, and Lockhart said that that should be
enough time. Stay in your room as much as possible, he
warned her; the last thing they wanted was for Strasser to
spot her.

She also had to get in touch with Moscow as soon as
possible. She said that she would telegram her GRU
contact in Berlin, who would then be able to radio her

news to Moscow. Hopefully they would get some information back within a week. Lockhart would send another message via Stafford to London, but that might take time, if indeed London even replied.

For a few days, Lockhart could do little more than wait. Occasionally, the unit would receive news of the Allies' advance, although Lockhart suspected that any news was heavily censored and manipulated. Nevertheless, a picture of the Allies' success was emerging, especially with the news that Cherbourg had been liberated, thus providing them with a port. In the east, the Russians were making huge advances. If the Nazis were going to use sarin, thought Lockhart, then they would use it soon.

The news of these advances and the continued threat that they would soon be sent to Dresden made the men edgy. With the exception of Stafford, the non-fascists – Hull, Andreae, Marston, Allan, Malcolm and Nichols – were demanding to be sent back to their POW camps, whatever the consequences. Even the fascists – Maclaren, Catchpole, Simpkin, Smith and Prain – were getting flaky, and had said to Pugh, who they still regarded as their spiritual leader, that they too were uneasy; were there not jobs out of uniform that could be found for them?

For Lockhart, these stirrings were a mixed blessing. The men's realisation that being caught by the Allies as members of the BFC was hardly an attractive prospect meant that most would be more susceptible to his plan. However, it was likely that a mutiny might soon take place, which would doubtless ensure the demise of both the unit and Lockhart's plan.

Strasser remained subdued, compliant. He spent most of his time preparing for the move to Dresden, an activity that depressed him because he knew that Lockhart would eventually put a halt to it. There were many days when he was tempted to break Lockhart's hold over him, but he calculated that the risk was too great. If he had Lockhart shot, then that would certainly result in two things – the unit's end, and Leni going to the SD. Just one of those events would be bad enough, but both would ensure his death, either in front of a firing squad, or somewhere on the ever-encroaching Russian front. He resolved to sit tight, although he was fearful of what Lockhart was going to ask of him, fearful that it would make him complicit, that Lockhart would make him a traitor. One night, when cleaning his gun, he thought about putting it to his head, but he stopped himself. Like Lockhart, he thought, he had too much of a will to live. Suicide was too cowardly. Part of him needed to see Leni again, but he knew that he couldn't. It was best if he never contacted her again.

It came as no surprise to Lockhart that Moscow responded first. Some bugger in Baker Street or Whitehall was doubtlessly sitting on his dispatches, dismissing them as bunkum. Or perhaps they hadn't arrived, held up by the German censors. But other members of the BFC – including Stafford himself – had sent and received post, so why would the Germans pick on his inane-looking correspondence to Hattie in Belsize Park? There was no reason – it had to be a delay in London. Presumably, warned by Cairo and coded letters from POWs in Thorn and Posen, they regarded anything to do with him as being deeply suspect. That was fair enough, but maddening. Thank God for the Russians, he thought, thank God for them.

'Here it is,' Leni said, passing Lockhart a small rolled-up piece of yellow paper. 'You've caused quite a stir,' she added. 'Moscow had never heard of sarin, but they've certainly heard of the rockets. It seems as though the Gestapo captured your friend Nicolas just too soon.' It was Friday afternoon, and they were sitting in her room in the guesthouse. The old landlady said that normally she did not allow male visitors, but Lockhart's uniform and a ten Reichsmark note were enough to shut her up.

Lockhart unfurled the paper.

Most likely location for rockets KOHNSTEIN MOUNTAIN near NORDHAUSEN. Factory called MITTELBAU. Destroy at all costs.

'Are you all right?' asked Leni. 'You've gone white.'

It hit him right between the ribs, and it hit him hard. So here at last was what Nicolas was tapping. 'Mitt' was Mittelbau. That had to be it.

'Lockhart!'

He read the message again. 'Destroy at all costs.' Easier said than done.

'John!'

Lockhart looked up.

'Hmm?'

'Are you all right?'

'Yes,' he said after a pause. 'Quite all right.'

'You look as though you've seen a ghost.'

Lockhart smiled ruefully.

'No, but I think I'll be seeing one soon.'

'What?'

'Nothing.'

Leni nodded and moved on.

'We're to go to Hanover tomorrow,' she said. 'To meet a friend, a friend who has the plans.'

'The plans?'

'The plans to Mittelbau. We're to meet in the Grosser Garten at lunchtime. There is a maze there, and we are to meet in the centre of that at . . . Are you listening to me?'

'Yes. Meet in the middle of the maze at lunchtime. Sorry, I just think I'm a little tired. The idea of these rockets has stopped me from sleeping.'

'You're not the only one. At least you can get out – it hasn't been much fun being cooped up here for the past few days.'

'I'm sorry, but you'll have a day out tomorrow.'

Leni pretended to return Lockhart's cheering smile.

'Sorry,' Lockhart repeated. 'There's nothing I can do.'

Leni sighed.

'Sorry as well,' she said. 'I'm a bit tense. And I've run out of cigarettes.'

'These plans,' said Lockhart. 'Who are they from?'

'I don't know. All I know is that we're to meet a woman wearing a blue headscarf reading the *Volkischer Beobachter*. She will leave the paper on the bench in the centre of the maze, and we will then pick it up. In it will be the plans. I don't know how detailed they are or anything else about them.'

'It's a start,' said Lockhart. 'In the mean time, I need to speak to Strasser.'

'What about?'

'Well, we need a few things. It's time he stuck his neck out.'

Strasser was incredulous. Lockhart's list of demands was intolerable, absurd.

'There's absolutely no way that I am going to issue you with any of this equipment!'

Lockhart sat in front of him, cockily chewing on a biscuit that he had taken off a plate on Strasser's desk, taken without even asking.

'Carl,' said Lockhart, '*Carl*. You have no choice. You have to help me, otherwise . . .'

'That's enough!'

Lockhart was being condescending towards him, playing with him. He had half a mind to get up and shoot him here and now.

'And what are you proposing to do with all this equipment?' Strasser asked.

'That's my business. All you have to do is supply it. Come on – I thought this was your line of work, procuring weapons. You must have some old pal who can help you.'

Strasser thought briefly of Max, his colleague back in Berlin. Max with his one ear, probably still sitting in that small office with the ferocious Frau Buch. Max wouldn't ask too many questions; he would be willing to help out an old friend. If he had to ask him, he would.

'I'm afraid I don't,' said Strasser, shuffling some papers in front of him. He just wanted to get Lockhart out of the office.

'I don't believe you.'

Strasser shook his head and leaned back.

'I'm sorry, Lockhart – you can threaten me as much as you like, but I really cannot help you. Practically every gun, every round, every piece of explosive is going to the front line. What it's not doing is staying here in Germany.'

'I still don't believe you,' said Lockhart. 'I *know* you can help me. You know you can help me – you know you *have* to help me. If you don't, I shall simply ask our mutual friend to go to her superiors and tell them about your indiscreet behaviour. I don't think they will be entirely happy to hear about it.'

Strasser slammed his hand down on the table.

'Listen! I am not going to help you! Now get out!'

'No.'

Damn him! Lockhart was being downright impudent. Strasser unbuttoned his holster.

'If you don't leave . . .'

Strasser's words trailed off. The still-seated Lockhart had beaten him to it, and was already pointing a Luger at his chest.

'What . . . do you think you're doing?'

'What does it look like?'

The fool! It wouldn't be loaded.

'You're aiming an empty gun at me,' said Strasser.

'Is that right?'

Lockhart cocked the weapon.

'I know perfectly well you don't have any ammunition for that gun.'

Lockhart smiled.

'Well, Carl, there's only one way to find out. Do you want to take that chance?'

No he didn't. Lockhart had probably found some ammunition – presumably that bitch in Berlin had supplied him with it. Fucking whore. He should never have got involved with her, never opened his mouth.

'There's something else I need, Carl.'

'What?'

'A lorry. I also need a lorry.'

'A lorry! Anything else you might need? A fucking villa perhaps?'

Lockhart uncocked the Luger.

'No thanks, Carl. But it's good of you to be so thoughtful.'

They arrived at the Grosser Garten in Hanover at midday. Lockhart was impressed with the huge formal gardens, which were thronging with families, soldiers on leave, couples arm-in-arm – all enjoying the heat of the day. With his pay, Lockhart had bought himself a jacket, a casual shirt, some shoes and some trousers. They were badly made, and felt rough, but he blended in with the crowds far better than he would have done had he been wearing his uniform. He had even found a holster in the stores at the St Michael Cloister, into which he had slipped his Luger.

At her suggestion, Leni had put her arm inside his. It made them look more natural, more like just another couple.

'It's nice to be out at last,' said Leni.

'I bet,' said Lockhart. 'I expect your landlady thought you were mad staying in the whole time.'

'I pretended I was ill.'

Although they were indulging in small talk, their eyes were darting around the park, taking in every figure they thought looked suspicious. There was a chance, and they both knew it, that Leni's network had been compromised, that the whole meeting in the park was a set-up.

'Have you noticed anyone?' Lockhart asked.

Leni shook her head gently.

'No – I don't think so.'

'It's almost impossible to tell. Anybody here could work for them.'

They walked slowly, like lovers. Lockhart found Leni's grip comforting, but he promised himself not to get distracted, to keep his mind on the rendezvous.

'What time is the collection?'

'One o'clock.'

'I'd prefer it,' said Lockhart, 'if we went there now. I'd feel a lot happier if I knew my way round this maze. Besides, if she's already there, I'll want to abandon it.'

'Why?'

'Because it'll look like a set-up. Nobody can sit and pretend to read the *Volkischer Beobachter* for an hour. It's not that interesting. If she's the genuine article, she won't want to hang around, and will get there just before one.

But if she's a plant, she might get there early, in case we do. She'll be happy to wait, because she's got nothing to fear.'

Leni nodded.

'All right,' she said. 'Let's go then – it's at the other end.'

They walked past the parterre gardens, the fountains, the vendors selling boiled sweets. For a few moments, Lockhart could almost feel that there wasn't a war on; that he was on holiday, taking an idle stroll on a sunny day. They reached the entrance to the maze.

'Can you see a map?' Lockhart asked. 'Or anyone selling one?'

They both looked around fruitlessly.

'Well,' said Lockhart, 'we'll just have to hope that it's not too complicated. Your friends certainly chose one hell of spot.'

'It's not my fault,' said Leni.

The hedges were about seven feet high and made from yew.

'Have you ever been in a maze before?' asked Leni.

'Once,' said Lockhart. 'At Hampton Court.'

'What was it like?' she asked.

'I must have been about ten – all I can remember is that I got lost. How about you?'

'Never.'

'Well, this is going to be fun, isn't it?'

Leni couldn't resist a slight giggle.

They entered the maze.

'All right then,' said Lockhart. 'Left or right?'

'Right,' said Leni, 'let's go right.'

'Fine.'

They walked for about ten yards and then turned left and left again. What worried Lockhart most was that the maze was quite busy, with several children running around, as well as plenty of other couples. Most of the men were in uniform.

A dead end.

'Well, I suppose that had to happen,' Lockhart said.

'Sorry,' said Leni.

Lockhart pretended to strangle her.

They made their way back to the entrance and turned left and then took two right turns. They were presented with a fork.

'I say left,' said Lockhart. 'Right would take us back near the entrance.'

'Whatever you say - you're the expert.'

Another dead end.

'Damn!' said Lockhart. 'I'd be enjoying this if I was here for some other reason. How are we going to get out of here in a hurry?'

'We'll be all right,' said Leni. 'We'll just have to remember the sequence of turns and then reverse them.'

After ten minutes, they had reached the centre, where there were two benches and a sun dial.

'I don't see her,' said Lockhart.

All they could see were three couples, and a family, which must have consisted of at least six strikingly blond children. Lockhart looked at his watch - it was coming up for half past twelve.

'I wouldn't mind doing this one more time,' he said.

'Let's both memorise the turns and then compare notes back at the entrance,' said Leni.

'Good idea,' said Lockhart.

Back at the entrance, they found they agreed.

'So, it's left, right, left, then three rights, four lefts, three rights, two lefts,' said Lockhart.

'That's what I make it,' replied Leni.

'Easy enough to remember – after the initial left right left, there are two sets of rights and two sets of lefts. The rights come in threes, and the lefts in four and then two.'

Leni looked mildly exasperated.

'You do make life complicated for yourself!'

Lockhart suddenly started.

'What?' asked Leni.

'Don't turn round, but I just saw her going in.'

'Does she have a scarf on?'

'Yes, a blue one.'

'Good. Let's follow her.'

'No,' said Lockhart. 'Leave it for five minutes. Give her a chance to sit down and read the paper. We'll get there bang on one.'

'Well, we can't just stand here.'

Lockhart looked around.

'Let's go and get some sweets or something.'

'Or maybe some flowers?'

'Flowers?'

Leni was pointing to a flower salesman.

'Are you being serious?'

*   *   *

Lockhart looked at his watch again. Ten to one.

'You ready?' he asked.

Leni nodded.

They walked back into the maze, Leni clutching a single dark red rose. Lockhart felt on edge, the same as he had felt when he landed in Crete, the same sense of dread that he was walking head first into a trap.

'Slow down!' hissed Leni.

Lockhart did so. She took his arm once more and pecked him on the cheek.

'Relax,' she whispered.

They walked on, occasionally glancing at their fellow visitors, who showed no sign of interest in them. Leni was right to hold his arm – it made them look ordinary, unremarkable.

As arranged, the woman was sitting on a bench looking at the *Volkischer Beobachter*. Because of her scarf, it was hard to tell her age, but Lockhart guessed she must have been in her mid-thirties. She was wearing glasses, and she was slightly plump. She didn't even glance at them when they arrived.

Together, Leni and Lockhart feigned immense interest in the sun dial, comparing the time it showed to the time on their watches. Out the corners of their eyes, they took in those around them. A couple sat on the other bench, and another couple with a child were walking around. There was also a young and tubby Wehrmacht leutnant on his own. Lockhart wasn't worried about him. If anything, he was more concerned about the couple with the child. They were the ones who looked the most innocent, and in his book that made them the most guilty. This was a damn stupid place, he thought, a damn stupid place.

The leutnant was walking near the woman. She looked up at him, which caused him to nod his head gently at her.

'A lovely day,' he said.

'Isn't it,' said the woman.

'I love coming here, although I don't get the chance very often.'

For Christ's sake! Couldn't this pipsqueak leutnant just bugger off?

The woman buried her head in the paper, but the leutnant wasn't going to leave her alone.

'So you live in Hanover, Fräulein?'

Dammit, thought Lockhart, he was trying to pick her up!

The woman merely nodded at him. Good – hopefully he would get the message.

He did so, and walked away awkwardly, as though the conversation hadn't taken place. The woman then stood up. Too soon, thought Lockhart, too soon. She left the newspaper on the bench. The last thing he wanted to do was rush over to it – that would look too obvious. But then the leutnant might pick it up – that would be a greater disaster. Lockhart had to avoid that happening.

He nudged Leni and together they turned towards the bench. Lockhart's dread that this would be the moment they would be arrested was soon replaced by the realisation that the leutnant was also heading towards the bench.

Lockhart quickened his step and reached the bench first, sitting down and picking up the newspaper.

'I'm sorry, Leutnant,' said Lockhart, 'but my fiancée and I had been waiting for this bench.'

The leutnant looked puzzled.

'Excuse me?'

'This bench. My fiancée and I were waiting for it. We were here before you.'

The leutnant narrowed his eyes. Don't cause any hassle, Lockhart was thinking, just go away, do the decent thing.

The leutnant must have read his mind, because he clacked his heels together, and performed a half-salute.

'I apologise, sir,' he said, and then turned to Leni. 'Forgive me, Fräulein.'

'That's quite all right,' said Leni.

They reached the station fifteen minutes later, looking for all the world like any other couple who had just had a row.

'Damn!' said Lockhart, looking at a notice covering the timetable. 'There was an air raid last night – there won't be a train for at least another hour and a half.'

'We'll just have to wait,' said Leni.

They stepped on to the platform, which was teeming with what seemed to Lockhart to be a representation of every section of German society. There was the wounded soldier, hobbling on crutches and one leg, his uniform dishevelled. There was the fatherless family consisting of four young children and a pallid mother. Widow, thought Lockhart, there was no mistaking it. There were the scores of factory workers, sitting on battered suitcases, waiting to be taken to the next place where they might be able to scrape together a few Reichsmarks to send home. There was the group of young and rowdy soldiers, noisily belting out a marching song. And in amongst them all, men in uniforms, so many different uniforms. Wehrmacht, SS, police, railway, even some from the post office, all proudly wearing their costumes, showing that they fitted in, their uniforms saying, 'Here, I am this sort of person, this sort of cog.'

Lockhart counted at least ten pictures of Hitler around the station. There he was, surrounded by children in national dress – the father to a nation. Or the triumphant leader, at the head of a force of men – the Führer as warrior. And a copy of an oil painting, its subject composed – Hitler the statesman. In amongst these posters there were others that invited good citizens to behave in the way the Reich saw fit. 'Do not waste your coal', 'Join the SS', 'Keep fit', 'Report anything suspicious' – this accompanied by the figure of the Shylock-style Jew, all nose and treacherous grin.

It was impossible to find anywhere to sit, so Leni and Lockhart leaned against a wall. Lockhart took the newspaper, and was desperate to examine the plans, but he thought better of it, telling himself that even to look at them sitting on a lavatory would be too dangerous. No, they would have to wait until they got back to Leni's room in the guesthouse.

The sound of a distant train whistle made many heads turn.

'Come on,' he said to Leni, 'let's get to the front of the platform. I don't want to miss it.'

However, everybody else had had the same idea, and they were caught in a surging crush. With a little brute force, they managed to position themselves in the second row from the front. Lockhart was glad they weren't right at the front, for the force of the crowd could have pushed them on to the track. The train could be heard clearly now, its eager rhythmic chuff starting to fill the station.

But it didn't slow down. Instead, it whistled several more times, and raced through the station. It was a goods train, carrying wagon upon wagon of – what? Lockhart looked at the small slits at the top of each truck. They were covered in barbed wire. It was only when the seventh or eighth wagon had gone past that he realised that the white shapes in the slits were faces.

'Jews!' someone shouted.

'Bye bye, Jews!'

'Have a nice trip!'

This caused a lot of laughter.

Lockhart and Leni watched in silence. He had heard about this, seen it in reports back in London, but nothing could have prepared him for the actuality. They were treating them like cattle on their way to slaughter. The train must have been thirty wagons long – enough for about two thousand of them, two thousand *people*, two thousand lives that were about to be worked to death, two thousand lives about to be extinguished. He hated everyone on that platform, despised those who had laughed. He wanted to round them all up and make *them* endure days on end in wagons whose insides were coated with the effluence of their fellow passengers, many of whom would perish before the journey's end. He knew that to reciprocate hatred wasn't the answer, but how could he feel anything else? These were the people, this jeering mob of savages, who had taken away his wife, killed her, and with it had killed a part of him.

Since she had arrived, 10678 had been tempted every day to go into the wood. It would be so easy, and once there, she could stay for ever. There would be no more camp, no more work, no more pain. She imagined that he was there too, hiding somewhere among the trees, calling out for her, looking for her. And he would find her in a small clearing, find her and Amy building a pile of cones.

'These cones are meant to be you, Daddy,' Amy would say to him, and he would run forward and take them in his arms, lift them both off the ground, letting their feet kick the air in excitement. And they would stay like that for hours, just hugging and kissing and crying, being together, being a little family, a little family safe in the woods, safe from the world outside.

She hated herself, hated herself for leaving them. She had been impetuous, but she had to save her mother – it wouldn't have been right just to have left her to the invaders. It had to be worth the risk, and even though he didn't understand that, she knew she had to do it. It would only take a week, just one short week. After all, she said to him, they had been apart for far longer.

Her mother told her she was a silly girl, that she had made arrangements, that there was no need for her to have come all the way over. But Anna knew that her mother was grateful, aware that it would be much safer for her back in England. Give me a day to pack, she said, and then we can go. Just one day, Anna had insisted, and no longer, please, Mother, really no longer. Tomorrow we must go, for Bernhard is waiting.

And then they came, from the skies. Anna and her mother tried to get on a train, but there were no trains. Thousands of people were trying to go west, everyone except for those who had decided that it was not worth it, that it was better to stay put. But Anna and her mother tried – they *had* to leave. They paid a neighbour handsomely to drive them as far as possible, but the roads were clogged, and the police turned them back. So they walked, leaving everything but a suitcase containing photographs and jewellery.

At the end of the day, she knew they were not going to make it. Her mother told her to go on, go home, go back to your family, but Anna could not abandon her. Leave me, her mother insisted, my life is nearly over anyway, you should save yourself – John and Amy need you. Anna was torn apart, but her mother was right – they would never make it. That night, their last night together, they stayed with a farmer, who did not ask for any money. They slept badly, sharing a small bed, and the next morning they said goodbye, in the mud of the farmyard, the sound of geese filling the air.

* * *

She never found Bernhard – he and his boat had gone. He had been strict with her about when they had to leave, and no doubt he had gone as soon as he heard the news. She cursed him, but perhaps he was right. Nobody else was willing to make the voyage, not for all the money in the world, so she was trapped.

She decided to head back to her mother. It took her two days, and when she arrived, she noticed the neighbours' curtains were twitching. It was not until she had been knocking on her mother's door for five minutes that Mrs Kruyper from next door eventually came out. She had looked worried, clutching her necklace. You had better come in, she said to Anna, come in and sit down. So Anna went into Mrs Kruyper's house, and Mrs Kruyper said that there was no other way to say it, but they had found her mother yesterday. Found her where? Found her with her head in the oven, said Mrs Kruyper. They said that she had looked very peaceful, very serene, that she had obviously not suffered. Obviously, said Anna, wondering how much more wrong they could have been.

Their train arrived an hour later. The crush to get on it was appalling, but somehow Lockhart and Leni managed to secure themselves some standing room in the corridor alongside the first-class compartments. Their only comfort was that the journey should take no more than thirty minutes. After that, it would be a fifteen-minute walk to the comparative safety of the guesthouse.

The train had remained stationary for at least ten minutes, which caused Lockhart some anxiety. Leni could see in his eyes that he was troubled.

'Why do you think we aren't moving?'

'I don't know,' said Lockhart. 'I'll see if I can have a look.'

Unfortunately, the corridor and its windows faced away from the platform, so Lockhart had to step into the compartment next to them. The compartment contained six men, two of whom looked like complete thugs, Lockhart thought. Gestapo? Or was he being paranoid? He noticed that the air reeked of cigarette smoke and stale sweat.

'Can you see why we're not moving?' Lockhart asked, bending down to look out of their window.

A collective shaking of heads. Lockhart peered out, but could see no reason for the delay. All he could make out were a few angry prospective passengers who hadn't been able to get on the train, and the odd guard. He noticed that they were all looking in the same direction, down towards the locomotive. Lockhart stepped further into the carriage, to the obvious annoyance of its occupants.

With his face to the window, he craned his head to the left. There was obviously some commotion about three carriages down, and he thought he could make out the uniform of a civilian policeman or two, as well as that of a junior SS officer who had his back to him. He squinted hard, trying to make out what they were up to.

The policemen were removing men from the train and presenting them to the officer, who was then inspecting their papers. Lockhart wanted to jerk his head back from the window, but stopped himself. Instead, he moved away slowly and looked around the compartment with a casual smile.

'I think they must be looking for a fugitive or something,' he said.

A sigh from the occupants. The two men whom he thought to be Gestapo briefly looked at each other and then returned to their newspapers.

'We'll be here for fucking hours!'

'I've already been here for three!'

Lockhart shrugged, as if to say that it was not his fault; that they shouldn't blame the messenger. He stepped out of the compartment and stood next to Leni, who looked apprehensive.

'What is it?' she asked.

Lockhart didn't want to whisper, so he told her the truth as nonchalantly as possible, hoping that she would remain calm.

'I'm not sure,' he said. 'There are some policemen and an untersturmführer hauling people off the train. Probably looking for someone.'

Leni nodded, while some of their fellow standing passengers moaned.

'But we could be here for ages,' she said, her eyes looking straight into his.

'I know,' said Lockhart, chewing his lip. 'I was rather hoping we'd be able to get back home soon – I'm bloody starving.'

They were both thinking on their feet, hoping

desperately that the other would come up with an idea. They both knew that if they got off the train, that would attract attention. But they also knew that if they stayed, they might be caught. They both knew that the woman in the scarf could have been a traitor, or been captured and opened her mouth. It was Lockhart who broke their silence.

'Well, darling,' he said, 'I don't know about you, but if I stand here any longer my bladder will burst.'

Leni laughed, but her expression was one of 'can't you do better than that?'. In truth, he couldn't. It was the only near-innocent reason he could think of for getting off the train. But he couldn't abandon her.

'Do you need to go as well?' he asked. His tone was gentle, quiet, that of the thoughtful lover. Nothing would have been worse than booming out such a commonplace question.

'I'd like to,' she said fiercely, obviously not finding the idea attractive, 'but I think we might lose our places. You go. I'll wait. We women are better at doing so.'

Lockhart turned to the passenger next to him – a middle-aged man who was sweating keenly.

'Sir, you wouldn't mind making sure that we don't lose our places?' Lockhart asked. 'I would be very grateful.'

'Not at all! And perhaps you could go for me while you're there!'

The man laughed heartily, as if he was the first to make such a joke. Lockhart joined in the laughter.

'I'll do that for you!'

'I'll tell you what,' said the man, 'I wouldn't mind borrowing your newspaper whilst you're there.'

Lockhart froze. He could think of no reason why he should not temporarily surrender the paper. Leni coughed.

'Excuse me,' she said.

'Yes, dear?' said Lockhart.

'Well, it's a little embarrassing . . .'

'Yes?'

'Well, I think I do need to go, and, uh, the lavatories often have a shortage, you know, a shortage of paper . . .'

Lockhart shut his eyes in relief. The woman was a genius.

'Forgive me, Fräulein!' said the man, raising his hat. 'I quite understand what you're saying!'

'I'm sorry,' said Leni, nodding her head from side to side like a bashful schoolgirl. 'You know how it is.'

'Quite so! My wife and I sometimes have to do the same at home!'

'So, shall we go then?'

'Yes,' said Leni.

With a plethora of 'sorrys' and 'thank yous', Lockhart and Leni managed to wheedle themselves through their fellow passengers. The most risky moment would be when they were on the platform. If the SS officer was looking in their direction, well, they would just have to run.

Thankfully, the platform was still fairly crowded, and they stepped off the train into a throng of passengers. Lockhart caught a glimpse of the untersturmführer and his police officers – they had advanced half a carriage towards them.

'Which way are the lavatories?' Lockhart asked.

'Over there!' said Leni, pointing to the sign.

They couldn't have been in a worse position, for the lavatories lay halfway between them and the search party. Lockhart took a deep breath – at least he had the Luger.

'All right,' he said. 'We should both go into the same one.'

'But that'll look—'

'No, it's best we stick together. We'll go into the men's. You go ahead of me, and I'll cover you.'

Together, they walked slowly along the platform. Lockhart kept his eyes on the search party, who were in the process of ordering all the men off the next carriage. The untersturmführer still had his eyes glued to the train, rather than those on the platform. Lockhart just had to hope that some sharp-eyed little policeman didn't spot them. He thanked God for the blandness of his clothes, relieved that he had temporarily eschewed his BFC uniform, with its distinctive Union Jack and three lions.

They were now a few yards from the lavatories. The search party was engaged in hauling out some reluctant passengers, who were complaining that they were going to lose their places. Lockhart was grateful for the fracas – it meant that they should be able to slip into the lavatory unnoticed. If there was anybody in there, they would have to say that the ladies' was out of order.

The men's lavatory was empty. They were presented with a row of cubicles, behind each of which was a window large enough for them to get through. Lockhart hoped it wouldn't come to that, but better a window than no window.

'Here, let's go into this one,' Lockhart whispered.

They shut themselves into a cubicle in the corner. Now all they could do was wait for the train to be searched, and for it to leave. Lockhart estimated that they would be here for another half an hour. Too bad. At least they were off the train, where they were likely to have been caught.

The door to the lavatory opened, which caused Lockhart and Leni to hold their breath. They listened to the sound of footsteps, and then a cubicle opening two or three doors down. Sod's law, thought Lockhart, that whoever it was hadn't just come in for a leak. The man started to go about his business noisily, so noisily that they almost started to laugh. It was nervousness that was making them want to do so, thought Lockhart, sheer bloody nervousness.

After a few minutes, the man finished. As he flushed the chain, Lockhart felt himself and Leni relax slightly. The man got out and walked to the wash basins, turned on the tap and uttered a small curse that there wasn't any soap. He cursed again when he realised that there wasn't a towel on which to dry his hands. His footsteps made their way towards the door, and then paused.

'Are you all right in there?'

Lockhart and Leni froze.

'Are you all right in there?' the man asked again. 'You seem very quiet.'

'Yes thank you!' Lockhart croaked back. 'I think it must have been something I ate!'

The man chuckled a little.

'Thanks for asking though,' said Lockhart.

'That's all right!'

And with that, the man walked out. Leni and Lockhart exhaled together, feeling the relief streaming through them, a relief they wouldn't have felt if they could have seen the man leave the lavatory, walk up to a policeman, and tell him that he thought someone was hiding in one of the cubicles.

Lockhart reached for his Luger as soon as he heard the sound of marching boots. Leni's eyes widened.

'You're not!' she whispered.

Lockhart put a finger to his mouth.

The lavatory door slammed open.

'Out!'

Lockhart coughed.

'Sorry?' he groaned, trying to sound ill.

'I said out!'

'I'm terribly ill.'

'I don't care! Just open the door! We're looking for a dangerous terrorist!'

'But I'm not a terrorist.'

'Open the door or we'll kick it down and arrest you!'

Lockhart guessed there were two of them. He looked at Leni, who appeared to be as terrified as he felt inside.

'All right, all right,' said Lockhart. 'Give me a few seconds, will you?'

'Fine! But we don't have all day!'

Lockhart passed the gun and the newspaper to a quizzical Leni, who looked even more so when he removed his jacket.

'What are you doing in there?' the policeman shouted.

'I'm nearly there!' Lockhart shouted back.

He took the gun from Leni and pointed at the lavatory chain, indicating that she should flush it. As the water gurgled noisily through the system, Lockhart quickly wrapped the jacket around his right hand and the Luger. It was the best silencer he could hope for in the circumstances.

He started coughing as he opened the door. He was presented with two civilian policemen, neither of whom had their weapons drawn. More fool them.

'Come with us!' the nearer policeman shouted at him. Just as he was finishing his command, he looked over Lockhart's shoulder at Leni.

'What . . .'

It was to be the policeman's last word, a word that Lockhart used as his cue. He aimed his jacket at the man's stomach, and fired. The policeman bent violently double, a shocked look defiling his face, and then fell on his side, gasping hideously. The other policeman did not stand a chance; Lockhart shot him as he was gazing in a stupor at his downed colleague. The bullet went through his heart, killing him before he had even cracked the back of his skull on the edge of a wash basin. Lockhart briefly considered putting another round into the first policeman, but thought better of it: he needed the ammunition, and he didn't want to make any more noise than was necessary. The jacket had done a reasonable job deadening the noise of the gunshots, but they would still only have half a minute at most in which to escape.

'Get the window open!' he shouted at Leni.

Lockhart unwound the jacket from his Luger, and put the pistol back in its holster. It felt hot, and it burnt a little, but he ignored the pain. He put the badly scorched jacket back on, if only to cover the gun. He turned round to see Leni hauling herself up to the window ledge.

'How does it look out there?'

'It looks clear!'

'Good! Come on, get out, get out!'

Leni swung her legs over the ledge and leapt out. Lockhart stepped on the lavatory bowl and heaved himself on to the ledge. The window overlooked a narrow roofless corridor, into which Lockhart jumped. He landed heavily, feeling a slight twinge in his ankle.

'Shit!'

'Are you all right?' Leni asked.

'I'll be fine!'

'Which way?'

'Let's get back into the open, in amongst the crowds.'

They walked briskly towards a door that Lockhart guessed would take them into the main ticket hall. He listened out for any commotion in the lavatory, but so far there was none. As soon as the bodies were discovered, there would be one hell of a pandemonium. He opened the door slightly, and peered out.

The hall was busy, but as far as he could tell, there were no policemen. Lockhart opened the door, and stepped out.

'Take my arm!'

Leni held him tightly, very tightly. He could feel her trembling.

'Give me a kiss on the cheek.'

She kissed him hard.

'We're dead,' she whispered.

'Not yet we're not,' said Lockhart through gritted teeth, doing his utmost to present a picture of serene calm. 'All we have to do is to walk to the exit and disappear into the crowds.'

'And then what?'

'And then we'll have to find another way of getting back to Hildesheim.'

'What did you have in mind?'

'I don't care, so long as it's not a bloody train.'

They reached the exit and stepped out into the sun. The square was crowded with people sitting at cafés, taking in a beer and the heat, trying to forget about the air raids and the shortages.

It started after they had gone only a few steps. They heard the whistles first, and then the sounds of shouting.

'Just keep walking,' said Lockhart. 'Don't try and run. We're just another couple, remember.'

He noticed that people were glancing up from their drinks, looking towards the station. He turned his head too. It would have looked strange, out of place, if he was the only person to ignore the gathering commotion.

'Please tell me,' he said to Leni, 'that you've still got the newspaper.'

'It's under my arm.'

'Whatever's in it had better be worth it.'

'It will be.'

They were at the end of the square, about to duck

down a side road. Lockhart couldn't resist one look back. A couple of policemen were standing on the steps of the station, looking frantically around the crowded square, their guns at the ready. They were blowing their whistles with all their might, but to little effect, as the crowd did not know what to do. Lockhart allowed himself a quick smile, and then he and Leni peeled off from the square.

'What we need now,' said Lockhart, 'is a car, or a motorbike.'

'Or somewhere to lie low,' said Leni.

'No - we've got to get out of here as soon as possible. The longer we wait, the tighter their noose. At the moment, they're still confused, still searching for us around the station. We need to get out of Hanover before they circulate our descriptions.'

'Where are we going to get a car from?'

'We'll just have to steal one.'

'How?'

'I'll do it at gunpoint if necessary.'

For the next ten minutes they walked the streets, looking for a suitable vehicle. They were hardly spoilt for choice. Cars were a luxury item, used only by top officials. A motorbike would be more practical, and less conspicuous. Lockhart had noticed that a few civilians still rode them, despite the exorbitant price they had to pay for petrol on the black market. It was simply a case of waiting for a motorcyclist, stopping him, and stealing his bike. It was desperate, Lockhart thought, but there were no other options.

But there was no need for a drastic hijacking. As they made their way down a badly bombed street, Lockhart noticed a glint out of the corner of his eye. It came from inside a garage of a wrecked house.

'That looks hopeful,' he said.

'What does?'

'That – in there.'

It was a motorbike, its shiny surface visible in the darkness of the garage. Lockhart looked up and down the road. There were a few other pedestrians, but nobody in uniform. He stepped into the garage – it smelt musty, and part of it had collapsed on to a once-handsome Mercedes. However, the large BMW motorbike looked intact. Shelves bearing every form of tool imaginable lined the walls. Whoever owned this garage must be a rich man, Lockhart thought.

'That would have been nice to drive away in,' said Lockhart, pointing at the car.

'A little ostentatious, don't you think?'

'Just a little – and I wouldn't have liked to try and get it past all the rubble on the streets.'

'Do you know how to ride these things?' Leni asked.

'Sure,' said Lockhart.

'But won't you need a key to start it?'

Lockhart laughed.

'Not at all – just a strong right leg!'

Lockhart unscrewed the cap to the petrol tank and peered inside. It must have been half full – plenty to get them the thirty miles or so to Hildesheim.

'We're in luck. Give me a hand pushing it out of here, and let's get going.'

Within a few minutes, they were under way, Leni's arms wrapped tightly around Lockhart's chest. Initially, Lockhart's control of the motorbike was somewhat haphazard, causing several gasps from his passenger. However, his confidence quickly improved, and he was soon riding as competently as he had done in Crete. That time it had been Anna's arms around him, on the way back from the monastery at Arkádi, after they'd had their first kiss. Lockhart recalled the sun setting behind them, casting their long shadows out in front. He had sworn then that he would never forget that ride, telling himself that it was the best moment in his life. But now the memory of it was too painful.

'Do you know which way you're going?' Leni shouted over his shoulder.

'Sort of!' Lockhart shouted back. 'I'm trying to head south-east!'

The roads were in an appalling condition – the Allies had obviously visited Hanover many times, and vast parts of the city simply consisted of rubble. It made for difficult riding, and Lockhart became increasingly frustrated, wondering whether they were ever going to get out of the place. With every minute, he knew that the chances of being trapped by a roadblock got greater, and he cursed loudly every time they came across an impassable road. He was following his nose, estimating the direction by the position of the sun.

'I'm almost tempted to ask someone the way!' he said.

'Don't!' shouted Leni. 'They'll only remember us! Keep going this way – it feels right to me. And don't go too fast! I don't want to fall off the back!'

'I'll do my best!'

Leni was right – the road they were on appeared to lead out of town. This was the most likely place for a roadblock, thought Lockhart, somewhere on the outskirts. He considered his options. His SS *Personalausweiss* might just get him through – he could say that he had been visiting Hanover with his girlfriend. But he and Leni would match any description that had been circulated – it was too hopeful to assume that he would simply be able to pull rank. The other option was to ignore the roadblock altogether, but he did not fancy his chances. He was not a good enough rider to attempt any daredevilry – he had pushed his luck far enough today. And if he sped away from a roadblock, it would be Leni who would get the bullet in her back, not him. He couldn't do that, couldn't cold-bloodedly sacrifice her. Perhaps it would be best if they abandoned the bike and set off across country, attempted to walk back to Hildesheim. But then they would look like fugitives and somebody would be bound to report them.

Get the violence in first. It came back to him, like a mantra. If the roadblock was not too heavily manned, then they could come at it with guns, or rather *gun*, blazing. Better to go out like that; better than being tortured and strung up with piano wire. That bloody untersturmführer – this was all his fault. Lockhart slowed the bike down and came to a halt.

'Why are you stopping?'

'Because I think we need to work out what we're going to do if there's a roadblock.'

Lockhart outlined their options. He was surprised by Leni's ready agreement.

'Fine,' she said. 'Pass me the Luger. How many rounds has it got left?'

'Six,' said Lockhart, handing her the weapon.

Leni checked it over.

'You know these things like to jam, don't you?'

'So I've been told.'

'Well, we'll just have to hope that this is one of the better ones.'

'You're sure you know how to use it?' Lockhart asked.

Leni gave him a withering look. Lockhart gunned the engine and pulled away. Leni held on to him with her left arm, and held the Luger behind his back in her right hand.

'By the way,' she shouted, '*go slowly* through the roadblock – that way I'll be more likely to hit.'

Lockhart saluted.

As they left Hanover, Lockhart thought for a few cruel minutes that they were in the clear. The road was nearly empty, apart from the odd staff car or lorry, and they were making good progress.

'At this rate,' he bellowed over his shoulder, 'we should be in Hildesheim in half an hour!'

Leni didn't reply, for she had seen what Lockhart evidently hadn't – a line of traffic.

'Look!' she shouted.

'Shit,' said Lockhart under his breath, cursing his optimism.

There must have been at least ten vehicles in the queue. Lockhart pulled up behind a small Opel, no doubt being driven by some self-important official. He looked ahead – the roadblock appeared to be impromptu, consisting of not much more than two cars parked across the middle of each carriageway. Traffic from either direction, after being inspected, was allowed to pass through the narrow gap. There were large drainage ditches on either side of the road, which ruled out any attempt to go past the outside of the roadblock. Lockhart took a deep breath – they would have to go through the middle. He turned to Leni.

'What I suggest we do,' he began, 'is get through immediately behind this car. Hopefully we'll be too quick for them.'

'And what if they start shooting?'

'That's your department.'

As they edged forward, Lockhart studied the soldiers manning the checkpoint. There were six of them, four of whom were wearing badly cut suits: Gestapo, definitely Gestapo. The other two were SS NCOs, brandishing MP40 machine guns. If Leni needed to shoot anybody, it would have to be them.

'Do you see the two SS men?' asked Lockhart.

'Sure.'

They were now only three cars away from the roadblock. Lockhart readied himself, fearing that they might be spotted before their turn came. But with the Gestapo having to check traffic from both directions, their attention was reserved for those vehicles immediately before them.

'Hold tight,' said Lockhart. 'When I move, it's going to be quick.'

They inched forward. Now there was only the Opel between them and the roadblock. Lockhart started revving his engine in readiness, causing one of the Gestapo men to flash them an irritated look. Lockhart smiled back idiotically – it was more natural to act impatient.

Lockhart watched the Opel driver hand over his papers, which were studiously inspected. The Gestapo man seemed to take ages switching his look between them and the driver, seeing if they tallied. Lockhart could feel his heart pounding fiercely, readying himself for the coming burst of action. He and Leni could be dead in half a minute, their mangled bodies full of machine-gun rounds, crushed under the motorcycle. He dispelled the image as he watched the Opel driver take back his papers and put his car into gear. The Gestapo stepped aside to let the Opel go through. Now, thought Lockhart, now.

The motorbike pounced forward. He could feel Leni holding on so tightly that she almost pulled him away from the handlebars. He steered to the left of the Opel, and had to swerve violently to avoid the car queuing in the other direction. The engine was making the most ferocious whine, and Lockhart changed into second gear. He could feel Leni's weight shift in the saddle behind him, and then the unmistakable sound of the Luger firing, not once, but twice. He changed into third – by now they had gone at least sixty yards, far enough to be out of effective range.

'What happened?' Lockhart shouted.

'I hit them!' Leni screamed.

'Hit who?'

'The two SS!'

'You're sure?'

'Yes!'

Lockhart changed into fourth as he overtook a lorry. Nobody would be able to catch up with them, thank God. The motorbike could outpace any of the vehicles at the roadblock. Leni's marksmanship was astonishing. To be able to hit both targets from the back of a hurtling motorcycle was extraordinary.

'Great shooting,' he yelled. 'Amazing!'

Lockhart couldn't see Leni's smile, but it was one of elation and relief, deep relief that she was actively fighting for her parents, for what was right. She was making a difference, and doing it with someone she wanted to hold like this for a very long time.

They reached the edge of Hildesheim twenty minutes later. Lockhart had expected a roadblock, but there was none. He decided the best thing to do would be to ditch the motorbike and then get back to Leni's guesthouse on foot. A small copse provided the perfect spot, and Lockhart rolled the bike into some deep bushes. That would have to do – he didn't want to ride it any further.

They walked arm-in-arm back to the guesthouse. They were both shaking uncontrollably – they would need a drink, but there was no time for that. Lockhart's uniform was in Leni's room, and he desperately wanted to get it back on – something he'd never thought he would feel.

The clothes he was wearing would need to be destroyed, but for the mean time they could be stuffed into Leni's cupboard.

It was half past four when they walked into the guesthouse, the landlady once more sweetened by a few Reichsmarks pressed into her hand. Together they lay on the small bed, their brains in a turmoil of exhaustion and overexcitement.

'The plans!' said Lockhart.

'Don't worry, I've got them.'

Leni pulled the dog-eared *Volkischer Beobachter* from underneath her top and handed it to Lockhart. He stood up and opened the newspaper, letting a medium-sized brown envelope fall on to the floor. He picked it up, slit it open, and pulled out a folded piece of thin paper – it was a blueprint, thought Lockhart, a bloody blueprint. He walked over to the small dressing table and pushed Leni's meagre toiletries to one side, some of them falling on to the floor.

'Thanks,' Leni said sarcastically.

With Leni leaning over him eagerly, Lockhart unfolded the blueprint, revealing a detailed map of Mittelbau. It appeared to consist of two parallel tunnels, each over a mile long. These were connected by cross-tunnels, each around six hundred feet long, and numbered from 1 to 46. These were clearly the halls in which the rockets were assembled. Lockhart quickly scanned them – number 20, for example, was labelled 'Tolerance inspection', number 38 'Assembly of ailerons/tail section'. It was not clear what halls 43 to 46 were for – Lockhart guessed this was where the chemical warheads were fitted.

As he studied the plan, he felt his eyelids beginning to droop. He was absurdly tired. But there was no time for sleep, not now. What he needed to find out, more urgently than anything else, was how a gas that could kill millions could be safely destroyed. It came to him a few minutes later, as he lay on the bed with Leni. He kicked himself that he hadn't thought of him before. The Test Tube, that was who he needed. *He'd* know, and – what was more – he was in Germany.

Oflag IX A/H was a castle high above the town of Spangenburg, about forty-five miles south of Hildesheim. It housed Allied officers, some of whom had been POWs since 1940. Among them, Lockhart had got Strasser to discover, was Barham, Lt. Edward, Royal Artillery, POW number 1197. Why did Lockhart want to go there? Strasser had asked. Because Lieutenant Barham was an old friend and he wanted to see him for a drink. Lockhart could tell that Strasser was deeply suspicious, but, with his hands tied, he supplied Lockhart with the necessary papers, along with a letter to the camp commandant, saying that Hauptsturmführer Lockhart was recruiting for the BFC.

Spangenburg Castle was a grim place, thought Lockhart. A light rain was falling, making the greyness of the castle more gloomy, more forbidding. Poor Test Tube, what a place to have been stuck in all these years. Had he tried to escape? Lockhart remembered that Barham was notoriously clumsy – he doubted whether any other officer would care for him as an escape partner.

Lockhart walked over the drawbridge and presented himself to the guard under the vaulted gateway. He was nodded through, and found himself tripping over the badly laid cobbles, thinking that they would have been obstacle enough for any escaper, let alone The Test Tube.

'John? What the hell . . .?'

'Hello, Ted.'

Lockhart stood up and shook Barham's hand. After much cajoling by Lockhart, the commandant had given them ten minutes alone and the use of a small interrogation room in the German side of the castle. The furniture consisted of nothing more than three rickety wooden chairs and a solid table, upon which Lockhart had placed a packet of cigarettes.

'But what are you doing here? And that *uniform*! Don't tell me you're . . .'

'No, Ted, I'm not. This isn't what it looks like.'

'But you'll forgive me for *asking*. I don't want to seem *rude*, but it's not every day that an old Merton chum comes *swanning* into your POW camp wearing an SS uniform!'

Good old Test Tube. He was just the same, thought Lockhart, complete with his scratchy hair (although a little balder), and his thick-rimmed glasses (with an arm missing, but maybe they were like that at Oxford). He still spoke rapidly, half an octave higher than most people, and overemphasised certain words.

'Cigarette?' Lockhart asked.

'No, but I'll take some all the same. *Barter.*'

'Please – take them all.'

Barham left the packet on the table.

'So come on,' he said. 'Why are you here? What are you doing? Come on, come on.'

Lockhart told him the truth – all of it. He owed it to him. After he had finished, Ted took a cigarette, which Lockhart lit. They sat in silence, Lockhart feeling uneasy, hoping that Test Tube had believed him.

'I . . . I . . . don't know what to say,' Barham stuttered. 'It just seems *too* fantastic. *All* of it.'

'But Ted, it's *true*,' Lockhart insisted. 'And I need your help. You must know how to deal with this gas.'

'I'm not *sure* if I do.'

Lockhart's shoulders slumped.

'Please, Ted, you must trust me. Can't you see how important this is? If the Germans use this gas, then thousands, maybe *millions*, might die. It could alter the whole war. Can't you see that?'

Ted shook his head.

'It's just not possible, nothing can be *that* toxic.'

'So you think the whole thing's bunkum?'

Barham pushed his glasses back up the bridge of his nose and looked at Lockhart.

'Well, I've *certainly* never heard of such a gas. Why can't you tell me more? What's it *made* from?'

Lockhart shook his head.

'Sorry, I was hoping you might know, or might be able to guess. Couldn't you at least tell me how they deal with other poison gases? There must be some way of getting rid of them.'

Barham looked at the floor and scratched his head with the hand holding the cigarette. Lockhart noticed that some ash fell into his hair.

'The only way I can think of . . .' said Barham.

'Yes?'

'. . . is to find some other chemical that will neutralise it.'

'How the hell am I going to find that?'

Lockhart regretted showing his exasperation.

'Perhaps if you got hold of the *formula*, I *might* be able to help you.'

Lockhart shook his head.

'No, sorry, Ted, there's no time for that. If the Germans are going to use it, they're going to use it soon. Please, *think*.'

This was followed by a lot more head-scratching.

'Well . . . actually . . . no,' said Barham. 'No, it's ridiculous.'

'What? Tell me.'

'I suppose you could try *blowing* it up.'

'But surely that would release the gas?'

'Not if you blew it up in a *chamber*. You'd need something pretty heavy-duty, but it would *probably* work . . .'

Ted was speaking quickly now.

'We can safely assume that the sarin is stored in *liquid* form, because it's much more stable to store poison gas in that way. That'll mean that it's kept in *highly* pressurised containers, which would presumably be mounted on your rockets . . .'

'How big would these containers be?'

More scratching.

'Well, if this *sarin* is so bloody deadly, you wouldn't need very much of it, would you? I'd guess that each container wouldn't be *much* larger than a half-bottle of wine.'

'What then?'

'*Simple.* You place all your containers in your chamber, put a *small* amount of explosive in it, seal it, and then detonate it. Bingo!'

'How much explosive, Test Tube?'

'Ooh – I'd say no more than a *pound* of dynamite. That would easily do the trick, going off in an enclosed space. We don't of course know how many *containers* there are, but I'd say that if you used, I don't know, something the size of a normal fifty-*gallon* oil drum, you'd be able to blow up at least a hundred and fifty to two hundred containers at a time. The residue in the chamber would be pretty ghastly stuff, but it would be *relatively* harmless and unusable. This is all *hypothesis*, of course.'

'So could I use a normal oil drum?'

Barham started laughing.

'Good God, no! That would simply blow apart! You need something that can take the pressure.'

'What then?'

'Well, it would *have* to be immensely strong. Be able to take a lot of force.'

'Where am I going to get that?'

Barham turned his palms up.

'That's *your* problem. Try a factory.'

'Will you join me, Test Tube?'

'Sorry, John, I can't.'

'Why not? You'd be an enormous help.'

'I can't. I'd be useless. Anyway, I'm needed here.'

'What for?'

'I'm making some smoke bombs. We're organising a mass breakout, and we want to cause as much *confusion* as possible.'

Lockhart was nearly speechless. All he could say was 'good luck'. He expected this would be the last time he saw Test Tube. He couldn't imagine both of them surviving the war.

At first, Marston had said that he could not make the Monday morning run, but Lockhart had insisted, telling him that a bad knee was no excuse. Marston had whined, saying that the doctor had told him to put his leg up for a few days, but Lockhart said that doctors spoke nonsense, and what Marston needed was some air and exercise. Had Marston been more strong-willed, it would have been difficult for Lockhart to persuade him to come along, but thankfully he was more obedient to rank than a twinge in his leg.

The men were assembled outside the cloister, dressed in their regulation PT kit, which consisted of black shorts, running shoes, and a white sleeveless vest which bore the SS runes in black. Lockhart jogged on the spot in front of them, and continued to do so as he spoke.

'We'll be going on our usual run today,' he began.

The men groaned. Lockhart smiled.

'So that's through the woods, the normal circuit around the fields – twice – and then back here, through the woods again. Now that the ground is so hard, I see no reason why we shouldn't be able to do it in under ninety minutes.'

Another groan.

'And one more thing. I don't want us to separate. It's no good the quicker ones amongst us – such as you, Stafford, and you, Hull – racing ahead just so they can get back to use the baths first. In an advance, we could go no faster than the slowest, and today that would appear to be Marston. So then, if Marston lags behind, you all have to help him. You may even have to carry him. Is that clear?'

'Yes, sir!'

Poor Marston, thought Lockhart. Normally he would never have insisted that he come on the run, but he needed all the men together, away from the ears around every wall and corner.

'Right! Let's go then!'

Lockhart started off and the men reluctantly followed. They were not as fit as they had been a few months ago, but they were still in much better shape than at the beginning of the year.

After only a few hundred yards, Marston stopped running.

'Sir!' he shouted. 'I really can't go any further!'

'All right,' said Lockhart. 'We'll have to carry you. I'll take you first, and then everybody else will have a go, starting with Allan and working through the alphabet.'

Lockhart lifted Marston on to his back. Although he

couldn't have weighed more than ten stone, he was heavy enough to cause Lockhart a lot of difficulty as they ran up the medium gradient towards the woods. He was determined to make it, to show the men that he was willing to exhaust himself for the sake of one of them. The woods were still quarter of a mile away, and Lockhart reckoned that he should be able to manage.

After a few minutes, Lockhart was finding the going tough – very tough. Although the hill was not that steep, its incline was trebled by Marston's weight.

'Would you like me to take over now, sir?' Allan asked.

'No,' gasped Lockhart, 'I can manage.'

When the woods were a hundred yards away, Lockhart felt ready to collapse. Allan had once more asked to take over, but he was again refused. Lockhart felt his arms shaking as they started to buckle, and his calves felt tighter and tighter with every step. He was taking huge gulps of air, getting as much oxygen to his muscles as possible, and almost felt ready to pass out.

'Do you want me to get down, sir?' asked Marston.

'No . . . bloody . . . way,' panted Lockhart; the woods were only fifty yards away.

Marston's request gave him extra vigour, and he even managed to run-cum-stumble a little quicker than he had done over the previous few hundred yards. By the time he reached the woods, his legs and arms were in agony, but he made sure he put Marston down gently, not wishing to cause his knee any further damage.

'Well done, sir,' said Hull. 'That looked bloody hard – I don't think I could have done it.'

'Of course you could, Hull,' Lockhart panted. 'You could have carried him up one-handed. Right, let's carry on. Allan – it's your turn. Changeover point is the clearing, the one with the old summerhouse.'

They reached the clearing ten minutes later, although Allan, despite Lockhart's exhortations, had had to hand Marston over to Andreae before they got there. Lockhart didn't mind too much – it emphasised to the men how impressive it had been getting Marston up the hill.

'Right, let's stop here!' Lockhart ordered.

'Stop, sir?' asked Catchpole. 'But normally we—'

'I know, but I'm feeling generous, and besides, I've got something to say to you all. Sit down, sit down.'

The men did so, crumpling gratefully on to the ground. Lockhart remained standing, and let himself catch his breath, taking time to compose himself. He studied the men's faces. Some of them were looking up at him, their expressions curious; others were staring down at the ground between their legs. Malcolm was even stripping the bark off a stick, something that Lockhart remembered doing at prep school as he sat on the ground listening to a master prattle on about the rules of cricket. Schoolboys, that was what they were, he thought, just a bunch of schoolboys.

'What I'm about to talk to you about,' said Lockhart, 'is our future. I know that you're all worried about what's going to happen to us, now that the Allies and the Russians seem to be closing in. Well, it's very simple. If we're caught, then we'll get tried. And we'll be found guilty, even those of us who aren't fascists. And if we're found guilty, then some of us may well be sentenced to death. The lucky ones will get a mere twenty-five years breaking rocks on Dartmoor. Believe you me, we are traitors, men, every single one of us, even though each of one us thinks that he's not.

'We've all joined this unit for different reasons. Some of you, like Maclaren and Pugh, seem to have a lot of sympathy for the Nazis. Others, like you, Hull, and you, Andreae, are in it because you wanted out of your POW camp, wanted an easier life. And there are those such as you, Malcolm, who're here in order to get out of trouble, to avoid an unpleasant punishment.

'But these reasons no longer matter. There are many ways into this corps, and as I see it, there are many ways out. We can go to Dresden, and end up fighting the Russians, who are, let's not forget, our allies . . .'

'Not mine,' mumbled Prain surlily.

Lockhart ignored the comment.

'. . . and more than likely get killed as cannon fodder on the Eastern Front. Way out number two is to mutiny. I don't fancy that either – we'd be put in an SS punishment camp and wouldn't last the winter. Way out number three is to go back to our stalags, for those of us who came from one. No thanks once again. Way out number four is to escape. Again, even more unappealing – if you're caught, you'll get shot as a deserter. So what does that leave us with?'

Lockhart paused and looked at the men. They stayed silent, all waiting eagerly for what he was about to say.

'We've all made mistakes, men,' Lockhart continued. 'I'll be the first to admit that I have. As you know, I joined this unit because I wanted to save my wife. Well, now I've found out that she's dead, and that she's probably been dead for ages.'

A murmur went through the men.

'That's right,' said Lockhart. 'I allowed myself to be tricked – that's my mistake. Don't ask me how I was tricked, or who did it, because I won't tell you. Anyway, I want to make up for my mistake, make up for the fact that I've betrayed my country. I don't deny that I want to do something that may even get me off the hook when the Allies eventually get here, as I have no doubt that they will.

'But it's not just about saving my skin. It's about saving all our skins, doing something that will make each of us feel proud.'

'What did you have in mind?' said Catchpole.

'Yes, sir, what is it, sir?' asked Malcolm.

'Patience,' said Lockhart with a smile. 'I'm coming to it. What I'm offering you is a way out that doesn't involve shame. A way out that will make a difference to many; that involves doing something decent, something that you'll be proud of for the rest of your lives, because as things stand, I'm not proud to be a member of this unit. Don't get me wrong, I'm proud to lead *you*, but I'd rather lead you all somewhere better than an ignominious death.

'My way involves risk, but bearing in mind the alternatives open to us, it's a risk worth taking. If it works, then we will have saved the lives of many innocent people, people who stand to die for no reason at all.'

Lockhart could see that the men were all staring at him, hanging on to his every word.

'What I have in mind is very simple. Not far from us here is a mountain called Kohnstein. Buried in it is a concentration camp, not an ordinary concentration camp, but a huge underground factory called Mittelbau. In this factory they make rockets that the Germans intend to arm with a nerve gas called sarin, a gas so deadly that it can kill–'

'Rubbish!' shouted Maclaren. 'The Germans would never use gas!'

'Is that so?' asked Lockhart. 'What makes you such an authority?'

Maclaren didn't reply.

'Come on, Maclaren? Why don't you tell me?'

The men all turned to look at Maclaren, but he kept his gaze fixed to the ground.

'I'm sure,' Lockhart continued, 'that the Nazis are perfectly capable of using gas. A regime that wants to eradicate an entire race is hardly a regime that will have any qualms about destroying a few more millions of people.'

'Did you say millions?' asked Allan, incredulous.

'Yes, Allan, yes I did.'

'But . . . but where are these rockets going?'

'London.'

The men gasped, momentarily struck dumb. After a few seconds, most of them started to speak as one, firing questions and comments at Lockhart.

'What do you intend to do about it?' asked Catchpole, his voice riding over the babble.

'It is my intention to go to Mittelbau, and destroy the sarin.'

'Are you joking?' asked Simpkin.

'You'll get us all killed!' shouted Hull.

'Yes, Hull, that's entirely possible. But wouldn't you rather die trying to stop something this evil than live to see it being executed? Would you be happy to carry on in the knowledge that you stood by and let millions of people die? I know I wouldn't. It would be shameful, despicable, odious; in fact, it would be evil in itself to do nothing.'

Lockhart spoke in that vein for a further five minutes, during which time their collective opinion changed dramatically. Lockhart thought they reacted well, even the fascist element. He looked at his watch. It was already half past eight – Strasser would be expecting them back at nine, and he didn't want to arouse his suspicions by having the men returning as though they had been for a gentle stroll around town. Now was the time for the crunch.

'All right,' he said. 'Before we go, I want you to put your hand up if you do *not* wish to take part.'

A pause that set his heart crazy, crazier than it had been when carrying Marston up the hill, and then, to his relief, only the hands of Maclaren, Simpkin and Smith went up. The remaining ten kept theirs down, with a few, such as Hull and Andreae, resolutely folding their arms. The ten looked at the three, who appeared to become increasingly self-conscious.

Lockhart saw that Smith's hand was wobbling, and after a few seconds it fell back down. Maclaren and Simpkin did their best to look confident, with Maclaren even stretching his hand up further, but after a few moments, Simpkin's hand came down as well.

'Put your fucking hand down!' Hull shouted.

'That's right,' said Stafford. 'Do as he says, put it bloody down!'

'Quiet!' Lockhart ordered. 'I want Maclaren to volunteer, not be press-ganged into it. Well then, Maclaren, are you quite sure?'

Maclaren was sneering, his top lip twitching furiously. Lockhart stared at him, and then looked round at the others, most of whom seemed ready to beat him up.

'Why's your hand not up?' Maclaren said to Pugh. 'It should be up, dammit!'

'I'm sorry,' said Pugh. 'I know which side my bread's now buttered.'

Maclaren glared at Pugh, and then let his hand fall violently to the ground.

'Goddammit!' he shouted. 'This is madness!'

'Well done, Maclaren,' said Lockhart. 'I'm glad you've agreed to help. I'm glad *all* of you have agreed to help. It goes without saying, of course, that not one word of this goes any further. Is that understood?'

'Yes, sir!'

Lockhart noticed that Maclaren stayed silent.

'I said, Maclaren, is that understood?'

'Yesss, sir,' Maclaren hissed sarcastically.

'Good. Right. Halfway round the fields, back through the woods, and then at a sprint all the way back. And Catchpole, I think it's your turn to carry Marston.'

The men got up. All were quiet, stunned by what

Lockhart had told them. But perhaps the person most stunned was Lockhart himself, who was doing his best not to look as exhilarated as he felt. He knew that the cement that held the men together was weak, but it was a bond all the same, and it might set stronger. He would have to keep his eye on Maclaren, and if necessary be as ruthless as possible.

As they ran round one of the big fields, Pugh managed to get alongside Lockhart and speak to him without the others hearing.

'What would you have done if Maclaren had kept his hand up?' he puffed.

'Oh, that's simple,' said Lockhart. 'I'd have shot him.'

For a few moments, Pugh stopped running, and watched Lockhart. It didn't take him long to realise that Lockhart would quite readily have shot any one of them.

'So do you think they will follow you?' Leni asked.

'What?'

'*The men* – do you think they will follow you?'

'Fifty-fifty,' said Lockhart. 'Some are up for it, but there are one or two who might waver. But they've been training together for a long time now, so there is *some* cohesion. I doubt many of them would want to let the others down, even in combat.'

They were in Leni's room that same afternoon, studying the blueprint. Lockhart had something else on his mind, something more engaging than the loyalty of the men or the layout of the factory. Leni had noticed that he was distracted.

'What is it?' she asked.

'What's what?' Lockhart replied, slightly irritated.

'You seem angry or something, distant.'

'No, I'm fine.'

'Come on.'

There was never going to be a good time to tell her, Lockhart thought, and this time was as bad as any. He looked up from the blueprint and gazed into her enquiring face.

'What?' she said. 'What do you want to tell me?'

Lockhart looked back down at the plan and pointed to hall number 4.

'You see this hall here?' he asked.

'It says "Prisoner accommodation".' Leni shrugged. 'What about it?'

'I'm very interested in hall number 4.'

'Why?'

'Because that's where Anna is.'

November 1985

She had written once a year to the Russian Embassy, as the enigmatic Kirov had suggested, but she knew that the replies were as automatic as a photocopier. It was worth a try, though; you never knew, and Russia was where the files were. She had to keep trying, even if she always received the same bland response. It hadn't changed in over twenty years:

> Dear Miss Lockhart,
> The Embassy of the Union of Soviet Socialist Republics thanks you for your enquiry concerning your father. We regret . . .

And so on. The only thing that changed was the name of the functionary at the foot of the letter, but that was of no consequence. Never again were there to be any sympathetic and hurried phone calls, like the one from Kirov. What had happened to him? He was obviously a kind man, kind enough to put his job on the line for a strange Westerner in the middle of the Cuban Missile Crisis.

And then Gorbachev came to power, and announced his programme of reforms, a programme that showed the West that there was a different man in the Kremlin. There was *perestroika*, his catch-all term for this programme, as well as meaning the intended restructuring of the economy. And then there was *democratizatsia*, *novomyshlenie* – new thinking towards the West; *glasnost* – openness.

It was the last two that had Amy pricking her ears as she listened to the radio news in the bath. Surely this was her opportunity? They would *have* to help her now; it was their new policy to open up and be more friendly to the West. Well, they could start with her. She could be their test case. She could see it now – 'British Woman Unlocks Moscow Vaults'. Well, why the hell not? Someone had to be the first, and she was as deserving as anyone.

Predictably, Hugh scoffed at the idea when he came in to brush his teeth – a lot of 'leopards don't change their spots' and 'it's all a façade'.

'You only trust Gorbachev because you want to trust him,' he said.

'That's possible, but it's not going to do any harm.'

'The only harm it's doing is getting your hopes up before he dashes them back down to the ground again.'

'We'll see.'

'Yes, we will. And your friend Gorby will have me to deal with when I have a ratty wife for the next couple of weeks.'

Amy smiled.

'I expect he's got other things on his mind.'

'I'm sure he'd find some time for you.'

Hugh pretended to pick up a phone.

'Ronnie,' he said in a Russian accent, 'look, I really cannot talk right now, because there is this most important woman from England on the phone.'

Amy flicked some bath water at him.

'Hey!' Hugh exclaimed.

He filled up his tooth mug from the cold tap, rinsed his mouth, spat the water into the sink, and then emptied the rest of the tooth mug on to Amy in the bath.

'Not fair!' she screamed.

'I'm just pouring cold water on your idea,' said Hugh with a wicked grin.

'Not a chance,' said Amy.

Chapter Nine

FOR A MINUTE, Leni remained speechless.

'Do you mean to say . . .' she began, and then trailed off.

'What?' said Lockhart.

'Do you mean to say . . . that this is all about saving your wife?'

Lockhart shook his head.

'It is, isn't it?'

Lockhart continued to shake.

'I don't believe it!'

'Please, Leni!'

But she couldn't be stopped.

'You selfish bastard! You're going to risk all our lives just so you can see her again, aren't you? Go on – admit it!'

'That's not true!'

'Of course it is! How could it not be?'

Lockhart briefly shut his eyes and breathed out heavily through his nose.

'Please, Leni,' he said quietly. 'Please will you let me explain?'

But Leni would not be mollified.

'You're not interested in the gas. It's just a convenient excuse, isn't it? Just a way of convincing people like me and those poor fools in the unit to help you. Do you know how many people have already risked their lives for you? Do you realise that my parents will be killed if I get caught? Haven't you thought for one—'

'Leni! For God's sake, shut up! Will you let me explain?'

Leni stopped herself and held out her palms to him.

'All right,' she said. 'It had better be good.'

'It's a coincidence,' he said, 'just a bloody coincidence. I was first told where Anna was when I was in Crete. I had never heard of Mittelbau, had no idea where it was, or what went on there. And then, when I was in Berlin, when I heard Nicolas knocking through the wall, he tapped the word 'Mitt' when I asked him where the sarin was. But he was dragged off to his death before he could finish. Of course, when I first heard 'Mitt', I immediately thought of Mittelbau, but I dismissed it, thinking that such a coincidence was far too unlikely. It was only last week, when that telegram arrived, that I knew for certain.'

Leni raised her hands, as if she was about to say something, but let them fall back down to her sides.

'What do you want to say?' Lockhart asked.

'So . . . so do you think she's alive?'

Lockhart looked down at the blueprint, looked down at hall 4.

'I don't know,' he said, 'I really don't know. But something tells me that she is.'

'And so that's why we're going.'

'No!' Lockhart snapped.

Leni started.

'No!' he repeated. 'That's NOT the reason. The reason we're going is the same as it always was – to destroy the sarin. Whether my wife is there or not is secondary, and even then, secondary only for me – I would expect it to be of no relevance to anyone else. I would never ask anyone to risk their life just so I could save my own wife.'

'So you're going to forget that she's there?'

'Yes.'

'But how can you not look for her when you think she could be alive?' she asked.

'Because,' Lockhart replied, 'her life is worth no more than any other.'

'But she's your wife.'

'Just because she's worth more to me doesn't mean that she's worth more than anyone else in the world. I'd rather my wife died than two innocent people, let alone the countless others who might die.'

'You can't really think that. Most people would rather let others die before sacrificing their own wife or husband.'

'I expect they would,' said Lockhart. 'That's what's happening here in Germany. There is a monster on the loose, and people don't want him to eat their families. So they feed him with those they don't know, or pretend not to know – the Jews, the Gypsies, the handicapped, homosexuals, criminals. And the monster is eating them by the million, stuffing his face with the families of strangers. But those strangers are worth just as much as the families you do know. Who you know is just an accident – knowing people doesn't make them worth more.'

'And you include Anna in that?'

Lockhart paused. He looked Leni straight in the eye.

'Yes,' he replied. 'Yes I do. It hurts me more than anything to say that, but how can I possibly claim that her life is more precious than anyone else's? Anna is my wife because I met her. I could have met someone else and married that person instead, but would that have made Anna Green any less valuable in the eyes of the world? No. Don't get me wrong: she and Amy *are* my world, and I would do anything to save them. But what I won't do is let millions of others die just because I want to save my wife.'

'You realise that you might be the one who ends up killing her? If we succeed at Mittelbau, then she might well die.'

Another pause.

'I'm aware of that. But the principle doesn't change.'

'I can't . . .'

'What?'

'I can't believe you're being so logical about it.'

Lockhart allowed himself a wry smile.

'Believe you me, I'm not feeling very logical. I'm feeling the opposite, if anything.'

'So how can you be so logical?'

'Because I have to be, Leni. I have no choice. There'll be a time when I'll be able to scream and shout, but that's not now. It wouldn't help.'

They remained in silence, a silence that Leni eventually broke.

'So what you're telling me is that you're willing to shoot your own wife rather than shoot two complete strangers. Is that what you're saying?'

'Yes.'

'But would you, could you *actually* do that? If the three of them were actually standing in front of you, you'd shoot her?'

Slowly, Lockhart folded up the blueprint. He could feel the tears coming, but he stopped them.

'Ask me when we get to Mittelbau,' he said.

'You're ducking the question.'

Leni's tone was gentle.

'Yes,' he said quietly, 'yes I am. Only a saint or a monster could answer that question confidently. I'm somewhere in between, or at least I hope I am.'

Max had been wary at first, had wondered why on earth Strasser needed two dozen MP40 machine guns, twelve Walther P38s, thousands of rounds of ammunition, thirty-six grenades, and two dozen sticks of dynamite.

'What do you want to do?' he had asked down the crackling line from Berlin. 'Blow up Hildesheim? I knew you hated the place, but not that—'

'Please, Max,' Strasser had said. 'I need it for our move to Dresden. I'll pay you back in some way, I promise.'

'What the hell are you doing in Dresden?'

'We're joining the pioneer school.'

'Well, don't *they* have all this sort of kit?'

'Apparently not. I've been asked to bring as much as I can by the commander there, otherwise he won't take us. And if we can't find a home, then I'm sure that Berger will find a far more unpleasant place for us to go.'

'Christ, Carl! You know this is worth at least a week at Kitty's and a lifetime's supply of schnapps?'

'Whatever you want, Max.'

'I was joking! Come on, Carl, what's the matter with you?'

'Nothing. Can you help me or not?'

There had been a silence.

'Max?'

'Yes, I'm still here. You just don't sound yourself, that's all.'

'I promise you, Max, I'm all right – just under a lot of pressure. Can you help? You could put it down as "Emergency Requirement for Eastern Front" or something.'

Max had breathed heavily down the line.

'Everything's an emergency, but all right, Carl, I'll do it. It'll probably be the end of me, but I'll do it because it's for you.'

'Thank you, Max, thank you.'

'But I won't be able to do something like this again. All right?'

'Fine. And I owe you.'

'You certainly do! You should get it all in a few days.'

'Thank you, Max.'

'Don't worry about it. I'm looking forward to my week at Kitty's already.'

Max was as good as his word, and a few days later, on Friday afternoon, a lorry arrived at the St Michael Cloister. Lockhart was also there to receive it, along with a few members of the unit, who were manhandling the heavy crates.

'I take it that the lorry is for us as well?' Lockhart asked.

Damn, thought Strasser, he had forgotten about Lockhart's fucking lorry. Lockhart could obviously tell from his expression that he had done so.

'Come on, Carl,' said Lockhart. 'Don't tell me that you've forgotten.'

'No, I hadn't – there just aren't any lorries to give you.'

Now it was Lockhart's turn to look blank. Good.

'What about this one then?' Lockhart asked.

'This lorry will be going back to Berlin.'

That smile again. It infuriated Strasser, that cocky smile of Lockhart's. He should have just shot him back at Genshagen. Then he wouldn't have been in this mess.

'No it won't,' said Lockhart. 'Because I'm going to commandeer it.'

'That's out of the question!'

'Really?'

'Yes! It is a court-martial offence!'

'Well, that's just too bad.'

Enraged, Strasser watched the Englishman walk over to the two lorry drivers, who were standing some distance away having a cigarette. He could see from their faces that they were stunned by what Lockhart was telling them, presumably informing him that there was no way they could surrender their lorry to him, even if he was a hauptsturmführer, and they mere privates. However, just as Strasser thought that Lockhart was being put in his place, he watched him take a wallet out of his tunic, and pass the men a fistful of banknotes. He was bribing them! Strasser could have him shot for that, but he knew it was impossible. Lockhart had warned him that if anything happened to him, Leni would tell the SD about Strasser's loose tongue. Seething, he watched Lockhart walk back towards him, his expression triumphant.

'There we go, Carl, the British Free Corps now has its very own lorry.'

Strasser stayed silent. Whatever it was that Lockhart was planning, it was clearly important. He wasn't just intending to escape, because he could have done that some time ago. So what was he up to? What was it that required not only all this equipment, but the men as well?

Surely it was now time for Strasser to stop all this, stop being taken advantage of. There were three options open to him. He could simply call in the SD – that would put an end to it, but it might well put an end to him as well. Or he could turn a blind eye, and let Lockhart carry on. But that would also guarantee Strasser's demise. The third option was simply to kill himself, but the idea of throwing his life away was anathema. Once, he would have been willing to die for the Reich, but not any more. He felt conned, cheated. They had been swindled, all of them, sold a pup about the greatness and goodness of Germany. What had he done that felt so good and so great? Nothing. He felt ashamed, almost crippled by a lack of pride. All those bodies he had left behind, all that grief, all that destruction.

There was a fourth option, but he shrugged it off. It was unthinkable, and he felt guilty for letting it cross his mind.

That evening, Lockhart gathered the men together in their common room. A portrait of the Duke of Windsor was hanging on the wall, but there was an absence of any Nazi insignia, except for the BFC's tattered recruiting poster showing the Nazi flag and the Union Jack side by side, held aloft by glorious marching ranks. 'Our Flag Is Going Forward Too' read the caption, which seemed ironic to Lockhart, aware that the Nazi flag was going anywhere but forward. The Americans and the British were making huge advances in the west, and the Russians were thrusting forward equally strongly. It made Lockhart realise that there was no more time to lose – if the Germans were going to use the sarin, they were going to use it soon, to try to halt any further Allied advances, make them think again.

The thirteen men were sitting in a variety of tatty chairs, some of which had been pinched from bombed-out buildings in town. Standing in front of a blackboard he had wangled, Lockhart looked at each of them in turn. They all seemed nervous, apprehensive. Pugh gave him a wink, Hull, Andreae and Stafford knowing nods; the rest caught his eye, save for Maclaren, who avoided his gaze. He would have to watch him, thought Lockhart, he could ruin everything.

'I'll give it to you straight,' Lockhart began. 'We leave on Sunday morning.'

They gasped as one.

'But sir,' said Andreae, 'that's not enough time!'

'You're right,' said Lockhart. 'It isn't enough. But we don't have any more time. If the Germans are going to use the sarin, then I suspect they'll use it soon.'

'Couldn't we get the RAF to bomb it?' asked Allan.

'I wish we could,' Lockhart replied. 'But there are two problems there. First, as Stafford here will tell you, London has been singularly uncommunicative over the past few weeks. And even if they did order an air raid, I expect it would fail, because the gas and the rockets are buried deep within a mountain. A raid would do little more than knock down a few trees, perhaps take out some satellite camps. No, we actually have to get inside and deal with it.'

'But how?' asked Allan.

'Patience! I'm coming to that.'

Lockhart turned to face the blackboard, and spent a couple of minutes chalking up a simplified plan of Mittelbau. He had remembered every detail of the blueprint, had got Leni to quiz him repeatedly on the layout, which materials were stored in which hall, and so forth. There was no need to tell the men the complete layout – it would only confuse them. The basics were all that they required.

'The place we are going to is called Mittelbau,' said Lockhart. 'It is a factory built into the Kohnstein Mountain near Nordhausen, about a hundred kilometres from here. On Sunday morning, we will drive there in the lorry, dressed in our uniforms, although we shall have to strip them of the BFC insignia – Simpkin, I'd like you to see to that. Upon arrival, we shall present ourselves to the commandant. We will say that we have been sent from Berlin, and tell them that we are delivering some machinery, as well as forming a new guard detachment.'

'What if this doesn't work?' Hull chipped in.

'It will,' said Lockhart, producing a piece of paper from his tunic pocket, 'because I have typed orders from Berlin to that effect. I expect I will be told that they are not expecting us. I will answer that that's not my fault – they can either take it or leave it and incur the wrath of the supposed signatory – a certain Brigadeführer Karl Kammler. I'm gambling that they'll take it. The last thing anyone is expecting is a raid carried out by an SS unit.'

'And what happens when we're actually in the plant?' asked Pugh.

'Simple,' said Lockhart, pointing to the blackboard. 'We make our way to hall number 44 here, which is where I suspect the gas is held. It may be at this stage that we'll have to engage the enemy, but I'm hoping that the bluff will hold. We'll then park the lorry as close to the chemical store as possible, and deal with the gas.'

'But how?' Maclaren asked.

'I'll tell you that in a moment,' said Lockhart.

'There seems so much that can go wrong,' said Catchpole. 'We could be stopped at any moment. Someone could smell a rat . . .'

'I know, I know,' said Lockhart. 'But if you've got a better idea, then let's hear it. Remember, simple plans have less to go wrong with them. Don't forget, Mittelbau is a vast place – they have such comings and goings and every day. We'll be just another set of faces, just another unit of bored men looking forward to a Sunday afternoon off. And because it's the weekend, those on duty will probably be feeling a little more slack.'

'It sounds mad!' said Prain.

'Perhaps,' said Lockhart, 'but it would be a greater madness not to try. Just imagine the whole of London choking to death on an invisible cloud of gas. It would be the worst terror on earth, destruction and murder on a scale never seen before. We can't just sit by and let it happen. Many of you have families in London – are you willing just to let them die? And where will they hit next? Manchester? Liverpool? The whole British population could be eradicated. Just think of it for a minute.'

The men did so, most of them with their arms folded, looking at the floor or out of the window. Each thought of his family back home, trying to imagine a terror that was almost inconceivable. They pictured their mothers, their girlfriends, their fathers – all choking to death. They saw heaps of bodies lying in the streets, a vision so grim, so evil, that a collective shudder went round the room.

* * *

'And where do we go if we get away?' Prain asked.

Lockhart had thought about that, but had put it low down on his list of priorities. In his heart, he knew that the chance of any of them getting out alive was appallingly slim.

'I have a contact who has a safe house in Nordhausen,' said Lockhart. 'We will make our way there afterwards.'

'Who's your contact?'

'I cannot tell you,' said Lockhart, for the simple reason that there was no contact.

'What I'd like to know,' said Smith, 'is *exactly* how we're going to deal with the gas.'

Lockhart noticed Smith's use of the word 'we'. It was a good sign, an excellent sign.

'I'm glad you asked me that,' said Lockhart. 'Because some of us are going to pick it up tomorrow morning.'

'Pick what up?'

'All in good time, Smith, all in good time.'

At seven o'clock the next morning, a lorry pulled away from the St Michael Cloister. It was a commonplace event – lorries came and went nearly every hour, ferrying groups of SS men to parts of the ever-diminishing Reich. Lockhart had deliberately neglected to tell Strasser, preferring instead to face the music – if there was any – on his return.

'So how are you finding it?' Lockhart shouted above the noise of the engine.

'It's very good, sir,' replied Malcolm. 'I wish I'd had one as good as this back home!'

Alongside them in the front were Pugh and Hull.

'Where the hell are we going?' Pugh asked for the umpteenth time.

'It's not far now,' said Lockhart, studying a map.

They had been driving for an hour, and he could sense that Pugh and Hull were deeply frustrated at being left in the dark.

'But . . .' said Pugh.

'You'll see, don't you worry.'

Ten minutes later, Lockhart suddenly turned to Malcolm.

'Here! Stop here!'

Malcolm did as he was told. Lockhart looked out of the passenger window to see an elegantly arched gatehouse, which stood before a half-timbered complex consisting of a church, a cloister and numerous barns and outhouses. On the other side of the road was a huge orchard that stretched into the middle distance.

'What the hell is this place?' asked Hull.

'A sodding monastery!' Pugh exclaimed. 'Are we going to *pray* that the gas destroys itself?'

'Better than that,' Lockhart grinned. 'Come on, Malcolm, in we go. And let's not bump into the gatehouse. We need the monks to think we're decent sorts.'

Back at Hildesheim, the four men unloaded their cargo in full view of the rest of the unit. It consisted of a heavy steel drum about six feet tall, with a small copper pipe sticking out from near the bottom. On top was a heavy lid, screwed down with at least a dozen bolts. Another pipe came out through the centre of the lid.

'What the hell is that?' asked Maclaren.

'I know what it is!' said Marston.

'What?'

'It's a still, isn't it?'

'That's right,' said Lockhart. 'It is a still. A still which until two hours ago contained fermenting schnapps.'

'And what in the devil's name are we going to do with it?' asked Catchpole.

'This,' said Lockhart proudly, 'is the chamber in which we will destroy the sarin.'

'How?'

Lockhart told them about Barham's theory.

'A still is the only container I could find,' he said, finishing the lecture, 'that should be able to withstand the pressure of a small explosion.'

'And what if it doesn't?' asked Pugh.

'Then some of the gas will escape. Next question.'

There weren't any.

The rest of that Saturday was spent making hurried preparations. Lockhart and Stafford set about converting the still into a chamber. The plan was to pack the sarin around a pound of explosive, which would be detonated by a timer fuse. Lockhart was concerned that the pipes would prove to be the weak points, but Stafford, who had characteristically wangled a blowtorch, sealed them up.

Malcolm gave Nichols a crash course in how to drive the lorry – Lockhart had decided that it was essential to have at least two men capable of doing it. Simpkin managed to obtain some plain SS rune collar patches, which he sewed on to all fourteen uniforms, as well as unpicking all the BFC insignia off them. Lockhart made the rest of the unit check, and then double-check, that all the weapons worked, as well as priming the grenades.

By six o'clock in the evening, all that remained for him to do was to have his conversations with Leni and Strasser, one of whom he wanted to join them tomorrow, the other who he wanted to stay behind. He would talk to Strasser first, and then go to the guesthouse.

He found Strasser in his office, staring out of the window, his hands clasped behind his back.

'You seem very busy today, Lockhart,' Strasser said, turning round with an insincere smile on his face.

'I am indeed.'

'Do you want to tell me what it is you're doing?'

'As a matter of fact, I do.'

Nothing could have caused Strasser's mouth to fall open more suddenly.

'What?'

'I'd like you to know – I think it's only fair.'

Lockhart sat down.

'Go on,' said Strasser.

'Do you have anything to drink first?'

Strasser narrowed his eyes. Lockhart knew that Strasser was never a big drinker, but he also knew for a fact that the German kept some schnapps in his desk for medicinal purposes. Strasser opened his drawer and produced the bottle – it was 'Woeltingerode', from the Kornbrennerei monastery, the same monastery that had so kindly yielded its finest and strongest still to the polite young SS officer. Lockhart also noticed that the bottle was two thirds empty – Strasser had obviously been taking a lot of medicine of late. He poured two glasses and passed one over to Lockhart.

'Here's to you, Carl,' said Lockhart, raising his glass.

Strasser raised his own glass mirthlessly and drank with Lockhart.

'Thanks for that,' said Lockhart, putting his glass back down on Strasser's desk.

'So?' said Strasser, obviously impatient.

'I'd like to begin by asking you why you're a Nazi,' said Lockhart.

Strasser looked taken aback.

'I do not see why this is relevant.'

'It's very relevant. Please answer the question.'

Strasser shrugged.

'It's simple. The Nazis have given Germany back its pride, restored it to its rightful greatness. You have no idea what it was like before '33, with the poverty and the strikes, the inflation and the hardships. People were eating rats! I'm not joking! We were on our knees, and the Nazis changed all that. It was hard not to become one.'

'So you're saying that you weren't one from the start?'

Strasser lit a cigarette, taking his time about it. Lockhart refused his offer of one.

'I wasn't – no.'

Strasser looked almost ashamed.

'Carry on,' said Lockhart.

'But I became one when I saw how much good the Nazis had done, how they had turned the country the right way up. I joined the SS because I wanted to serve my country . . .'

'Why didn't you just join the Wehrmacht?'

'Because the SS is the elite. And when you're asked if you want to join the elite, its pretty hard to say no, especially as a young man. Of course I wanted to join the SS – no young German wouldn't.'

'What about the Jews?'

'What about them?'

'Do you care what's happening to them?'

Strasser took a long drag and poured himself and Lockhart another glass of schnapps.

'You have to understand that the Jews were holding us back throughout the twenties and the early thirties. They had a stranglehold on everything . . .'

Lockhart scoffed, and scoffed loudly.

'I know it's hard for you to understand,' Strasser continued, 'but it's true. The Jews were standing in the way of Germany, infecting us—'

'All right, all right,' said Lockhart, holding out his hand. 'Even if that were true, which it plainly isn't, do you think that's any reason to slaughter them?'

'We do not slaughter them!'

'Oh?'

'We put them to work, like the rest of our enemies.'

'Really?'

'Yes.'

'And you wouldn't say that it was the intention of the Nazi party to exterminate them?'

Strasser paused, removing a small piece of tobacco that had stuck to his bottom lip. He shook his head slowly.

'No. That is not correct. When the war is over, they will all be shipped to Madagascar. In the mean time, as enemies of the Reich, they should be put to work.'

Lockhart shut his eyes. It was hopeless. He would have to try another tack.

'All right, all right,' he said. 'But do you genuinely believe in this war?'

'Of course!'

'You just *had* to invade all those countries, did you?'

Strasser shook his head as if Lockhart's question was so naive, so banal, that it hardly seemed worth asking.

'Naturally. Somebody had to save them from Communism.'

'I see. And that's worth all this fighting, all this death?'

'Yes,' said Strasser. 'I think it's worth dying for freedom, don't you?'

'I happen to agree with you there, Carl. But what you're offering is hardly freedom, is it? Try telling any one of your Jews that he's free. Or one of your disabled people. I don't see many of them around. Do you think the Poles, the French, the Czechs, the Greeks and God knows who else feel free under you? If they did, why would they be fighting you, why would they resist?'

'Those who resist are Communists.'

Lockhart thought of Manoli, who was about as Communist as Churchill.

'Take it from me, you're wrong. My friends in Crete weren't Communists. *Some* of them were, but most weren't. And I think it says a lot that the Communists and the non-Communists are willing to join forces against you.'

Strasser shrugged once more. Lockhart scrutinised him. In another time, Strasser would have been an ordinary middle-class German, earning a decent salary, bringing up a decent family, but now even someone as intelligent as him had been tricked, conned into believing the rants of a madman.

'I don't think you believe what you're saying,' said Lockhart.

'That's your business.'

'I think you know that this war is a giant mistake, a mistake based on aggression and nothing else. You just want to get your own back for the last one, that's all. You dress it up in worthy-sounding ideals, but it's just plain violence. Perhaps we're to blame for that too, perhaps we should have let you keep some of your power after the last war, let you feel better about yourselves. Instead, you festered, grew resentful, then suddenly snapped back, and how! Well, you're losing again, Carl, and once more Germany is facing ruin. Well, I think it's gone beyond countries and borders and Communism now, because what I want to do tomorrow has got nothing to do with that.'

'You had better tell me then,' said Strasser.

'Sarin,' said Lockhart. 'Ever heard of it?'

'No.'

'It's a gas, a very nasty gas indeed. It can kill millions . . .'

Now it was Strasser's turn to scoff.

'Don't,' said Lockhart. 'I'm being serious. It exists. In fact it's not that far from here, underneath a mountain called Kohnstein. And do you know what is being planned for this gas, what is being planned in your name?'

Strasser shook his head.

'It's going to be put on rockets and aimed at London. I expect that's about the limit of their range. And when those rockets strike, they will kill millions, yes millions. And for what? It's not going to stop the war. If anything, the Allies will push even harder, if that's possible. All you'll achieve is murder on the hugest possible scale. This isn't about freedom, Carl, this isn't about who's right, fascists or Communists or those of us in between. This is about wanton savagery.'

'I don't believe you,' said Strasser. 'I don't believe this sarin exists. Anyway, how did you find out about it?'

'*That* I am not going to tell you. But let me assure you, Carl, that it does exist.'

'And what are you going to ... Of course! You ... you're going to try to destroy this, this sarin.'

Lockhart nodded.

'That's right, tomorrow morning, in fact.'

'How?'

'I'll only tell you that if you decide to help me.'

Strasser coughed on his cigarette.

'H ... help you?'

'Yes. But before you agree, let me assure you of something.'

'What?'

'That if I found out that the Allies were intending to do the same thing, I would try to stop them as well.'

'No!'

'I'm being serious, Carl.'

Strasser looked straight at Lockhart. Gone was any trace of warmth or humour – Lockhart's expression was as defiant as it had been before the firing squad.

'Forget Germany, forget Britain,' said Lockhart. 'Just think of the people who might die. They're just people, Carl, that's all they are. People.'

Strasser looked at his desk. In his heart, he knew Lockhart was right.

Lockhart reached the guesthouse by eight o'clock. He found Leni in a state of great agitation.

'I'm sick of being cooped up!'

'I'm sorry,' said Lockhart.

'You'd better have brought something to drink.'

'This I can do for you, Fräulein,' said Lockhart, mock-formal.

He produced a bottle from behind his back. It was champagne, nothing very spectacular, but spectacular enough for a small bar in the middle of Hildesheim.

'You're forgiven,' said Leni, bursting into a smile. 'But we'll have to drink it from mugs, I'm afraid.'

'Well in that case, we'd better save it.'

Leni looked at him – he was being deadly serious.

'What? Do you mean it?'

'Yes I do. I'm not drinking champagne from a mug.'

'You're joking! You are, aren't you?'

'Of course I am!'

Leni fetched the mugs from her table and held them out. Lockhart noticed a sealed stamped envelope on the table.

He unwrapped the foil and prised open the cork, doing so as quietly as possible. He wouldn't want the landlady to hear the sounds of such revelry. The champagne was warm, and as a result it sprayed inside Lockhart's hand and down the bottle, dripping on to the threadbare rug.

'Whoops!' Leni exclaimed.

Lockhart poured out two half-mugs and set the bottle down on Leni's bedside table. He took a mug from Leni and raised it.

'To tomorrow?' he said.

'To tomorrow.'

The champagne tasted pleasant enough, thought Lockhart.

'So is everything in place?' asked Leni.

'I think so,' said Lockhart. 'The men know what they're doing. The equipment is all in order. We even know the way.'

'And how are the men?'

'As well as can be expected.'

'And Maclaren?'

'I'm not sure. I've got both Catchpole and Stafford keeping an eye on him. If he tries going anywhere, I've told them they can kill him – I'm not risking anything.'

'Pugh?'

'Seems fine.'

'I don't trust him.'

'I don't trust any of them.'

'You have a point there.'

Leni drained her mug. Lockhart poured her another measure.

'This is going down well,' said Leni. 'Anyway, how are you feeling?'

'Nervous. I can't deny it.'

'Same here. By the way, what sort of pistol will I be using tomorrow? I hope you've got me a P38, because I don't want to use a Luger.'

'Ah, I was hoping we could talk about that.'

'Yes?'

'I don't think it's a good idea for you to come.'

Leni looked at him over the top of her mug.

'I'll assume,' she said, 'that this is another one of your jokes.'

She took another swig.

'I'm sorry, Leni, it's not.'

Leni slammed the mug down on the bedside table.

'What?'

'You can't come,' said Lockhart, 'because having a woman amongst us will only cause the guards to be suspicious.'

'What rubbish! You can say I'm a prisoner, a scientist, anything you damn well like, you know that! I'm as useful to you as any one of those idiots in your unit. You saw how I dealt with that roadblock! And now you're telling me – have the *nerve* to tell me – that I can't come along?'

'I'm sorry, Leni, but my decision is final.'

'Oh it's *your* decision, is it?'

'Yes it is!'

'Well you try stopping me! I haven't come this far just to stay in this shitty little room. I haven't risked everything to take a back seat! You're taking me along, and it's as simple as that!'

'No, Leni,' said Lockhart calmly. 'It's not an option.'

He knew it was pointless even trying to get to sleep, but he tried anyway. There was no going back. By tomorrow evening he could be dead, having failed in both destroying the gas and finding Anna. He knew that the chance of achieving either was slim, but he had to try. Death was something that he now accepted; its proximity, its violent inevitability. He was willing to die, no matter how much he loved Anna and Amy, because he knew it was right. It would happen tomorrow, he was sure, one way or another. He prayed that it would be quick, that when it happened he wouldn't know about it – a bullet to the back of his head; a shot straight through his heart; a sudden incineration in a massive explosion.

Whichever way it came, he would embrace it. He had done as much as he could. If he lived, then he would know he was charmed, but he wouldn't live. He deserved death, it beckoned him on with a comforting smile. His parents would be there, as would Richard. Manoli too. Even Worstead. And maybe Anna was there, waiting for him to arrive, asking him why it had taken him so long. Together, they would watch over Amy, making sure that Anna's sister did a good job. Amy would be all right, but they would miss her, miss her madly. He imagined their tears falling through the sky, falling like rain on to Amy, and she would look up, knowing that they were up there, and maybe she would smile.

Lockhart got up at five o'clock. He hadn't slept, but he didn't feel tired – there was too much adrenalin. Funny, he thought, as he shaved, that was probably the last time in his life that he would lie in a bed. This would be the last time he shaved, the last time he looked in a mirror. He smiled ruefully and splashed cold water over his face, rinsing the shaving soap away. He would look smart for Anna and his Maker.

He knew he should eat, but he didn't feel hungry. He would get the men up first, tell them to be ready in ten minutes to load up the lorry, after which they would have breakfast. He walked down the silent corridors and opened the door to the unit's dormitory.

'Up!' he shouted. 'Down by the lorry in ten minutes!'

Like him, they had barely slept, and some were already up, checking their weapons. They looked at him in silence, their young faces registering the deep terror that this might be their last morning, that today they might all be swept away. The poor buggers. For a moment, Lockhart felt guilty that he was leading them to their deaths, but he knew that it wasn't his fault. It was their duty to go to Mittelbau; it was their duty to ensure that their fellow countrymen were not murdered in their millions. And it was his duty to see that these men did theirs.

This was their chance to atone, to make good. Today,

they were no longer traitors, but brave men; not yet heroes, but brave all the same. Even if history got it wrong, each of them would face his individual end knowing that he was doing something right. Better a young righteous death than a traitor's drawn-out seedy shuffling to oblivion, dying in some obscure seaside town in his eighties, always looking over his shoulder, his heart black with shame and guilt.

The men assembled at the lorry within ten minutes. Catchpole had lined them up, and Lockhart walked up and down their two small ranks, inspecting them in the cool light of dawn. They were well turned out, even Maclaren. Lockhart said a few words of encouragement to each man, geeing them up, letting him know that he was looking out for them. He preferred to spend a few seconds of intimacy on each man than dole out a general pep talk. It was important, even if they were terrified, that they felt capable, felt that they were being supported. Of course each man was an island, thought Lockhart, but they were connected by causeways, causeways built on mutual support. Those links would be their only chance of survival.

'Right,' said Lockhart, looking at his watch, 'I want the lorry loaded up in ten minutes. After that, breakfast. We shall be leaving at six o'clock and no later. Malcolm and Nichols – check the lorry over. I don't want us breaking down. Catchpole – you supervise the loading.'

'Yes, sir,' said Catchpole, his voice quavering a little.

* * *

By five to six, the men were once more lined up next to the lorry.

'Is everything ready, Catchpole?'

'Yes, sir!'

'Have you checked every man's weapon?'

'Sir!'

'Grenades primed?'

'Sir!'

'The chamber?'

'Sir!'

'Hull?'

'Yes, sir?'

'I want you to carry a small pack of explosives and fuses, just in case. Never take it off, I repeat, never take it off.'

'Yes, sir!'

'Malcolm?'

'Sir?'

'Is the lorry in good order?'

'Yes, sir!'

'Right, let's get on board. I'll sit in the front with Malcolm, the rest of you in the back.'

Malcolm dropped the lorry's tailgate, and the men climbed aboard. Catchpole waited until the last had got on, and then turned to Lockhart.

'Sir?'

'Yes?'

'I was wondering, sir, whether you wished me to sit in the front. There is room for three and I thought—'

'That's all right, Catchpole,' Lockhart replied. 'I'm

afraid there won't be room, because I'm expecting one more at any moment.'

'Sir?'

'Yes. We shall be fifteen strong, not fourteen. I thought we could do with another pair of hands.'

'May I ask who, sir?'

'There's no need, because that pair of hands is walking right towards you.'

Lockhart pointed over Catchpole's shoulder. Catchpole turned to see a very familiar figure indeed – that of Carl Strasser.

'But . . .' said Catchpole.

'I'm so glad you could join us, Hauptsturmführer,' said Lockhart.

Strasser let out a sort of grunt in return, a grunt obscured by the noise of the lorry starting up.

For the first ten minutes of the journey, Lockhart, Strasser and Malcolm sat in silence. Hildesheim was still sleeping, and the roads were deserted. It was a lovely time of day, Lockhart thought, the time of day when he used to go out for a run, despite Anna's protestations that he should stay in bed. When they reached open country, Lockhart decided to speak. His tone was solemn, respectful of Strasser's decision.

'You're still sure about this?' he asked.

'Yes, John, yes I am.'

That was the first time Strasser had used his first name. He himself had called the German 'Carl' plenty of times, but he had used it derisively, as a term of false endearment.

It made him pause; made him feel reassured that Strasser's decision was sincere. It was time, if he was going to go into battle with the man, to show Strasser that he trusted him.

'You know that if you decided to drop out,' said Lockhart, 'then I would tell Leni not to speak to the SD.'

'That's good of you,' Strasser replied. 'I appreciate it. But let me assure you that my mind is made up. What you said last night . . .'

Strasser stopped.

'Yes?' Lockhart prodded.

'Let's just say that you made me feel ashamed. Your telling me that you would be doing the same if the British had made such a terrible weapon, well, it made me think. I don't care if I die as a traitor. I need to do something good for humanity, not the Reich. There have been too many firing squads, too many razed villages, too many killings for me to remember. My life is stained with too much blood. I'm no longer proud.'

For a while, Lockhart didn't reply. There was nothing he could say. Strasser had come to the end of his own personal road – he was either going to find a turning off it, or he was simply going to stop.

'One thing,' said Lockhart.

'Yes?'

'Do you think you're the only one?'

'The only one with doubts?'

'Yes.'

'Oh no. There are the fanatics, of course, but there are many who I'm sure are already planning their escape.

Argentina, I hear, is the most favoured destination.'

'If we survive this,' said Lockhart, 'I shall make sure that when the war is—'

'We're not going to survive.'

Lockhart looked out of the window to his right. They were driving past a field of barley, the crop's ears quite still, a pink light washing over them. Strasser was right, but he didn't want to tell him so in front of Malcolm. With his eyes still on the field, he spoke.

'You know, Carl, I feel ancient, old enough to be my own grandfather. I feel as if I am carrying the whole of time on my shoulders, and I'm exhausted, bloody exhausted. When I went to Crete, I was a young man, but in just a few months, I've become very, very old.'

'I've been feeling like that since my second week in Russia.'

'Then perhaps it's time,' said Lockhart, and he turned round to Strasser. There should have been tears in Strasser's eyes, but Lockhart knew that they would have dried up long ago. Instead, Strasser was just staring through the windscreen, at a place that was neither near nor far, but somewhere else altogether.

According to the map, they would have to enter Mittelbau from the east, passing through a concentration camp called Harzungen. They would then have to make their way to the north of the mountain, where Lockhart assumed they would have to pass another, more stringent checkpoint. It was one thing to let a lorry into a concentration camp, but another to allow it into the mountain itself.

They arrived at Harzungen just after eight o'clock, having driven through towns and villages that Lockhart couldn't help but notice were picturesque. The inhabitants who were awake didn't give them a second glance; it was just another military lorry ruining the peace of their Sunday morning. Occasionally they passed other detachments of SS and Wehrmacht, causing Lockhart's heart to jump, but they showed as little interest in them as the civilians did.

The concentration camp looked very new. As they neared its entrance, Lockhart saw, through the barbed wire, row upon row of low wooden housing blocks, and a road passing between them. There appeared to be a lot of activity – there were lorries, prisoners constructing more housing blocks, prisoners marching in ranks, prisoners digging. He was too far away to see their expressions, but their bodies suggested they were broken, beaten, resigned. His mind turned to Anna, wondering whether she was here; they could be less than a few hundred yards apart. Malcolm's voice snapped him out of his thoughts.

'What's the plan, sir?'

'Just drive up to the gate and stop when you're told to. If you're asked any questions, just act dumb. Hauptsturmführer Strasser and I will deal with the guards.'

'Yes, sir.'

Malcolm edged the lorry a few more yards forward until they drew up at a solid-looking crash barrier. There must have been at least six guards milling around, all wearing the uniform of the SS Death's Head formation.

They looked tough and unpleasant, their faces hardened by brutality. Butcher had had that same look, Lockhart thought, that cold stare, that expression of permanent hatred. Their eyes expected to find fear, and their search was often fruitful. Once again, Anna invaded his thoughts, and it was with a huge wrench that he managed to dispel her. If she *was* here, if she was alive, then he would meet her. He had no doubt of that.

'Come with me,' he said to Strasser. 'I think we'll need to deal with this lot together.'

'Sure,' said Strasser.

They stepped down from the lorry and approached the nearest guard. Lockhart could see that the man was writing down the registration plate of the lorry. Officious little bastard, thought Lockhart, a view reinforced by the man's absurdly overblown Heil Hitler.

'Heil Hitler, Rottenführer,' Lockhart saluted back. 'We have an important consignment for Mittelwerk.'

From his blueprint, Lockhart had learned that 'Mittelwerk' was the name of the factory itself.

'You have the necessary documentation?' the rottenführer asked with a slight sneer.

Lockhart produced the forged papers from his tunic, and handed them with a slight tutting to the guard. He affected a tone of disdain, as any man of his rank would when confronted by a petty-minded NCO. To have been too polite would have looked unusual. Men like these were accustomed to being kicked around – it was what made them the monsters they were.

The guard studied the papers closely.

'It says here that you have some vital equipment for the factory.'

Lockhart rolled his eyes skyward.

'Indeed we do,' he replied. 'Otherwise I wouldn't be here, would I?'

The guard ignored the comment.

'I would like to inspect this equipment.'

Lockhart looked at his watch.

'Rottenführer,' he said, 'I do not have the time for you to inspect my lorry. This load needs to be delivered as quickly as possible.'

The guard looked almost amused. Part of Lockhart rashly felt like producing his pistol and gunning the man down, but he knew that it would be better to be patient. It was Strasser who spoke next.

'Perhaps we'd better let him.'

Lockhart knew that he was right.

'All right, all right, Rottenführer,' said Lockhart, stressing the man's rank to remind him of his place. 'Why not come round and have a look? If it makes you happy, then go ahead.'

The guard waved one of his comrades over, and together, the four men walked round the lorry. Marston and Hull were sitting nearest to the back.

'Lower the tailgate,' Lockhart said to Hull, 'and let these two on. They want to inspect our consignment.'

'Yes, sir,' said Hull.

For a moment, Lockhart worried whether Hull's Norfolk burr came through even in those few words of German, but neither of the guards seemed to detect anything unusual in his voice. With the tailgate lowered, the rottenführer and his fellow guard climbed up to make their inspection.

'How many men are in here?' the rottenführer asked, his tone surprised.

'I told you this equipment was important,' Lockhart replied.

'But you really need all these men to go into the plant?'

'That's what the papers say, Rottenführer, or did you neglect to read that part?'

The rottenführer said nothing. Lockhart could see him looking at the still, although he couldn't see his face. He turned to Strasser, whose calm expression helped to steady Lockhart's nerves.

'What is this thing?' the rottenführer shouted out. 'It looks like a schnapps still to me – we have one back on the farm.'

Lockhart couldn't speak. They were going to fail before they had even got over the first fence, all because they had the rotten luck to have a sodding farm-boy for a guard.

It was Strasser who replied.

'What it is, Rottenführer, is none of your business!'

'I'm sorry, sir, but my orders—'

'All you need to know is that it is important scientific equipment for Mittelwerk. I barely know what it is myself! You can put down what you like on your form, but what we're not going to do is stand around discussing technical matters.'

The rottenführer turned round.

'But . . .'

'No "buts", Rottenführer,' said Lockhart. 'You've had your look. Fill in your form, do whatever it is you have to, and then let us proceed. Is that understood?'

The rottenführer stepped down with his comrade. For a moment, Lockhart thought that he was going to continue in this officious vein, but he obviously had no desire to wage war on two hauptsturmführers.

'All right, Hauptsturmführer,' he said. 'All you need to do is fill in and sign this form. You'll need it when you get up to the mountain.'

He passed Lockhart his clipboard. Lockhart scanned the form quickly – it was dense, and contained at least twenty boxes he had to fill in. Shit. If the guard didn't get the better of them, then bureaucracy would.

'Pen?' asked Lockhart wearily, casually holding out his hand. The rottenführer passed him a cheap ink-pen.

'Carl,' said Lockhart, 'you'd better help me fill this in.'

Together they went through it, entering spurious details about the origin of the cargo – 'Berlin' – an exact description of the cargo – 'research equipment' – although they paused when they came to entering the name of the officer supervising the cargo. Lockhart knew that it would be foolish to enter a British surname on the form.

'Here, Carl,' he said, 'do you want to be the officer for this one?'

He hoped that Strasser didn't think that he was being cowardly, that he was being a shirker. Strasser hesitated. After what seemed an age, he took the pen from Lockhart, and then entered his own name before filling in the rest of the form. Lockhart noticed that he also put down his old unit, rather than admitting that they were members of the BFC. He handed the form back to the rottenführer, who looked it over with a disdainful eye, before tearing the form off the clipboard, exposing a sheet of carbon paper underneath, and giving it to Lockhart.

'There you are, *Hauptsturmführer*,' he said, stressing Lockhart's rank in retaliation for Lockhart's similar tactic, showing the other man that he was not concerned at his seniority, or at least did not want to appear so.

'Thank you, Rottenführer,' Lockhart replied, his voice lacking any sarcasm. He would rise above playing such games.

They got back into the lorry's cab, not daring to speak until they were clear. Malcolm started the engine, and inched forward as a guard slowly raised the barrier. They were a step nearer, thought Lockhart, but he knew that from here on the steps would get a lot bigger.

Nothing could have prepared Lockhart for the full horror of the concentration camp. He didn't think that people could get so thin, yet here they were, skeletons that moved, their yellowing skin stretched tightly over their bones. Their faces looked up at him, and Lockhart felt not only revulsion, but guilt at having that reaction. With every head that turned towards him, Lockhart imposed Anna's face on it, waiting for the moment when the imagined face matched the face in front of him. Perhaps, just perhaps, it would be better if she was dead. It felt awful to think that, but the extent of the suffering of those in front of him was all too horrifically apparent. He didn't want her to be enduring this, spending each day in such pain and hunger. And, selfishly, he knew that he couldn't deal with seeing her like this. He had to think of the mission, he had to think of the millions who could die if he didn't stay in control, not only of himself, but also of the men.

'My God.'

It was Strasser. Malcolm had stayed silent, just shaking his head at what he saw.

'My God,' said Strasser again.

'I'd thought you'd have been to a concentration camp,' said Lockhart.

'No.'

'Really?'

'Really. This . . . this isn't what I had expected.'

Lockhart wanted to shout at him, to say to him, 'What *did* you fucking expect?' He wanted to rub his face in it, make him apologise with every breath Strasser had left. But he knew that Strasser too was seeking atonement, that he was with them because he wanted to undo all this, and to undo what he himself had done. Strasser was making the ultimate apology. Like Lockhart, he knew that he wouldn't be around to see the night fall.

'If only . . .' Strasser began, and then trailed off.

'If only what?'

'If only everybody in Germany could see this.'

'Then what?'

Strasser turned to Lockhart.

'And then I think it would stop. Then I think we would realise what we were doing to ourselves.'

'But you *must* have realised.'

Strasser was shaking his head.

'No. We all *knew*, but we didn't *realise*, we didn't see the reality.'

'It's still here. It's still going on. Look at them, Carl! Just look at them!'

Strasser shut his eyes.

'Your wife . . .'

'Yes?' said Lockhart.

'I'm . . . I'm so sorry.'

'Is there something you haven't told me?'

'No. I'm just sorry, just so very, very sorry.'

Whatever the depth of Strasser's contrition, Lockhart was not going to accept any apology. This was the man who had been threatening to execute both him and Anna no more than a few months ago. Only actions would speak now, actions that would save people, not torture them, not kill them.

'Let's just get on with it, shall we?' said Lockhart. 'We can talk about this later.'

Strasser smiled weakly. Fifty yards ahead of them, just to the right of the road, they watched a prisoner fall over. Lockhart couldn't tell whether it was male or female, an adult or a child. What he did know was that he had witnessed the end of a life; a life ended because somebody had decided to find a difference where there was none. And so what if there was a difference, he thought, so bloody what?

The mountain loomed high over the camp. Thickly wooded and with shallow, graceful slopes, it looked the picture of tranquillity. But knowing what lay within, it also looked impregnable, forbidding. As Malcolm changed gear, readying the lorry for the climb to the entrance, they left the camp behind, and entered the forest. The Germans had chosen their site well. There was no way that bombers could deal with this place, and a band of resistance fighters – well, such a thing didn't even exist, at least not in the Reich itself. Their way was the only way; they *had* to get it right, there wouldn't be another chance.

The road through the forest was peppered with warning signs, requesting that drivers should not exceed thirty kilometres per hour, and to take care on the blind bends. Their progress felt slow, desperately so. At one point, Malcolm had to stop and pull over, because he had heard the sound of a loud horn from round a corner.

As they waited for whatever it was to pass, Lockhart became aware that the ground was starting to vibrate. Whatever was coming was clearly massive. There was not just one, but six of them, six flat-bed trucks each carrying a single rocket. Lockhart, Strasser and Malcolm gasped as the convoy went past. Each rocket must have been at least fifty feet long, from the tip of their pointed nose cones to the base of their fins.

Lockhart felt a slight panic; a chill that these rockets already contained the sarin, that what was passing them was enough to kill everybody in London. He felt almost sick, sick that they were too late. But then, he told himself, there was every chance that those rockets had contained conventional warheads, that the sarin was not yet ready.

There was only way to find out, and that was to keep going.

After the last truck had passed, Malcolm gunned the engine, and put the lorry into first gear. Lockhart looked down at the ground below his window, noticing that the road was littered with pine cones. Malcolm started to pull away.

'Wait!' Lockhart barked.

'What is it?' Malcolm asked, jamming on the brakes.

Lockhart opened his door and jumped to the ground. If she was here, he would give her a pine cone – she had always liked them, had baskets of them back home. Amy could paint it one day. He stood, walked forward warily, and picked one up. The one he had selected wasn't the best cone, not the most symmetrical, even a little on the rough side, but it was his cone now. He put it in his pocket and climbed back into the lorry.

'Sorry about that,' said Lockhart. 'Just a little talisman.'

'I think we'll need a lot more than just the one,' Strasser said.

After a couple of minutes, they approached the entrance to the mountain, which consisted of a huge archway cut into the rock. Lockhart remembered from the blueprint that this was the smaller of the entrances, but it was still well guarded. There was a guardhouse on the left side of the arch, and two large metal gates in the archway across the road itself. Lockhart could see at least a dozen guards outside the guardhouse. There were prisoners too, some of whom were marching towards them, presumably being herded back to the camp. Once again, Lockhart looked for Anna amongst their faces, simultaneously clutching the cone inside his pocket, but he stopped himself. For the purposes of the mission, she was not here. She was an irrelevance compared to all those other people he was here to save; just one life set against so many thousands, so many millions.

What surprised Lockhart was the lack of infrastructure around the entrance. Apart from the guardhouse, there were no other buildings. It was discreet, quiet, and presumably practically invisible from the air. It felt eerie, almost otherworldly. It seemed incredible that there was a vast factory only a few yards away, and yet there was hardly any sign of it. It could have been the entrance to nothing more than a modest coal mine. It wasn't ominous enough, Lockhart thought, to act as the gateway to an underground hell that was producing the instruments of mayhem.

Malcolm stopped the lorry at the request of a young untersturmführer – a junior officer. It was just as Lockhart suspected – things were getting a lot tighter, a lot more problematic. Once again, he and Strasser got down from the cab.

'Good morning, Untersturmführer!' Lockhart said, breezily.

'Heil Hitler, Hauptsturmführers!' the officer replied. Lockhart was relieved to see that he had returned his smile.

'And what have you got for us this fine Sunday morning?' asked the untersturmführer.

Lockhart handed over the documents, resolving that

he wasn't going to be seduced by the young officer's friendly manner. It would be too dangerous to allow himself to be lulled into relaxation. It anything, he had to be more on his guard than when dealing with a sour old NCO.

'I see this comes straight from the top,' said the untersturmführer. 'Signed by the Brigadeführer, no less.'

'That's right,' said Lockhart. 'It's an extremely sensitive piece of equipment.'

The officer took his time studying the papers. He looked slightly puzzled.

'Is there a problem, Untersturmführer?' Lockhart asked.

The man looked up at Lockhart and smiled.

'No, I don't think so,' he said. 'Why? Should there be a problem?'

'No,' said Lockhart with a shrug. 'But you know what it's like. The more forms there are, the more hassle there is.'

'Quite! If only you knew how many of these forms I have to look at every day!'

He started to hand the papers to Lockhart. Just as Lockhart reached out to take them, the untersturmführer pulled them back.

'There is *one* thing,' he said.

'Yes?' said Lockhart, doing his best not to show concern. Inside, his heart had started to throb unbearably hard.

'It's probably nothing,' the untersturmführer said. 'I'm sure it's just an administrative thing, but normally I get the first form in duplicate. I keep one, you keep the other. Do you not have it?'

'No,' said Lockhart, 'I only received the one you've seen. Did you get another one, Carl?'

'No,' said Strasser. 'This was all we were given.'

The junior officer tapped his chin with his finger, evidently deciding whether to let them through. He was clearly enjoying his moment of authority over these two senior officers.

'You see,' he continued, 'I'm not authorised to let you through unless I have both forms. I'm sorry, but that's the way it is.'

What would be natural? Lockhart asked himself. Indignation would be the most likely response if one were guilt-free.

'I know you have your orders, Untersturmführer,' he said with an air of forced patience, 'but what are we supposed to do? Drive back to Berlin to pick up another sheet of paper? Wait for one to arrive in the post? You can see that our consignment is urgently required.'

'Yes, yes, I can see that. It's just that I do not have the authority to let consignments into Mittelwerk without the necessary documentation.'

Fuck, thought Lockhart, the man was implacable. It was time to call his bluff.

'Isn't there someone you can phone, Untersturmführer, someone senior to both of us?'

Before the officer could reply, another lorry drew up behind them.

'Please wait,' said the untersturmführer. 'Let me deal with this other lorry. Look – why don't you pull up over there and then I'll come back to you?'

'Fine,' said Lockhart, with a hint of annoyance. 'Fine.'

The two men got back into the cab, and Lockhart told Malcolm to park the lorry a few yards from the entrance, but to keep the engine running.

'What's the problem, sir?' Malcolm asked.

'Red tape,' said Lockhart. 'Bloody red tape.'

Lockhart turned to Strasser.

'What do you think?' he asked.

'I'd say we're in trouble,' Strasser replied. 'Whoever he phones isn't going to have heard of us. When he finds that out, I wouldn't be surprised if he has us all arrested.'

'Shit,' said Lockhart. 'We're so damn close! I've half a mind just to storm through those gates.'

Strasser chewed it over.

'Maybe that's not such a bad idea,' he said. 'We all know that surprise counts for a lot.'

'But we'll probably get massacred before we've even gone a few yards.'

'I don't fancy our chances after our untersturmführer has made his phone call,' said Strasser.

'You're right,' said Lockhart.

They sat in silence for a moment. Lockhart looked back at the other lorry, and saw the untersturmführer going through the routine of bureaucracy.

'If he lets that lorry through,' said Lockhart, 'perhaps we could charge through immediately after it.'

Strasser thought about it before replying.

'I can't think of a better idea.'

'What do you think, Malcolm?' Lockhart asked. 'Do you think you could do it?'

Malcolm breathed out slowly, deliberately. Lockhart almost expected him to say, 'It'll cost yer.'

'I don't think it should be a problem, sir.'

'Good man, Malcolm. So, are we agreed?'

Strasser nodded.

'This is it then,' said Lockhart. 'Remember, it's hall 44 we're after. I'll go and tell the men in the back. They'll need to open fire if necessary. In fact, I'll join them there – is that all right with you, Carl?'

'Malcolm and I should be able to manage.'

Lockhart held out his hand. Strasser shook it.

'Thank you, Carl,' he said. 'Thank you.'

'Thank me when we get inside.'

Lockhart stepped out and walked around the lorry. He noticed the untersturmführer look up briefly from his paperwork.

'What's going on, sir?' Hull asked when Lockhart reached the back.

'Help me up and I'll tell you.'

Hull held out his hand and Lockhart pulled himself up with it, almost leaping over the tailgate. As soon as he had stepped into the darkness of the lorry, he could smell the fear emanating from the men. Twelve pairs of eyes shone in the darkness, reflecting the light that was creeping in through the back.

'Men,' Lockhart said quietly, 'there's been a slight hiccup.'

The men held their breath – not a sound came from them as they absorbed Lockhart's words.

'There's been a problem with the paperwork, and we're

being denied access. We've been told to park here and wait for our permission to come through. I don't fancy the chances of that, so what I've planned is this: there's a lorry just behind us, which is about to go in. We will drive in immediately behind it and take our chances. We have little choice. If we sit here, we'll get rumbled. I'd rather we took this opportunity, no matter how small.'

Some of the men nodded.

'I'd like Catchpole and Stafford to sit at the back, and return fire with me if necessary. The rest of you I want to lie on the deck. Any questions?'

'Er . . . there's one thing,' said Pugh.

'Yes, Pugh?'

'We've got a visitor.'

'A visitor?'

'Yes. An old friend of yours.'

That last voice was not Pugh's; it was not even a man's. It came from the back of the lorry. Lockhart knew immediately whose voice it was.

'Leni?' said Lockhart.

'At your service – or is that not an option?'

Lockhart did his best not to shout out loud.

'Jesus Christ!' he exclaimed. 'What the hell are you doing here?'

Leni stood up.

'I thought you could do with another pair of hands.'

'But how did you get here?'

'I climbed on board just before you were about to set off.'

'Who is this woman anyway?' asked Hull.

'She's . . . she's . . .' Lockhart began. 'It doesn't matter. She's here now. I assume you're armed.'

'Only with the Luger – I don't expect you've got a spare P38?'

'Afraid not,' said Lockhart. 'You'll just have to manage with what you've got.'

He wanted to berate her, to give her a dressing-down, but it would be counterproductive. Perhaps it was for the best – as Leni had said, she was another pair of hands. The sound of the other lorry starting up interrupted his thoughts.

'All right!' he whispered loudly. 'On the deck! Catchpole and Stafford – you get up here with me.'

In the cab, Strasser watched in his wing mirror as the other lorry started to move off.

'You're ready, Malcolm?' he asked.

'Ready as I'll ever be.'

For a moment, Strasser thought himself mad, idiotic even, for being here. There must have been some way, he thought, some way that he could have got rid of Lockhart and Leni without risking his own life. He was going to die, because not only had he had been blackmailed, he had allowed himself to be. But perhaps it wasn't too late. He could get out of the cab right now, and surrender himself to the untersturmführer. He might have a chance then, a chance of saying that he had been forced here at gunpoint, that he'd had no choice.

But then the images of the camp back to him. The

smell, the sense of menace, those hollow looks of fear and degradation, the masks of those who knew they were going to die. Too much death, too much killing. He had seen those rockets go past. They didn't have Germany's name on them, but the name of a madman, a maniac, a murderer. Lockhart had said he would be doing the same if the English were planning to do something similar. Strasser had found that hard to believe, but he could now see that Lockhart was obeying a code that had nothing to do with borders or territories, but everything to do with morality, a sense of values that stemmed from an innate decency and not from a twisted belief. Was that worth dying for? Yes, Strasser thought, yes it was. There was a freedom in that, that nobody could take away from you: the freedom to die – or be killed – for your own values.

Strasser looked ahead. The huge gates were opening to allow the other lorry to enter the factory.

'You see the gates, Malcolm?'

Malcolm nodded.

Strasser looked in his wing mirror once more. The other lorry was now passing out of its field of view, and into the corner of Strasser's right eye. He could also see the untersturmführer walking back towards them.

'Here she comes,' said Strasser calmly. 'Get ready . . .'

The engine still in neutral, Malcolm pushed his foot down hard on the accelerator. Strasser could see the quizzical look on the face of the untersturmführer as the whining sound of their lorry's engine filled the air.

'Now!' Strasser shouted. 'Now! Now!'

Malcolm lifted his foot off the clutch, and they lurched

violently forward, kicking up a mass of loose stones and dirt into the face of the untersturmführer. Skilfully, Malcolm tucked himself in directly behind the other lorry. All he could hope for now was that it wouldn't stop.

The lorry shot forward with such a violent jolt that Lockhart, Stafford and Catchpole were almost sent over the tailgate and on to the ground. But somehow they managed to hang on, and witnessed the look of consternation that crossed the untersturmführer's face before it was obscured by the cloud of dirt. Come on, Malcolm, Lockhart was thinking, come on, you can do it, just get us in.

They had at least ten yards to go, and Lockhart feared that one of the sharper guards would have time to let off a round or two. Not that he would hear it, because the noise of the lorry was terrific, enough to drown out the sound of gunfire.

His worst fear was realised just as he was thinking it. Although Lockhart couldn't see him through the dust, a guard who had been standing slightly further back from the untersturmführer had opened fire at the back of the lorry. One of his shots had met its target, and that target was Stafford. The bullet entered the front of Stafford's neck, tore through his windpipe and shattered his neck vertebrae before exiting through the canvas roof of the lorry. The force of the impact knocked Stafford back into the lorry, where he fell on top of Hull. Lockhart looked down briefly to see Stafford's hands clutching frantically at his neck, blood frothing up from his mouth, along with a curdling, bubbling groan.

Lockhart's first reaction was anger, swiftly followed by revenge.

'Open fire!' he shouted to Catchpole, and together they opened up with their MP40s on the guards.

The effect was immediate and brutal. Lockhart watched the untersturmführer's body being knocked back violently, pieces of flesh flying off his face. At least three other guards were felled in the initial burst, one of whom must have been the bastard who had hit Stafford. Good; all Lockhart could think was good, excellent, he was glad that he had killed him.

'Aim for the guardhouse!' Lockhart yelled.

He leaned partially out of the back of the lorry, and he and Catchpole did as much as they could, squeezing off a few long bursts at the windows and the guards. It should be enough to stop the alarm being raised, thought Lockhart, at least for a minute or so. SOE had taught him that it took a defending force, caught by surprise, at least two minutes to get its act together. A lot could be achieved in two minutes, Lockhart thought, a hell of a lot.

After a few seconds, it suddenly went dark. They were inside the factory.

Strasser had heard the shots, just audible over the noise of the lorry. His instinct was to duck, get out of the line of fire, but instead he brought his MP40 up to his window. For a second, it occurred to him that he was about to fire on his own countrymen, that he was about to commit the ultimate act of treachery, that he was about to betray everything that he had been groomed to believe in. It was too late for such niceties; they were useless now. He opened fire, felling at least two guards. They didn't stand a chance, their young forms punched back with a ferocious force, each of them absorbing at least half a dozen rounds. At least they would have died immediately, he thought, a small consolation.

Lockhart quickly took stock as he watched the gates close behind them. They were driving down a tunnel, just as the blueprint had indicated. His eyes were growing accustomed to the gloom. On the ground he started to make out rows and piles of bodies, bodies partially clothed in striped uniforms, bodies twisted into grotesque shapes. Prisoners, arranged into work gangs, shuffled alongside. But Lockhart didn't have time to feel nauseous or horrified, as much as a large part of him wanted to.

As yet, after half a minute, there was no alarm going off, which was a relief. Guards looked up at them as they went past – it wouldn't be much longer before those same guards, alerted by a klaxon, would open fire. So far, the tactic of surprise was paying off. But try telling that to Stafford, he thought. He looked back down – Hull was leaning over Stafford, trying to tend to him, but Lockhart knew it was useless. The poor bastard. All because he had picked a fight with someone who he had thought was a traitor. He had done the right thing, and had continued to do so, even at the risk of ruining his own reputation, even at the risk of facing the gallows in Wandsworth Prison. At least he had been spared that. If only one of them survived, that person would be able to restore their reputations, ensure that history regarded them not as traitors, but as men who had chosen to do the right thing, even if they were destined to fail.

But they were not going to fail. Every ten to fifteen seconds, they drove past a hall, which gave Lockhart the opportunity to glimpse what was going on. In the gloom, he could make out assembly lines, rocket parts being hoisted, showers of sparks arcing up from huge casings, and prisoners everywhere, thousands of prisoners. They were going past hall 29 – 'Combustion chamber storage' read a sign. If anything, the din seemed to magnify as they continued deeper into the mountain, and soon it got so loud that Lockhart would have to shout to make himself heard.

Hall 30 went past – 'Soldering'. He began looking at the faces of the prisoners, trying vainly to find Anna, but it was no good. He had to stop thinking about her, do as he had promised, forget about her, no matter how hard it seemed. He told himself that she would be dead – nobody could survive here for longer than a few weeks. It was a circle of hell, nothing less.

He didn't notice the hand on his shoulder at first. It was Leni's, trying to pull him back so she could shout in his ear.

'Where are we?' she yelled.

'Getting close!' he yelled back.

They had just gone past hall 38 – 'Aileron assembly'.

'Shouldn't we be getting off?' asked Leni.

'Not yet – it's best if we keep going!'

* * *

But Lockhart couldn't see what was happening in front. For the past minute and a half, Malcolm had stayed tucked in behind the other lorry. It appeared that the driver in front hadn't a clue what had gone on, but it would only be a matter of time, Strasser thought, before he would come to a stop.

That happened just outside hall 40 – 'Maintenance'. Malcolm had to slam on the brakes, narrowly avoiding running into the back of the lorry.

'Shit!' Strasser shouted. 'Try and get round him!'

'I can't! I'm too close!'

'Reverse! Reverse!'

Malcolm wrenched the gearstick into reverse, and lifted the clutch. Nothing.

'Come on, man!' Strasser shouted.

'I'm trying!'

Frantically, Malcolm juggled with the gearstick, crunched it into reverse, stepped hard on the accelerator, lifted the clutch, and still the lorry didn't move.

'It's broken, sir!'

'Shit!'

Strasser jumped down from the cab, running past confused-looking prisoners and guards. Still no alarm, he thought; how long would that last?

Lockhart looked down at Strasser's anxious face.

'What's happened?' he shouted.

'We're stuck!' said Strasser. 'We can't get round the lorry in front!'

'Can't we reverse?'

Strasser shook his head.

Just their luck, thought Lockhart. He turned to face the men. Briefly he took in the fact that Stafford was no longer with them, his body now quite still.

'All right! This is where we get off! Hull, Pugh, Nichols, Andreae – you take the still and come with me! The rest will stay here with Strasser and hold this position. Now move!'

'What about me?' Leni asked.

'You stick with me,' Lockhart replied.

As Lockhart jumped down from the lorry, the alarm went off. The noise was deafening, making communication all but impossible. He had to yell in Strasser's ear.

'Can you stay here and hold this position? I'm going to take some of the men and the still to 44!'

Although Strasser had heard Lockhart, he was momentarily stunned by the presence of Leni, who had appeared at Lockhart's side.

'What in God's name is she doing here?' he yelled.

'Don't ask!' Lockhart shouted back. 'I had no idea either.'

Leni looked at Strasser, her face reflecting the surprise on his. There was so much she wanted to say to him, but she knew that any conversation would be pointless, with or without an alarm, whether they were in a factory or a bedroom. Instead, she smiled at him, hopefully not an arrogant smile, but a kind one, a smile that wished him well, her dear Carl. He smiled back, as well as he could under the circumstances, Leni thought.

*   *   *

Within half a minute, the men had got the still off the lorry.

'Let's go!' Lockhart shouted, and ran forward with Leni, past the sides of the two lorries.

'Come on!' he shouted at Malcolm, who was still sitting in the cab.

Lockhart looked back, to see the four men carrying their still doing their best to keep up. They ran past hall 41, which was vast – at least forty feet high, carved out of solid rock. A single rocket stood in the middle of it, surrounded by scaffolding.

Hall 42 – 'Heating and ventilation plant'. Hall 43 – 'Mechanical systems'. Lockhart swallowed. They were nearly there, nearly at the object of a quest that had started in a cell in Berlin. Lockhart stopped, waiting for the others to catch up. He had his last orders to issue.

Strasser had seven men to fight off any advance from the north entrance – Maclaren, Catchpole, Marston, Simpkin, Smith, Prain, and Allan.

'Catchpole!' he shouted. 'You stay here with Marston, Simpkin and Prain! The rest come with me!'

'I'm not going anywhere!' shouted Maclaren.

'Why not?'

'Because you'll get us all killed!'

Strasser had been in with this situation before. Cowardice was infectious; even the finest troops could contract it, let alone this mob. There was only one way to deal with it, and that was to stop it getting a toehold. He raised his MP40 at Maclaren, and before Maclaren could even stick out his hand, before he could even scream for mercy, Strasser had abruptly squeezed the trigger, extinguishing the infection.

The rest of the men didn't need asking again. Strasser ran forward with Smith and Allan, weaving their way between the prisoners, many of whom were cowering on the ground. In the noise and confusion, the guards were standing around gormlessly, a situation that Strasser exploited by shooting any guard he saw. Smith and Allan followed suit, and soon they were on the offensive, creating a buffer zone between the north of the hall and Lockhart. Strasser thanked God that they were defending a tunnel, which made it impossible for them to be outflanked. It was probably the best position to defend if you had a small body of men, thought Strasser. The guards would *have* to take them head-on.

Lockhart got Malcolm and Andreae to take up position on the other side of hall 44. Thankfully, there had been no commotion from that end of the factory, only from where they had left Strasser. Because the lorries were in the way, none of them had seen Maclaren's execution, and even if they had, none of them would have mourned his passing.

Quickly, Lockhart described his plan. He, Hull and Leni would storm the hall, dealing with any resistance, and then come back and fetch the still, which would be guarded by Pugh and Nichols.

'Ready?' Lockhart shouted.

The men, and Leni, nodded.

He started running, his machine gun at the ready. He would shoot anybody he saw, unless they were wearing a prisoner's uniform. Anybody else in hall 44 was guilty, and would have to die. Nothing was going to stop him now, nothing. He was in a rage, not just a fighting rage, but a rage emanating from somewhere deeper, a rage that wanted justice, atonement. He would have it, he would bloody well have it. He had got this far, got to the entrance of hall 44, and he wouldn't be stopped by anybody.

They turned right into the hall, and he started shooting, firing at anybody in a white coat, anybody in a military uniform. As he fired, he took in the layout of the hall. Three rockets lay on their sides, their open tips pointing away from the entrance. Towards the back of the hall was a large metallic building, about the size of a cricket pavilion. A huge black cross was painted on it, as well as a skull and crossed bones. That had to be the sarin, he thought; that had to be it in there, that was their goal.

Lockhart changed his magazine, and ran forward, along the length of the rocket in the middle. So far there had been no resistance, and Leni and Hull were hard on his heels. But he carried on firing, decimating those in front of him. He reached the front of the metallic building, catching his breath. In front of him lay the bodies of those he had just killed, the redness of the blood spreading through the fabric of their white coats like ink on blotting paper. Some workers and prisoners were kneeling in front of them, begging for their lives. There was no time to reassure them.

He kicked open the door to the metal building.

'In here!' he shouted at Hull. 'Leni! Take my machine gun! You guard the entrance.'

He passed his MP40 to Leni, swapping it for her Luger, and rushed into the building with Hull. They were in a laboratory, towards the back of which were at least a hundred, maybe a hundred and fifty, small metal canisters marked with black crosses – sarin, enough to wipe out everybody on the bloody planet. Lockhart allowed himself a small moment of joy – it was just as Test Tube had expected it to be.

Four scientists faced him, their hands in the air.

'Don't shoot!' one of them screamed. 'Please don't shoot!'

Lockhart could tell that he meant it. One round hitting one canister would mean a vile death for all of them.

'Get out!' shouted Lockhart. 'Get out!'

He motioned them towards the door with his Luger.

'Right, Hull,' he said. 'You get this lot out of here, take Leni, and come back with the still and Pugh.'

'Move it!' Hull shouted at the scientists. 'Move it!'

The scientists did as they were told.

Strasser had to retreat. Someone had got the guards under control, and they were starting to fight back. The element of surprise was now lost, but it must have worked for at least two minutes. That had bought them plenty of time, Strasser thought, so long as Lockhart was having no difficulty in hall 44.

Along with Smith and Allan, he fell back to the position the others had taken by the lorry. From there, they should be able to hold off any attack for a while yet. He didn't doubt that they would be overrun, but he would do his best to make sure that Lockhart could do his.

After no more than a minute – but what seemed like an hour to Lockhart – Hull, Leni, Pugh and Nichols returned with the still.

'Set it down here,' said Lockhart, his voice calm, pointing to a spot just next to the rack of canisters.

They did so.

'Hull and Nichols, you guard the entrance to the hall. The others will help me.'

Hull and Nichols, ran off.

'I'm sure I don't need to tell you,' Lockhart began, 'that these canisters need to be handled with great care. Ignore the noise around you, ignore the gunfire, ignore the alarm. We've only failed when we've been killed. Understood?'

Leni and Pugh nodded.

'Pugh, I want you to take the canisters off the rack and pass them to Leni. Leni, you will then pass them to me. I shall pack the still. When we've got halfway, I shall place the explosive with a ten-minute fuse. That will give us enough time to pack the remaining canisters and seal the lid.'

'One question,' said Leni.

'Yes?'

'Are we going to stay here until it goes off?'

'Yes,' said Lockhart, 'I will. Someone has to make sure that it works.'

'You're mad,' said Leni, 'but I'll stay too.'

'There's no need,' said Lockhart.

'But . . .'

'No arguments! To work.'

For the next two to three minutes, they worked efficiently, if nervously. At one point, Pugh nearly dropped a canister, but saved it just before it fell. The chances were, said Lockhart, that it might not have broken, but it was just as well to treat the canisters as though they were crystal.

'That gunfire is getting louder,' said Leni.

'Ignore it,' said Lockhart. 'Concentrate on this.'

Within another minute, they were halfway. Lockhart took a stick of explosive from his backpack, and, with trembling hands, set the fuse for ten minutes. There was no going back now, but he felt calm, in control. This was his job, his entire world. For the next ten minutes, he was no longer a husband, a father, an archaeologist – his only role was to destroy the sarin.

'Come on! Let's pack the rest in!'

Their ammunition was running low, and the guards were attacking them with an ever-increasing ferocity. Marston and Simpkin had already been shot dead, and Strasser had to resort to throwing some grenades down the tunnel. He had not wished to, for fear of killing any of the prisoners, but there was now no choice. His decision was based purely on numbers – better for a few to die here than for millions to perish in London. Better for him to die as well, and he knew that time would soon come.

Within five minutes, they had packed the still with the remaining canisters. Now they simply had to replace the lid, and pray. The first few bolts went on easily, until they came to the eighth of the twelve. The wing-nut wouldn't twist down properly, as though the thread of the bolt had got mangled.

'What's wrong with it?' Leni asked.

'The bloody thing won't go on,' Lockhart grunted.

'Quick!' shouted Pugh. 'We can't have much more than two or three minutes!'

Lockhart ignored him and tried twisting it, but it wouldn't budge. But for the want of a wing-nut that worked, he thought, a city had fallen.

'Get me some pliers!' he shouted.

Leni and Pugh scrabbled around the laboratory.

'There aren't any!' Leni yelled.

'There must be!'

Meanwhile, Lockhart tightened up the remaining four nuts. Would that be enough? Would the eleven bolts and the rubber seal suffice?

'For Christ's sake!' he shouted. 'There have to be some! We're in a bloody factory!'

Lockhart looked at his watch. There was only a minute to go. The firing was hard to ignore now; it was getting close, very close.

'I've got some!' shouted Pugh.

'Throw them here!'

Pugh did so, but his throw went wide, causing Lockhart to have to rummage for them under a workbench. He reached for the offending wing-nut, and with all his strength, twisted it. At first it wouldn't budge, but with another wrench it did so. As quickly as he could, he screwed it down, and as it reached the end of the bolt, he noticed the lid closing on to the still a fraction tighter. That, he thought, might make all the difference.

The guards were no more than ten yards away. Strasser had only one magazine left, and the others were running similarly low. Sooner or later, a machine gun would be brought up, and then they would be decimated. He desperately wanted to know if he had bought Lockhart enough time, but he couldn't run and find out. Perhaps Lockhart was already dead, perhaps he had already failed, and this battle was just a senseless massacre. But Strasser had faith in Lockhart, an instinctive belief that because Lockhart was right, he would win. It was the only straw that Strasser had left, and he clutched it tightly.

They stood round the still, as if they were communing with it, Lockhart thought. With only thirty seconds to go, they all knew that the steel container in front of them could be the means by which they were transported to another world. In that sense, it did have the power of a divinity; it was something that could be communed with. In these last few seconds, Lockhart thought of Anna and Amy, playing images of them through his head, remembering them at their happiest moments – in Crete, on their wedding day, at Amy's birth. He had loved, and he had been loved, and that was enough.

Leni fought hard to control herself. Although she desperately wanted to live, part of her wanted the explosion to rip her to pieces, to vaporise her. As far as the SD was concerned, she was already dead – killed by the bomb that had destroyed her flat – and no doubt her parents had been informed of her death. What she didn't want was to survive and be captured, because then her parents would also be executed. And she couldn't bear that, even if in some afterlife she could tell them that she had risked all their lives so that so many others might live. Perhaps they would understand; perhaps they would forgive her.

Lockhart looked at the nervous faces of Leni and Pugh, smiled at them, and then looked at his watch. He noticed that it was still morning. It couldn't be, he thought, *surely* not. What an inane thing to think, he said to himself, and then it happened, with a sort of hollow thud. The sides of the still bulged dramatically outwards, but remained intact. The lid stayed on. Was there gas coming out? If he was still alive, then there couldn't be. He heard nothing, just the sound of his own breathing. He felt more alive than ever, as though what he was seeing was more than real.

For a moment, he almost fainted. Was this it? Was he dying? No. He was still alive. He looked back at the other two, and heard himself say:

'We've done it! We've gone and bloody done it!'

Slowly, their faces lit up. Leni had tears in her eyes.

'You fucking genius!' Pugh yelled. 'You fucking genius!'

'Don't thank me, thank Test Tube!'

'Who the hell is Test Tube?'

'I'll tell you later,' said Lockhart. 'Come on – let's get out!'

They paused, took one last look at the swollen still, and then ran. As they did so, Lockhart wondered whether they had really succeeded. What if even just one of the canisters was intact? He kicked himself for worrying – nobody would be able to open the still and live. Any canisters that remained undamaged were utterly inaccessible.

They got back into the main tunnel, ducking as the occasional round flew past them. Down to the left, Lockhart could just about make out Strasser and a couple of the others.

'We've done it!' Lockhart shouted. 'We've done it!'

But all he saw was Strasser's hand go up in the air, waving Lockhart away. That was Strasser's apology, the ultimate apology. He was going to let them get away, and Lockhart was going to accept it.

Lockhart turned and ran, following Leni and Pugh. Up ahead there was light coming in from the southern end of the tunnel. If they could just make it there, they might be safe. He hoped that Hull, Nichols, Malcolm and Andreae had managed to secure them a passage out, but God knew what lay outside.

A few yards up ahead there were some thirty or forty prisoners being herded forward by a couple of guards. They were screaming, terrified by the noise of the alarm and the gunfire. Lockhart drew level with them, and then passed them. He only had a couple of hundred yards to go and he would be out, out into the air, out into the light.

As she ran, Leni knew that she *had* to get out, that if anybody was going to do so, it would be her. She wanted to write this down, to make sure that future generations would know what had happened. Lockhart, Strasser, the rest of the unit – they would all be regarded as traitors for posterity unless someone made a record. She would be the one to do it, and nothing was going to stop her, not the guards, not the SD, not even the whole of the Wehrmacht. The truth, she thought; she was running for the truth.

He didn't know what made him turn round. Whatever it was, it was a delayed reaction. But the force was as great as if he had been knocked round by a punch. He stumbled, staggered, and looked back at the group of prisoners. There was something about them, an aura that separated them from the others he had seen. What was it? What the hell was it?

He walked back towards them, as if he was being led by a vision. He was staring, staring intently at one of the prisoners. She was slightly taller than the rest. Her hair was short, very short, but it was the right colour. She was walking in the same way as when he had first seen her, first seen her long legs tripping over those piles of ancient masonry. She had been wearing a large sun hat then, and carrying a small knapsack, and he had laughed at her stumbling attempts to keep up with Dr Buchan. And he remembered her brown eyes, and her defiant expression, and how he had been mesmerised. He remembered shaking her hand, finding the formality funny, but knowing, even then, that he always wanted to be with this woman, that he would always fight for her.

Lockhart reached into his pocket and brought out the pine cone. He was dreaming now, surely he was, as he ran up to her, shouting her name. And she looked up, as if she had been summoned by some presence that had stepped out of a void, stepped out of a time that had been forgotten, brushed away. He watched her eyes, rendered dull by years of captivity, light up in the way that they always had done. It *was* her, and he could tell from her face that she knew it was him, her John, her darling husband.

He was only feet away now, and she had lifted her hands up to her mouth. They were going to hold each other, be together again. They would get out of here, and they would get back to Amy, and they would live as a little family once again, grow old together, and always hold each other, never let each other go.

The first bullet entered him at the top of his right leg, causing him to fall backwards. No, he didn't believe it. That guard hadn't fired at him, that couldn't have happened. He tried shooting the guard, pulling the trigger, but the gun had jammed. All he could hear was a scream, but he didn't know if it was his. He looked at her, could see her mouth stretched wide, could see her face shaking, going red.

He kept his eyes fixed on her, waiting for the next round to hit him. Please don't cry, he wanted to say, I'm here, I'm here for you, I've come all this way, please don't cry. He clutched his stomach – it was on fire, something must have hit him there too, but he didn't know where from, because his eyes never left her. He tried smiling, because he was happy, so very happy that he was back with his wife. That was really all he had ever wanted.

Epilogue

June 1986

AT LEAST SHE could see the field. Usually it was the orange foam armchairs horseshoed around the wood-panelled television. Or it was the dining room with its light green walls and strip lighting. Or at twilight the tired ceiling from the discomfort of her small bed, the mattress of which was as dead as its last three inhabitants. But at least she could see the field. If she brought her chair to the window, and looked across the kitchen roof and over the car park, there, through a gap in the firs, lay the prettiest field of linseed, its blue flowers so subtle she sometimes thought they were a trick of the light. After lunch, she would stare at the field, longing to walk through it, but her legs weren't so good, and besides, there was nobody here who would take her.

This was her third June at the home. She had made no

friends. Except for the necessary pleasantries with the helpers, her mouth was only for eating and drinking. Some had wanted to talk – even to have whole conversations – but she was suspicious and had ignored them. Far better to die an unfriendly enigma, without the shame. Too many had tried to find out, and the memories gave her pain. Each one came wrapped in guilt, uncertainty, anger and self-loathing.

The letters were the worst. Enquiries, no matter how well-meaning, unpacked years of attempted forgetfulness. She would scan each one, picking out the few words common to them all, and then she would put them in one of her carrier bags. Now she no longer opened them, and they would go straight into the bags, which were arranged neatly at the bottom of the cheap wardrobe, next to the pair of shoes she wasn't wearing.

The bags too were unopened. She wondered whether she would be set free if she threw them away, shedding her past and starting again with what little time there was. But she couldn't do that – it wouldn't be fair to him, no matter what he had done. So they remained unopened, their photographs, letters and diaries neither examined nor discarded, in a state, like her, of being somewhere in between.

All she now had to look forward to were the visits from Amy, who came as often as she could. She would be coming today, at tea-time, said she had some important news, something so special, something for which she had been fighting for a long time. 'Oh not that,' she had said, but Amy told her this was different, this was *it*, Mum. Well, she doubted that.

Amy was breathless in her telling, and at first her brain felt too muddled to take it all in. Something about a female Russian agent's testimony, found in Moscow, saying that he was not a traitor, saying that he'd wanted to blow up some secret gas. Something about him only joining the BFC because he wanted to save his wife.

'This Russian agent was in fact a German, Mum,' Amy said, 'called Leni Steiner. She escaped from the factory disguised as a prisoner. In her testimony, she says that she was the only one to get out of the factory alive.

'Do you see now, Mum? That's what Dad was doing in your factory! And now we know why – because of this gas. That's why he was there – he wasn't on their side, he wasn't a traitor. He was *pretending* to be one so he could destroy this sarin. In fact, it looks as though he saved the whole of London, or maybe even changed the whole outcome of the war. It's incredible! The MOD say that he's going to get a pardon, along with the rest of the unit, and will probably even get a medal.'

'But this girl, Leni, why didn't she say something before?'

'According to the records in Moscow, she was arrested near the end of 1944. She had been hiding on a farm near your factory, but somebody betrayed her and she was sent to Belsen. They think she was executed in December. Apparently, the Nazis sent a bill to her parents for the cost of her execution.'

She opened her mouth, but no sound came out.

'Mum?'

She was holding it, cupping it in her hands. It wasn't the best pine cone, not the most symmetrical, perhaps even a little on the rough side.

'What's that, Mum? What have you got there?'

She smiled through her tears.

'Oh, nothing much, dear. Just something your father once gave me.'

Historical Notes

THE BRITISH FREE Corps came into being towards the middle of 1943. It was incorporated into the Waffen-SS at the beginning of 1944. Around fifty men joined the BFC, although at any one time there were never more than thirty, the number that Hitler stipulated the corps should reach before it went into action on the Eastern Front. Many of the members of the BFC were either fascists or simpletons, and discipline was a problem.

The British Free Corps met its end in Berlin in May 1945. Some accounts claim that its members did actually fight the Russians, although this is unlikely, as many deserted.

The British had long been aware of the existence of the BFC, as word had got back from POW camps, where the Germans had attempted recruitment drives. After the war, BFC members were tracked down and court-martialled. The sentences were surprisingly lenient, ranging from life sentences to modest fines. The traitor John Amery, however, was famously executed at Wandsworth Prison.

Interested readers can visit www.guywalters.com, where they will find a history of the BFC, complete with photographs, biographies, an extensive bibliography and links to other relevant sites.

However, there is only one place to turn for the complete history of the BFC, and that is Adrian Weale's excellent *Renegades*, his definitive account of the corps. They might also find great interest in *Patriot Traitors*, his comparative biography of John Amery and Sir Roger Casement.

Devotees of the Public Record Office in Kew might wish to know that the records of the courts martial of, and testimonies by, members of the BFC are contained in the classes WO71 and HO45.

The code used by Lockhart to formulate his letter to 'Hattie' is a simplified version of the code invented by MI9, the wartime British secret service that taught the armed forces how to escape, and also how to evade capture. Fans of cryptography will find a full explanation at www.guywalters.com, as well as in *From Colditz in Code* by J. M. Green and Robert Hale, which is out of print.

As far as the author is aware, the Nazis never intended to employ sarin, a gas they had created before the war. Hitler had an abhorrence of the use of gas in a military capacity, believing it would lead to the mutual destruction of both the Allies and Nazi Germany. It is also supposed that his experience of being gassed in the trenches of WWI may have influenced his opinion. Readers scarcely need to be reminded that Hitler was more than willing to use gas away from the battlefield.

The A4 project to build V2 rockets was indeed masterminded by SS-Brigadeführer Hans Kammler, who disappeared after the war. More people died manufacturing V2 rockets than as a result of their use. It is estimated that every operational rocket cost the lives of six workers.

Some of the locations in both Crete and Germany are necessarily fictional.

Readers concerned at Lockhart's inability to revive Dr Rudolph should be aware that cardio-pulmonary resuscitation was not in practice in the 1940s.

Flint

Paul Eddy

'Breathtaking' *Independent on Sunday*

Grace Flint is the best undercover cop in the business: driven by a need to put herself into the most dangerous situations. Until an operation to trap big-time money-launderer Frank Harling goes wrong, and for the first time Grace is completely at the mercy of a violent criminal. And mercy is not a word in his vocabulary.

After months of surgery, although Grace is physically restored to an icy beauty, her superiors fear that her mind and personality must have been irreversibly damaged. But Grace is determined to track down the man who almost destroyed her. Even if it means going it alone. Even if it means stepping back into her worst nightmare.

'Eddy has created a female action heroine in the classic tradition . ... high-octane stuff' *The Times*

'Eddy's forte is the taut description of danger . . . full of passages that won't easily be forgotten' *Sunday Times*

'Flint is a great heroine . . . the best thing to come out of the Met since Lynda La Plante's DCI Jane Tennison. She'd give Thomas Harris's Clarice Starling a run for her money too' *Mirror*

'An absolutely cracking literary debut reminiscent of Patricia Cornwell at her best' *Arena*

0 7472 6424 4

headline

Now you can buy any of these other bestselling
Feature titles from your bookshop or
direct from the publisher.

FREE P&P AND UK DELIVERY
(Overseas and Ireland £3.50 per book)

Tom Clancy's Net Force: Point of Impact		£6.99
Created by Tom Clancy and Steve Pieczenik, written by Steve Perry		
American Gods	Neil Gaiman	£6.99
The Forgotten	Faye Kellerman	£5.99
From the Corner of his Eye	Dean Koontz	£6.99
Nothing But the Truth	John Lescroart	£5.99
The Jury	Steve Martini	£6.99
Burnt Sienna	David Morrell	£6.99
Revelation	Bill Napier	£6.99
1st to Die	James Patterson	£6.99
The Runner	Christopher Reich	£5.99
No Good Deed	Manda Scott	£5.99

TO ORDER SIMPLY CALL THIS NUMBER

01235 400 414

or visit our website: www.madaboutbooks.co.uk

Prices and availability subject to change without notice.

AS GOOD AS
FATHERLAND
OR YOUR MONEY BACK

We at **headline** are convinced that you'll find *The Traitor* as good as *Fatherland*. If you disagree, we'll give you your money back.

To claim: send your book and till receipt along with a short letter stating why you are dissatisfied to:

> The Traitor Refund Offer
> Headline (Marketing Dept)
> 338 Euston Road
> London
> NW1 3BH

Allow 28 days for receipt of payment, which will be by cheque. Offer closes 31 December 2002.